SLAYERS

PLAYING WITH FIRE

C.J. HILL

OTHER TITLES BY CJ HILL
(AKA JANETTE RALLISON)

Slayers (under pen name CJ Hill)
Slayers: Friends and Traitors (under pen name CJ Hill)
Erasing Time (under pen name CJ Hill)
Echo in Time (under pen name CJ Hill)
Son of War, Daughter of Chaos
Blue Eyes and Other Teenage Hazards
Just One Wish
Masquerade
My Double Life
A Longtime (and at One Point Illegal) Crush
Life, Love, and the Pursuit of Free Throws
The Girl Who Heard Demons
How I Met Your Brother
Playing The Field
The Wrong Side of Magic
My Fair Godmother
My Unfair Godmother
My Fairly Dangerous Godmother
All's Fair in Love, War, and High School
Fame, Glory, and Other Things on my To Do List
It's a Mall World After All
Revenge of the Cheerleaders
How to Take The Ex Out of Ex-boyfriend
What the Doctor Ordered (under pen name Sierra St. James)

SLAYERS

PLAYING WITH FIRE

Slayers: Playing With Fire
By Janette Rallison
Copyright © 2016

This is a work of fiction. The characters, names, places, incidents and
dialogue are products of the author's imagination and are not to be
construed as real.

No part of this book may be reproduced in any form whatsoever
without prior written permission of the publisher except in the case
of brief passages embodied in critical reviews and articles.

ISBN: 978-0-9906757-3-0
Cover design by Claudia McKinney
Cover © 2016 by Janette Rallison
Formatting by Heather Justesen

To everyone who believes in perseverance and in dragons.
Not necessarily in that order.

SYNOPSIS OF THE FIRST TWO BOOKS

Brant Overdrake's family had kept dragons on the remote island of St. Helena for generations. He was a dragon lord, a man able to connect to a dragon's mind and make the dragon do whatever he wished. His family always cared for the dragons in secret, but Brant had greater ambitions. He planned to use the dragons' electromagnetic pulses as weapons. When dragons screeched, they sent out an EMP pulse that destroyed electronics, rendering cars, phones, computers—most technology—useless. He moved to Virginia and started laying the groundwork for a future takeover of America's government.

When transporting a pair of dragon eggs, his wife had unexpected early labor and he was forced to make an emergency detour to an airport near DC. (Labor comes at inconvenient times. If you don't believe this, ask me about my last labor, which lasted eighteen hours. It was *quite* inconvenient. And painful.) While the dragon eggs were at the airport, the general population was exposed to their signal.

This was unfortunate for Overdrake because the dragons had a natural enemy—Slayers. Slayers were descendants of the knights who killed dragons in the Middle Ages. If a person with Slayer genes came in contact with a dragon or dragon eggs while in utero, the person's genes were activated, turning them into a Slayer. The child then grew up with an innate interest in dragons and inborn athletic skill.

The summer before her junior year of high school, Tori Hampton, a senator's daughter, enrolled in Dragon Camp in the hopes of understanding her obsession with dragons. (She was a socialite, yes, but not a *spoiled* girl, despite what the hardcover book flap of Slayers claims.) Jesse and Dirk, the blessed-with-good-looks captains of the camp teams A-Team and Team Magnus, introduced themselves at registration and took her to the camp's secret secondary location. (I'm not kidding about the good looks part. I based Dirk on Dirk Benedict. If you don't know who that is, google his pictures from *Battlestar Gallactica*. You see what I mean?) At the secret camp, Tori met six other teens, all close to her age. She found out that they were actually training to fight real dragons and that she herself was a Slayer.

When Slayers came within five miles of a dragon (or the dragon simulator that Dr. B developed to help the Slayers train and complete missions) their powers turned on. The Slayers always had highly attuned senses, but when their powers were triggered they had extra strength, night vision, and the ability to leap ten to fifteen feet in the air. They also had an individual skill. Jesse could fly, Bess threw shields up, Kody could throw both freezing blasts and fireballs, Dirk saw what the nearest dragon saw, Shang and Lilly extinguished fire, and Rosa and Alyssa healed burns.

Slayers who had the same skill set were counterparts, which meant they could read one another really, really well. Also, when in the same vicinity, Slayers could tell where their counterparts were without looking. It was a skill that helped while fighting and made the group more tight-knit.

Two days into camp, Tori discovered she could hear what the nearest dragon heard. It seemed like a useless and disappointing skill as dragons didn't generally hear much that would help the Slayers fight them. She also found out that she was counterparts with Dirk. Their skills weren't exactly the same, but close enough to give them the counterpart abilities.

Dirk developed feelings for her; she developed feelings for Jesse. (I did mention that Jesse was hot too, didn't I?)

When Tori overheard vets near a dragon give information about the dragon eggs location, she realized her skill was not as useless as she first imagined. She and the other Slayers planned a surprise attack on the location in order to destroy the dragon eggs. Because, as the old saying goes, it's easier to kill your dragons before they hatch. Okay, that isn't actually an old saying, but it should be.

Where was I? Oh yes, telling you about the ill-fated surprise attack. It was a surprise, although mostly the Slayers were surprised because they were ambushed. If you haven't read the first book (and you should, because it's awesome) I'm going to have to disappoint you here and tell you that Dirk is actually Brant Overdrake's son, a traitor who was sent to camp to spy on the Slayers.

However, as the Slayers were being ambushed, and were trapped in Overdrake's enclosure, Dirk had a change of heart about betraying his friends. He then double-crossed his father by helping Tori save the others. At this point Tori found out she could also fly.

It was a surprise to her, but not to Overdrake, because he already knew what readers won't learn until the second book—that Tori is actually part dragon lord. Her ability to hear what the dragon hears—that's not really a Slayer skill, it's a dragon lord one.

This, by the way, was supposed to be the big reveal in *Slayers: Friends and Traitors*. And would have been quite a surprise to many people if the publisher hadn't given away that plot twist on the back blurb. Which they did. Yeah, authors generally don't have any control over what goes on the back of the book.

Anyway, I keep getting off track. So after the Slayers

escaped, Overdrake set a dragon on them. Dirk's dragon. He had to help his friends fight and kill it in order to save their lives. In case you haven't figured it out yet, Overdrake isn't a very nice person.

In book two, camp ended and the Slayers went back to their homes. Tori heard the eggs hatch, got together briefly with Dirk, and had her father search for Ryker, the missing Slayer.

I haven't mentioned him yet, even though book one starts out and ends with him. (Hey, it's hard to summarize hundreds of pages down to three.) When Dr. B first told Ryker's parents that their son was going to be a Slayer, instead of letting Dr. B train him, Ryker's parents moved without a forwarding address. Well, you can't blame them really. Would you let your son fight huge, flying carnivores that breathe fire?

Tori's father was able to track down Ryker's address, because he worked for the government and let's face it; you can't disappear from the government. They know where you are.

On Halloween, Overdrake kidnapped Alyssa as a way to lure the Slayers into another ambush. He knew they'd go after her. As the Slayers met for the mission, Tori let Dirk know that her father had tracked down Ryker and told him he lived in Rutland, Vermont. While Dr. B prepped the Slayers for the mission, Tori sensed Dirk's anxiety about the mission—he was plagued with guilt for betraying his friends—and she figured out who Dirk was.

What follows is an awesome chase scene through DC, which you really should read sometime. Plus, you should visit DC because it's a really cool place. (And when you go to the Jefferson Memorial, you can imagine me stepping off the area between the columns to see if a dragon would fit through them. This is the sort of dedicated research authors do.)

The Slayers retrieved Alyssa, although sadly her memories

and powers were gone. Slayers had an Achilles heel, so to speak. If they were drugged to the point of unconsciousness, the pathways in their brains that gave them powers were destroyed. The Slayers not only lost their powers, they didn't even remember being Slayers.

It was a very sad and yet funny scene because Alyssa thought they were all crazy.

Moving right along. Tori realized she had put Ryker in danger by revealing his address to Dirk. This is probably a good example of why you shouldn't trust hot guys. Just saying. The Slayers then flew to Vermont to find and convince Ryker to join them. Overdrake's men reached Ryker's house at roughly the same time and a fight ensued. When you read that scene, please appreciate it because I had to rewrite it like, six times.

The Slayers found out that not only was Ryker a Slayer, but his cousin Willow was too. Their addition was especially good news because the Slayers numbers had been dwindling. They just lost Alyssa, and in the backstory of book one, they'd lost two other Slayers, Leo and Danielle. You need to know about them because they come into play in book four. At this point, you may be wondering if I regret writing a book with so many characters. *Yes.* I mean, of course I don't—although I will never *ever* write a series with so many people in it again. The poor audiobook reader had such a hard time doing different voices for them all.

Back to the storyline. Dirk realized that his father was going to attack the Slayers' plane. As they were flying home, he warned Tori. The Slayers were able to jump out of the plane before the dragon ripped the thing apart. One more author's note here: I wanted to make that scene as authentic as possible, so I went skydiving. If you read that book, imagine me thousands of feet above the ground trying to convince the skydiving instructor that I'd changed my mind and didn't want to jump after all. They don't listen to you at that point. You're strapped onto them and they just pull you right out of the plane. But I digress.

Anyway, another fight ensued and in this one, Tori was briefly able to enter the dragon's mind. She couldn't control the dragon. Overdrake had too firm a control on the dragon's mind, but he was angry that she tried and told the dragon to ignore the rest of the Slayers and kill her.

As you may have guessed, the dragon wasn't successful. Because if the dragon was, the book would have ended very badly, and I would have gotten angry emails from readers. I'd rather not get those.

So, that pretty much should bring you up to speed. Oh, one more piece of information you need. Dr. B lived on St. Helena with Overdrake. In fact, his father worked for Overdrake. His younger brother, Nathan, was a Slayer who was killed by Overdrake's father. (You can read the novella for free at

http://www.tor.com/2013/10/08/slayers-the-making-of-a-mentor/)

PROLOGUE

THE DOWNSIDE OF BEING MARRIED
TO A DRAGON LORD

Thirteen years ago

Bianca Overdrake's entire future hinged on the results in the doctor's envelope. She took it from him with a shaking hand. "I hope I'm having a girl."

Hoping wouldn't affect the outcome, but the words popped out anyway. They'd been replaying nonstop in her mind through the entire exam. A girl. A girl. It has to be a girl. A daughter wouldn't inherit dragon lord genes and could live a safe life.

The doctor smiled. "You'll find out when you open the envelope."

Was his smile sad? Happy for her? She couldn't tell.

She tucked the envelope into her purse, left the office, and climbed into her Cadillac. All the way to her friend Ruth's house she felt numb, too exhausted to deal with the future and its uncertain twists and pitfalls.

Bianca had meant to go somewhere private to open the envelope. She couldn't bring herself to touch it, though. Not yet.

Her future wasn't the only one in question. Dirk's was too. Her son was only five, too young to understand the decisions she had to make, and much too young to lose a mother. And yet, she might have to disappear, leave him and everyone she knew. She had the baby's safety to consider. She had to be a mother to that child too.

Bianca pulled up to Ruth's house. Dirk was playing there with Ruth's son, Thomas, while Bianca had gone to the OB's. She hadn't told Dirk about the baby. He wouldn't be able to keep that sort of news a secret from his father, and Brant didn't know about the pregnancy.

She was four months along, and her baggy clothes wouldn't hide her secret for much longer. If the baby was a girl, Bianca would claim that she hadn't told Brant beforehand because she had worried about having another miscarriage. Over the course of their marriage, she'd had three. But this baby was healthy, on track, its heartbeat swishing a strong rhythm at every checkup.

After so many losses, so many children she never got to hold, Bianca loved this baby fiercely already.

She went to the door, repeating the mantra: Let it be a girl. Brant would be disappointed, but he also wouldn't train her to be a fighter in his upcoming war. Daughters couldn't control dragons the way sons could.

Bianca rang the doorbell, and a few moments later, Ruth answered. She was petite, with blonde hair and delicate features that belied her true personality: Ruth was a force to be reckoned with.

She looked Bianca over, as if trying to read her expression. "You're not crying. It must be good news, then. A girl?"

Bianca shook her head and pulled the envelope from her purse. "I had the doctor write down the ultrasound results. I haven't opened it yet."

She'd been afraid that if she started sobbing on the exam table, the doctor would wonder why. But he didn't question her when she asked for the results to be sealed in an envelope. Women did that sort of thing all the time. They planned reveals at baby showers or special events.

Ruth opened the door wider and stepped aside. "You can't put it off forever."

"I know." Bianca walked into the living room, glancing around for Dirk.

He came roaring into the living room, laughing as he and Thomas chased each other around with foam swords. Dirk spied Bianca, and his blue eyes lit up.

"Mommy!" he yelled, and rushed over to give her a hug. He didn't let go of the sword. If it had been real, he would have impaled her.

Bianca knelt down and gathered Dirk into a hug, shutting her eyes as she pressed her cheek to his mop of blond hair. He was so small and soft, and he smelled of peanut butter and laundry soap. She couldn't ever leave him, no matter what the results said. Why had she ever entertained it as an option? For Dirk's sake, she'd stay with Brant and make the relationship work.

Dirk wriggled out of her embrace, oblivious to her adoration and done being hugged. "Can I stay longer?" he asked. "Thomas and me are still killing stuff."

"What are you killing?" Bianca asked.

"Monsters," he replied. "The big kind that have lots of crazy arms."

Bianca nodded, forcing a smile. "We can't have those wandering around the house. You and Thomas had better take care of them."

"Yeah," Dirk said, raising his sword like a banner.

Thomas lifted his sword in the same gesture. "Yeah!" he shouted, and the two boys dashed out of the room to parts of the house unseen.

Bianca slowly got to her feet. She still clutched the envelope, rumpled a bit now.

Ruth motioned for Bianca to follow her to the couch. She kept her voice low in case the boys came back. "Finding out your baby's gender is supposed to be exciting." She plunked down on the couch, shaking her head. "Why are you so worried about what Brant thinks? A normal husband wouldn't care one way or the other."

Bianca sank into the loveseat, still clutching the envelope. She hadn't told Ruth everything about her life. She hadn't mentioned how Brant kept dragons in an enclosure on their property, or explained that he wanted sons to help him control the dragons. But Ruth did know that Brant wanted to attack the government someday, that he was dangerous.

"Brant wants sons," Bianca said flatly. He needed them. Only boys inherited the ability to link minds with dragons, so only boys could control them.

Ruth's cup sat on the coffee table. She picked it up and took a sip. "I don't know why you stay with him. You're not happy and haven't been for a long time."

Bianca had been happy with Brant once, or at least, she'd been awed and enamored. Out of all of the women who'd swooned at his wealth and charisma, he'd chosen her. She'd been poor and ordinary, and he'd told her he would make her a queen. She'd been too flattered to think about what his desire for power would mean to her children.

After Dirk was born, though, she understood. Brant wanted to raise their son to be a terrorist. He wanted to pit him against the government and engulf him in his own personal war. Nothing she said on the subject, no amount of begging, reason, or tears could sway her husband.

Bianca's hands began to tremble. She clenched them to keep them still. "Brant would never let me take Dirk away from him. If I want to keep my son, I have to stay."

Ruth replaced her cup on the table with a thud. "Not if you get a half-way decent lawyer."

It wasn't that easy. "The law doesn't matter to Brant. He would take Dirk and disappear. If I ask for a divorce, the only way I'll ever get to see Dirk is if I give Brant full custody. That way, he won't feel threatened, and he'll let me visit."

"Or he'll be spiteful and never let you visit."

That was a possibility too. Brant could be spiteful.

Ruth leaned forward, putting her hand on Bianca's knee. "Maybe you're the one who should take Dirk and disappear."

Bianca had considered the idea, had thought of it every day of her pregnancy. "Brant would have every FBI agent, police officer, and *private investigator in the country searching for us." As well as some less-savory bounty hunters.*

"Brant's rich, not omnipotent. He doesn't have that much pull."

He had more pull than Bianca liked to admit. He was already placing his own people in the government, making alliances that would help him later. "If I took Dirk, and Brant found me . . ." She didn't think he'd actually have her killed, but she didn't want to test the theory or find out how much revenge he'd exact. "He wouldn't just take Dirk away from me. He'd take the baby, too."

And if the baby was a boy, Brant would train him to be a dragon lord. What would her second son's chances of survival be against artillery and tanks?

Ruth's eyes were still on her, heavy with sympathy. "There's got to be something you can do."

Bianca smoothed out the envelope on her lap. "Maybe I'm worried about nothing. I might be having a girl."

Ruth let out a sigh, letting Bianca know she'd missed the point. "And having a girl would somehow erase your marriage problems?"

Bianca didn't answer. Before she could think about it anymore, she opened the envelope. Let it be a girl, *she thought, and took hold of the slip of paper.*

One sentence was written on the paper: Congratulations, you're having a boy!

A son.

Oh no.

A wave of dizziness swept over Bianca. She put her hand to her mouth and tried to breathe. Her eyes stung, watered.

"Are those relieved tears or upset tears?" Ruth asked. "What is it?"

A death sentence, *Bianca thought.* He'll fight armies, face gunfire and missiles. *Both of her children would end up dead.*

Ruth took the paper from her hand and read it. Instead of

slumping into the couch like Bianca was doing, she sat straighter. "You don't have to stay with Brant. Take Dirk and go to a safe house."

The room felt like it was closing in. The future already seemed to be twisting away from her, changing into something dark and perilous. Bianca shook her head wearily. "Brant has too many connections. He'd find out where the safe houses are."

Ruth was undeterred. "Then go somewhere else, somewhere he won't suspect." She pulled her cellphone from her pocket and opened her contact list. "My brother lives in North Carolina. He's single and lives in a four-bedroom house, so he has plenty of room. You and Dirk can stay there until you get back on your feet."

The offer made Bianca laugh. Not happy laughter; disbelieving laughter. "Your brother would take in a stranger with a dangerous ex who's looking for her?"

"Wesley's a great guy. He'll understand." Ruth began texting. "Really, you'll like him. And maybe living with him for a while will show you what normal men are supposed to be like."

Bianca couldn't run with Dirk; Brant wouldn't calmly accept that sort of loss. Especially since Dirk was the only other dragon lord around. Brant would have people investigating every friend Bianca had ever made. And he would become increasingly violent in his methods of finding information.

If Bianca wanted to escape her marriage and protect her unborn child, she'd have to do it without Dirk. This knowledge had haunted her for the last four months, rearing its head every time she wondered about the baby's gender. Now she felt the weight of the decision suffocating her.

"I have to go alone." Bianca's words were no more than a choked whisper. "He'll let me go if he doesn't know about the baby." She gulped, and her hands tightened around the envelope, crumpling it. "After he's born and I make sure he's safe, maybe I'll be able to . . ." Figure out a way Brant couldn't track her down. Find a place beyond his reach. "To come back and take Dirk." It was a faint hope, a plan that would endanger both her and the baby, but right now, she couldn't bear the thought of losing Dirk altogether. It was hard enough to think of not seeing him until after the baby was born.

Ruth fingered her phone, clearly unhappy with Bianca's decision. "When you come back, Brant might not let you spend any time alone with Dirk. He might suspect your intentions."

He probably would, but Bianca would have to deal with that problem later. She had no choice but to leave, not unless she wanted both of her sons dead. She might or might not be able to protect Dirk from Brant's plans, but she could still protect this baby.

Ruth's phone buzzed with a text. She glanced down at it and smiled. "Wesley says, 'sure'. I told you he was a great guy."

Good. Then it was decided. Bianca took the doctor's note from Ruth and tore it into pieces. She couldn't leave any evidence of the baby, no matter how slight the chance Brant would find it. "I'll go to North Carolina," she said. "I need to leave right away. Today." She had some money hidden away and could withdraw a few thousand in cash from the bank to tide her over. "This evening, I'll call Brant and tell him to pick up Dirk here. I'll tell him that I want a separation, and that I need time to think things over by myself for a few months." She'd have to get rid of her cell phone so he couldn't trace her. What else did she need to do?

"Are you sure you can be ready to leave so soon?" Ruth asked.

"I have to," Bianca said. "If I let myself take time to think about going, I won't be able to do it." She got up and made her way to Thomas's room.

She found the boys on the floor, surrounded by stuffed animals. "I thought you were killing monsters," she said. Her voice sounded too high, unnatural.

"These are the monsters' hostages," Dirk said.

A five-year-old shouldn't know what hostages were. One more

thing to thank Brant for. "You said I could stay longer," Dirk said with a frown. "It isn't longer yet."

"I know," she said. "I have to go somewhere, so I'm leaving you here for a while."

Leaving you, leaving you. Would those be the words he remembered when she'd gone?

"Okay." He turned back to Thomas and the stuffed animals.

She knelt on the floor beside him. "Give me a hug goodbye."

He wrapped his arms around her neck. She cried despite herself and couldn't let him go.

"You're squeezing me," he protested.

"Sorry." She released him and wiped at her tears. It was a hopeless task. More tears came.

Dirk saw her face and his blue eyes went wide. "What's wrong?"

"Nothing. Sometimes mommies just cry."

He watched her, probably debating whether to believe her. She took deep breaths and did her best to compose herself. She'd have plenty of time to fall apart later. She needed to be strong for a few more minutes.

"I want you to remember two things," she said. "Can you do that?"

He nodded solemnly.

She reached out for his hand, felt his small fingers wrapping around hers. She wanted to engrave the memory of this moment into her mind so she'd never forget it. She held up one finger. "I love you." She held up a second. "And I'll come back for you. Will you remember those two things?"

He nodded again.

She gave his hand one last squeeze. "I love you, and I'll come back for you." Then she stood up and left.

CHAPTER 1

Only one thing could ruin a night of soaring on a dragon, and that was Dirk's assignment: scouting military bases in Maryland for possible attack. Bases weren't shown on public record satellite images, and his father wanted photographs of them to analyze. While Dirk was out, he was also supposed to decide on a couple of east coast cities to cripple during their first strike.

Choosing them was harder than he expected. He'd been mulling over cities all night and still hadn't come up with a single one that would satisfy his conscience. He couldn't use the dragon's electromagnetic pulse on Philadelphia or New York. Both had too many people, which meant too much suffering. But even smaller cities had hospitals. If all of the electronics in a city were fried, anyone on life support would die within minutes. The point of the first strike wouldn't be to kill, but to instill fear, show what the dragons could inflict even without landing.

He took a turn around Baltimore's business district. Perhaps he could purposely miss the hospitals. But a partial strike would tick off his father. He'd call it sloppy work.

Dirk circled the city one last time and then decided to check out some areas near DC. On a whim, he leapt off the dragon and flew on his own. He had to make sure his flying skills didn't get rusty, and besides, he enjoyed the sensation of speed and the feel of wind rushing around him.

He gave Khan the mental command to fly ahead and used the updraft to gain height. *Head southwest*, he told the dragon. The words were directed from Dirk's mind to Khan's. Speaking wouldn't have done any good. Dragons didn't obey their masters because they wanted to. They did it because dragon lords connected with their minds — mentally hacking into their brains and forcing the dragon to obey their commands.

Dirk could feel Khan's frustration at the new instruction. He'd been flying fast for nearly three hours, and Dirk had just told him to fly away from home instead of toward it.

For an hour, Dirk and Khan zoomed over lit-up cities, sleepy suburbs, and dark land that looked like a messy quilt. Farms maybe, or parks. When he grew tired, he climbed back onto the riding seat tethered to the dragon's back. He should probably start acting like a dragon lord again. Time to figure out which cities to suggest to his father. Dirk let several possibilities run through his mind, judging each on importance and strategic location. Population. Resources. Transportation routes.

The city that kept popping into his mind was McLean, Virginia. Not for potential destruction, but because Tori Hampton lived there. Tori, his counterpart.

Years ago when Dirk had first gone to camp, he'd seen the Slayers match up with their counterparts. People with the same dragon-fighting ability had a bond, a way to read each other as though they'd known each other their whole lives. They could also sense each other's presence. Knowing where your counterpart was and what they were likely to do helped in a fight.

Dirk had always figured he couldn't have a counterpart.

After all, he wasn't a Slayer; he was a dragon lord pretending to be one so he could spy on them. But then Tori had arrived at camp—a senator's daughter, a socialite with a model's face, the last sort of person he'd expected to be a Slayer. And inexplicably, the two of them were counterparts. It was one of those surprises life liked to throw at you when you thought you had things under control.

Dirk was so used to living a double life that he'd never expected anyone to see beyond the act he put on, let alone understand him. But Tori had understood him too well. She'd stolen his heart with unintentional ease, then figured out who he was and told the other Slayers.

Boston. Chicago. McLean. It would be so easy to fly to her house for a visit.

Dirk hadn't seen her for two weeks, not since the mission when Tori outed him as a dragon lord, but she still messaged him online. Mostly trying to convince him to leave his father. A lost cause, really.

Fortunately, he didn't need to rely on technology to contact Tori. She was not only a Slayer, she was half dragon lord which meant she automatically connected to whichever dragon she was closest to. Specifically, she heard whatever it did. Living in McLean, she was generally closest to the dragon nursery, and he'd learned from trial and error that of the two fledglings there, she always connected to Vesta. But if Dirk flew near her house, she'd connect to Khan. Then Dirk could speak aloud, and she would hear anything he said.

He headed that way, letting his mind roam to Tori: Her long brown hair, mint-green eyes, the tilt of her head that made her look both sophisticated and vulnerable. He knew her every expression, including the smile that had been just his, a smile she'd given him even when she'd started dating Jesse.

Thirty minutes later, Dirk was ten miles from McLean. Close enough by far for Tori to connect with Khan. The city lay below him, the streetlights lit like candles glowing in the darkness. Only a few cars lumbered through the streets. Most people were asleep at this hour. He skimmed through the air, feeling like Peter Pan about to stop at Wendy's window.

In the story, Peter lost his shadow at Wendy's, and he went back to search for it. That part had never made sense to Dirk as a child, but it did now. Tori had a piece of Dirk too. Not his shadow. Nothing so insubstantial.

He flew toward an area of McLean dotted with mansions and sprawling yards. "Tori, wake up. I have a proposition for you." He couldn't be sure she was awake, but he went on. "I'm not far from your house. If I come in range, will you fly out to meet me?"

Tori's powers, like those of all Slayers and dragon lords, turned on whenever a dragon came within five miles. Then she could fly, had extra strength, and had night vision.

"I want to talk," he said. "I want to show you what a dragon is really like. Give me your answer."

He took his phone from his pocket, went to the site where they exchanged messages, and waited to see if she would answer. After a moment, she did.

I already know what a dragon is like, thanks. Why are you flying around in the middle of the night?

He ignored her question. "I mean I want to show you what a dragon is like when he isn't attacking you. They're amazing, Tori—sleek and powerful. If you gave yourself a chance, you'd love them. You're half dragon lord. This is what you were born for."

He waited for her response to show up, hoping she'd say yes. The two of them could sail over the city, effortlessly gliding underneath the stars, and forget they were enemies for a while.

I'm pretty sure I was born for travel, chocolate, and sleeping in. You keep telling me I'm part dragon lord, but we couldn't be counterparts unless you were part Slayer. Why can't you be loyal to that side for a change?

Dirk wasn't sure she was right. At least, his father didn't want to admit that Dirk's genealogy, or worse, his own, might be contaminated with Slayer genes. Dirk repeated his father's explanation to Tori.

"The original Slayers and dragon lords both used dragon DNA to create their powers. That's why the two groups have similar abilities." Slayers weren't the only ones with extra strength, night vision, and if they were lucky, the ability to fly. Dragon lords had all of those abilities too. "Crossover in other areas was bound to happen. If more dragon lords were around, some of them would probably have counterparts too."

He had no way to test that theory, because he and his father were the only other dragon lords around.

"Say you'll meet me," Dirk persisted.

Did I ever mention that your last dragon tried to eat me?

"I'll make sure this one behaves."

Right. I'm not even sure you'd *behave.*

He laughed and missed Tori all over again. "I'll make sure I behave too. When I come close enough that your powers turn on, fly out of your window, straight up. I'll watch for you."

Her words appeared on his phone screen fast now. Each sentence by itself. Dirk could tell she was angry.

I can't fly off with you at three in the morning for a rendezvous.

You seem to have forgotten that we're on opposite sides of the whole your-father-wants-to-take-over-the-country issue.

You already betrayed us and tried to lead us into traps, twice.

How can I trust you anymore?

He winced. He didn't like to remember his betrayals. Last

summer he'd led the Slayers into an ambush in a dragon enclosure. In the middle of the fight, he'd had a change of heart, and he got them back out again—a fact that made his father set up the second ambush last Halloween. That was when Tori had figured out who he was.

"I was trying to protect the Slayers, not hurt them." Dirk had told Tori the same thing before, but she refused to see his point of view. "If they lose their powers, they won't fight dragons and get hurt. Do you think I *want* to see my friends killed?"

In theory, taking away Slayer powers should have been an easy thing. When Slayers were drugged to the point of unconsciousness, the brain pathways controlling their abilities were destroyed, turning them into normal people again. What's more, a Slayer who'd been drugged lost all of their Slayer memories. They didn't remember ever having powers.

The problem was that Slayers had highly acute senses even when their powers weren't turned on. They could tell when someone around them had a spike of adrenaline that signaled fear or an impending attack. It was hard to take a Slayer by surprise.

"I've never wanted you to lose your powers," Dirk insisted. "I want you to start using your dragon lord ones. Come out, and I can show you how."

Maybe you want to kidnap me. That way you'll eliminate one of the flyers who can kill your dragons.

"I'm not leading you into a trap. I'm your counterpart. You'd know if I were lying."

I didn't before.

"Yes, you did. That's how I got caught."

Well, I couldn't tell the first *time.*

Dirk kept Khan in a circling pattern. The dragon glided,

wings outstretched over winding roads. "You hadn't known me long enough yet."

I spent most of the summer with you at camp and never realized you were a traitor.

He didn't answer right away. He wasn't sure whether to admit that after the first ambush, he'd switched sides. He hadn't been pretending at camp. His loyalties really had been with the Slayers then. But when summer ended, common sense kicked in again. He was a dragon lord. With or without his help, his father would take over the country. So Dirk had to help. His father's revolution would be less violent and more humane if Dirk had a part in it.

"Well," he said, "you apparently learned how to tell when I'm being deceitful. You'd know now."

She didn't answer for a full minute. He imagined her sitting in the darkness of her bedroom, her long hair messy with sleep as she stared at her screen, debating.

"Come," he whispered.

I'm not a dragon lord. Not if they're like your father—playing God with other people's lives. I can't do what you're doing.

"Come," he said again. "Maybe you can convince me the error of my ways. I'll let you try."

If you want to talk, let me choose the time and place. And I can already tell you that it won't be three in the morning. What are you doing flying around Virginia anyway?

Was she fishing for information—something to pass on to the Slayers? He couldn't give any hint of the coming attacks, or of the cities that would be affected. Otherwise the Slayers would be waiting.

"It has to be now. I can't hear your voice, so I can't tell whether you're lying. If I let you choose the time and place, you would almost certainly lead me into a trap."

You don't trust me, but you expect me to trust you?

"You can hear my voice."

That doesn't mean I can trust you.

He thought she'd finished writing, and he was forming a response, when she added, *That will always be our problem, won't it? How can we trust each other?*

Maybe their counterpart senses worked better over large distances than he'd thought. He knew she wouldn't ever come and meet him, if for no other reason than to make a point that she didn't trust him anymore—punishment for his betrayal.

He'd offered her a chance to meet a dragon: to touch it, to fly on its back and see the world how it should be seen, but she'd turned him down to make a point.

He shut off his phone and slid it into his pocket. "I'll let you get back to bed." He turned the dragon away from McLean, cutting a quick line into the night air. "While you fall back asleep, remember this. Last summer, I helped you destroy my own dragon instead of letting it kill the Slayers. And on Halloween, I could have kidnapped you when we were together, but I let you return to the Slayers. And then I saved all of your lives by warning you that a dragon was about to attack your plane. You have more reasons to trust me than I have to trust you. But I'm the one who made you the offer tonight, and you're the one who refused it."

She probably had a reply to that. He didn't check his phone to see it. That was one of the only benefits of these one-way conversations. He could always have the last word.

He flew back toward Pennsylvania, toward the dragon enclosure hidden in the middle of forest land. This time as he deliberated over cities again, he considered them with less compassion. His father thought Philadelphia was a strategic choice. Fine. Philadelphia would be city number one. He'd avoid as many hospitals as possible, and the rest of the population would have a firsthand look at how the colonials once lived.

Maybe he'd make McLean his second choice. Let Tori live without electricity for a while. It was petty he knew, vengeful.

Then again, he was his father's son.

CHAPTER 2

By the time Dirk walked into the house, his temper had worn off, and he was worrying again that crippling Philadelphia was too much for a first strike. He found his father sitting in the living room, maps spread in front of him, waiting for a report.

Dirk sat down beside his father, noting the map and the cities circled on it.

"Did you have any trouble with the military bases?" his father asked.

"No." Dirk put the camera on the table. Dragon scales absorbed radar, so none of the equipment on the base had detected him coming or going.

His father picked up the camera and reviewed the pictures. "I've decided you should hit New York City on the first night. That'll throw a wrench in the machinery of world trading. Which reminds me, I need to move my stocks to Tokyo."

Dirk hid his reaction, didn't let any emotion show as he thought of the eight million people who lived in New York City. How many hospitals were there in a place that big? Was it even possible to avoid them all? He picked up one of the pencils and tapped it against the table. "Strategically speaking, I don't think New York should be first on our strike list."

"New York is the largest city in the country." His father spoke with exaggerated patience, as if he didn't like explaining the obvious. "More people live there than in most states. If you combined Wyoming, Vermont, Alaska, both Dakotas, Delaware, Montana, Rhode Island, and Maine, their populations would still be smaller than New York City. It is one of the most, if not *the* most, important targets. Unless we take it out the first night, the government will send anti-aircraft to protect it."

"Which is why we leave it alone," Dirk countered. "As long as New York is functioning, the government will have to protect it. They'll tie up a large portion of troops and artillery there. If we take New York out first, the government will spread those troops out around the rest of the country, making it harder to strike other areas. Besides, we want to keep the most productive cities functioning. We'll need the profits."

His father considered the argument. "You make valid points." He put the camera down and sent Dirk an approving look. "You may yet become another Alexander."

His father's standard for military genius had long been Alexander the Great. More than once, his father had told him how Julius Caesar wept when he turned thirty-one, because Alexander had conquered so much more territory by that age. Dirk's father always ended the story by saying, "but you will best them both. You'll help take down the most powerful country on earth before you turn twenty."

Dirk was two months shy of eighteen. His father was ahead of schedule.

Dirk leaned over the maps, noting that Boston was circled. So were Chicago, Atlanta, and Baltimore. "I think we should hit small targets at first. Our goal is to instill fear, not destroy the places we want to control."

His father returned his attention to the map, making notations next to port cities. "We need to show a force of power. Japan didn't surrender in World War II after normal bombing raids. It took two—not one—atomic bombs to convince Japan that they couldn't win. Do you think they would have surrendered if the US had dropped those bombs on small villages?"

"Maybe," Dirk said. "The Japanese would have seen the bombs' power either way."

His father let out a scoff, indicating that he didn't think Japan would have been so reasonable. "The bombs were a good thing because they ended the war, ended all of the killings. Fewer than a quarter of a million people died in Hiroshima and Nagasaki. Sixty million died from the other effects of the war. The same principle will be true when we rule. The country will suffer losses during the first attacks, but in the long run, everyone will be better off."

When his father talked about the revolution, he always insisted the country would be better off in the long run, and usually Dirk believed him. That was harder to do tonight with the memory of flying over cities fresh in his mind.

His father leaned back in his chair, surveying Dirk. "Which cities do you suggest?"

"Philadelphia and Florence, South Carolina."

"Florence?" his father repeated. "I've never even heard of it. What strategic advantage would it give us?"

"Taking out a small city will instill more fear. If we only hit big cities, everyone else will think they're safe. They'll be more defiant. If we take out a small city, people will realize that no one is safe. *Anyone* could lose their technology."

His father nodded. "True." He moved the map of the east coast, revealing a map of the United States beneath it. "But it's more important to obtain our strongholds during the first strike." He tapped his pencil against the western coastline. "I'll have troops waiting on both sides of the country. Boston, Baltimore, and Norfolk, Virginia will give them footholds in the east, and Seattle and Portland in the northwest. The southwest will be more complicated."

Complicated because his father didn't have a dragon enclosure there. He'd built facilities to house and hide his dragons in the Midwest, the East, and the wooded West, but hadn't bothered with the Southwest. Most of the land there was too open, barren of trees and cover. Attacks in that part of the country would have to be launched from their Oregon base.

"We need to take out the military bases in California on the first night." He circled Vandenberg and Edwards. "I don't know if it's worth pushing Khan up to Portland after we've taken care of California. I don't want to overtire him."

"When will you take Khan to the West?" Dirk asked. That move would signal that the attacks were about to start.

His father's gaze left the map and examined Dirk's expression. Dirk tried to look only interested, not worried.

After a moment of scrutiny, his father returned his attention to California. "You don't need to know those details right now."

Message received: Dirk's father still didn't completely trust him. Ever since he'd freed his friends from the dragon enclosure last summer, his father had treated him like an employee— giving him as few details as possible, always questioning his loyalty.

And his father didn't even know that Dirk had warned the Slayers about the second dragon attack. If his father ever figured out that bit of deception, he'd never let Dirk go near the dragons again.

No, that wasn't true. Dirk's father wanted his help, needed it so he could attack multiple fronts. Dirk was the only other person in the family who had the power to control dragons. Bridget, his half-sister, had no powers. Girls typically didn't. Tori probably had them only because her Slayer genes somehow gave her access to her dragon lord abilities as well.

But he wouldn't be his father's only son for long. His stepmother, Cassie, was pregnant with a boy. If Dirk didn't prove his loyalty, then in another decade or so, he'd be replaced.

"If you don't need me for anything else," Dirk said, standing, "I'll go to bed." After all, if his father wouldn't share details, he couldn't expect Dirk to stick around.

His father looked as if he wanted to protest, but remained silent.

Dirk went up the stairs, flying so his footsteps didn't wake his sister or stepmother. He paused in front of Bridget's room. She was only seven years old. Too young to realize any of what was going on.

He continued down the hallway, wishing he had someone to talk to. No one understood his divided loyalties or the frustration that came from having no one who trusted him. Worst of all was the feeling that he'd lose no matter what. Someday he would have to fight the Slayers, his friends, and he was powerless to stop any of it from happening.

When he got to his bedroom, he kicked off his shoes in the general direction of the closet. He didn't turn on the light. No need; he could still see in the dark. His phone had died during the flight home, so he plugged it into the charger on the desk. His gaze fell on his computer. Tori had probably written him back.

He told himself to ignore her and go to bed, but somehow

found himself sitting at the desk and logging on. She was the person who came closest to understanding him. Maybe that was the real reason he couldn't let her go.

A new message from Tori sat at the top of his notifications. *I do think about you saving us—and I'm grateful for it. Really grateful. I know you have good intentions, and you don't want to hurt anybody. That's why I don't understand why you're staying with your father. You can still come back and join the Slayers. Dr. B would find a place for you to live. I want you to come back.*

Her words melted him, made him want to fly straight to McLean and spend the rest of the night talking to her. But he couldn't go back to the Slayers. Not now. He'd turned his friends into enemies, and although Tori was blind to that fact, he wasn't. The Slayers would never forgive him for what he'd done or who he was, and they would certainly never trust him again. Seeing them would only be a painful reminder.

He wrote back: *You only feel the way you do because you went to a Slayer camp and trained to kill dragons. If I'd found you first and taught you about dragons, you wouldn't be trying to destroy them. You'd be looking for ways to protect them. Don't you think you owe it to yourself to learn about your dragon-lord half before you decide what you do with the rest of your life?*

She probably wouldn't answer for a while. She had most likely gone to sleep after sending the message, but just in case, he would leave the screen open while getting ready for bed. As he pushed his chair away from the desk, he noticed his father standing behind him, hovering a few inches off the ground. He had silently flown into the room, and was now reading over Dirk's shoulder.

"You still talk to her?" His father managed to sound both amused and reproachful. "Passing along secrets?"

"Of course not." Dirk hid the spike of panic gripping him.

Had anything in Tori's messages revealed how he'd warned her about the second dragon attack? He skimmed the screen. No, her reply said only that she was grateful he'd saved them. She could have been talking about the time he'd let them out of the dragon enclosure and saved them from losing their powers.

His father shouldered his way closer to the computer, and then scrolled through the rest of the messages, reading each one.

Irritation flared through Dirk. "Do you mind? That's a private conversation." Tori's texts showed only half of most conversations. Dirk had been speaking for many of them, not writing. Still, he nearly turned off the monitor on his father. He only stopped himself because doing so would make him look like he was hiding something.

His father ignored his protest and kept reading. Dirk had already erased most of their earlier conversations, a precaution he was suddenly glad he'd taken. His father wouldn't be happy to know how often he and Tori had talked over the last couple weeks.

When his father finished reading, he straightened. "Why did you ask Tori to meet you tonight? What game are you playing?"

"She's a dragon lord," Dirk said. "I want to convince her to join our side. Didn't the messages make that clear?" He turned off the computer and stood up. "She knows what side I'm on. I wonder why you don't."

His father relaxed his stance, pleased with Dirk's reaction, pleased with this new evidence of his loyalty. "Well . . ." his father said, lengthening the word while he thought. "I admit that having another dragon lord around would be helpful. But Tori seems to think she can turn you into Slayer. How do I know she's not right?"

"Because I'm still here. If I wanted to switch sides and leave, I could have done it tonight."

"She asked how you justified your actions," his father said, referring to one of their earlier conversations. "What did you tell her?" He'd figured out that when only Tori wrote, Dirk had been talking to her near a dragon.

"I told her sometimes you need a revolution to improve a civilization."

"True enough." Dirk's father nodded. "But you shouldn't bother with justifications. Alexander didn't depend on votes to obtain his power. No one elected Genghis Khan. Men of action conquer. Plain and simple. You and I have dragon DNA. Nature gave us the ability to conquer, and that gives us the right to do it."

"Tori isn't a fan of Genghis Khan or Alexander the Great. Go figure. She needs better reasons."

His father glanced at the computer as though he could still see Tori's messages there. When he spoke again, his voice was neutral; the tone he used when concealing his thoughts. "Perhaps you're right, and we'll find a way to bring Tori to our side. I won't forbid you from trying as long as you keep me informed." A smile spread across his lips, one that was calculating. "Perhaps I'll even think of a way to help you."

Dirk bristled. Maybe it was because of his father's smile. It made his words seem sinister. "Don't," he said. "Let me handle her. I know how her mind works, and you—well, you've already tried to kill her twice."

His father held his hands up, conceding the point. "And I'm beginning to see the folly of that strategy. You're right—if we'd found a way to engage her dragon lord side instead of triggering her Slayer instincts, things might be very different now." He let his hands drop, then tapped one against the side of his leg, still thinking, doing more of whatever calculations were running through his mind. "Perhaps it's not too late." Another smile. "Have you thought about the fact that if the two of you married, your children would all be dragon lords, even your daughters?"

Dirk stared at him in surprise, unsure how to answer. Was he serious? Plotting something? If so, what? It seemed weird that in one conversation, his father had gone from hating Tori to discussing the benefits of marrying her. Dirk had always figured that if he did persuade Tori to switch sides, his father would need just as much persuasion to trust her.

"Stop looking so suspicious," his father said with a laugh. "I'm allowed to change my mind once in a while." He held up a hand, making a pledge. "I promise I won't try to kill Tori again. Unless, of course, it's really warranted."

"Thanks," Dirk said, still guarded. Perhaps his father was just changing tactics. Perhaps he wanted Dirk to set up a meeting with Tori so he could capture her. Is that why he wanted to be kept informed?

His father must have seen the doubt. He let out a sigh and went toward the door. "It's been a long night, and we both need sleep. Just promise to do your part in the revolution, and I won't care who you choose for a girlfriend. Agreed?"

"Agreed," Dirk said. But despite his father's words, he was more worried about Tori's safety than he had been before.

CHAPTER 3

Ever since Tori had learned she had superpowers, she'd been making a mental list of their drawbacks. Foremost on the list today was that people didn't respect her private time.

At least Dr. B never had. It didn't matter that she specifically told him she was going to see *Wicked* today—or that she and her sister had purchased the tickets seven months ago. He decided to call a Slayer meeting at the same time anyway.

While Tori sat in the red velvet seats of the Kennedy Center waiting for the musical to start, her watch phone beeped. And beeped again. Should she keep ignoring the sound or give in and answer?

Aprilynne, her older sister, glanced at the watch and rolled her eyes. "I can't believe you wore that thing here."

No one with any style or taste would believe Tori wore it anywhere. It was a high-tech Slayer phone disguised as a watch, and a sadly dismal fashion choice all wrapped up into one piece of clunky black plastic wrist-wear; completely tacky.

The beep was Jesse's chime. He was probably calling her to ream her out about skipping practice. Again. In her defense, it was harder for her to get away than it was for the rest of the Slayers. Tori had a busier schedule, and she frequently had bodyguards tailing her. One sat in the row behind her now.

Aprilynne cast Tori another reproving glance before flipping open her program. "You better turn off whatever alarms you have on that watch. You don't want it going off during the performance."

Tori pushed a button on the side twice, a signal that she'd call Jesse in a few minutes when she got to a private location. The show was a Saturday matinee and didn't start until one. She had twenty minutes to make her apologies to him and return to her seat. Plenty of time.

Tori forced a surprised gasp for Aprilynne's sake. "I set the alarm to remind myself to call Jesse and cancel a date. I can't believe I forgot. I'd better call him before he leaves to pick me up."

"Jesse?" Aprilynne repeated. She'd met him once, and if she didn't exactly approve of their clandestine relationship, she at least understood Jesse's draw. Tall, dark, handsome, and all that.

"I'll be right back." Tori slung her purse over her shoulder, got to her feet, and waved to Lars, the bodyguard who doubled as their driver. He was a burly, humorless guy who hardly spoke to Tori, frequently scowled at her friends, and exuded an air of general hostility. "I'm just going to the lady's room," she told him. "No need to come with me." She scooted past the other chairs and hurried out of the theater before he could complain. She was supposed to stay with Aprilynne at all times so Lars could keep an eye on them both.

The wide, red-carpeted hallways of the Kennedy Center were filled with patrons making their way to theaters. Tori wound through the crowd in the grand foyer and took the elevator upstairs. The upper theaters were smaller, so fewer people milled around the hallways. From there, she headed out to the balcony, a vast structure more proportioned for giants than the average arts patron looking for fresh air or a view of the Potomac. A cluster of people stood smoking by one of the fountains, but otherwise, the balcony was empty. Tori strolled to the railing thirty yards away and turned so they couldn't see her having a conversation with her watch. She always felt ridiculous talking to her wrist, like she was part of a hokey spy movie.

She pushed the button sequence to reach Jesse. "You called?"

"Glad you picked up." His deep familiar voice came over the speaker, a sound that always made her heart purr a little. "You were supposed to meet us fifteen minutes ago. Location Alpha."

The Air and Space Museum. Dr. B insisted on clandestine language, and ever since Dirk betrayed them, all the code names had changed.

"Where are you?" Jesse asked.

"At the Kennedy Center, just like I texted everyone. I couldn't get away."

"You've missed every practice this week."

Meaning three. Which was way too many sessions for Dr. B to hold during the school year.

"It's been a busy week."

Jesse let out a disapproving grunt. "You're the other captain. You can't keep missing practice."

Granted, Tori was A-team's captain, but Dr. B had only given her the job because she was a flyer. When he made the assignment, he hadn't known she was part dragon lord. If he had, he probably would have done things differently.

"People's lives are depending on you," Jesse went on. "What's more important than defending your country?"

Tori checked over her shoulder to make sure no one was near. "Right now, *Wicked*. With the Broadway cast."

"You'll lose your edge if you don't train."

Even though the people by the fountain hadn't moved, Tori couldn't shake the feeling that someone was watching her. She moved toward the side of the building for more privacy. "I'm sure Dr. B will work me twice as hard next time to make up for it."

"Wrong," Jesse said, and not on the phone. He'd landed by her side.

Tori jumped in surprise and put her hand to her chest.

"See?" he said with a smirk. "You've lost your edge. You didn't hear me coming." His brown hair was mussed by his flight, and his dark eyes looked triumphant. He wore a navy blue jacket that was a little beat-up but still looked good on his broad shoulders. Well, really anything looked good on Jesse. He was handsome in a serious, down-to-earth way, which was twice as attractive because he didn't realize the sway of his looks.

Tori turned off her watch's phone function. "It's not nice to sneak up on people." In her defense, it was hard to hear a flyer approaching; they made no sound.

"Yeah," he said, drifting closer, "and Overdrake hasn't been nice to us on more than one occasion." Jesse's eyes were still on hers. "That's why you can't skip training."

She took a step backward, which wasn't usually what she did when Jesse was around. The two of them had secretly met in DC more than once, pretending to be normal teenagers who did things like date and hold hands in movie theaters. "Tell Dr. B I'll make the next practice for sure. I can't disappear from the Kennedy Center right before a performance." She held her hands up in apology. "I'm a presidential candidate's daughter. I'd have every security guard in the building searching for me."

Jesse smiled. Not one of the flirty smiles he gave while they were tucked away in some café having covert french fries. It was a smile of determination that said he knew he was going to win this argument. "Just tell your sister you're leaving. Then no one will worry."

"I don't want to leave." Tori planted her hands on her hips. "And don't you dare fly off with me."

He glided closer, still smiling. He'd been around a dragon simulator, so he had his powers. She didn't, which meant she couldn't do anything to stop him from hauling her into the sky.

She took another step backward. "I've been waiting seven months to see this show. A good boyfriend would be understanding."

He shrugged, not looking sorry. "We agreed that while we were at practice, we would put our relationship aside and act only as Slayers."

"I'm not at practice," she said.

"But I am." He moved closer, then stopped and let his gaze drift over her, taking in her tight-fitting skirt and heels. "Okay, I need a thirty-second break from being a Slayer to tell you that you look amazing."

"Thanks." She didn't mean it.

"And also, I'm sorry I have to do this." He glanced at his watch. "Ten seconds left. That's not nearly long enough to kiss you."

Oh, she wasn't going to let him kiss her. She shuffled backward. "If you fly off with me, someone will see you. Probably a lot of someones. Several pedestrians, and whoever is looking up at this balcony, will question their sanity. Do you want that on your conscience?"

Jesse was apparently unconcerned with the mental wellbeing of random people passing by. "I said I was sorry." He flew over, grabbed Tori around the waist, and pulled her to him. "Dr. B ordered me to bring you back. I'm Team Magnus's captain. I've got to set a good example, remember?" He shot into the sky, going fast and high.

Tori put her hands against Jesse's chest and let out a groan that was swallowed by the wind. "Next time you call, I'm answering you in the ladies restroom—and I don't care who hears the conversation."

That was another problem with the watch phones. Not only did you look stupid talking on them, you sounded stupid talking in code words—or worse yet, forgetting to talk in code words and saying things like, "I haven't seen any signs that the dragon lord is stalking me."

Jesse kept his eyes on the sky, twirling midair to adjust his direction. With his powers in full force, he was immune to the cold air rushing around them. Tori, however, shivered as she watched the Kennedy Center shrink in the distance.

"What am I supposed to tell Aprilynne?"

"You'll think of something."

Easy for him to say. Every time she went to a practice, she had to sneak off or come up with a plausible excuse for being absent for several hours. This frequently made her look flakey, selfish, and secretive.

Jesse zoomed higher until the cars below seemed like multicolored beaded necklaces curving through a maze of blocks. Tori usually loved flying. Sailing through the air made her feel free and powerful. And she usually loved being in Jesse's arms. But now she was cold, and the wind was making her hair whip around her face in tangles. A perfectly good hairstyle ruined.

"You owe me a date to *Wicked*," she said. "And I expect good seats."

He laughed in a way that was far too charming for someone who had just wrecked her afternoon. "I'll do my best."

She reached for her purse. "Aprilynne might have already turned off her phone, and then she's going to . . ." With Jesse's arms around her, she couldn't manage to open her purse without spilling the contents. "This really isn't the best position to fly in."

He'd leveled out, tilting to soar horizontally, and was holding her in an awkward reclining position.

She expected him to turn her to face the same direction. Instead he put his hands under her knees and flipped her around, carrying her like a bride.

She pulled her cell phone from her purse, still miffed. "Now we're acting out scenes from Superman?"

He gave her another smile. "If the cape fits . . ."

She ignored him and called Aprilynne, shielding the phone as best she could from the wind. "Slow down," Tori told Jesse. "I need to hear my sister."

Jesse slowed a little, but not enough to make much difference. If Tori's hearing hadn't been exceptional, she wouldn't have been able to hear what Aprilynne was saying.

"Tori, where are you? Why are you calling me?"

She was flying high in the air over a grid of apartment buildings. The trees below wore their last change before winter, leaves of yellow, red, and orange. "Um, I've had a change of plans. See, Jesse went to a lot of work for our date, and now he's laying this major guilt trip on me." She gave him a pointed look. "You'd think he'd be more understanding since I've had our tickets for seven months, but no, he's being completely unreasonable, and demanding I go with him. He'll drop me off at home later. Don't tell Mom and Dad, okay?"

"Are you serious?" Aprilynne's voice was incredulous. "You're the one who insisted we come to this play, and now you're making me watch it by myself?"

"Sorry."

"Can't you just get Jesse a ticket? Throw Dad's name around. I bet they can find him a seat."

"I wouldn't feel right doing that." That, at least, was true. Her father's fame was something Tori endured, not reveled in.

"But you feel right about ditching me for Jesse?"

"I'll make it up to you."

Aprilynne let out a huff. "You've had a lot to make up for lately. When are you going to stop making apologies and start making things up?"

"I make up things all the time," Tori protested, then glared at Jesse when he laughed at the phrase. "And by *make up* things, I don't mean lies. . ."

Aprilynne hung up, obviously ticked.

Well, that went great.

"Freudian slip?" Jesse asked.

Tori slid her phone back into her pocket. "The rest of you have it easy. Your families can't question where you're going or what you're doing." After Overdrake had discovered the Slayers' addresses, Dr. B sent men posing as FBI agents to the other Slayers' homes. The parents were told that their children had witnessed a drug cartel crime and had agreed to testify in the federal case. Because of that, the whole family were given new identities and relocated in the Witness Protection Program.

Dr. B moved the families to Virginia and had been finding new jobs for the Slayers' parents ever since. Whenever he held a practice, the other Slayers told their parents that they were needed for the case. The parents couldn't ask questions about the ongoing legal situation. Problem solved.

But Tori hadn't been part of the relocation. She couldn't be. Not when her father was a senator. He would have checked his government sources and found out that Dr. B's men weren't really FBI. And even if Dr. B had found a way to make himself look legitimate, her dad wouldn't have changed his identity. He'd already spent millions of dollars on his presidential campaign.

Tori hoped the bodyguards and precautions her family took would not only keep disgruntled constituents away from their home, but also megalomaniac dragon lords.

She shivered again. Her outfit didn't offer a lot of warmth in the high altitude, and the wind rushing across her bare legs and arms made goosebumps bloom on her skin.

"Hold on to my neck," Jesse told her. "I'll give you my coat."

She put her arms around his neck, too cold to refuse. She ignored the feel of his muscles under her arms, wouldn't let herself get distracted by his closeness.

He let go of his hold on her to shrug out of his jacket. Not long ago, dangling from a guy's neck thousands of feet above the ground would have freaked her out. Over the last few months, she'd spent so much time in the air that she had to remind herself not to let go of Jesse's neck, because she couldn't fly on her own.

Jesse circled her waist with one hand so he could give her his jacket with the other. She slipped it on, enjoying the warmth of the material and the way the coat smelled like him—some sort of spicy scent she could never quite identify.

The landscape spreading below showed that they'd left the DC area, but they weren't headed to the gymnasium where they'd held practice lately.

"Where are we going?" she asked.

"North Carolina."

"Long flight. You're going to get tired."

"I'm just flying to the van. A jet will do the rest."

He was serious. Dr. B wouldn't send them on a trip to another state if it wasn't important. Which meant this wasn't practice; it was a mission. That's why Jesse had really come for her: She was supposed to act as A-team's captain.

She pulled the jacket around her tighter. "What's in North Carolina?"

"Hopefully a clue to the dragons' location. One of Dr. B's sources reported someone in Huntersville selling actual dragon scales on the black market—five thousand dollars apiece."

"Why would anyone want to buy a dragon scale?"

Jesse flew lower, gliding toward a high school surrounded by fields and bleachers abandoned for the weekend. "Scales are fireproof and bulletproof, and, according to Chinese lore, if you grind them up and eat them, they'll give you long life and cure everything from madness to heart problems."

The Chinese were clearly optimists.

In the parking lot, Tori spotted a lone white van waiting for them. Dr. B's van. Jesse veered toward it. "The scales in North Carolina might be fake, but if not, the seller must be one of Overdrake's men making some money on the side. No one else would have access to dragon scales. We need to find him and convince him to give us the dragons' location."

"Convince him how?"

"The guy wants money. Hopefully a big enough bribe will work."

Tori smiled, thinking over the implications. The Slayers finally had a lead that could give them an advantage. If they could find the dragons' location, they could plan a surprise attack.

"Where exactly is the guy running his business from?"

"Exactly where you'd expect someone to sell dragon scales—one of the country's largest Renaissance fairs."

CHAPTER 4

A few minutes later, Tori and Jesse climbed into the white fifteen-passenger van. She'd expected to see all of the Slayers inside, with Dr. B behind the wheel. Instead, Bess sat in the driver's seat, and Ryker was the only other passenger.

Bess was tall and athletic looking, with shoulder-length brown curls she did her best to tame and blue eyes that often had a mischievous glint to them. Lately those eyes had spent a lot of time gazing in Ryker's direction. At 6' 4", he was the tallest of the Slayers, with short, dark hair and features ready-made for an action-movie hero.

"Hey, stranger," Bess said as Tori sat in the seat behind her. "How was *Wicked*?"

Tori clicked her seatbelt. "Wish I could tell you."

Bess started the ignition and headed across the parking lot toward the street. "Don't worry about missing the play. We'll have plenty of wicked stuff to deal with today."

"Where is everybody else?" Tori asked.

Bess stopped at the exit, checking for traffic before she pulled onto the street. "They're loading the jet with our equipment. My dad wants to leave as soon as we get there."

Bess was Dr. B's daughter, a fact the two of them did their best to forget during practice. Dr. B because he didn't want to show favoritism. Bess because she didn't want to receive it. A lot of times, his favoritism involved giving her long commentaries about how she could improve her performance.

Jesse motioned to Ryker. "Let's fill Tori in on the mission."

Ryker moved from the front seat to sit on Tori's other side. He had a tablet opened to the North Carolina Renaissance Festival website, his blue eyes all concentration.

Tori liked Ryker; she did. And she was relieved to have another flyer in the group. But she couldn't help feeling a twinge of resentment toward him. He was not only Jesse's counterpart—a role she'd once hoped was hers—he was a natural leader too. Smart, confident, and never at a loss for what to do. The other Slayers acted like it was only a matter of time before he took over as A-team's captain.

Jesse leaned toward Tori. "We don't know exactly where the dragon scales are being sold, just that it's in the back room of one of the buildings in the Renaissance festival, and the seller goes by Rudolpho. He meets prospective customers of his most expensive items only by appointment. We're hoping that if we flash around enough money, we can find him."

"I can hardly wait to flash around money," Bess called cheerfully from the front. "It's always been a lifelong goal of mine." She was rarely serious unless someone was about to be killed. This was one of the reasons Tori liked her so much.

"We'll split into three groups to search for Rudolpho," Jesse went on. "Theo will stay with the simulator in the festival parking lot to run surveillance."

Theo was a tech genius Dr. B hired years ago, and he took care of all things electronic or computer related.

"Once someone finds Rudolpho," Ryker said, "they'll signal for backup."

He tilted the tablet toward her, which now showed a

tourist map of the festival grounds. "The fair is on twenty-two acres surrounded by another two hundred and fifty acres of woodland. It's got dozens of permanent buildings, twelve stages, and over a hundred craft shops." He pointed to an area in the middle of the map. "I'll take Willow and Lilly and cover this part." He circled another spot. "Kody, Shang, and Dr. B will look here. You, Jesse, and Bess take this area."

Tori gazed at the map, memorizing as much of it as possible. "What if Rudolpho doesn't go for the money?" She hadn't had a lot of experience with bribing people. It was one of the few things Dr. B hadn't covered at camp.

Ryker zoomed in the screen, enlarging the shops area. "Then we'll have to use another form of persuasion."

She could guess what that would be. She gestured to her heels and the skirt hugging her legs. "You should have told me what we were doing. I'm not dressed for a fight."

Ryker gave her a pointed look. "You knew we had practice today." He glanced at Jesse, waiting for him to agree.

Jesse just grinned. "Hey, I have no complaints about Tori's outfit." His eyes shifted to her. "I already told you that you look amazing, right?"

Bess slowed for a red light. "My dad brought some clothes for you. I can't say they're fashionable, but at least they won't be so restrictive."

Ryker moved the map, as though a different angle would give him more information. "If we can't find a way to get the truth from Rudolpho, we'll bag the guy and take him with us. Theo rigged up some tranquilizer darts that connect to the bottom of our watches."

"Wait," Tori said. "We're going to kidnap someone?"

Ryker shrugged. "Only if we can't convince him to cooperate."

Tori's gaze went to Jesse to see his reaction. He looked unsurprised. He already knew about this part of the plan and had agreed to it. She let out a sigh. "Kidnapping is a federal offense. That means jail time."

"This is war." Jesse's voice became soft, asking her to understand. "We can't always play by the rules. You know that. Sometimes the ends justify the means."

"Funny, that's what Dirk said to justify his father's actions."

Jesse had the grace to wince at the comparison, but he didn't change his tone. "Yeah, except that we're trying to *protect* the nation, not take it over."

True. And they'd already had a turn on the slippery slope of justification. Last summer they invaded Overdrake's compound, hoping to destroy a pair of dragon eggs. If they'd been caught, the police would have charged them with breaking and entering with the intent to destroy personal property. The risk had seemed worth it. But this . . .

"Did I mention that my father is a presidential candidate?" Tori asked. "Having his daughter commit a felony would look really bad for his campaign."

"I guess so," Ryker said. "But dragons destroying cities would look even worse."

Jesse's tone was gentler. "Maybe she's right. Maybe she should sit out on this part and join the teams after we have intel on the dragons' location."

Ryker shook his head. "Who knows how many men Rudolpho has or what sort of security he's using? Tori can't sit out. We need as much help as we can get."

And there were Ryker and Jesse, sitting on either side of her, acting like captains as they decided the matter without her input. She lifted a hand to get their attention. "How are we going to sneak an unconscious body out of a Renaissance fair?"

Jesse opened his mouth to speak, then caught a look from Ryker, and nodded at him in answer instead. This was one of those counterpart things—understanding each other with less information than other people needed. "It's better if you don't know the details," Jesse said. "That way if we get caught, you can honestly say you didn't know what we were planning."

Ryker leaned back in his seat. "Besides, we're not kidnapping anyone. In fact, we're not doing anything illegal. See? Now you can tell the feds that I assured you this is all a normal business deal."

"That's right," Bess chimed in. "You're just our high-end shopping consultant."

As if the FBI would let her off that easy. She'd have to make sure she didn't get caught. "If Rudolpho is one of Overdrake's men," she pointed out, "he'll know that teenage Slayers are hunting for the dragons. He might even recognize us."

With a flick of her hand, Bess brushed off the objection. "My dad's got disguise stuff on the jet—hats, glasses, wigs. Things like that."

"But we'll still look like teenagers," Tori said. "Just different teenagers."

"We've got an hour until we land in Charlotte," Bess said without concern. "That gives us time to practice looking like innocent tourists."

Tori didn't press the issue. Bess meant there wasn't a better solution, and she had a point. Even if Dr. B rounded up enough trusted adults and gave them the task of finding Rudolpho, they wouldn't have Slayer training or abilities. Bess could throw shields up that blocked dragon fire and bullets. Kody's skill was shooting freezing blasts and fireballs. Shang and Lilly could extinguish fire, and Rosa specialized in healing burns. No one knew if Willow had an extra power. None had manifested yet, but her other Slayer abilities were enough to make her an asset. All of them had acute senses, extra strength, night vision, and could leap ten to fifteen feet in the air.

So the Slayers had to be the ones hunting for Rudolpho. No one else could do it, even though Overdrake's men knew the Slayers existed and were most likely watching for them.

And facing one of Overdrake's men would be worth it if doing so led them to the dragons.

"What if this is one of Overdrake's traps?" Tori asked. "He could have set up shop here, knowing that Dr. B would eventually find out about the scales and send us in to dig around."

Ryker shook his head at the idea. "Even if Overdrake is behind the operation, he won't know we're coming today. We'll just have to be careful."

Jesse pulled his attention away from the map to look at her. "As captain of A-team, don't you think looking for the scales is worth the risk?"

She hesitated, but only for a moment. "Yes."

* * *

When the group reached the private jet, the other Slayers were already onboard, dressed in jeans and T-shirts with their jackets slung over their seats. They looked like an average group of teenagers. Well, mostly. The guys were all more athletic than average, and Shang was probably dressier, wearing a polo shirt and brand-new jeans, their creases still visible.

At camp, he'd always been the most organized one—never forgetting a schedule, never late for practice. He was also the only reason the guys' cabin hadn't been heaped with trash and dirty clothes. He insisted that messiness was bad feng shui.

Lilly sat by Shang, her nails painted a don't-mess-with-me black and her long hair bleached platinum blonde. The last time Tori had seen it, it was regular blonde. Miss a few practices, and you missed the makeovers.

Lilly barely glanced over, which was the amount of attention Lilly usually paid to Tori, so she didn't mind. As long as Lilly followed orders when Tori was acting as captain, it didn't matter if she ignored her the rest of the time.

Kody, who was also on A-team, gave Tori a playful salute. He had short blond hair and a body builder's physique: all hulking, broad shoulders and biceps as big as salad plates. He was too good natured and friendly to care that Tori—who had years' less experience than he did—was in charge of the team. Besides, when he got it in his mind to do something, he generally disregarded the captains anyway, so being under her command probably didn't seem like much of an imposition to him.

Willow and Rosa motioned for Tori and Bess to come sit in the seats near them. Willow was tall, thin, and had the sort of natural grace that belonged to dancers and tree nymphs. Today her curly blonde hair was twisted into a bun, making her look like she ought to be at a rehearsal for *Swan Lake*. "I told you Bess wouldn't crash the van," Willow told Rosa. "They're all in one piece."

Ryker dropped into a seat behind them. "We would have been here sooner if Bess had let me drive."

Bess sent him a patient smile. "You're not allowed to drive the van again until you understand the difference between the beltway and a NASCAR racetrack."

"Oh, I understand the difference," he said with mock offense. "One has more traffic to get around."

Rosa shook her head at him. She was petite and pretty, with

china-doll features and dark brown hair that hung loose down her back. She was also the gentlest of the group and had the habit of worrying about the rest of them. "You know," she said directing her gaze to Ryker, "you won't be much use to us in a body cast."

Willow nodded in agreement. "And if you do something stupid that puts you in one, I'll sign your cast, 'I told you so.'"

She was Ryker's cousin and had no problem ribbing him. Which, Tori decided, partially made up for the way the rest of the girls acted all deferential and flirty around him. He'd been with the group for only a few weeks, so he still had *hot new guy* status, whereas the other guys were just boring, everyday hot.

Dr. B stepped from the flight deck into the seating area, carrying a plastic shopping bag. At practices, he usually wore Dockers and a button-down shirt, the sort of outfit you'd expect a professor of medieval history to wear. With his wavy gray hair and wire-rim glasses, he'd always looked the part of a dignified intellectual.

Today, he was dressed in a belted tunic, leggings, and pair of knee-high leather boots. Tori blinked and stared.

"I know," Bess said in a whisper. "I told him not to wear that, but he thinks it'll help him blend in with the Renaissance crowd."

Dr. B noted Tori's presence and smiled. "Good to see you. Looks like we're ready to go."

Jesse was still up near the front of the plane. Dr. B handed the plastic bag to him. "Give this to Tori so she can change, won't you?" Then he motioned to the group. "Seatbelts on, everyone." Without waiting, he returned to the cockpit to fly the plane.

Jesse walked down the aisle, sat beside Tori, and reluctantly handed her the plastic bag. His reluctance should have been her first clue that something was wrong.

"Just so you know," Bess said, "I told him you'd hate it."

Oh no. A sinking feeling went through Tori's stomach. She reached into the bag and pulled out a dress with a long brown skirt and maroon corset. The shirt had poofy, flowing white sleeves—some sort of Renaissance servant's dress. "I'm supposed to wear this?"

"Yeah," Willow said in an apologetic tone. "You get to be a saucy barmaid."

The label on the costume did indeed read, "Saucy barmaid."

Tori gazed around at the rest of the Slayers in their jeans. "Come on, this is a joke, right?"

The plane began taxiing down the runway. Jesse put on his seatbelt. "Dr. B wants one of us in costume in case we need to access any staff-only areas."

Rosa shrugged sympathetically. "I'd trade, but you wouldn't fit into my clothes." Rosa was a half a foot shorter than Tori.

"Sorry," Bess said. "I refuse to put on anything that makes me look like I'm wearing a matching outfit with my dad."

Willow lifted her shoulders and let them fall. "I don't have the figure to pull off a saucy barmaid. The costume would look stupid on me."

Tori sat back in her seat with a huff. "It'll look stupid no matter who's wearing it."

Lilly finally pulled herself away from her conversation with Shang. "If you don't like it, don't show up for the next mission in a cocktail dress and heels."

"This isn't a cocktail dress," Tori said. "It's from Dior's casual line. If you want to insult someone, you should at least be accurate."

Bess gestured to the overhead compartment. "And to

complete your outfit, your boots are in there with the rest of the gear." She meant her fighting boots: black, steel-toed, fireproof boots. Not exactly period wear, but the dress was long enough to mostly hide them.

Shang, who shared counterpart abilities with Lilly—but not her impatience toward Tori—said, "Lots of people dress up at these things. No one will think twice about your barmaid outfit."

"Unless they're really thirsty," Bess added. "Then they'll order you to go to ye olde tavern and fetch them a frothy brew."

Tori leaned her head back against her seat. This was going to be a long day.

CHAPTER 5

At three o'clock, the group walked through the gabled gates of Fairhaven and into the expansive grounds. Tori strode along with the others, pretending not to hate her outfit. The two- and three-story buildings, complete with high-pitched roofs and wood trim, seemed as though they'd been plucked from a fairy tale. Nearby, a flute player trilled out a tune while jesters juggled pins for a crowd. People in jeans mixed among those dressed in ball gowns, all of them slowly flowing down the wide dirt streets.

The simulator was back in the parking lot, so the Slayers could use their powers. Helpful, but also distracting. The noise from the musicians and the shuffling crowd felt louder, the scent of the different foods was more pungent. Turkey, roasted nuts, coffee, bread, and beer mixed together with the sweat of tourists—all of it heightened.

Dr. B gave everyone last-minute instructions before they split into their groups. "Remember, subtlety is the better part of stealth. Use as little force as necessary. We don't want anyone to remember we've been here."

Under her breath, Bess whispered, "Then you shouldn't have worn leggings."

Tori was glad to finally head off with Jesse and Bess to

search their area. If Tori had to hear Ryker call her, "Wench," one more time, she was going to slap him with her barmaid satchel. It held enough stacks of hundred dollar bills to make a decent weapon.

Along with her dress, Tori wore a curly black wig and a serving cap. Bess had on a pair of hipster glasses and a blond wig she kept swishing over her shoulder. Jesse wore a baseball cap pulled low over his forehead, glasses, and a bulky jacket. Not much of a disguise. He was still handsome enough to draw attention from passing girls.

The group strolled by a blue-and yellow-striped tent, where a king and queen held court and loudly discussed the burdens of royalty.

Jesse side-stepped a man sweeping by on stilts. "Watch your purse," he told Tori. "This would be a bad time to be pickpocketed."

He was right; she carried the price of one dragon scale plus ten thousand in bribe money. The other groups had been given the same amount, which made Tori wonder, not for the first time, where the mysterious Sam, who funded the Slayers, got his money.

"Five thousand dollars per scale," Jesse muttered. "If I'd known they sold for that much, I would have pried some off the last two dragons we killed." He glanced at Bess. "Is your dad going to sell the ones he took?"

Bess shook her head. "He's experimenting on ways to break them. Although I have to say, I think he's developed an unhealthy attachment to them. He's always getting them out and staring at them. Soon he's going to give them names like *Shnookums* and *Precious*.

Tori hadn't remembered Dr. B taking scales from either of the dragons they'd killed, but she'd been in a state of sickened shock at the time and hadn't paid attention to that sort of thing. She hadn't wanted to look at the dragons, to see their broken forms and know she'd been responsible for their deaths.

That was the problem with being half Slayer and half dragon lord. Her genetics had programmed her to kill dragons, but unfortunately also made her feel guilty about it afterward.

Tori wound past a family heading the opposite direction. "I wonder if the Chinese are right about dragons having medicinal uses. What if we were to kill them all and then found out their scales could cure cancer?"

Bess and Jesse exchanged a look, one that indicated that they thought Tori was being naive about medicinal uses. Jesse said, "I'm willing to take that chance."

"Ditto," Bess said.

They made their way around a stage where belly dancers clanged their finger cymbals and swayed to an exotic, soulful tune.

"Overdrake is the real problem," Tori insisted. "If we take care of him, the dragons would—"

"Still be huge, flying carnivores who want to eat us," Bess finished. She turned to Jesse, peering over the rim of her glasses. "Is there any way to unplug Dirk from her mind? I think he's brainwashing her."

"I wish there was," Jesse said. He didn't like that Dirk could talk to Tori any time he wanted. "And speaking of dragon lords, have you talked to your parents about moving, Tori?"

The fact that Overdrake knew where Tori lived worried all of the Slayers, especially Jesse, and most of all, Tori. But the problem wasn't an easy one to fix.

"I tried. I made up stories about seeing suspicious men scoping out the house, and I told my parents that I thought political whackos were going to break in."

"Didn't that concern them?"

"Oh, they're concerned—about me. They think I'm getting paranoid. They checked the footage of our security cameras and didn't see anything worth worrying about."

Although, Aprilynne had suggested that a family of boogey men might have moved in down the street and were waiting for the opportunity to relocate under Tori's bed.

Tori adjusted a strand from her wig that kept knocking into her face. "I'm just going to have to depend on our security system, the bodyguards, and our German shepherd to keep me safe."

Jesse frowned. "It's not enough."

"I don't know. Brindy's a pretty smart dog." Not remotely true. Brindy was hopelessly trusting and would allow burglars entrance to the house or lead them to the valuables as long as they gave her dog treats in the process.

Jesse's gaze went to Tori's and stayed there. He was probably trying to look stern, but somehow managed to look like a brooding cologne model instead. "You're not taking this seriously."

Tori pulled her attention away from him and surveyed the surrounding shops. "Dirk said his father promised not to hurt me." He had assured her of this fact more than once during their talks.

Jesse let a grunt. "Yeah, and we know how much Dirk's word means. Overdrake has already sent two dragons to kill us. I don't think he cares what he promised Dirk."

Jesse had a point, but what could she do about it? She had no way to convince her parents to move.

The group spent the next hour trudging into buildings, perusing the wares, and asking if Rudolpho was around. Since Tori carried the money, it fell to her to play the part of the interested buyer.

"You've got to be the one," Bess had said at the first shop. "Jesse and I would have a hard time faking being rich, but you don't have to pretend."

They'd gone into five stores, and in each one Tori had acted like she knew that Rudolpho would be inside, that she had connections who had directed her to that place to meet him. And in each shop, the proprietors looked at her as if she was confused and perhaps not all that bright.

Jesse and Bess would have a hard time faking they were rich. Right. They were just smart enough to avoid the role of confused/half-crazy buyer. Well, that would teach Tori to skip out on practices where they planned these sorts of things.

They wandered into The Black Unicorn Shoppe, and Tori pretended to eye the silver tiaras while she scanned the store. Several tourists milled among the goods. A woman dressed in a blue corset stood behind the counter, ringing up purchases. A man in a tunic and leggings helped a middle-aged woman with a dragonfly necklace. No watchful security men seemed to be guarding anything of value.

Bess, Jesse, and Tori meandered across the room, admiring shelves filled with pewter knights and unicorn figurines. So many dragon prints hung on the wall, they looked like they were part of a parade. The artists had gotten the color completely wrong. Dragons weren't brown or grayish, lizard-like colors. They didn't have to blend into their surroundings. They were flashy, proudly wearing the colors of danger. The dragons she'd seen were red and bright blue.

The shopkeeper finished helping his customer and strolled over. "Sir, my ladies, may I be of service?"

Tori gave him a bashful smile. "I hope so. I'm looking for something special."

He swept his hand toward the shelves. "We've many a special trinket here. What, pray tell, has caught your fancy?"

"Actually, I want to speak to Rudolpho."

The man paused, hesitated, and took in Tori again. He seemed to note how young she was. "Do you?" he asked, still measuring her.

"I hear he sells some, um, authentic souvenirs." She sashayed closer. "Dragon scales. Don't worry. I have cash." She reached into the cloth purse. While she did, she hit the button at the side of her watch that contacted Dr. B and let him hear her conversation. She pulled out a stack of hundreds and flashed them at the man. "Can you take me to Rudolpho, please?"

Dr. B's voice immediately came through the earpiece hidden in Tori's ear. "You've found him?"

Tori smiled at the shopkeeper again. "Seeing Rudolpho is really why I came to the fair." That should answer Dr. B's question.

The man nodded at the sight of her bills. "He usually requires an appointment, but if you give me your name, I can ask if he's available."

Tori slipped the money back into her purse. "Tell him Emily Morgan would like to see him." Tori had chosen the name because everyone knew a few Emilys. Emilys were hard to keep track of.

The man gave them a slight bow, said, "Wait here," and went through a door behind to the counter.

Jesse turned so the woman at the counter couldn't see his face. "We're at The Black Unicorn," he whispered into his mic.

In Tori's earpiece, Dr. B reported the news to the other teams. They'd convene here soon. "Theo," he said. "You've got the horse?"

"And the armor," Theo answered. "I'm heading to the shop now."

Horse? Armor? What were they planning to do if Rudolpho didn't cooperate? She really should have insisted they give her those sorts of details.

Then again, maybe Jesse was right. If things went wrong, she could honestly tell her parents she didn't know what had been on the day's agenda. She would just hope that none of their watches were confiscated. The police might notice that the timepieces had each been equipped with a tranquilizing dart.

Dr. B's voice came over her earpiece. "Be sure to examine the scale to make sure it's genuine before you offer money. Authentic scales have an interlocking micro pattern."

Tori had never looked at a scale up close, but she'd seen enough of the real kind that she should be able to identify one.

Her phone buzzed in her purse. She pulled it out, checked the screen, and let out a disheartened sigh. "Bad news."

Jesse's gaze swung to her. "What?"

"My parents know I'm AWOL. They want to know where I am and when I'll be home."

"Oh," he said, relieved, and went back to scoping out the store. "Tell them we're at a movie, it's about to start, and you have to turn off your phone now."

Tori typed in the sentence, sent it, and slipped her phone into her purse. "I hope this mission doesn't take all day. I'm still on probation for disappearing last time."

The shopkeeper came back and made a summoning motion to Tori while holding open the back door. "This way, please."

When Bess and Jesse followed after her, the shopkeeper raised a hand to stop them. "Only one buyer at a time in the room."

"But we're with her," Bess protested.

"Then I'm surprised you don't already know the rules," he said. "One buyer."

Tori faltered, but couldn't think of a way around the rule. "Fine." She flicked her hand in Jesse's direction. "Can you get me a soda while you wait? This dress is hot." She was really giving him an excuse to leave the shop and scout around the building until the other Slayers arrived. Bess would stay inside in case Tori needed backup.

He nodded. "I'll see what's around."

Tori trailed after the man, hoping Rudolpho could be easily bribed. That would make the meeting so much simpler.

The man led her down a short hallway, and then took her up a flight of stairs. "I hope I don't trip," she said to let the other Slayers know where she was going. "It's so hard to navigate stairs in a long dress."

A narrow hallway waited at the top of the stairs. He led her down it, bypassing two doors and coming to a stop at the third. "First things first," the shopkeeper said, still maintaining the British accent. "I need to make sure you're not, as you Yanks say, packing heat." He picked up a metal detector wand that hung by the door and ran it over her.

She held her hands up, showing they were empty. "Security already checked our bags when we came into the fair. For a place that sells swords in every other shop, you people worry a lot about weapons."

Satisfied she didn't have a gun on her, the man hung the detector up and opened the door. "This way."

A portly, middle-aged man dressed in nobleman clothes sat behind a large desk. He had sharp eyes, graying brown hair that brushed against his shoulders, and an overgrown, bushy beard. Tori wondered if the beard was period accurate, or whether he just didn't like to shave.

A hulkingly tall man in regular clothes stood in the corner of the room, arms folded, watching her. Probably Rudolpho's security. The dark jacket he wore on his sizable chest undoubtedly hid a firearm.

Tori stepped into the room, automatically surveying it for tactical information. It was medium-sized with a window on the back wall. No other doors besides the one she'd come in. The window faced the forest, not the festival grounds. If she had to fly out of it, at least she wouldn't be videotaped by tourists in the process.

A tapestry depicting a unicorn hung on one wall. Two crossed swords and a heraldry shield hung on the other. Green opaque curtains blocked the view but not the sunlight. Which meant Tori couldn't destroy the overhead light to get the advantage of fighting in the dark with night vision.

The shopkeeper who'd taken Tori to the room followed her in, locked the door, and leaned against the wall. If things went badly, Tori would have three men to take care of, and at least one of them was armed. Could she bribe them all? She hoped so, because her watch only shot one dart. There hadn't been room for more than that. Bess and Jesse were supposed to be around to help with crowd control.

Tori made her way to a chair that sat in front of the desk, ignoring Rudolpho's penetrating stare. Several different magnifying glasses lay on the desk, along with a lamp and a long, black box. The keypad on the box told her it was a safe.

Rudolpho leaned back in his chair, revealing an oversized stomach. "You're younger than my usual clients."

"Thank you," she said, as though it was a compliment and not a statement of suspicion. "I do what I can to keep up my appearance. That's one of the reasons I'm interested in dragon scales. I have it on good authority that taking powdered scale promotes long life."

Rudolpho steepled his fingers, a pose of confidence. "Quite

true, although grinding them isn't an easy task." His gaze went over Tori again. "I'm always curious to learn how people find out about my business. Who should I thank for referring you?"

She didn't hesitate with her rehearsed answer. "I met a man in DC's Chinatown who spoke highly of you—an artifact dealer named Lee." When Rudolpho showed no recognition of the name, Tori shrugged. "He may not have given me his real name. Some of his artifacts weren't exactly legal."

Rudolpho smiled though she wasn't sure if he believed her or whether the smile was because he found her story amusingly easy to see through. He gestured at her purse. "Before I show you a scale, I need to make sure you have sufficient cash. The price is five thousand dollars. No refunds."

She opened her purse, wondering how far away the other Slayers were from the building. It would have been nice if Dr. B was issuing instructions through her earpiece, but he remained quiet. For the most part, Dr. B let the Slayers run ops themselves and intervened only when he had information to add.

Tori took out a stack of hundred-dollar bills, one containing five thousand dollars, and fanned the bills out on the desk. "Can I see a scale now?" All of this would be a lot of effort for nothing if the scale turned out to be fake.

Rudolpho eyed the money then pushed a few buttons on his safe's keypad. The top unlatched, he flipped it open, and revealed a blue dragon scale. It was about the size of Tori's palm, the bright blue bleeding into purple at the tip. He picked up the scale, laid it on the desk, then handed her a jeweler's magnifying glass.

He didn't have to bother. She'd recognized the scale as soon as she saw it: one of Kiha's. On Halloween, the Slayers had killed that dragon in a deserted part of the Catskill Mountains.

The sight of the scale made Tori gulp, made the memory come back in searing force—the fear as she fled through the trees from Overdrake and his dragon, the bullets and fire.

Had one of Overdrake's cleanup crew cut off some of Kiha's scales before disposing of her? The scale looked smaller than the ones she'd seen on the dragon's torso and chest. Perhaps it had come from some small area—around her claws or from her face.

Tori took the magnifying glass and held it to her eye to examine the scale. Dr. B had said scales were made up of small, interlocking parts. Under magnification, this scale appeared to be made of blue crystals, like an exotic sapphire. How odd that something so beautiful belonged to such a deadly creature.

She ran a finger across the scale. It was as smooth as polished stone. She hadn't expected that. Funny, she'd fought two dragons—been torched, bludgeoned by wings, and even connected with a dragon's mind—but she'd never run her fingers over a scale until now.

She set the jeweler's glass down. "Looks authentic." The words were for the Slayers listening on her earpiece. The trail here was real; one they could follow. And Rudolpho would lead the Slayers to Overdrake, whether he wanted to or not.

CHAPTER 6

Tori picked up the scale and let the weight of it press into her fingers. It was heavier than she imagined, more substantial. "Where did you get this?"

Rudolpho gave her an indulgent look, as if she were a child who'd asked for the moon. "My suppliers are private. I'm sure you understand how these things work."

"Of course." Tori placed the scale back on the desk and pulled the second stack of hundreds from her purse. "Ten thousand. You see, I'm more interested in finding your supplier than I am in buying the scale."

"I'm sorry," he said, unmoved by the money in her hand. "A good dealer never reveals his sources. That would mean creating competition for myself."

"How about fifteen thousand? I have friends here with more cash."

Rudolpho squinted at her in disbelief. "Fifteen grand? You have that much money to spend?"

"I have a deep interest in dragons." She shrugged and fluttered her hand in an attempt of nonchalance. "If you sell scales, you've got to expect that people will want to see the dragon."

Rudolpho stroked the end of his beard, watching her.

"There's nothing left to see. Dragons are extinct. That's why their scales are so valuable." He spoke easily enough, expecting her to believe his words.

"Are you sure they're extinct?" she asked.

He made a huffing noise to let her know the topic wasn't worth discussing. "Do you want to buy the scale or not?"

He might not be one of Overdrake's men after all, but he had to know someone who was. That scale was real, and it must have come from Kiha. Tori pushed the stack of money toward him. "I want to know the dragons' location."

Without another word, Rudolpho picked up the scale, tucked it back into the safe, and shut the lid with unmistakable finality. "I'm afraid I can't help you. My sources aren't for sale." He sent the shopkeeper a look that said, *I'm through. Take care of her.*

The shopkeeper stepped away from the wall toward Tori. "I'll show you out. You and your friends are not to bother Mr. Rudolpho again." No accent this time. His words came out low and firm.

In Tori's earpiece, Jesse said, "The other Slayers are almost here. Which room are you in? Back, front? Left, right?"

The room was in the back of the building, but Tori wasn't sure whether he was asking for directions based on facing the front of the building or facing the rear.

"Back . . . to bargaining," Tori said, not leaving her chair. "I don't know what the right price is, or what's left to negotiate. But how does twenty thousand sound?"

Rudolpho let out a small laugh and waved her away. "I was willing to believe someone your age could come up with five grand—although trust me, I check for counterfeit bills. Your problem is that you stretched your credibility too far. You don't really have ten thousand, let alone twenty. Go find someone else to hustle, and stop wasting my time."

"Check the bills," Tori said, gesturing to money. "Check them all."

Rudolpho shook his head. "I've got real customers to worry about." To the shopkeeper, he said, "See her outside."

Really? Tori thought. *You're turning me down because I don't look rich enough?* The other Slayers were going to think *that* was hilarious.

She slid the money into her purse, slung it over her shoulder, and stood. "You're making a mistake."

The shopkeeper took hold of Tori's arm, more than willing to drag her from the room. As he peered at her, his eyes focused on her ear, and his hand tightened on her arm. "What's that?"

Oh no. If he could see her earpiece, then Tori's wig no longer covered it. He knew she was wired. This was about to get very bad.

Jesse and Bess were too far away to help. Tori would have to take care of this herself. Three against one. Well, that was just a normal day at Slayer practice.

The shopkeeper reached for her ear. She yanked him forward, sending him tumbling onto the desk. The security guard stepped from the corner and headed her way, reaching into his jacket for his gun. That left her no choice. Rudolpho might be the target, but she had to take out the guard. She aimed her watch at his neck and pushed the release button.

The man flinched, slapped the dart from his neck, then went for his gun again. The drug wouldn't take full effect for at least a minute, probably longer with his body mass. Until then, she'd have to dodge bullets.

The shopkeeper straightened, pushing himself away from the desk. With one leap, she placed herself behind him. Hopefully the security guy wouldn't shoot his own man to get at her.

Rudolpho glared at her from the desk but didn't join the fight. He obviously thought she didn't stand a chance against his men, that she was about to be subdued.

The shopkeeper turned and lunged at her, bending at the waist. No good. She was losing her shield. She dropped to a squat and used the man's momentum to flip him over her shoulder and into the back wall.

The thud and groan behind her told her he wouldn't be a threat for a few seconds, but she still had two men to deal with, one of them armed. Time to improve her odds. The code word for requesting backup was "crowd." Tori was about to say it, then remembered they'd changed the word after Dirk's betrayal. What had they switched it to?

The security guard leveled his gun at her. No time to think about code words. "Uh," was all she got out before she sprang sideways, half leaping, half flying toward the nearest wall. A pop sounded from the gun, and a bullet whizzed by her shoulder. Too close. Even with a silencer, the noise still sounded loud in the small room.

"T-bird?" Jesse asked, using her code name. "What was that noise?"

She was concentrating too hard to answer. She pushed off the wall to the desk and grabbed the safe. It probably weighed fifty pounds, but felt like nothing in her hands. In one smooth motion, she flung it at the security guard.

Jesse spoke in her earpiece again. "What's going on? Are you still in the building?"

The safe hit the guard in the chest and he flew backward, arms flung out to his sides, until he smacked the wall with a thud. She hoped he would drop the gun, but as he slid to the floor, he kept hold of it. That was dedication to the job. Who said you couldn't hire good help anymore?

It would take him a moment to aim at her again. Rudolpho was still sitting at his desk, gaping at her in open-mouthed shock. She ignored him. The shopkeeper was coming up behind her, panting out determined breaths.

She ran to the nearest wall, took three steps up it, and grabbed the hanging tapestry. As she flipped back down to the floor, the wall hanging ripped away. She flung it at the security guard, covering him in the woven hunt scene. That should keep him from shooting for half a minute. How many seconds were left before he passed out? Ten? Twenty? What if the tranquilizer didn't completely work on someone his size?

"Not crowd!" she said into her mic. "You know what I mean."

She dashed to the next wall, took two steps up it, and kicked the shield from its spot. She caught it on the way back down and spun around to face the shopkeeper. He kept a wary distance now that he'd seen that she was dangerous. She'd meant to fling the shield into him, but waited when something metallic flashed in his hand. As he raised his arm, she realized what he held—a pair of ninja stars.

Seriously? Only at a place where people got all geeky about weapons would someone be armed with ninja stars.

As the stars whizzed toward her, she lifted the shield, blocking them. They thunked harmlessly into the metal and pinged to the floor.

Rudolpho had been rifling through a desk drawer, now he came toward her, a stun gun in hand.

"'Not crowd'?" Jesse repeated in her ear. He obviously didn't know what she meant. "Beta, has T-bird come back out of the room?"

"No," Bess said.

Before Rudolpho could use the stun gun, Tori kicked at his

hand. Her long skirt tangled around her legs, and a rip sounded as her foot connected with his arm. Stupid dress. Say what you wanted about Wonder Woman's skimpy crime-fighting outfit; at least the thing never tripped her during a kick.

The weapon flew from Rudolpho's grip and slid under his desk. He swore and stepped backward, shaking his hand in pain.

"Go in," Jesse told Bess. "Something's wrong." It would take them a couple minutes to get inside and then figure out which room she was in.

Rudolpho looked over Tori's shoulder, where the security guard was trying to get the tapestry off himself. "Shoot her!"

The man hadn't passed out yet? Tori flung the shield toward the shopkeeper and lunged at Rudolpho. Grabbing his arm, she pulled him in front of her and held him there.

"Wait, don't shoot!" Rudolpho called.

The security guard unsteadily got to his feet, swaying as he stood. His eyes were glassy, his hands wavering as he tried to focus.

The shopkeeper rushed at Tori, probably meaning to knock her down and break her grip on Rudolpho.

Fine. Right before the shopkeeper plunged into her, she let go of Rudolpho and stepped back. The shopkeeper slammed into his boss and sent him sprawling against the wall. She grabbed the shopkeeper by the arms, pinned them behind his back, and spun him around. New guy as a shield, but basically the same situation.

"Shoot her!" Rudolpho rasped from his spot on the floor. "She's robbing us!"

"Don't shoot!" the shopkeeper called in disbelief.

That was the thing about employee loyalty: Sometimes it only went one way.

Tori never found out which instruction the guard would have obeyed, because the drug finally took effect. His head lolled, and he toppled forward. The sound of his crash to the floor was almost as loud as the sound of the door splintering from its hinges behind her.

Bess stepped into the room, arm raised, and hand on her watch, ready to shoot a tranquilizer dart. Her gaze flew between Tori holding the shopkeeper, and Rudolpho, now cowering on the floor.

"Situation?" Bess asked.

"Shoot the guy by the wall," Tori said. "Subtlety didn't work out so well."

Rudolpho raised his hands in protest. "No!" he croaked. "I'll tell you what you want!"

Bess swung her arm in Rudolpho's direction and shot. The dart penetrated his cheek, making him grimace. He wiped at it wildly. "Why did you do that?"

The shopkeeper stopped struggling in Tori's grip as if fear had taken hold of him. "I don't know anything about his contacts," he stammered. "Rudolpho was the only one who met with the guy."

Tori didn't release him.

Bess addressed Rudolpho. "You have sixty seconds to tell us where you got the scale, or we'll have to haul you out of here and get the information from you in a different way."

"Don't make us do that, Rudolpho," Tori added sweetly. "I've got a busy day as it is."

"I don't know where the scale came from," Rudolpho said in a shaky voice. He raised his hands in surrender. "But I'll tell you what I know. My contact is Connor. He lives in Huntersville. We always exchange goods at the post office, but I had him followed once, so I know he lives on Grassy Creek

Drive. Brick house with black shutters. A two-story. I can get you the address. It's in my phone." Still raising his hands, he got to his feet.

"Stay where you are," Bess said. "I'll get your phone."

Jesse's voice came over Tori's earpiece. "I'm heading up the stairs." He was letting her know so she wouldn't mistake him for one of Rudolpho's men.

"It's in the . . ." Rudolpho slumped back to the floor. He blinked at the desk blankly, and his fingers made strokes at the air.

Tori didn't hear Jesse come up the stairs. Her first indication he'd arrived was the shopkeeper flinching in her grasp. Then she saw a tiny dart sticking out of the back of the man's neck. Jesse had shot him.

"I don't know anything about this Connor guy," the shopkeeper sputtered, indignant. "Why are you drugging me?"

"No one is going to hurt you," Tori assured him. She shook her head at Jesse. "I can't believe you took that shot. You could have hit me."

"Not with my aim. Some of us don't skip out of practice." Jesse sent her a meaningful look as he walked into the room. His gaze ran over her, checking for injuries, and then he glanced back at the stairs. "The others are keeping the sales clerk busy, but someone is bound to come up here before long. We've got to hurry."

As if in answer, a scratching noise came from the window.

"What's that?" the shopkeeper asked. "What are you doing?"

"I don't know," Tori said, holding onto him more loosely now. "I missed the planning meeting. Want to lie down?"

Everything she said felt odd. For the last few minutes, roughing up unsuspecting merchants, she'd felt like the villain.

The shopkeeper didn't answer. He was gawking at the window and the outline of a person floating outside.

Jesse pushed aside the curtains and opened the window. Ryker hovered outside, standing in the sunshine against a backdrop of fall trees. His arms were full of knight armor, a shiny leg sticking out one way, an arm piece poking out another. He handed some of them to Jesse and flew in with the rest. Jesse strode over to Rudolpho, lifted the man's head, and put the helmet on him.

The shopkeeper began to sway in Tori's grip, so she helped him to the floor. While she did that, Ryker, Jesse, and Bess strapped armor onto Rudolpho's unconscious form, maneuvering his arms into the costume as though he was a large, middle-aged doll.

That's how they'd planned on getting the man out of the fair—disguised in armor and sitting on a horse. The armor would hold him in place, and no one would recognize him or realize he was unconscious.

Tori sighed. "He gave us the address. Why are we taking him?" She'd hoped the illegal portion of their trip to the Renaissance fair was over. Apparently not.

"Because he might have lied." Jesse latched shut the armor around Rudolpho's chest. "We won't get a chance to question him again for a while, so we'll keep him until his info checks out."

She understood the logic, but didn't like the situation. "We're going to end up as a story on one of those crime shows— and I'm the one who did most of the assaulting."

Jesse lifted Rudolpho so Bess and Ryker could slide his metal pants on. "Speaking of which, why didn't you ask for backup earlier? My clue you need help shouldn't be the sound of angry men swearing at you."

"I forgot the signal, but I said, 'Not crowd.'"

"Which I thought meant you didn't want backup." Jesse shifted Rudolpho, tugging up the leg armor. "I thought you'd forgotten that we changed the word."

"I remembered." Tori felt along her wig. Some of the pins had come loose during the fight. She fastened them back in place. "I just couldn't remember what we changed it to."

"It's 'reverse,'" Jesse said.

Reverse. Because when you put a car in reverse, you back up.

Rudolpho was ready, ensconced in a knight's outfit that, if not completely authentic, at least did a good job disguising him. Ryker put his arms around the man's torso and hefted him toward the window as easily as if he were a child.

Lilly's voice came over the earpiece. "You're about to have company. The sales clerk sent someone to check on you."

"We're leaving," Jesse said. "Aspen, is the way clear?"

"Still clear," Willow answered. "But your horse is getting antsy."

Without another word, Jesse glided just out of the window, then turned back, reaching for the unconscious man. Ryker handed him to Jesse then flew out himself. Tori followed, carrying Bess.

Once on the ground, they split into groups and walked out of the fair, casually, unnoticed. Dr. B led the horse. Metal braces in the back of the armor kept Rudolpho securely upright and in place. Several passing tourists waved at the knight, but he never waved back.

CHAPTER 7

Tori had to wait until Dr. B drove the Slayers to a motel in Huntersville before she could change out of her barmaid costume and into her battle gear: Black bulletproof jackets and matching pants, both with plenty of pockets for weapons and ammo. The outfits were stiff, but the protection was worth losing a little mobility. And best of all, with her helmet on, she'd be unrecognizable so her picture was much less likely to end up splashed across the tabloids.

The Slayers left Kody to guard Rudolpho while the rest of them drove to the address he'd given them. If his information panned out, he would be set free. Dr. B didn't seem to worry about Rudolpho going to the authorities to report being kidnapped. He wouldn't want to tell the police about his business. According to Dr. B, scales weren't the only thing the man sold on the black market. He also had a variety of stolen artifacts from countries who weren't as adept at protecting their antiquities as they should have been.

Connor's neighborhood was in an upscale area not far from the festival grounds. By the time the Slayers reached it, darkness was settling in, providing them with cover. Colonial-style houses with manicured lawns backed up against an undeveloped stretch of land that looked like it had aspirations of one day becoming a golf course. Connor, whoever he was, clearly had money.

How well did Overdrake pay his men? She had no idea what the going salary rate was for minions. Perhaps Connor needed to supplement his income with some clandestine sales to pay his mortgage.

Dr. B parked the van a few houses away. He brought up a satellite picture of the home on his laptop and waited for Theo to access additional material from a blueprint database he'd hacked into.

Rosa, dressed in her normal clothes and using an infrared sensor, took a walk past the house to see how many people were inside. She always did reconnaissance. With her petite size and innocent-looking features, no one ever suspected her being up to anything.

After a few minutes, she returned and climbed back into the van. "Two people are in the house, both on first floor."

By then, Theo had pulled up the house's schematics. While Dr. B handed out equipment, the Slayers surveyed the layout, committing it to memory. Four bedrooms upstairs, everything else downstairs.

"They've got an alarm," Theo said, reading a stream of numbers on his laptop. "But it's not turned on right now." He grunted and shook his head. "Nobody ever activates their systems when they should. You'd think Overdrake's men would be more careful."

Yes, you would. Tori hoped an unarmed system didn't mean they were about to break into some innocent person's home. An invasion of this sort would be hard to explain to a couple of random strangers.

"I'll call the attack plan." Jesse said. His eyes shifted to Tori in explanation. "I know you want to stay out of this one as much as possible."

She wasn't sure whether to protest being excluded or not. When Jesse called the plans, he had a tendency to put her in the safest position. A sweet but unnecessary gesture.

"Lilly and Rosa," he went on, without giving her time to decide, "you have outside reconnaissance. Jump the fence, tranquilize any dogs, and do an updated scan of the house to make sure the targets haven't moved locations. See if the back door is locked. If it is, stay in the yard unless someone calls for backup." He sent Tori a look. "And the code word for backup is?"

"Reverse." She sent him a look right back. "If I had really needed your help, I would have found a way to ask sooner, but I was taking care of things pretty well by myself."

Jesse tilted his chin down, unhappy with her response. "Three armed men attacked you, and you didn't think you needed help? Overconfidence leads to mistakes." He didn't add, although his expression implied, that her safety was of more than casual importance to him.

That was the problem with dating the other captain—he worried about her too much.

"Only two of them were armed," she said, taking one of a tranquilizer guns from Dr. B. "I mean, ninja stars hardly count."

"We'll talk more about that later," Jesse said, unconvinced. "When we're alone." He returned his attention to the computer screen.

He obviously didn't get as sidetracked as she did by the thought of them being alone.

Jesse pointed to an upstairs window at the back of the house. "Ryker, if the back door is locked, fly here, cut the glass, and go inside. Tori, you carry Willow and follow after Ryker. When Theo gives the all clear, Ryker will fly downstairs and open the back door for Shang, Bess, and me."

Tori's phone buzzed. She took it out of her jacket pocket to check the screen. Her parents had texted, asking when she'd be home.

Jesse stopped his instructions. "I thought you turned that off."

"I had to turn it back on. A movie would be over by now." Tori opened the message, then texted back a reply. "I'm telling my parents we're getting something to eat and the service is really slow." After all, she still had an hour-long flight home to account for.

"Don't forget dessert," Rosa put in.

"And the making out afterwards," Bess added. "Jesse will take you to a romantic overlook in DC for that."

Tori coughed in disbelief and put her phone back into her pocket. "Like I'd tell my parents that. They'd never let me out of the house unchaperoned again."

"Just imply it," Bess said.

"Um," Jesse said, breaking into the conversation. "We need to get back to the mission." He turned to Tori and lowered his voice. "Please don't ever tell your parents anything that will make them sic Secret Service on me." His eyes went back to the screen, and he stared at it blankly. Another moment went by. "Where was I?"

Ryker let out a small laugh. "Apparently deep in thought about a romantic overlook in DC."

"I remember," Jesse said, "I was putting Ryker in danger. He'll fly downstairs, open the door, and he, Shang, Bess, and I will surround the targets. With the element of surprise, we shouldn't have much of a fight."

Willow leaned over the computer, scrutinizing the floorplan. "What are Tori and I supposed to do upstairs while the rest of you are downstairs?"

Jesse's gaze flicked briefly to Tori, then went back to the diagram. He pointed to one of the upstairs bedrooms. "This window has a ledge. Someone could use it to escape the house. You and Tori will stand guard at the top of the stairs to prevent that from happening."

"You need two people to do that?" Tori asked, eyebrow raised.

Jesse didn't look at her. "Two people are in the house, so yeah, it makes sense to have two of us waiting at the top of the stairs."

Uh-huh. Jesse just wanted her someplace safe and out of the action. Really, she forgot one code word, and he lost all confidence in her.

A protest sat on the edge of Tori's tongue, but she bit it back. She'd already participated in this mission more than was prudent—especially if any of Rudolpho's men ended up going to the police and were able to give a description of her. Better to lie low during this part of the mission.

Willow let out a huff. "You think I don't know how to fight, don't you?"

Jesse shook his head, perhaps too quickly. "No, tactically, it's always better to keep some players in reserve."

Yeah, Tori didn't buy that excuse, and she doubted Willow did either.

Ryker checked his tranquilizer gun, then put it in its holster. "No one's going to do much fighting. Once Connor and his accomplice are surrounded, they'll give up." He patted Willow on the shoulder. "Your job will mostly be making sure Tori doesn't ditch us like she usually does during practice."

"Hey," Tori said, adjusting her neck mic. "I can't help it if I have other commitments."

"Consider it girl bonding time," Ryker added, ignoring Tori. "You can talk about guys."

Tori put in her earpiece. "And I know which guy we'll be talking about first."

Dr. B handed out the last of the tranquilizer guns. "Remember, do your best to keep out of sight."

If anyone saw people in black clothes and helmets breaking into a house, they'd no doubt call the police. Theo was monitoring the police scanner. If any calls went out, he'd hear them and warn the Slayers.

Dr. B returned to the driver's seat and guided the van toward the house, glancing up and down the street to check for wandering pedestrians. Satisfied the van wasn't being watched, he stopped a little way from Connor's house, then hit the button to open the side door.

Rosa and Lilly slipped outside. They hurried across the side lawn, shadow-like, and disappeared into the backyard. A couple of minutes later, Lilly's voice came over the earpiece.

"No dogs. The back door is locked. Ryker will need to go in and open the door. Scanner is still picking up two people downstairs—one in the family room, and I think the other is in the den."

"Understood," Jesse said, and gestured to the other Slayers. "Proceed as planned."

Jesse, Ryker, Willow, and Tori poured out of the van.

Nothing will go wrong, Tori told herself. *Whoever Connor is, he isn't expecting us. He couldn't be.*

In truth, this mission would probably be less dangerous than some of her past practice sessions. Even so, her adrenaline pumped in a way that set her nerves on edge. She ran toward the house, silently keeping pace with the others. Ryker leapt over the fence without breaking stride. Jesse went over next, also clearing the top in one fluid motion.

"Flyers make it look so easy," Willow muttered, and

leaped, kicking her legs up like a pole vaulter. Tori flew over at the same time, and wondered if she should grab Willow midair and help her over, but Willow managed to straighten her legs and land on her feet. Tori dropped down to the ground and waited for Willow to come around behind her and take hold of her shoulders. Carrying another Slayer was easier that way because it left the flyer's hands free.

Ryker glided up to a second-story window, a glass cutter in one hand and a suction cup in the other.

"This is so awkward," Willow said, gripping Tori's collar. "I hate dangling off of other people."

"Just don't let go." Tori took to the air, moving slowly. Willow was the only Slayer who hated flying—something Dr. B kept saying would lessen with practice. So far, it hadn't. Tori could feel Willow's fingers digging into her jacket.

Tori hovered behind Ryker and waited. He cut the glass with fast, practiced strokes, outlining a large section of the window. After that was done, he placed the suction cup on the middle of the glass and pushed inward. The pane made a small creak, a feeble protest, as it came loose. He maneuvered the cut portion onto the floor by the window, then flew into the room.

"Careful not to touch the edges." Ryker's voice was only a whisper. During a mission, the Slayers kept their voices low, but their neck mics picked up the sound well enough.

Tori leaned forward, stomach down, and gingerly slid through the window, making sure she didn't bump Willow into the cut glass.

She found herself in what was probably a guest room. A bed with an ornately carved white headboard stood by the far wall with a pale cedar chest at its foot. A rose quilt lay on top of the bed, matching a flower arrangement sitting on an antique dresser. Wainscoting and crown molding tied the whole theme together.

"Wow," Tori breathed out.

"What?" Jesse asked over her earpiece, concerned.

"Nothing." Tori straightened, but didn't land. It wouldn't do to have anyone downstairs hear footsteps. "I just hadn't expected any of Overdrake's men to decorate shabby chic."

"Oh," Willow cooed, peering around. "I love that armoire."

Ryker looked over his shoulder at Tori and Willow. "Would the two of you stop admiring the furniture and get in position?" He opened the bedroom door and glided out.

Tori went across the room, silently carrying Willow. Right before they reached the door, her gaze landed on the dresser and zeroed in on the framed picture of a young teenage boy. Blond hair, blue eyes, familiar face, cocky grin. The resemblance couldn't be a coincidence.

She let out a gasp. "There's a picture of Dirk in here."

"What?" Willow's head swung around, and she squinted at the frame. She'd never met Dirk, but she'd seen a photo of him.

The picture on the dresser must have been an old one, taken during Dirk's junior high years. He stood at the top of some rock formation, smiling as though he'd conquered it.

"If that's Dirk," Willow whispered, "this must be Overdrake's house. *He's* the one selling dragon scales?"

Rosa's voice came over the earpiece urgent with worry. "You guys need to get out of there. This must be a trap."

"Captains?" Dr. B asked, waiting for their opinions.

If Overdrake was selling scales, would he expect the Slayers to find out about it and come here? Was this some elaborate setup?

"I doubt it's a trap," Jesse said sounding more excited than apprehensive. "If it were, Overdrake wouldn't leave pictures of Dirk lying around for us to find. He doesn't know we're coming."

Tori looked back at the window. The yard was empty, unchanged. Part of a neighbor's house was visible, but the rest was shrouded by trees. "Does the infrared show any signs that people are converging on the house?"

"Negative," Dr. B said. "We haven't picked up anyone moving closer."

"Then we continue," Tori said.

Lilly broke into the conversation. "Why would Overdrake have a house in the suburbs with no security?"

"He may have houses in several locations," Dr. B answered. "That would make disappearing easier."

"Selling dragon scales seems like a sloppy way to earn extra money," Shang said.

Tori turned to Dirk's picture again, and her pulse started to hammer. Was this his house? Could he be one of the people downstairs? The thought filled her with an optimistic and completely unreasonable happiness.

Dirk was her enemy. He was dangerous.

But she wanted to see him.

Part of her was certain that if the Slayers could get him away from his father, they could turn him back to their side.

She used her counterpart sense to search for him, seeing if she could feel his presence nearby. She didn't. Yet she felt *something*, a sort of vague familiarity. Was she imagining it because she wanted him to be here?

She must be. The idea of capturing Dirk and un-brainwashing him was so appealing that she was creating wisps of his presence. "I don't think either of the people downstairs is Dirk," she said. "But I'm not certain."

"If Overdrake is in the house," Dr. B said, "he'll put up a fight."

"We're ready for him," Jesse answered.

A soft click sounded over the earpiece—Ryker unlocking the back door.

"We're going in," Jesse said.

Tori quietly sailed to the top of the stairs and set Willow down by the banister. The two of them stared into the darkened staircase and listened.

They waited as a minute ticked by. Only soft creaking sounds came from below. Then Jesse's voice—both over the earpiece and coming from a room downstairs—said, "Put your hands up where we can see them."

A woman screamed, a sound like a startled bird. Dirk's stepmother?

Footsteps pounded across the floor. The woman screamed again.

"We don't want to hurt you," Bess said. "We just want to talk. Put your hands up so we know you're unarmed."

Tori waited, unconsciously gripping her hands into fists at her side.

A moment later Jesse said, "We've got a woman contained in the den. Obviously not Connor. Where's our man?"

"On his tail," Ryker said. "But it's not Overdrake. Too young."

Too young? Could it be Dirk after all? No, Ryker had seen a picture of Dirk. He would have recognized him.

A door slammed. "He went into the laundry room," Ryker said.

The guy had probably been trying to make it to the garage door, seen Ryker, and locked himself in that room instead. A dead end. According to the blueprint, the laundry room had no window. But Connor might have weapons stashed there.

Tori didn't need to point that out to Ryker. They'd all had those sorts of details drilled into them at practice.

"We need a shield," Shang said.

"On my way," Bess called.

The woman in the den was speaking to Jesse, but Ryker's voice was louder. "Come out of there!" he yelled. "Hands above your head!"

No one answered from the laundry room. Only the woman's voice came over the line, high pitched with fear. "Who are you? What do you want?" She spoke with a slight British accent, the same sort Overdrake had.

"We want information," Jesse said.

"Don't hurt us," the woman pleaded. "We're unarmed."

The fear in her voice sent prickles of guilt into Tori's stomach. She did her best to push them away. This lady wasn't some innocent bystander. She was connected with Overdrake—an assistant or a secretary, someone who knew about the dragons and was helping him raise money to fund his upcoming attacks.

Willow covered her mic so her words wouldn't be picked up. "I guess Ryker was right about these people not fighting. You know, I sort of expected more from Overdrake's henchmen."

So had Tori. Was it possible the Slayers had burst in on an unfortunate house sitter?

"Chameleon," Dr. B said, "What do you mean, your man's too young? Did you get a visual on him?"

"He's a kid," Ryker said. "fourteen, maybe."

Tori inwardly sighed. She'd had most likely missed *Wicked* to terrorize Renaissance fair merchants and house sitters.

"We need the dragons' location," Jesse said. "That's all we want from you."

"The what?" the woman replied. "Who are you?" If the woman didn't know about Overdrake's business, she probably thought Jesse was crazy.

Ryker was still talking to the kid in the laundry room. "Come out here. Your mom won't like it if I have to break down the door."

In the den, Jesse went on. "Rudolpho gave us your address. We know you're involved with the dragons."

Ryker's voice: "Hey! Put the fire extinguisher down. Now!"

A hissing indicated the kid had ignored Ryker's instructions and sprayed the foam. Ryker cursed. Apparently the kid's aim had been accurate.

Willow took a tentative step toward the stairs. "Do you guys need some, uh, reverse?"

"No," Ryker snapped. "I'll take care of this." Then he called, "Jump him!"

Something crashed into a wall.

"Sorry," Shang said, "The kid is fast."

Willow turned to Tori, head cocked to better hear what was going on downstairs. "So what exactly are we supposed to do in this sort of situation?"

Tori shrugged. "We're supposed to be bonding and letting the others take care of things." She leaned against the banister. "Let's talk about fashion."

Jesse probably wouldn't appreciate her sarcasm during a mission, but really, what did he expect? He and Ryker had taken charge of everything and sent her and Willow to guard an empty stairway.

"I think overalls are always a bad choice," Tori said.

"I agree," Willow said.

In the den, the woman was emphatically denying any knowledge of Rudolpho or dragons.

Ryker hadn't subdued the teenager yet. "Come away from there," he said. Then, "We both know you're not really going to throw that chair."

A crash sounded somewhere below. "Okay," Ryker said, "your mom is going to be ticked about that."

Willow peered down the staircase. "Are you sure we shouldn't help?"

"They haven't said, 'reverse.'"

The boy shouted, "Get away from me, all of you!"

His mother must have heard him. Light-switch fast, the fear in her voice turned to anger. "What are you doing to my son?"

"Nothing," Jesse said, then added, "Chameleon, bring the kid in here so his mother can see he's safe."

Another crash. "Working on it," Ryker said.

"How hard can it be?" Jesse asked, clearly bothered.

Scuffling sounds. "He's strong," Shang said. "Slayer strong."

"Can't be," Ryker said. "Wrong age. He's not old enough."

Tori straightened, Shang's words repeating in her ears. *Slayer strong?*

Forget her post; she had to see the kid herself. As she flew down the stairs, she heard footsteps coming up them. And then he stood in front of her. The boy in the picture. Not Dirk, and yet enough of a lookalike to be a younger version of him. He had the same face shape, the same surfer boy blond hair and startling blue eyes. He wasn't as tall as Dirk, and yet he was still tall enough to make her think that he might reach Dirk's 6'2" in a few more years. Dirk didn't have any brothers. How was it that this stranger looked so much like him?

When he saw her standing there, floating off the floor, the boy stopped. He seemed to not know whether to fight his way past her or turn away and run.

"Who are you?" she asked.

Perhaps it was the urgency in her voice, or perhaps it was

just surprise that one of the people invading his house was a girl. Whatever the reason, the boy's gaze swung to hers, trying to see her face through her smoky visor. The moment of hesitation cost him. Ryker flew up from behind and wrapped his arms around the boy's chest, pinning his arms to his side. Then Ryker flew the kid, kicking and struggling, toward the den.

Tori followed, skimming through the air.

"Let me go!" The kid thrashed in Ryker's arms, legs flailing. "You better not hurt my mom!"

Ryker tightened his grip. "Your mother isn't the one I'm thinking of hurting."

The group rounded the corner into the living room and nearly ran into Dr. B. He had always overseen missions from a distance, never joining in the fighting, and yet today, he'd abandoned the van and come inside. He wasn't armed or even disguised. Ryker and Tori both hesitated, staring at him in disbelief.

"Put the boy down," Dr. B said. "We've frightened him enough."

Ryker didn't move, didn't let go of the kid.

But the boy seemed to realize that something had changed. He stopped thrashing and took deep breaths.

"Jaybird," Dr. B called, using Jesse's code name, "bring the woman into the living room so we can talk civilly about this situation."

Ryker reluctantly lowered the kid to the ground and let him go. The boy pushed away from Ryker, glaring at everyone. "Who are you?" he demanded.

Dr. B looked the boy up and down. "I should ask you the same question. However, I believe I already know the answer, Connor."

At the name, the kid's gaze snapped to Dr. B, and some of the angry flush drained from his cheeks, replaced by pale dread.

"Is that your real name?" Dr. B asked calmly, almost conversationally. "Or is Connor just a name you gave Rudolpho? Did you tell him you were someone's delivery boy? Hard to believe he'd make deals with someone as young as yourself."

Bess eyed the kid. "Maybe he was using *Conner* as an adjective."

Conner, or whatever his name was, clamped his lips together in defiance. "I don't have to answer your questions."

Jesse walked into the room, towing a middle-aged, blonde woman by the wrist. She was thin and pretty, the sort who looked like her clothes had always been on the cusp of fashion. Her hair was twisted in a French knot, her makeup perfectly applied.

Her blue eyes fixed on Dr. B and widened in surprise. "Jameson? Is that you?"

Jameson? Dr. B's first name was Alastair.

Dr. B showed no confusion, gave no denial of the name. "Hello, Bianca."

The two regarded each other, unspeaking, but the emotion in their eyes, their familiarity, showed that they had a history. Judging by the pain in Bianca's expression and the accusation in his, it wasn't a good one.

That's when Tori remembered: Dr. B had changed his name when he left St. Helena. And he'd mentioned Bianca before. She was one of his old girlfriends—the one who married Overdrake.

Bianca was Dirk's mother.

CHAPTER 8

"I'm sorry for the intrusion," Dr. B said calmly, as though this were a social call and not an attack. "We didn't know this was your home. We've come for information about the dragons' locations."

"I don't keep up with Brant's whereabouts." Bianca pulled her wrist away from Jesse and strode over to her son. She looked him over, checking to make sure he was okay. When she was satisfied that he was unhurt, she turned and stood protectively in front of him. Her gaze darted around the room, taking in a toppled couch, an overturned end table, and a side chair that now lay in pieces on the floor. The chandelier still swayed in a reproving rhythm.

"And why would you think I'd tell you anything after you broke into my home and destroyed my things?"

"Actually," Shang said, joining the semicircle they'd made in front of Bianca. "We didn't do any of this. Your son did."

Bianca gawked at the broken chair. "Aaron couldn't have."

The boy, apparently Aaron, surveyed the wreckage as well. He seemed surprised to see bits of broken wood strewn on the floor. "I didn't mean to. It was the adrenaline, I guess."

"He's Overdrake's son," Dr. B said flatly. "The simulator triggered his powers. He has extra strength right now."

Bianca stiffened and lifted her chin. She looked statuesque standing there, even though she was a good inch shorter than Aaron. "He's not Brant's son. We divorced years ago, before Aaron was born."

Dr. B shook his head, an unspoken sigh on his lips. "Bianca, there's no point in denying it. He looks too much like Dirk."

Tori had thought Bianca looked shocked when she'd first seen Dr. B, but now her eyes went even wider. "You know Dirk? You know what he looks like?"

Dr. B nodded wearily. He walked over to the toppled end table and lifted it, setting it right. "Dirk pretended to be a Slayer and trained with me for several years. We only recently found out who he was."

Bianca's hand went to her chest. "Where is he?"

Dr. B picked up an overturned candle and picture frame and returned them to the table. "I don't know." He straightened the frame. "I suppose Dirk is wherever Brant and the dragons are. I hoped that whoever was selling dragon scales to Rudolpho could give me that information."

"Selling dragon scales?" The words fell from Bianca's mouth in disbelief. She turned and landed a penetrating gaze at Aaron. "You sold the dragon scales?"

He gulped and shrank back. "Sorry. I didn't think that . . . I mean, the guy at the fair was willing to pay a lot for them, and you said we needed money. I didn't think they were actually real . . ."

She gestured pointedly at the Slayers. "Do you see why I didn't sell them? Do you see what danger you put us in?"

Dr. B pushed aside a broken chair leg with his foot. "You're not in danger from us, but would you be if Brant found you?"

Bianca didn't answer, just adjusted her position so she stood between her son and the Slayers again. She whispered to Aaron, "Don't tell them anything."

"Bianca," Dr. B said with more firmness. "If we found you because of the dragon scales, so can Brant." His gaze went to hers, demanding her attention. "Would you be in danger if he found you?"

She still didn't speak, although Dr. B seemed to read an answer in the stubborn set of her shoulders and the trembling of her lips: Yes, she would be in danger.

Dr. B's voice grew soft with sympathy. "I'm sorry. I'd hoped things would turn out differently for you."

Bianca's expression wavered. She swallowed, let out a tired breath, and slumped a little. "Brant doesn't know he has another son. I left so he wouldn't find out." She sent Dr. B a pleading look. "I don't want Aaron to have anything to do with his father."

Tori spoke without thinking. "But you left Dirk with him? *That* was okay?"

The accusation hung in the air. Tori could feel the other Slayers staring at her.

A flash of pain went through Bianca's eyes, replaced immediately by coldness. "You wouldn't understand my reasons."

"You're right," Tori said. "I don't. And neither does Dirk. How could you have left him and never even—"

"That's enough," Dr. B cut her off. "This isn't the place."

"Right," Bess said, drawing out the word uncomfortably. "We should get back to threatening these folks and leave family counseling to the professionals."

Aaron stepped out from behind his mother. "Who are you? What do you want with the dragons?"

"I've told you about them," Bianca answered, looking over the group as she spoke to Aaron. "They're Slayers, and they want to kill the dragons. *Now* will you believe that I'm not making up stories?"

"Slayers," Aaron repeated, examining the group more closely. He seemed to be trying to see their features beneath the reflections of their helmets. "So you guys have all kinds of powers, and you're like, obsessed dragon killers?"

"We're not obsessed." Bess said, sounding offended as she crossed her arms. "I mean, it's not like we do this sort of thing twenty-four/seven. We have day jobs." She hiked her thumb in her father's direction. "Or at least, he does."

"They're teenagers," Bianca said. She looked at Dr. B with a mixture of resignation and reprimand. "I should have known you would be the one training them. You weren't about to let go of the past, were you?"

"Not true," Dr. B said, matching her crisp tone. "It's not the past I can't let go of, it's the future. I've never wanted a future where Brant Overdrake is in charge."

Bianca took a step toward him. "And what about Dirk? Are you planning on killing him, too?"

"No," Tori answered emphatically. She'd thought about fighting Dirk, but somehow she'd never thought about the fact Dirk could be killed—that one of her friends could be the one to kill him.

Dr. B answered more calmly. "We've no wish to hurt Dirk."

"But you *might* hurt him?" Bianca asked. She shook her head scornfully. "You can see why I won't help you."

Tori folded her arms. "You're about eleven years late in worrying about what hurts Dirk." The other Slayers were still staring at her. She didn't care. She looked Aaron up and down. "And your son has got to be older than eleven, which makes me wonder if you're telling us the truth about when and why you left Overdrake."

Bianca's gaze swung to Tori, eyes narrowed. "It's so nice to be young and sure you're right. I remember being that way once myself."

Tori gestured to Aaron. "You're what, thirteen? Fourteen?"

"Twelve and a half," he said, looking to his mother for explanation. He didn't seem to know what to make of Tori's accusation.

"I left when Dirk was five," Bianca told him. "After you were born, I left you with a friend for a bit and went back for your brother." She paused as though it was hard to say the next words, as though even the memory had sharp edges. "I couldn't take him. Brant made sure of that." She wrapped her arm around Aaron and leaned in to him, shutting her eyes. "I'm trying to move on from that part of my life."

Tori had never told the other Slayers that she messaged Dirk online. They wouldn't understand. She was about to admit everything, to give Bianca Dirk's contact information, but the words died on Tori's lips.

Bianca was trying to "move on" from that part of her life. What did that mean? Was she trying to forget Dirk? Cut her losses? Would she risk talking to him? If Tori told Dirk that she'd given his information to his mother and then she *didn't* contact him, he'd feel rejected and unimportant all over again.

Bianca's eyes looked tight and tired. She kept her arm around Aaron, but addressed Dr. B. "When I left Brant, I took some scales that the dragons had shed. I wanted something to show Aaron that would prove the things I told him about his father were true. I don't know where Brant or the dragons are now."

Dr. B listened to Bianca's explanation, then remained silent for a moment more. Some sort of decision hung in that silence, although Tori couldn't tell what it was. He pulled his phone from his pocket, brought up an image, and walked over to Bianca. "This is a recent picture of Dirk."

Tori knew which picture it was—the one she'd taken in his

car last September. His blond hair was mussed, his blue eyes watching her with assurance. He had a half-smile on his face, but it was genuine. He was happy she'd come to see him.

The Slayers hadn't been allowed to take pictures of one another, but she and Dirk had broken the rule. After his defection, she'd given Dr. B a copy in case it would help him track Dirk down.

Bianca took the phone from Dr. B with shaking hands. Her expression softened, then crumbled. She put her hand to her mouth and let out a choked laugh. "No wonder you recognized Aaron. They look so much alike."

Aaron peered at the picture too, studying it.

Bianca held the phone closer, almost cradled it. "Dirk is so grown up. I can't believe how much."

"Yeah," Ryker said with a grunt. "Dirk's all grown up and taking over the world."

Dr. B sent him a stern look then returned his attention to Bianca. "I spent the last five summers with Dirk. You'll think I'm making this up, but he reminds me of Nathan. He has the same humor, charm, and I believe he has the same goodness, too."

Nathan was Dr. B's brother, a Slayer killed by Overdrake's father when he was only thirteen years old. It occurred to Tori that Bianca must have known Nathan, must have known what happened to him. Tears brimmed in her eyes, then ran down her cheeks. She didn't bother wiping them away.

"I don't think you're making it up. That's how Dirk was as a boy."

Dr. B extended a hand as if to comfort her, then seemed to think better of it. "I don't want to hurt Dirk. If anything, I want to get him away from Brant. Certainly, you must want to help me do that?"

Bianca didn't take her eyes off Dirk's picture. "I don't know where Brant is." Her voice had a note of suffering, of fear. "We used to live in Winchester, Virginia. On Dirk's eighth birthday, I went back again. I thought Brant would at least let me see him, but I found new people living in the house. They said he'd moved to Louisiana."

He hadn't. Overdrake must have just bought a new house in the same city, because Dirk had still been living in Winchester until last month when they'd found out who he was.

Dr. B nodded at the information. "We're aware of the compounds in Winchester. But thank you for sharing that information." He took his phone from her. "Tell me your number, and I'll send you Dirk's picture."

She hesitated, thinking over the request.

Dr. B let out a laugh, one that almost sounded amused. "Are you worried about giving it to me? If I need to contact you, wouldn't you rather I called instead of dropping by your house again?"

That seemed to convince her. She told him the number.

Good. That meant Tori could talk to Dr. B later about whether she should give Bianca Dirk's contact information or vice-versa.

While Dr. B forwarded the picture he said, "I apologize for the state we've left your living room in. I'd stay and clean up, but I need to return the Slayers to their homes." He slipped the phone into his pocket. "If you need to relocate, I can help make sure Brant doesn't find you."

Bianca put her arm around Aaron, her composure coming back. "We'll be fine."

She and Dr. B stared at each other silently for another moment. Tori wasn't sure what passed between them, but theirs was the gaze of people who knew each other well, and were calculating strategies.

"I'd like to talk to you later," Dr. B finally said. "Perhaps we could find ways to mutually benefit each other."

Her lack of enthusiasm at the suggestion was apparent, but she forced a smile. "I'll call you tomorrow."

And then, as though it had really been a normal visit, the Slayers left through the front door. Tori was the last one out. Before she left, she turned around and looked back.

Bianca's arms were around Aaron, her face buried into him. She was crying, her shoulders shaking. As Aaron watched the Slayers leave, his expression reminded Tori of one of Dirk's: Firm resolve.

Perhaps Tori had some sort of counterpart skill with Aaron too, because she knew what he was thinking.

I'll learn everything about you I can, and next time, I'll protect my mother. I won't let any of you ever bother her again.

Tori didn't go out the doorway. "We're not your enemies."

"Could have fooled me," he said.

"We're just trying to protect the country from dragons."

"Yeah," he said. "They're a huge problem. I often think, *If only someone would do something about our country's dragon infestation. I can't walk to school without batting one away.*"

He was determined to be their enemy. It felt like losing Dirk all over again. The other Slayers were already making their way to the van, but Tori turned off her mic and walked back to Aaron.

When he saw her come back inside, he straightened, and Bianca looked up, startled. "What do you want?" she asked.

Tori hated that they were afraid of her, although she couldn't blame them. She was an unknown assailant in a helmet. She did the only thing she could think of to lessen their fear; she took off her helmet and let them see her face, her expression, her eyes.

"I was Dirk's friend," she said. "I mean, I'm still his friend." Instead of explaining more, she said, "I want to see if Aaron has counterpart abilities like Dirk."

"If I what?" Aaron asked.

Bianca said nothing. She stared at Tori, incredulous.

Tori pulled off a glove. Back at camp, she hadn't known she was Dirk's counterpart right away. It wasn't until the third day when they'd touched, that her senses had zeroed in on him, bonded with him as though she'd known him all her life. No, that wasn't right. It was before they'd touched. With her eyes closed, she'd still known where he was.

"Shut your eyes," she told Aaron. "I'm going to hold up my hand, and I want you to tell me where it is."

From over the earpiece she heard Jesse say, "Where's Tori?" She didn't have much time until someone came back for her.

Aaron didn't shut his eyes. Instead he cocked an eyebrow at her. "Why do you want me to tell you where your hand is? Don't you already know where it is?"

Tori let out an aggravated sigh. "Hey, let me be the first to tell you that you're as smart-mouthed as your brother. Just do it. I'm seeing if you're like him in other ways."

"Counterpart abilities?" Bianca asked. "What are those?"

From her earpiece, Jesse said, "Tori, where are you?"

She flicked on her mic. "Talking to Aaron. Be there in a second." She turned the mic back off. She didn't have time for explanations. "Shut your eyes."

Aaron did, then flinched and jerked them open again. "What the . . ."

"What?" Tori and Bianca asked together. Bianca came around to better see his face.

Aaron looked from Tori to his mother. "Nothing," he said.

Liar. Something had freaked him out. Tori didn't have time to question him about it.

"I can tell you're lying," she said. "Now let me show you that you can tell when I'm lying too. Shut your eyes again and don't open them."

He did, this time bracing himself. Tori held her hand a few inches in front of his shoulder. "Do you know where my hand is?"

"Um, I'm guessing it's still at the end of your arm?"

He was worse than Dirk; he was a twelve-year-old version of Dirk. "Is that a no?"

When Dirk had done the test with her, she'd known exactly where his hand was to the point that she raised hers and put it exactly against his, matching every finger with his. But perhaps only two people could be counterparts. Perhaps the right genes were only one aspect of it.

With his eyes still shut, he pointed to Tori's hand.

Tori smiled. "Open your eyes."

He did and blinked in surprise. "How did I know?"

"You knew," Tori said, "because we've got counterpart abilities. When I'm close, you'll know where I am. You'll also know if I'm not telling the truth. So believe me when I tell you, the Slayers aren't your enemies."

Bianca shook her head, her lips pressed into a tight line. "We're supposed to believe you just because Aaron could tell where your hand was? You'll excuse me for remaining skeptical."

Tori heard footsteps approaching the doorway. "T-bird, what are you doing?" Dr. B sounded horrified. Most likely because she'd taken her helmet off and revealed who she was.

She hadn't expected him—the maker and worrier about all

the rules—to be the one who came back for her. She put her helmet on and headed for the door. "Coming. Sorry."

Dr. B stood there, waiting until she went out. He didn't speak until Tori was half way across the lawn, so he probably didn't mean for her to hear him speak to Bianca, but she had exceptional hearing. Dragon hearing. Thank you, DNA.

"Now you know one of my secrets," Dr. B said. "I trust you'll keep it as well as I keep yours."

"The senator's daughter was never here," Bianca replied.

"Who?" Aaron asked.

"Never mind," Bianca said. "We have things to talk about."

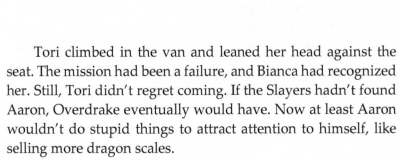

CHAPTER 9

Tori climbed in the van and leaned her head against the seat. The mission had been a failure, and Bianca had recognized her. Still, Tori didn't regret coming. If the Slayers hadn't found Aaron, Overdrake eventually would have. Now at least Aaron wouldn't do stupid things to attract attention to himself, like selling more dragon scales.

Knowing he was a counterpart was such an odd thing. She'd just met Aaron, and already she felt a protective streak for him. She'd have to do her best to dismiss the feeling. She would probably never see him again.

Dr. B started the van. "Seatbelts on?" The question was typical. Dr. B could lead them into danger one moment, and then turn into a concerned parent the next. As he pulled away from the curb, he called Kody and told him to release Rudolpho. No point detaining him longer. The address hadn't been a bluff.

The Slayers all took off their helmets, which were too hot and stuffy to keep on. Ryker glanced over his shoulder at the receding house. "We're not really going to just leave, are we? We need to post some sort of watch, keep those two under surveillance."

"Why?" Bess asked, running a hand through her hair to smooth it down. "Do you think they know something they didn't tell us?"

"The kid is a dragon lord," Ryker replied as though it were obvious. "That means he's potentially dangerous. We can't let random dragon lords wander around."

Rosa and Bess both glanced at Tori, then awkwardly looked away. Tori had never admitted to anyone except Jesse and Dr. B that she was half dragon lord, but she wondered if the others suspected. After all, they knew she was Dirk's counterpart.

"Not all dragon lords are evil," Rosa put in.

Ryker took off his gloves and laid them on the seat. "It's not a matter of being evil; it's a matter of genetics. Dragon lords want to protect dragons, and we have to kill them. Overdrake could find out about Aaron and use him. If we're not careful, the kid could turn into a huge liability. We might end up fighting three dragons at a time. We have to make sure that doesn't happen."

Dr. B cast a look at the Slayers through the rearview mirror. "Captains? What are your thoughts?"

Jesse unbuttoned his jacket, his dark eyes serious. "Being a dragon lord doesn't automatically make someone a liability. People choose whether to work for the good of society or against it."

From the passenger seat, Lilly rolled her eyes. "Says the guy who is dating a dragon lordess." She turned to Dr. B. "Come on, you can't have the captains decide this issue when one of them is a dragon lord."

"Dragon lords are always men," Bess reminded her. "The genes don't pass down to women. Tori can't be one."

If the other Slayers agreed, they would have jumped to Tori's defense. But no one said anything. Perhaps they felt the same way about her that Ryker did about Aaron—that she might be a liability.

Dr. B pulled up to a stop sign and looked around the van before proceeding through the intersection. "Have any of you had a reason to doubt Tori's loyalties?"

"Yes," Lilly said. "I doubted them when I found out she was a dragon lord."

A flash of anger went through Tori. "And I doubt your intelligence all of the time, but I try not to hold that against you."

"Tori's a Slayer," Jesse said firmly.

Bess tossed her helmet on the van floor. "Lilly's hair bleach is too strong. It's killed off her brain cells."

Lilly started to respond to that, but Dr. B cut her off. "Stop it, all of you," he snapped, showing more anger than he had all day. "Your best defense will always be unity. Lose that, and you'll lose everything."

No one said anything for a few moments. Bess glared at Lilly, something that seemed to have no effect on her. She stared back at Bess with self-righteous dignity. Rosa and Willow kept sending Tori sympathetic glances, which somehow made her feel worse. Jesse looked out the window, clenching his jaw in agitation, although she wasn't sure what he was upset about—Tori being a dragon lord, or Lilly trying to out her for being one.

"Has Tori done anything," Dr. B asked, composed again, "that makes any of you question her loyalties?"

A chorus of "No" went around the van.

Lilly said, "Dirk didn't do anything to make us question his loyalties, but then he led us into a trap."

Bess leaned back in her seat. "I have it on good authority that Tori isn't Overdrake's kid. In fact, I'm pretty sure we all know who her father is."

"I'm not being mean," Lilly insisted, raising her voice to emphasize the point. "I'm just saying that genetics make us who we are. We can't ignore that fact. Especially not when it comes to dragon lords."

"Genetics don't make us who we are," Jesse maintained. "Our choices do. Tori helped kill two dragons, and she unmasked Dirk. She's one of us."

Tori wanted to agree that her genetics didn't matter, to claim she was only a Slayer. She knew that everyone expected her to say at least that much in her own defense, but the memory of the last dragon attack was repeating in her mind. When the dragon had come after her, she had a clear shot at the dragon's heart—just for one second—and she hadn't taken it. Somehow she couldn't bring herself to kill the dragon, and she'd nearly paid for that mistake with her life.

She relived that moment sometimes, horrified at how close she'd come to death. If she found herself in that situation again, would she act differently? What if someone else's life had hung in the balance? What if Jesse hadn't been there to shoot the dragon before it reached her? Well, there was no ambiguity about that one. The dragon would have killed her.

Would some genetic part of her short circuit all reasoning during the next attack? "I'm not going to betray any of you or join up with Overdrake," she finally said.

"Okay," Ryker said, impatient, "We all love Tori. We're agreed on that. Now what do we do about dragon lord junior back there?"

Shang pulled off his gloves and laid them neatly across his lap. "We watch him. Dr. B should put some people on surveillance."

"And do what?" Bess asked. "Slap his hand if he does anything pro dragon?"

Jesse looked upward, thinking. "We should keep track of him for his own protection. Make sure Overdrake doesn't find him."

Rosa slid her helmet under her seat. "We already asked Bianca if she wanted our help keeping away from Overdrake. She said no. What more can we do?"

"It's like eating vegetables," Ryker said. "We force our help on them for their own good."

"Time for broccoli," Bess agreed.

"Willow?" Dr. B said, "What's your opinion?"

She shrugged, making a section of her curly blonde hair slide off her shoulder. "I've only been a Slayer for a few weeks. I don't know what to do."

Dr. B shook his head, refusing to accept her answer. "Ryker hasn't been a Slayer any longer than you have, and he has an opinion."

"That's because he has an opinion about everything," Willow said.

"And I'm usually right," Ryker added.

Lilly looked back toward the neighborhood. "He's right this time, anyway. We've got to keep track of the kid."

"Captains?" Dr. B asked. "What are your official positions?"

Bess let her head tip backward on the seat. "Is this one of those training moments when you ask people's opinions and then end up telling us why we're wrong? Because if it is, could you just cut to the chase?"

Dr. B didn't answer her. "Jesse?"

"It won't hurt to watch him," he said.

"Unless he figures out we're watching him," Tori put in, "and then he'll think we're invasive, or dangerous, or just plain creepy. We don't want him to see us as the enemy."

"Newsflash," Lilly said. "We *are* his enemy. And by the way, what were you doing in the house after we left?"

Tori unzipped her jacket. "I was trying to convince him that we're not the enemy."

Lilly waved a hand in Tori's direction, her black fingernails flicking the air. "See, this is exactly what I was talking about. It's genetic. She's making friends with other dragon lords."

Tori ignored her. "My opinion as a team captain is that we should train Aaron."

"As a Slayer?" Jesse asked, surprised.

"No," Tori said, letting her gaze fall on each of her friends so they would know she was serious. "I think we should train him to be a dragon lord."

She didn't get to say anything else, because everyone started speaking on top of one another.

"Are you crazy?" That was Ryker.

"Yeah," Bess said, "let's tell him our secrets so he can pull another Dirk on us."

Shang shook his head, lips pursed in disapproval. "Bad idea. Excessively bad."

"Told you so," Lilly said. Apparently she'd told the other Slayers many things about Tori and was enjoying being right about all of them.

Tori held up her hands to stop the barrage. "Has it ever occurred to you that we don't need to kill the dragons to win?"

Bess let out a moan and rubbed her eyes. "I can't believe this. I finally agree with Lilly about something." She sent Tori a firm look. "Of course we need to kill the dragons. They're weapons that will be used against us and every person in this nation. But mostly against us."

Tori still held her hands up. "The first dragon lords used their powers to turn dragons away from villages, not to attack them. Dirk may have been brainwashed by his father, but Aaron hasn't been. And neither have I." She could tell from their blank expressions they didn't know why she'd said the part about her not being brainwashed.

"Technically," she added. "You could say I'm a dragon lord."

She'd expected at least a little surprise at the confession. But the only reaction was a sigh from Jesse, some exchanged looks between Rosa and Bess, and Lilly's smug exclamation, "I *have* been saying so."

Tori ignored Lilly. "If Aaron and I learned how to access our dragon lord powers, maybe we could take the dragons out of Overdrake's control and stop him that way."

Silence filled the van while everyone considered the idea.

"It might work," Shang said. "In China, dragons are revered and considered lucky. The dragon lords who lived there must have had success controlling them."

Jesse's tone was more skeptical. "During our last fight with Overdrake, you got into the dragon's mind but couldn't budge Overdrake's control on it. What makes you think you'll ever be able to take control from him?"

Bess's mouth dropped open. "You knew back then that Tori was a dragon lord?" She turned to Tori. "You went spelunking in a dragon's mind and never told us?"

Tori looked back at her pleadingly, asking her to understand. "It doesn't change anything."

"Except our strategy," Ryker said, and he sounded excited about the possibility. "I don't know about bringing Aaron into the group, but Tori should definitely learn how to control dragons."

"I wish she could," Dr. B said. "Unfortunately, in all of my studies, I've never uncovered information about how dragon lords do what they do. They've kept their secrets to themselves."

"Dirk knows," Tori said. "He could teach me."

Jesse tilted his head, clearly unhappy with the idea. "Why would he do that?"

They wouldn't like her answer. Jesse especially. "When Dirk talks to me, sometimes I answer him online. Last night he flew with a dragon near McLean, and he wanted me to come out and see him. He told me that if I was around a dragon that wasn't attacking me, I would love it."

Jesse shook his head, his movements suddenly taut. "No. You should absolutely not go with him. It's another one of his traps. Overdrake sees you as a threat to be eliminated."

"Dirk could have eliminated me last October," Tori pointed out. "He didn't. He wants me to keep my powers so I can be a dragon lord."

Jesse was still shaking his head. "Don't go anywhere near Dirk. He's too dangerous."

"And fighting dragons isn't?" Tori asked. "When we agreed to be Slayers, we accepted that it would be dangerous."

Rosa looked at Tori sympathetically, as if she understood Tori's position but thought she was being naïve. "You won't be able to double cross Dirk. He's your counterpart. He'll know you're asking for information to use against him."

She was right, of course. Tori slumped into her seat, deflated. She hadn't thought of that. How could she get Dirk to teach her about dragons while hiding her motives for wanting to learn? "I can ask him to tell me things online. He can't tell whether I'm lying when I write."

"Dirk wouldn't go for it," Jesse said. "He's not that stupid."

Tori didn't want to let the idea go. Being able to control a dragon could be the difference between winning and losing a fight. "Maybe Bianca knows how to do it. She lived with Overdrake for years. He must have told her things."

"That's a possibility," Dr. B said, "an option worth exploring."

Bess stretched her legs into the aisle. "I hate to rain on your exploration, but Bianca didn't seem all that willing to talk to us."

Another inconvenient fact. Why was everyone so eager to point out that her plan wouldn't work?

"We'll have to find a way to convince her," Tori said, though she wasn't sure how. Bianca had obviously been afraid of Brant, maybe too afraid to give them any useful information.

"Wait," Willow said, breaking into the conversation. "I'm still trying to understand all this. I thought only guys could be dragon lords. How is Tori one?"

"I'm part Slayer, part dragon lord," Tori said. "Dirk told me that women probably inherit powers but usually don't have a way to access them. For some reason, when my Slayer powers turn on, it activates my dragon lord ones too."

Willow cocked her head in confusion. "So if your ability to fly and your hearing are actually dragon lord powers, what's your Slayer power? Shouldn't you be able to extinguish fire or heal burns or something?"

"My Slayer power must be flying," Tori said. "Any other power would have shown up by now." Which would perhaps explain why she'd sometimes felt like she had counterpart abilities with Jesse.

"And the fact you're counterparts with Dirk," Willow went on, "Does that mean he's got Slayer genes too?"

"I hope so," Tori said. "Because that would mean part of Dirk wants to be loyal to us."

"It would mean other things too." Dr. B suddenly slowed the van. "Bianca may have Slayer genes. Why didn't I think of that before?"

"Why does it matter?" Jesse asked.

Instead of answering, Dr. B turned the van around and pulled out his phone. "Booker, let surveillance know we're going back to the house. I need to speak to Bianca again."

"What?" Tori asked. "You already set up a surveillance team, and you let us sit here and debate the issue like it's not already decided?"

He didn't take his eyes from the road. "It's my job to train you as leaders. However, that doesn't mean I'm not still in charge of ground ops."

* * *

Tori and Dr. B walked up to the house while the other Slayers waited in the van. This time, they knocked on the front door. Tori still didn't know what he needed to talk to Bianca about, or why he was taking her with him to the meeting. She supposed he wanted her to hear anything Bianca might reveal about dragon lord powers.

Tori still wore her black jacket and pants. Her wardrobe choices for this meeting had been battle gear, a form-fitting skirt, or the Saucy barmaid costume. Battle gear just seemed like the best choice.

After a couple of minutes, Bianca cautiously opened the door. She didn't look happy to see them, and she didn't open the door wider or invite them in. "Back so soon?"

"I'm sorry to bother you again," Dr. B. said slowly, "but what I have to say is best said in person. I must warn you that you may have Slayer genes."

Tori had expected him to ask about how to control dragons, and wondered why he'd started with a warning instead. What good would it do Bianca to know about her Slayer genes?

"I don't," she said, her expression showing that she thought it was a ridiculous assertion. "If I had, my children would have been Slayers, not dragon lords."

"They would be both," Dr. B said. "At least, the first two would be."

The first two?

Dr. B continued, his gaze on Bianca's eyes. "I'm sure you understand the implications of what I'm saying. When you were pregnant with your third son, you didn't ever go near a dragon, did you?"

Bianca froze, just stared at Dr. B.

Another son?

Bianca didn't speak, but her mouth dropped open in a silent protest.

Dr. B motioned toward the living room. "I saw your family picture on the end table. You remarried. Aaron has a younger brother." Bianca still didn't speak. Dr. B's voice grew worried. "Bianca, you understand what I'm asking?"

Tori hadn't seen the picture, but she remembered Dr. B picking it up and returning it to the table. Bianca had a child with another man, a child who would have inherited only Slayer genes, not dragon lord ones.

The color drained from Bianca's face. Her eyes were stunned circles. "Why are you telling me this? Why would you think I have Slayer genes?"

"Because Tori has counterpart abilities with Dirk—"

"And Aaron," Tori added.

Dr. B didn't comment on that revelation. "Unless you have knowledge of dragon lords also being capable of having counterpart abilities, Dirk and Aaron have inherited Slayer qualities."

Bianca held up a hand to show that she didn't quite follow. "What are counterparts?"

Dr. B shifted his position into a pose of patience and used his teaching tone. "I didn't know about the phenomenon myself until I began training the children. Counterparts are Slayers that not only share skills, but also the ability to read one another.

Tori is counterparts with your first two sons, which indicates that they both have Slayer genes."

Bianca shook her head, perhaps hoping her refusal would keep his words from being true. "What Slayer abilities does Dirk have? Can he heal burns or throw force fields up?"

"No," Dr. B said, "but if his Slayer ability is flight, it would be indistinguishable from his dragon lord power."

"Indistinguishable?" Bianca said. "So if Dirk *is* part Slayer, Brant wouldn't know?"

"Brant knows that Dirk and I are counterparts," Tori said. "He probably understands the implications." Even if he didn't want to admit the possibility of Dirk or himself not being completely dragon lord.

Bianca's voice wavered. "The Slayer genes might not have come from me. They could have come from Brant's mother or grandmother—someone in his line."

"That's possible," Dr. B said. "But if he got those genes from you, then your youngest son would have inherited them too. So I ask again, did you go near a dragon while pregnant with him?"

Tori had thought Dr. B would want to find another Slayer, but the sympathy in his voice said otherwise.

"I can't have Slayer genes," Bianca insisted. "I can't."

Bianca's fear meant one thing: There *could* be another Slayer.

Tori wasn't sure whether she felt more hopeful or sick. The Slayers needed all the help they could get, but if the boy was Aaron's younger brother, he couldn't be more than ten. Too young to fight. And even if Overdrake's next attack didn't happen for years, how could the boy ever fight his own half-brother, or his brothers' father? That was too much to ask of anyone.

Bianca leaned against the doorframe as if too drained to stand. Dr. B took her arm, pushed open the door and led her inside. "You need to sit down."

"This can't be happening," she muttered.

He guided her to the living room couch. The broken chair still lay in pieces on the floor, untouched. "Was your youngest son exposed, then?"

She sank onto the couch, still pale. "I didn't do it on purpose. I went to see Dirk when he was about seven. I wanted to take him with me—I had a new life. All I needed was a way to get Dirk. I thought . . . I didn't know I was pregnant again. I wouldn't have gone near a dragon enclosure if I had."

Dr. B sat down next to Bianca. Tori, unsure what she was supposed to do, sat in a nearby recliner.

"I never would have endangered my child on purpose." Bianca swallowed hard, then let out a small cry. "What am I going to do? Brant wants to wipe out the Slayers. If he knows Dirk is half Slayer, he'll know that any other children I have might be too. What if he decides to find me to check?"

Dr. B put his hand on her arm, consolingly. "As you pointed out, the Slayer genes might have come from Brant. Or we might be wrong about the reason for Tori's counterpart connection with your sons. On the other hand, Brant might already be looking for you. How old is your youngest son?"

"Jacob just turned eleven," she said.

"Eleven," Dr. B repeated. "That's the age I began to train the other Slayers."

Bianca let out an incredulous cough and shook her head. "He's not joining you. I won't let him hunt dragons or break into people's homes."

"We don't break into a lot of houses," Tori said. "Mostly we run drills, shoot weapons, and play with fire."

Dr. B spoke without any sign he'd taken offense. "Jacob is too young to join us, but you can still protect your children by helping us fight Brant."

Bianca stood, agitated, and paced across the living room. "I can't fight him. He has armies and dragons."

"You don't have to fight him," Dr. B said. "We'll do that. But you have information we need. At least, I'm hoping you do."

Bianca didn't seem to hear him. "Jacob would be a flyer. Those are the most dangerous Slayers, the ones that go after the dragons." She wrapped her arms around herself, a poor attempt to hold herself together. "I only stayed in the states because I hoped—I don't know, I still hoped to find Dirk someday. But I've got to think of my other children. We need to leave the country."

Dr. B wasn't the sort of man who raised his voice. A terse tone was generally the closest he got. Now his voice went low with anger. "You've never been a coward. Don't teach your children that running away is the answer."

Her gaze snapped to his. "I won't let you use my children to satisfy your revenge."

His expression hardened. "All I want is to prevent Brant from wreaking havoc on this country. Don't tell me about the need to protect your children. My daughter has already fought two of Brant's dragons." Dr. B stopped and took a breath to compose himself. He clearly hadn't meant to tell Bianca about Bess.

"Your daughter?" Bianca stopped pacing to stare at him in surprise.

Dr. B nodded, let out a sigh. "When I left St. Helena, I didn't realize I was moving to the one place my pregnant wife would come into contact with dragon eggs."

"I'm sorry," Bianca said. "We never meant to expose anyone. Brant and I were en route to the dragon enclosure with some eggs when I went into labor with Dirk. We were forced to land at BWI. Everyone in the airport was in range of the eggs." A hint of weariness shone in her eyes. "It all comes around, doesn't it? The parts we play while hurting each other? Brant's father killed your brother. Your father killed Brant's father. Next it will be your daughter and my son."

"No," Dr. B said. "I still have hope for Dirk."

Tori felt Aaron's presence behind the wall separating the living room from the kitchen. He'd been there for a while, she realized. Perhaps during the entire conversation. Tori had been too caught up in the emotion in the room to notice him. She looked at the wall and wondered if she should tell Dr. B and Bianca that he was listening.

"I hope you're right." Bianca shook her head wearily. "Fate has dealt us both badly."

"Perhaps. But fate has also given us an opportunity today." Dr. B gestured to Tori, including her in the conversation. "We want to know how dragon lords control the dragons. Tori is half dragon lord. She needs to learn."

Bianca regarded Tori, then turned to Dr. B with obvious skepticism. "Women aren't dragon lords. You want to train Aaron. That's what this is really about."

"Women don't *usually* have dragon lord capabilities." Dr. B held up a hand, conceding the point. "But we've learned that if a woman also has Slayer genes, she can then access her dragon lord side."

Bianca stepped away from Dr. B, distancing herself from him. "Aaron is only twelve. I don't want him anywhere near dragons, and I certainly won't pit him against Brant and Dirk."

Ironic, Tori thought, that after hiding her dragon lord abilities for weeks, she finally wanted to claim them, and Bianca didn't believe her. "I've been inside a dragon's mind," Tori said, "but I couldn't take control from Brant."

"Of course not," Bianca still look unconvinced about Tori's claim. "Once someone has hold of a dragon's mind, it's nearly impossible for another dragon lord to shake off his grasp. And trust me, when Brant attacks, he'll have control of his dragon. Involving Aaron would be pointless."

Tori leaned forward in the chair. "What if we found a dragon when Overdrake didn't have control of it? He's not always in a dragon's mind, is he? You must have an idea where he built his other dragon enclosures."

Bianca raised an eyebrow. "*We*—meaning you and Aaron?"

"He wouldn't have to do any fighting with the guards," Tori said, "But it would be nice to have his help hijacking a dragon." After all, what if she only had some dragon lord powers?

Bianca dropped her voice to a harsh whisper. "I won't have Aaron involved. I don't even want him to know about any of this."

"Too late for that." Tori motioned to the wall. "He's been over there listening for a while now."

Bianca's head whipped around to look down the hallway. No one was visible there.

Tori shrugged. "He's in the kitchen. I don't have to see him to know. It's one of those counterpart things."

Bianca turned in that direction. "Aaron?" she called.

He stepped sheepishly out of the kitchen. Tori hadn't considered the possibility someone else could have come to the house while the Slayers had been gone, but Aaron wasn't alone.

A younger, brown haired boy stood with him—eyes large with wonder. "Does this mean I can fly?"

# CHAPTER 10

Tori studied the boy—Jacob. With his dark hair and eyes, he didn't look like Dirk or Aaron. He was tall, but still had the thin arms and full cheeks of a child. So young. Much too young to train to fight.

Bianca walked over to her sons, hands on hips. "No. And don't even think about jumping off something to try."

Dr. B stood as well. His gaze ran over Jacob as if judging him for combat ability. Perhaps he couldn't help it when it came to Slayers. "Testing him is easy enough. He's within range of a simulator right now. If he can see in the dark or has extra strength, then he's got Slayer genes."

Jacob brightened with excitement.

Aaron pointed at an empty recliner. "Jake, see if you can pick that up." In a confidential whisper, he added, "I threw the other one across the room."

Without hesitation, Jacob strode to the chair, took hold of its sides, and hefted it into the air. He held it above his head like he was lifting weights. Light weights. "This is so cool." He grinned and turned to his mom. "How long does it last?"

She stared back, unspeaking.

Dr. B ran a hand through his hair. "I'm sorry," he told Bianca.

Jacob set the chair down, letting it drop the last couple inches to the floor. "What about flying? How does that work?"

Tori answered because she didn't think Bianca or Dr. B would. "Your powers will only last for a half an hour after we leave, and you have to be in range of a dragon or a simulator for them to turn on again. Flying is tricky at first. Usually those powers don't kick in unless you're in danger."

Bianca took Jacob by his shoulders. She'd grown pale again. "You're not to put yourself in danger. Do you understand? You're not to have anything to do with Slayers or dragon lords." She turned to Aaron. "The two of you go upstairs. I'll talk to you later."

It was like watching Ryker's parents all over again, although Tori doubted Bianca would relent the way his parents had. Not with Aaron and Jacob being so young. Not with Overdrake being Aaron's father.

The boys hesitated, looking as though they wanted to ask more questions, but they headed up the stairs anyway.

After they'd gone, Bianca sank back down on the couch and put her head in her hands.

Dr. B sat next to her, fingers steepled across his knees. "If you want to protect your sons, help us defeat Brant."

She didn't answer.

"You do want to protect your sons, don't you?"

Her gaze went to Dr. B's eyes and stayed there. "If I tell you what I know, you've got to promise you'll never tell Brant about my children."

"Agreed," Dr. B said. "We don't want Overdrake to know about them any more than you do."

Bianca took a deep breath and held it as if it were a note in a song. "When Brant was teaching Dirk to connect to a dragon, Brant said to take the part of his mind that saw what the dragons saw, picture it as a door, and walk through it into the dragon's mind. Once there, his consciousness would join the dragon's."

Tori nodded. The time she'd gone into the dragon's mind, she hadn't thought about how she'd done it, but Bianca's description made sense—follow the link Tori already had and put herself on the other side of it.

"Dirk was supposed to find the dragon's control center, imagine the dragon's will as an object, and turn it into a shape he could grasp."

Turn it into an object? How was Tori supposed to do that?

Bianca paused, remembering. "Brant always turned the dragon's will into a knife he could wield, but Dirk didn't like that. I'd told him not to touch knives." She paused again, forcing herself to leave her memories and return to her instructions. "Once Brant controlled the object, he controlled the dragon."

But how specifically was it all done? Tori felt like she'd been given clues, not instructions. "How do I find a dragon's control center?"

"I don't know," Bianca said, shrugging. "I never heard that part. Brant went into the dragon's mind with Dirk and showed him how to find it."

Of course he did. Parents didn't teach a child to ride a bike by telling them about it. They put their kids on bikes and made them pedal. Tori's hopes for easy answers sputtered and sank. She would not only have to figure out how to ride the bike, she would have to find it too.

Dr. B frowned as he considered Bianca's answer. "What else do you know about controlling dragons?"

She ran her fingers across her lips, thinking. "When a dragon first hatched, Brant had to see the dragon to connect to its mind, but before long he could keep control of a dragon even when it was miles away."

"How many dragons does Brant have?" Dr. B asked.

"We brought Kiha and Tamerlane with us to America. Brant planned on leaving Khan and Minerva in St. Helena where it was safer. He used to go back there a couple of times a month to exercise them. After a year, that became too much trouble, so he brought them to the States too."

"We killed Kiha and Tamerlane," Dr. B said. "But new eggs hatched last September."

Four dragons to contend with. Tori had suspected as much. Dirk told her once that there were enough dragons for her to have one too, and they came in pairs.

Bianca's mouth fell open. "You killed two dragons? How?"

With a chain, an assault rifle, and a lot of luck.

Dr. B wasn't as specific in his answer. "Overdrake set the dragons on us. The Slayers simply did what they were trained to."

Bianca's eyes flickered in surprise, although Tori couldn't tell whether she was surprised Overdrake had set dragons on teenagers, or that they'd managed to defend themselves.

"So there are four dragons," Dr. B said grimly.

Bianca shook her head. "No. Dragon lords can force dragons to lay more eggs than they would in the wild. Before I left, Brant had four eggs from Kiha, two from Minerva, and he also planned on mating Minerva with Tamerlane. She was his favorite for breeding because she was the biggest. She could have laid another four by now. And Kiha could have laid another pair as well."

A chill raced across Tori's spine, and her mouth went dry. Too many dragons, so many that fear made it hard for her brain to add the figures and come up with an exact number. Fear and math weren't compatible. She forced herself to concentrate. Twelve eggs, four adults, but the Slayers had already killed two.

Dr. B reached the number a moment before she did. "Fourteen? That's madness. How does Brant expect to take care of that many dragons?"

Bianca lifted a hand in explanation. "He planned for the nation to become a different place, a place where he didn't have to keep them hidden. And he thought he'd have more sons to help." She sent a look in the direction of Aaron's bedroom.

"When will they hatch?" Tori asked.

Bianca shut her eyes, doing the calculation. "If Kiha's first set hatched in September, Minerva's first clutch will probably hatch within a year, and then more dragons could hatch every year or two."

Tori felt ill. How could the Slayers ever fight that many? They couldn't. They'd be killed. And if they didn't stop Overdrake, he would mate the hatchlings as well. "He can't think he'll control that many," Tori said numbly. "He must be planning on releasing them into the wild."

But there weren't that many wild places anymore. Most livable land was populated. Would that matter to him?

Bianca let out a bitter laugh. "I doubt he'd ever give up control of the dragons by releasing them. He knows some of them will be killed in combat, and he's making sure he always has a supply."

Fourteen dragons. More dragons than Slayers. Tori's mind wouldn't let go of the number, and her heart pounded in fear, in worry. The Slayers would have to find a way to destroy the eggs before they hatched.

Fourteen.

"Who is working for Overdrake?" Dr. B asked. "Where is he getting his army?"

Bianca shifted uncomfortably on the couch. "If he finds out I helped you, he'll kill me."

Dr. B leaned toward her, his eyes full of sympathy. "Remember what happened to Nathan. Then think of Jacob's safety. When he's old enough, Jacob will be drawn to fight the dragons whether you like it or not. How formidable of a foe do you want him to face?"

Bianca drew a sharp breath. "Venezuela," she said. "He's made deals with some of their leaders. He also has men inside the US government. People who give him information and will help him disable things when he attacks."

"Who are his men in the government?" Dr. B asked. "And what sort of things will they disable?"

"I don't know," she said. "Military things. He never told me specifics, just that he had sleeper agents installed in key positions. He's been planning this takeover for two decades." She raised her hands in a gesture of frustration. "That's all I know."

Dr. B nodded. "Thank you for your help." He stood to go, then hesitated. "Aaron and Jacob would be safer if they learned how to use their powers. That's what I've been doing for the last five years: teaching children to use their powers."

She didn't glance at Dr. B, just shook her head. For all her earlier bravado, she looked small somehow, sitting on the couch and trembling with emotion. She needed protection as much as her children did, but she was refusing Dr. B's help.

"If you change your mind," he said, "you know how to reach me." He motioned for Tori to follow him, and they left the house for the second time that night.

CHAPTER 11

On the ride to the airport, the other Slayers couldn't stop talking about the extra dragon eggs—guessing where they might be and when they would hatch. Tori sat silently staring out the windows, feeling defeated.

Ryker and Jesse were already conferring about new fighting approaches, busily discussing how to best battle multiple dragons at a time.

"It doesn't matter how many dragons Overdrake has," Kody said, leaning over his seat to talk to them. "He can only control two at a time."

"Possibly three," Ryker said. "If Aaron joins him."

"Overdrake doesn't have to control the dragons," Jesse said. "He could just let some loose on a city while he controlled others in a coordinated attack at another location. He'll want to spread us thin."

Right. Which was why they shouldn't attempt to fight on multiple fronts. Tamerlane and Kiha had both nearly defeated them. And those fights had been all of the Slayers pitted against one dragon. Against fourteen? No way. Why didn't the others realize that killing that many was impossible? What was it about Slayer genes that made her friends want to keep fighting when doing so was obviously hopeless?

Maybe it was just her. Maybe she wasn't as brave as the rest. Or maybe she was just more sensible. Aaron had accused Slayers of being obsessed with killing dragons. She was beginning to think he had a point.

Jesse gazed over at her, seeming to remember she was A-team's captain. "What's your input on this? Do you want to come up with some plays?"

She shook her head. "I'm still considering options."

The best option she could see was hanging up the superhero gear and moving to some nice, safe island. But she couldn't say that, and she couldn't walk away from her friends and leave them to fight fourteen dragons alone.

As Tori mulled over the problem, one thing became clear. To have any chance at success, the Slayers needed a completely new strategy, one that involved Tori learning to control the dragons. It was the only way she could save the Slayers. Dirk wouldn't teach her, not when he knew she wanted the information to defeat him. So how could she learn?

How?

She asked herself the question fourteen times.

CHAPTER 12

Aaron paced across Jacob's bedroom, his mind going in a dozen different directions. A lot of weird things had happened tonight. People broke into his house, he got extra strength from something called a simulator, and a teenage girl who his mother recognized told him she was his counterpart. The girl could tell where he was and if he was lying, so apparently being a counterpart was like being a mother on steroids.

He'd also found out he was half Slayer and half dragon lord, which meant he had powers, or at least would when he was near a dragon or the mysterious simulator.

But all of that wasn't as weird as what happened now when he shut his eyes. Instead of seeing the normal back-of-his-eye-lids darkness, he saw the inside of a cavernous room with boulders, ledges, bushes, and a pond. As though that wasn't creepy enough, a couple of times, other things flashed into his sight—a swishing clubbed tail armored with red scales and huge reptilian front legs with claws at their end.

A dragon. Or at least, part of one. It was massive, scary, and Aaron had no idea why it was in his brain now. Or rather, why he was in *its* brain. That's what he was seeing, he realized—whatever the dragon saw.

His mother had mentioned that dragon lords could connect

with a dragon's mind. That's what this must be, but he didn't like that it was happening and didn't know how to make it stop.

Jacob was sitting on his bed, twisting a fork into some obscure shape. He'd tested out his strength on other things first. He'd thought it was hilarious to stack Aaron's dresser and desk on his bed. Aaron had been in the process of putting Jacob's furniture in the bathtub when their mother came upstairs and demanded, in a less than patient voice, that they put everything back in its place. "The two of you need to learn to think about things before you act," she told them. It was one of her standard lectures. "Just once assess something before you do it." Then she went to make phone calls.

After that, Aaron and Jacob had jumped off Jacob's bed in an attempt to fly. Aaron had leaped the length of the room, and would have gone even farther if the wall hadn't been in the way. He'd smacked it hard enough that his hands went through, creating two jagged holes. The crash made so much noise, their mom came upstairs again. She told them, even less patiently, to stop destroying the house and go to sleep. Assessment fail.

Right. Aaron wouldn't be able to sleep for a long time, and if his mom wanted Jacob to sleep, she should have left him over at the neighbors. He'd been with one of his friends, but as soon as the Slayers left the first time, she called him home.

Aaron kept pacing while Jacob bent the fork as easily as if it were a pipe cleaner. He'd gathered all of the stray silverware and wire hangers in his room and had already made a bat, a truck, and a blob he claimed was a lion.

Aaron paused in front of his brother. "Do you see anything when you shut your eyes?" He didn't expect that Jacob did. Only Aaron had the dragon lord genes, but he still had to ask.

Jacob tilted his chin down, and gave him a look that said

he thought the question was the ultimate in stupid things to say. "No. Because that's the whole point of shutting your eyes. You don't see anything."

Aaron went back to pacing in silence. He didn't want Jacob to think he was losing his mind.

Jacob twisted the handle of a spoon into a snake lifting its head. "Where do you think we could get a simulator?"

"I don't know." Too bad he hadn't asked the Slayers more questions.

From the time Aaron was little, his mom had told him that Slayers hunted dragons and the dragon lords who took care of them. That was one of the reasons he couldn't tell people who his real father was.

When Aaron was younger, Slayers had seemed like goblins or werewolves, creatures lurking in shadows when the sun went down. He'd stopped believing in them years ago, stopped believing all of it. He'd thought the dragon scales were fake, made by someone to take money from gullible people.

Really, the whole situation was his mother's fault. If she hadn't also told him stories about Santa Claus, the tooth fairy, and the Easter bunny, maybe he would have believed her about the rest of it. But flying reindeer and dragons had the same credibility problem.

Now that the Slayers had broken into his house, the line dividing bedtime stories from truth had disappeared altogether. As incredible as it seemed, his father really was a dragon lord hiding out somewhere with a bunch of dragons. Jacob was a Slayer, and Aaron himself was part Slayer. He couldn't quite wrap his mind around that. His mother had always described Slayers in a way that made him picture sword-wielding ninjas obsessed with dragons and driven to pursue them.

But Aaron wasn't obsessed with dragons. Sure, he thought they were cool looking, and in a mythological fight, he would bet on them to wipe the floor with unicorns and mermaids, but he wasn't obsessed. And neither was Jacob.

"I hope we can buy a simulator," Jacob said. He'd started a new creation, and was twisting forks and a knife onto a spoon. "Because that way if your dad comes looking for me, I can punch him through a wall."

Aaron wished Jacob hadn't heard the parts about Overdrake trying to get rid of all the Slayers and possibly checking on their family.

"We're moving," Aaron said. "He won't find us." Their mom had been talking to Realtors on the phone all evening.

Aaron expected Jacob to be relieved. Instead, his brother's expression darkened with anger. He kept twisting metal. "Overdrake is the one who should hide from the Slayers. I don't see why we have to move. That's like lions moving to get away from a gazelle."

Aaron stopped pacing. "We're moving because you're eleven and stupid enough to want to punch a dragon lord. Hello, he's an adult with weapons and huge, flying hench-creatures. If you punched him, we would never find your remains."

"You're only saying that because he's your dad."

Aaron couldn't bring himself to respond to that. Overdrake wasn't his dad. Wesley was his real dad. At least, he had been until the separation four months ago. Jacob still belonged to Wesley, but Aaron didn't.

When Aaron had moved Jacob's dresser, a book fell off the top and slid halfway under his bed. Now Aaron's foot caught the edge of the book. He picked it up, ready to toss it on Jacob's bookshelf, but the title caught his eye: *An Illustrated Encyclopedia of Dragons*.

Jacob had a ton of books in his room. Their mother kept buying them, either in the hopes of turning Jacob into a reader or because she thought books looked good lined up on his shelves.

Jacob had never cracked open most of them. The dragon encyclopedia, however, was worn, and its pages were bent from use. Aaron used to give Jacob a bad time for liking dragon stuff, for encouraging their mother's stories, but Aaron thought Jacob had outgrown that sort of thing years ago. The worn book said otherwise. It had been on his brother's dresser. He'd been reading it lately.

That didn't seem like a good sign.

Aaron walked to the bookcase and ran a finger across the top of a row, not looking at titles but at the condition of the books. He passed over nearly ten with perfect, crisp pages before he found one that showed signs of use. Like the dragon encyclopedia, it hadn't just been flipped through; it had been read multiple times. He pulled it from the shelf. The cover showed a dragon and a sword-wielding knight.

Their mother wouldn't have bought this book. Jacob must have gotten it for himself.

That's when dread first took hold in Aaron's chest.

He ran his fingers along the top of the books again until he found the next worn novel among the ignored ones: *The Hobbit*. It had a dragon in the story too. Aaron put it down and went through the next shelf, pulling out three more books. Every one of them was about dragons. After that, he went through the next shelf, flipping books out to see which ones had been read.

The dragon ones. Always the dragon ones. How had Aaron missed this about his brother—that he only read dragon books? Aaron knew the answer to that question as soon as it crossed his mind. Jacob hid it because Aaron had told him that liking dragons was the same as liking Santa and his globe-trotting reindeer.

The sight of all the books lying in a pile made Aaron's stomach clench. Jacob was obsessed with dragons. He *was* going to be drawn to fight them. Just like that boy Nathan.

Their mother had told him the story about Dr. B's brother, how he'd snuck onto the Overdrake's plantation and been killed. She'd told the story with sadness and warning in her voice. She'd told the story to convince Aaron to never try to contact his father or anyone on that side of his family. They were ruthless people, the Overdrakes.

Now the story seemed like a horrible omen.

He shut his eyes but saw the dragon's huge, clawed legs stretching out.

"Hey, look at this one," Jacob said, bringing Aaron's attention back to the room. He held up his latest silverware creation.

Aaron didn't have to ask what it was supposed to be; he could tell by the wings and tail. A dragon.

"Pretty good, huh? Too bad for the dragon that I'm better." Jacob wadded up the silverware into a tangled, useless ball, then tossed it across the room into his garbage can. He let out a cheer when he made the shot.

It's won't be that easy to get rid of them, Aaron wanted to say. *They're huge. They can cut you in half with one swipe of a claw.* He didn't say any of that. It wouldn't matter. Jacob was a Slayer.

Sooner or later, Overdrake would attack the country with his dragons. How many years would it be until Jacob felt compelled to fight them? How long would it take for Aaron's father to kill all the Slayers?

Aaron didn't know what he needed to do to save Jacob, only that he had to do *something*. For a moment, he considered going to the Slayers for help, but quickly dismissed the idea. The Slayers wouldn't help to keep Jacob out of the fight. Dr. B wanted to train him, and then Jacob would die fighting with them. If Aaron wanted to keep his brother alive, he'd have to find a way to do it himself.

He paced some more. Only one solution seemed to have a chance of working. Aaron would have to give Overdrake what he wanted.

# CHAPTER 13

When Tori got home at nine, Brindy, the family's German shepherd, met her at the door, waving her tail in furry arcs. Her parents were considerably less enthusiastic about her arrival. Her father called Tori into the kitchen using a tone that suggested they'd be there a while.

She slinked into the room, all apologies. "I'm sorry I didn't tell you where I was going beforehand. I forgot about my date with Jesse, and he was really hurt. I had to go with him to make up for it."

Tori's father was tall, stately, and the source of her honey-brown hair and green eyes. Now he folded his arms and trained those green eyes on her. "You know the rules. When you want to go somewhere, you ask us. You don't tell us after the fact. We need to know what you're doing, who you're with, and when you'll be back. That would be true even if you weren't a candidate's daughter."

Her mother's blonde hair was styled and she wore a pair of black pants with matching blazer. She'd obviously been at some function earlier. She was emptying out the dishwasher, setting the dishes down extra hard in the cupboard. "You can't just disappear whenever you feel like it. I thought you'd learned that lesson after your last grounding, but apparently not."

"I did learn it," Tori said. "That's why I texted you from the movie, even though the theaters spend like, five minutes before each film telling you not to."

Her mother kept clanging plates, unappeased. "We know why you're sneaking off, and it has got to stop."

A breath lodged in Tori's throat. Could her parents know about the Slayers? Had someone seen her fly away from the Kennedy Center? Or worse, did anyone know what she'd done in North Carolina?

Her mother shut a cupboard and turned to face Tori. "I'm sorry that you and your boyfriend find your bodyguard bothersome, but you'll have to learn to deal with it."

They didn't know. It was both a relief and a disappointment. A disappointment because she hated keeping secrets from them.

"Well, there is that," Tori said. "Having Lars following me around sort of kills the romantic atmosphere."

"I can live with that," her father said.

He had three bodyguards who rotated the duty of watching him whenever he left the house, a fourth who went with her mother or sister as needed, and a fifth who drove Tori to and from school. Her parents could claim Lars was primarily a driver, but one look at his six-foot-five frame or the holster tucked not so inconspicuously in his suitcoat, and everyone knew he was more than a chauffeur.

Lately, whenever Tori went out in public, her parents sent Lars with her. It had become a hassle. In order to make it to her Slayer practices, she had to pretend she was going to a safe place like a friend's house and insist on driving herself.

Her mother wiped a rag energetically at a spot on the counter. "You have to take precautions. Any guy who doesn't understand that isn't worth your time."

Tori turned to her dad pleadingly. The country thought he was strong and decisive. In family matters, though, her mother was the strict one. He was the one who spoiled her.

He shook his head at her now. "Don't give me that look. I think every teenage girl should have a bodyguard. And speaking of unauthorized dates, when are you going to bring Jesse over and introduce him to us? I don't like you running around with people I haven't met."

Bringing Jesse here would only complicate matters. Her parents would ask about what his parents did and where he lived, and then her father would undoubtedly do a background check. For the time being, Jesse was undercover. His parents had quit their jobs and disappeared. How would that sort of thing look to her father?

Tori forced out a sigh. "I don't want you to meet him unless, you know, we're really serious. I mean, you guys aren't like normal parents."

Tori's mom tilted her head in a questioning manner. "We're not normal parents?"

Her dad nodded. "I think what she meant to say is that we're better than normal."

"I mean," Tori said, "your security detail would frisk him or something."

Her father flipped through a couple of pieces of mail that lay on the counter. "Only if he's a Democrat."

"See?" Tori said. "That's what I'm talking about. It would turn into an awkward political thing. It's better if Jesse and I meet in private. That way I don't have to worry about the media finding out about him and harassing him."

Her mother lifted a finger, making a point. "I'm sorry your father's job is putting a crimp in your social life, but sometimes we have to make sacrifices. From now on, you will let us know about your plans so we can approve them and decide whether you need extra security. No more keeping things from us. Understand?"

"I understand," Tori said. What else could she say?

"And you have to show Lars more consideration," her mother went on. "He was trying to keep an eye on you and . . ." She shook her head in frustration. "I don't know what you did, but the man is convinced you scaled down the side of the Kennedy Center to get away from him."

Tori let out a small, guilty cough. "I wouldn't do that. At least, not in a skirt and heels."

Her mother went back to wiping the counter. "To help you remember you need to follow our rules, you're grounded next weekend."

The edict had been unavoidable, but even so, the unfairness chaffed. She'd been out trying to protect the country. "Fine," she said, crossing her arms. "I don't suppose you and Dad ever went out without telling your parents where you were, or without toting around a large, humorless man who resembles Arnold Schwarzenegger."

Her father laughed, but stopped when her mother sent him a glare.

Tori headed out of the room, then remembered Bianca's information and turned back. "Dad, you shouldn't trust Venezuela. They're up to something."

Now it was her mother's turn to laugh. "You must have had some interesting conversations on your date."

Her father didn't smile. His eyebrows drew together in question. "What do you know about Venezuela?"

She couldn't tell him the truth, so she shrugged and found a vague explanation. "Their leaders don't seem to have America's best interests at heart." She walked out of the kitchen before he could ask her more questions.

After a few moments, her father spoke to her mother in a voice low enough that Tori shouldn't have been able to hear him. "We know one thing about Jesse now. He must be the son of someone on the foreign relations subcommittee. Those are the only people who know that Venezuela asked permission to do training sessions near our shores."

The comment stopped Tori in her tracks. She stood in the hallway, waiting for him to say more. He didn't, at least not about Venezuela, but what he'd already said made her heart pound. Was Venezuela taking steps to get into a better tactical position to attack? She wanted to run back to the kitchen and tell her father everything about Overdrake.

She couldn't reveal her Slayer identity, though. Her parents didn't even want her to go on dates without a bodyguard. They weren't about to let her fly off on missions to fight dragons. She walked up the stairs, went to her room, and called Dr. B.

She relayed the information, finishing with, "We've got to let the authorities know Venezuela is up to something."

His answer came over the speaker in reassuring tones. "I'm doing what I can to inform key officials. That's all we can do. If we let anyone know about us, we'll only end up jeopardizing ourselves. Remember, Overdrake has agents in the government."

After Tori hung up, she felt even more exasperated and powerless. Bad things were going to happen, and she couldn't do a thing to stop any of them.

She opened her laptop, logged on to talk to Dirk, and stared at his icon. She ached to tell him about his mother. He should know that his mom hadn't wanted to leave him. He should know that when she saw his picture, she cried.

Yet if Tori told Dirk about Bianca, he'd want to know how she'd been found and why they'd talked. He'd ask all kinds of questions. When Tori refused to answer, he might look for his mother himself. Finding her would lead him to finding his brothers.

She couldn't risk that. And yet, if Dirk knew about his mother, knew she loved and missed him, was there even the smallest of possibilities of him leaving his father to live with her?

Finally she wrote, *I've been thinking about you and what you said. Maybe I should learn more about my dragon lord side. I can't agree to meet you anywhere, not when I'm worried I could be walking into a trap. Could you teach me some other way?*

A pathetic attempt to learn how to control dragons without letting on that she wanted the information to defeat him.

She didn't hear back from Dirk right away, but hadn't expected to. She got ready for bed then checked her laptop again. Dirk had written back.

What do you have in mind?

She typed, *How about a video? You could do your own version of How to Train Your Dragon. Be sure to include scenes where they look adorable instead of deadly.*

A few seconds later, his reply showed up. *I don't think so. If you want to learn about dragons, you'll have to do it firsthand. And you'll have to trust me.*

His answer sounded terse. Was Dirk mad because she'd turned him down the first time? Or . . . a thought flashed through her mind. What if Overdrake had discovered that she and Dirk communicated this way? He might be the one writing. He might be the one trying to set up a meeting, not Dirk.

She nearly asked him to speak to her near a dragon, but decided against it. If Overdrake didn't know Dirk talked to her like that, she didn't want to tell him.

I'll talk to you later, she wrote, and then closed her laptop. She'd wait until she heard his voice and was certain a message came from him before she wrote again.

 # CHAPTER 14

Jesse was the last to be dropped off. For him, home was the hotel his family lived in while Dr. B worked out the last few relocation details. Jesse was used to the extra time with Dr. B, and was sure he planned to drive Jesse home last so he could talk about the teams. Usually he asked how Willow and Ryker were coming along, or commented on ways the captains could better utilize their players' skills during practice rounds.

Dr. B was the sort of person who had an almost unnerving calmness about him. He may not have inherited any super powers, but he had the ability to approach every situation like a military strategist. During Jesse's first year at camp, he'd learned not to expect more than mild sympathy for injuries sustained while fighting. Dr. B. didn't console the Slayers; he handed out advice on how not to get injured next time.

During the ride tonight, Dr. B spoke in that same calm tone. "Although the mission didn't yield the results we wanted, the teamwork was flawless. Everyone executed their orders well."

Jesse didn't comment. He was still bothered that Tori had forgotten the code for backup and didn't seem to think fighting three guys by herself was a big deal. If months of practice should have taught her anything, it was that overconfidence led to a quick death.

"I've been thinking about Tori," Dr. B continued.

Something he and Jesse had in common.

"How do you think she'll take it," Dr. B asked, "when Ryker replaces her as captain?"

Jesse tensed. "Are you trading out positions now?"

"Not yet. Ryker still needs more practice. Perhaps within a month or two. It makes sense to have the flying counterparts lead the groups."

It did make sense, especially since Tori had a hard time getting away for practices. Both teams probably expected the change, including Tori. Still, Jesse felt a sting of resentment on her behalf. "I don't know," he said. "The last dragon lord you demoted didn't take it so well."

Dr. B just laughed. "Point taken. But you trust her? Implicitly?"

"Don't you?" Jesse asked.

"After Dirk, I'm not sure I can completely trust anyone. But for now, yes, I trust her." Dr. B's gaze cut over to Jesse. "I'm afraid that if her loyalties change, you may be the last to realize it." He didn't add, although the implication was clear, *Love is blind.*

"Her genetics don't matter," Jesse said. "She's chosen to be a Slayer."

"Her genetics matter very much to Overdrake. He'll want to convert or neutralize any other dragon lords. We may be able to conceal Aaron, but Overdrake knows where Tori lives and where she goes to school. I'm afraid even her father's bodyguards might not be enough to protect her."

"So we'd better change that," Jesse said.

"Change a presidential candidate's home?"

"We're Slayers. We can find a way to change anything." Jesse considered the problem, planning out a strategy. "Especially if we have some explosives."

 # CHAPTER 15

On Sunday afternoon while Tori was in her room doing math homework, her father walked in. "I got a message from my office. A guy called claiming to know you and insisted he talk with you. Said it was urgent."

Dirk, she thought, and wondered what was so important. "Who was it?"

"An Aaron Smith."

Oh, Aaron. She hoped he was calling to give her helpful information and not a bill for damages to his house. "Yeah, I probably should talk to him. Did he leave a number?"

Her father dropped the paper on the end of her bed, giving her an annoyed look as he did. "My office shouldn't double as the relationship coordinator for your love life. And what about Jesse? Did something happen with him?"

"No." Tori picked up the paper. "Aaron is just a guy I know. And he's way too young for me."

"If you ask me, you're way too young for any of this. Boys can't be trusted, you know."

Tori started on her next math problem. "Weren't you a boy once?"

"Nope, I've always been a father." He left the room and shut the door.

A Skype account was written on the paper with the words, "Call me." She went to her laptop and did. Almost immediately Aaron appeared on the screen. He wore a white T-shirt and was leaning back in a chair, striking a pose that looked more like a businessman than a seventh grader. His blond hair was smoothed back, and his blue eyes had a confident gleam to them. His resemblance to Dirk struck her all over again.

"I see your mother told you who I am," Tori said.

"I figured it out myself. There aren't too many senators' daughters my mother would recognize."

Tori hoped she wasn't about to regret taking off her helmet. If he was planning some sort of blackmail . . . "What did you want to talk to me about?"

"I've got some questions," he said, then hesitated, as though he weren't sure how to ask them. Finally, he said, "I keep seeing dragon legs. Like, a dragon moving around inside a huge cave-like room. It's especially clear when I shut my eyes. Why is that happening?"

He'd connected with a dragon. Tori should have realized he would. This could be useful. "Have you seen anything that indicates where the dragon is? Any landmarks?"

"What landmarks would I see inside a cave? All I see are just a bunch of rocks, a pond, and overhead lighting."

"Dragon lords see what the nearest dragon sees. Once your powers have been activated, you always have a link. Didn't your mother tell you about any of this?"

"I thought it only happened when a dragon was close."

"You must be close enough." Maybe Overdrake was somewhere between Virginia and North Carolina. It was possible. Tori had no idea how close dragon lords had to be to connect. "Eventually the dragon will leave its enclosure. When that happens, look for clues to its location: road signs, distinctive buildings, that sort of thing, and then tell me what you see."

Aaron frowned, dissatisfied. "How do I make the dragon stuff go away? I have to shut my eyes to sleep, but then I can't sleep because I see all the dragon crap. Sometimes literally."

Well, that was one advantage to only hearing dragons.

"I want it to stop," Aaron emphasized.

Tori felt a pang of sympathy. When she first started hearing a dragon, it had been so bothersome and creepy to constantly have reptilian company. Seeing a dragon must be worse. "I'm not sure you can make it completely go away, but you can learn to minimize it. Dirk said he imagined his dragon sight as a window and shrank it."

Aaron shut his eyes in concentration. After a few moments he scowled. Shrinking the "window" must not be as easy as Dirk made it sound.

"Sorry I can't be more specific," Tori said. "I only hear dragons. I don't see anything."

Aaron's eyes flicked open. "Explain the whole counterpart thing again."

She spent the next few minutes telling him the basics. "It's not mind reading," she finished up. "It's only an ability to read each other really well."

Aaron had listened to her explanation silently. "I can't fool you or lie to you at all?"

She considered telling him, "No," so he wouldn't ever lie to her, but instead told the truth. "Actually, Dirk fooled me about himself for a long time. But I sensed when a subject made him uncomfortable or tense. When he lied to the Slayers before a mission, I knew something was wrong. I could tell he wasn't being completely forthcoming, and it made me wonder why. And then I figured out his identity."

"But you might not have," Aaron said.

"I think eventually I would have put two and two and fourteen dragons together."

He didn't ask her what she meant. "You said you were Dirk's friend. Do you have a way of contacting him?"

She hesitated. "Why do you ask?"

Instead of answering, he tilted his head, studying her. "Wait, did you have a thing with my brother?"

She lifted an eyebrow, wondering how he'd come to that conclusion. "That isn't really any of your business."

Aaron let out a laugh that reminded her of Dirk's. "You did. I can totally tell."

She sent him a forced smile and leaned toward her computer to disconnect the call. "It's been great talking to you, but I've got homework."

"I'm not done yet," he said, straightening. "I want to figure out how to be a dragon lord."

"Me too. Unfortunately, I can't help you with that."

"Actually, you can."

At first she didn't understand what he was talking about, and then the meaning became clear. She saw it in the firm set of his lips, in the determined lift of his chin, and in the emotion coming from him—bravery mixed with desperation. He wanted to contact Overdrake, and he wanted her help to do it.

"No," she said. "Absolutely not. Stay away from Overdrake."

"He can teach me how to control the dragons."

"Yeah, and then he can use you to hurt people. He wouldn't let you go back to your family."

Aaron shook his head. "Once I control a dragon, I can do what I want with it. I could kidnap it or turn it on him."

"That's a really noble idea. But you're twelve, and Overdrake has a deadly shot with a rifle."

"I'm closer to thirteen than to twelve."

"Which doesn't matter when it comes to bullets."

Aaron acted as though she hadn't spoken. "I'm pretty sure I can fool Overdrake, but if Dirk and I are counterparts, will he know I want to stop him?"

"Probably. Which is another reason it's a bad idea to put yourself in Overdrake's reach."

Aaron pursed his lips in thought. "Dirk fooled you for a long time; you said so. That means I could keep secrets from him too."

"But I wasn't actively trying to figure out if he was a traitor. I trusted him and never put him to the test. If you show up and ask how to control a dragon, Overdrake and Dirk both will be suspicious."

Aaron rolled his eyes. "I'm not an idiot. I won't even bring it up. I'll let Overdrake offer. He'll want to use me in his war— that's the whole reason my mom left."

Tori tapped her fingers against the edge of her laptop. Aaron was serious. He'd thought this through, he'd come up with an idea, and now wanted her help. "Does your mother know what you're planning to do?"

"Does *your* mother?"

Touché. Tori didn't answer.

"Adults think we can't do anything," Aaron said. "But they're wrong. That's why Overdrake won't see my betrayal coming."

The problem with talking to someone over a video call was that you couldn't reach out and shake some sense into them. "Look, you shouldn't go anywhere near Overdrake."

"Here's what I need you to do," Aaron said, ignoring her statement. "Contact Dirk and tell him you found me at the Renaissance fair, selling the dragon scales. It's mostly the truth, so he won't suspect it's a trap. Don't tell him you came to my house. I don't want him to find my mom or learn about my brother. Tell him he can find me near The Black Unicorn Shoppe. Next weekend is the last week of the festival. All I have to do is hang out there. Overdrake will send someone for me. I know he will."

"Yeah, I do too. That's why I'm not going to tell Dirk about you. Do you have any idea how much your mother would freak out if you went missing?"

The resolve in Aaron's eyes didn't waver. "I'll be at the fair next weekend. If Overdrake doesn't come, I'll find some other way to contact him, and then the whole thing will seem suspicious. If you want to help me stay safe, you'll do it my way. Contact Dirk."

Tori was being coerced by a twelve-year-old. For a moment she only stared at him. He squared his shoulders, showing her he meant everything he said. "We could figure out a way to pass information to each other," he added. "Maybe I'll even be able to tell you where the dragons are and how to control them."

He didn't need to come up with a way—it already existed. All he had to do was talk to her when he was around the dragon she was connected to. If Aaron's plan worked, it might be worth the risk to send him in as a mole.

She bit her lip, thinking. "The other Slayers probably wouldn't go for it." The last thing they wanted was another trained dragon lord to worry about.

"It's not up to them. This is my decision. Mine and yours."

"It doesn't work that way. We vote on things . . ." Her sentence drifted off as she thought of how the Slayers had reacted when she told them Aaron could be an asset. No one had believed her.

"It's my decision," Aaron repeated.

"What would I tell Dr. B when he reports you've been kidnapped?"

Aaron shrugged. "You can lie to him without being caught, right?"

"That doesn't mean I want to."

"Fine. Tell Dr. B the truth, but not anyone else. If you have another traitor in your group, I'll be chained up somewhere until this revolution is over."

Could it work? Could Aaron give them information about the dragons that would help the Slayers? Probably. He might even be their best hope for turning the tide in their favor. She'd already suggested to the other Slayers that they ought to train Aaron to use his powers so he could help them. The only difference was that Overdrake would be the one training him instead of Dr. B.

Sometimes you had to fight fire with fire. Maybe the best way to fight dragons was with dragon lords.

Still, if Tori went along with Aaron's plan she would be sending him into a lion's den—no, make that a dragon's den. "Why are you so insistent on learning to use your abilities?" she asked.

Aaron let out a snort like the reason should be obvious. "Because Slayers are drawn to fight dragons. I know what happened to Dr. B's brother. I'm not letting that happen to Jacob."

How could she argue with that? She felt the fierce protectiveness in his words. He was anxious about his brother, angry at Overdrake, and had a sort of pent-up energy that insisted he do something.

"Fine," Tori said. "I'll tell Dirk about you. But not until Friday. That will give you time to change your mind."

And time for Tori to come up with a different, better plan.

CHAPTER 16

On Sunday afternoon, Overdrake sat at his computer, checking the latest reports from his agents. He had dozens working for him, and even had some agents spying on other agents to ensure everyone's loyalty. Most of them were vastly overpaid for what they did. The information they turned in—when they had any—usually wasn't more than mildly helpful. But the exceptions were worth the money.

And the latest report from his man in New York might fall in that category.

When Overdrake had learned the Slayers' identities, he'd had his agents research their extended families as well. Dr. B might have moved the Slayers' families, but Overdrake was still watching the grandparents and cousins.

He'd toyed with the idea of kidnapping aunts or uncles and making demands, but had rejected the idea. He doubted the Slayers would give in to such things, and besides, kidnappings were messy. The FBI might get involved.

Still, keeping track of the extended family could pay off in other ways.

The email to Overdrake read: *Shang's cousin, Serena Cheng, will be married in Albany, New York, at five o'clock on Wednesday.*

A wedding. Serena's extended family would attend. And that meant Shang was likely to be there too.

Overdrake would make sure someone was waiting to greet him.

He clicked on the Slayers file to review Shang's data, but somehow his gaze went to Tori's name instead.

No matter how many other Slayers Overdrake got rid of, Tori would always be a problem. Because Dirk wanted to protect her.

It was ridiculous, really, the way Dirk was tying his hands. Overdrake had been planning this revolution for more than two decades. It had already cost an enormous amount of money and manpower, yet his son was letting his priorities be twisted around by a girl.

Well, Overdrake might have promised Dirk that Tori and her family were off limits, but that didn't mean he couldn't use his influence in other ways. He could show her that she wasn't safe. He could remind her that if she fought against him, she would pay a price.

Perhaps it was time to visit Tori's house.

 # CHAPTER 17

Instead of finishing up her homework, Tori found herself researching Venezuela. By all accounts, the country had more than its share of problems: economic instability, high inflation, political turmoil, and it was one of the most violent places on earth. American diplomats had to travel in armored vehicles. Unfortunately, Venezuela also had an advanced navy and air force, along with plenty of weaponry.

Charming. She should warn her father about them again. He needed to try and stop them from doing any sort of military exercises near US shores.

She went downstairs, walked into the den, and found him sitting at his desk, signing documents. She plopped down on an oversized chair in front of his desk. "You know how you've raised me to be politically aware and concerned about the country?"

He eyed her suspiciously then returned his attention to his papers. "Why do I have a feeling a request for money is couched somewhere in that question?"

"I'm not asking for money."

He signed a paper and set it onto a different stack. "I'm also not lifting your grounding. Even if you do want to go to some political rally or save-the-earth cause."

She rearranged one of the chair pillows so she could lean back. "It's not that either. I just wanted to talk to you about Venezuela and the exercises they want to conduct offshore."

Her father's gaze shot to hers. "That's not public information. How did you come by it?"

She couldn't answer that question. She'd heard it from him while she'd been eavesdropping, and she didn't want to let him know just how good her hearing was. "My sources aren't the point. The point is Venezuela has ulterior motives for those tests. We can't let their military anywhere near our borders."

He sat back in his chair, studying her. "It isn't up to me alone to decide those things. And tell Jesse he shouldn't talk to you or anyone else about what goes on in senate committees. His parent, whoever it is, could get in a lot of trouble for leaking details."

Tori didn't want her dad thinking about those sorts of rules or what he shouldn't be talking about. She forced an incredulous laugh. "Please. Government officials leak stuff all the time. That was the President's reelection campaign. He leaked things about his opponents and let the media campaign for him."

"All the more reason for me to be careful. I can't talk with my daughter about classified matters. The media would have a field day with that." Her father turned his attention back to his papers, ending the conversation.

But she didn't want it to end. "If the committee says yes, when will Venezuela do the exercises?"

Her father kept his gaze on his papers. She could tell from his expression that he was debating whether to answer. He liked discussing foreign affairs with her. He was always saying that most Americans were dangerously uninformed about the world around them, and he didn't want her to be that way.

He signed the paper on the top of the pile. "Venezuela has proposed different dates. That's one of the things the senatorial committee is discussing."

Tori didn't ask why Venezuela wanted to do their military exercises near the borders of the US. Whatever explanation they'd given was a lie. The exercises would either be an invasion, or practice for one.

Tori let out a cough of indignation. "Who on the committee thinks letting a foreign country's military near our shores is a good idea?"

Her father paused before signing the next paper. "Venezuela has one of the world's largest oil reserves. Some people think good relations with them would benefit our country. And they might be right. But that's the problem with these decisions. It's hard to know whether we're creating a friendship or leaving ourselves open to future aggression."

He hadn't given Tori any names of Venezuela's supporters, and she wanted them. Those people were most likely either Overdrake's men or people who were influenced by them.

What was the best way to extract their names? "So it's about oil? Are the pro-Venezuela people the same ones who want to drill in the US?"

Her father chuckled. "Of course not. Senator Ethington is the one pushing the initiative."

What?

"Senator Ethington?" Tori echoed. He was the frontrunner of the Democratic candidates; the man who would most likely run against her father. Could he be one of Overdrake's men?

"Senator Ethington only minds drilling for oil on our soil, not Venezuela's."

Tori didn't like most politicians on principle. She'd met too many. They were all smiles and charisma in public, but would cheerfully throw anyone to the wolves if it furthered their agenda.

But surely Senator Ethington wouldn't be involved with Overdrake and his plans for a takeover. Not a presidential candidate. He had to care about the nation's safety.

"I thought he wanted us to move to green energy. Who's convinced him we need Venezuela's oil?"

Tori's father gave her a look that said she should know better. "He touts green energy because it sounds good to the voting population. Less pollution, no oil spills. We'd all like that. But he's also a pragmatist and knows that people need to drive to work every day. He's already promised he won't expand drilling here, so he's got to get oil elsewhere. He was the one who reached out to Venezuela, and now they're putting our goodwill to the test."

Her father went on for a few more minutes, talking about the difficulty of balancing security with loyalty to the country's allies.

Through all of it, one thought kept repeating in Tori's mind. Senator Ethington had been the one to reach out to Venezuela. It was either horribly bad timing on his part, or he was one of Overdrake's men. When her father paused his lecture, she said, "Who else wants to let Venezuela run tests near our shores?"

Perhaps she sounded too eager. Her father's gaze went to her eyes, and then his voice changed from informative to comforting. "You don't have to worry about Venezuela. They're not going take on the most powerful nation in the world."

"You don't know that," Tori said. "Germany was a small country. So was Japan. England isn't that large, and for a while the sun didn't set on its colonies."

"Glad to see that your school is teaching you history, but I think we'll be okay."

School hadn't taught her about war and conquerors lately; Dirk had. He seemed to know about every invasion in history, and why it had or hadn't worked. Overdrake had drilled that knowledge into him, and Dirk had studied it like it was his personal playbook.

Again, Tori wanted to tell her father everything she knew. He needed to realize what the country was up against.

The words were on her tongue, but she couldn't say them. She had promised Dr. B she wouldn't reveal anything about the Slayers. If her parents knew she was training to fight dragons, they wouldn't let her anywhere near Dr. B or the Slayers again.

But that didn't mean she couldn't tell her father other things. Before she could talk herself out of it, she blurted out, "Someone is using the Venezuelan military to try to take over the country. We'll be hit with electromagnetic pulse that will cripple our infrastructure. I think it might happen within the year. And if I'm right, you can't trust Senator Ethington. He's involved with the Venezuelans."

Her father stared at her, caught between laughter and worry—not worry about the country, worry about her. "Where did you hear all of that?"

She stiffened, stung by his reaction. Although, really, what had she expected? She'd given him no reason to believe her, and she couldn't offer him the proof.

She crossed her arms. "You have sources you can't talk about. So do I."

"Jesse? Is he your source?"

She considered agreeing. Her father already thought Jesse knew about Venezuela's request. But that wouldn't work. Her father knew every committee member and would easily find out none of them had a son named Jesse. Maybe another cover story could give his supposed knowledge legitimacy. She quickly abandoned the idea. She shouldn't drag Jesse into this without his permission.

"No," she said at last. And knew she'd waited too long to make the word convincing.

"Uh-huh. Have the two of you been listening to some conspiracy podcast or something?"

"You don't have to believe me. But you should do what you can to keep Venezuela away from our borders, and you should also look into ways to protect the country from an EMP strike."

"EMP is a danger we're aware of." Her father smiled at her with more concern in his eyes than made her comfortable. "I know being a politician's daughter isn't easy. You've heard about the perils facing America since you were a toddler. But don't obsess about them. There's a lot to be optimistic about."

Great. He hadn't listened to her warning, he thought she was being paranoid, and now he was undoubtedly going to give her a lot of pep talks about having a positive attitude.

"This isn't about being pessimistic," she said.

Before her father could comment on that, her mother opened the door. She wore a coat, and her cheeks and nose were pink from the cold. "Brindy isn't in here, is she?" After a quick glance around the room revealed it was German shepherd-less, she added, "I can't find her anywhere. I let her outside a while ago, and she's disappeared."

Brindy was the sort of dog who firmly ignored her custom-made dog house in the backyard, as well as any intrigues their wooded three-acre backyard could provide. She preferred to spend her time sniffing for food that had fallen on the kitchen floor and devising ways to get around the no-dogs-allowed-on-the-couch rule.

Tori's father looked unconcerned. "She can't have gone past the fence."

Her mother lifted a hand, puzzled. "Maybe she dug under it or something. I've spent the last twenty minutes looking around and calling her. She isn't in the backyard."

Prickles of worry darted up Tori's spine. Her father was right; Brindy couldn't have just disappeared.

He only shrugged. "Maybe someone let her inside, and she's stuck in a room."

Her mother pulled off her gloves. "I already had Aprilynne check the house." She turned to Tori. "Would you walk around the neighborhood with Lars and see if you can find her?"

Tori didn't have to ask why her mother didn't send Lars to do the job by himself. Brindy wouldn't go near the bodyguards, let alone come when they called.

A few minutes later, Tori was trekking down the street, flashlight in hand, Lars at her side.

She swept the flashlight beam over bushes and between trees, yelling, "Brindy!"

Wind rustled the fallen leaves around their feet, and a neighbor's Great Dane rushed to the edge of its fence to bark at them. There was no sign of a German shepherd.

Tori kept walking, gripping the flashlight and listening for Brindy's bark while she swung the light into the shadows. "Brindy!"

Silence.

"Brindy!"

Silence.

"Brindy!" The farther they went, the more her call sounded desperate and alone.

Lars didn't call, just marched silently beside her, scanning for danger.

They spent an hour traversing the neighborhood. Tori kept

hoping that if she walked a little farther, called a few more times, the dog would appear. Past the next house, or the next, Brindy would bound toward her, tail wagging and completely oblivious to the worry she'd caused.

Every minute that didn't happen, another scenario presented itself. Overdrake knew where she lived. He'd taken her dog, maybe even killed her. Then when he attacked her at home, Brindy wouldn't be there to warn anyone.

When Tori finally gave up searching and went back to her house, she felt sick. Her parents were in the kitchen, and she went straight to them. "I think someone took Brindy to keep her from barking during a home invasion."

Her parents exchanged a concerned look. Not for Brindy, for Tori. "I don't think we need to jump to the worst conclusion," her father said soothingly.

Aprilynne, who had come into the kitchen for a snack, breezed by Tori on her way to the fridge. "How come you're so preoccupied with death lately? It's not healthy."

"I'm not preoccupied with death," Tori said.

"You thought some creepy guy was staking out our house."

"That means I'm preoccupied with safety, not death."

Aprilynne opened a yogurt and went to the garbage to throw away the lid. "If you want more bodyguards trailing after you, you can have mine."

Aprilynne had graduated last year, and was taking online university classes while she worked downtown at their father's campaign office. Mostly, she just saw the campaign staff, but she still had her share of security detail.

"No one is getting rid of their bodyguards," their mother said pointedly, looking at Tori, not Aprilynne.

Their dad walked over and put his arm around Tori's shoulder. "Honey, sometimes pets get lost. This isn't the first time it's happened. If Brindy hasn't come home by the morning, we'll put up flyers around the neighborhood."

Why wasn't her family worried about the obvious? "If Brindy got out of the backyard, someone else can get in."

Aprilynne took a bite of yogurt. "You think someone is going to dig under our fence like a dog?" She shook her head, then left the kitchen as though she didn't want to hear Tori's answer.

"Even if someone did dig under the fence," her mother said, "we have a security system."

But alarms could be disabled. Tori didn't press the issue. She went up to her room and sent a message to Dr. B telling him about Senator Ethington and reporting what had happened to her dog. She wasn't sure what she expected him to do about Brindy's disappearance; she just wanted to tell someone who wouldn't treat her like a paranoid child.

He wrote back, *I'll send someone to watch your house tonight, and we'll discuss long-term solutions. Make sure you don't leave home without a means of protection.*

Well, that would make going to school difficult. School had a no-weapons policy for students. What could she take to protect herself that the teachers wouldn't see as a weapon? A candlestick? A nail gun?

Despite Dr. B's assurances that someone was watching her house, she didn't sleep much that night. Brindy wasn't the sort of dog who made a lot of noise. She usually only barked when the doorbell rang. Still, the silence seemed wrong. Heavy. Where was she? Somewhere afraid and whining? Was she hurt? Dead? Even after Tori had pushed those images from her mind, she was always half listening for the creaking of the floorboard. Instead she heard the familiar thumps, shuffles, and wingbeats of a dragon.

CHAPTER 18

That night when Dirk went to the kitchen to rummage for leftovers, he found Bridget sitting at the table with a bowl of popcorn. A German shepherd stood attentively at her side. Bridget was throwing pieces of popcorn in the air and laughing as the dog snatched them in its mouth.

"Where did the dog come from?" he asked. The German shepherd wore a collar, but no tags.

"Daddy brought her home. She's visiting us for a little while. I'm naming her Peppermint because she's so sweet."

The family owned two Rottweilers, trained guard dogs. Neither were around now. "Are you saying we're dog sitting for one of Dad's friends?" Unlikely. His father didn't have those sorts of friendships. In fact, he had hardly any friends. He had allies, contacts, employees, and if you counted Venezuela, minions.

"I don't know who she belongs to," Bridget replied. "But she likes popcorn."

Dirk petted the dog's head, scratching her ears. She turned and licked his hand, then spent several moments sniffing him with interest. "It's dragon," he told the dog. "A new smell. Don't ever get too close to one." He gave her a last scratch then went to the sink and washed his hands. "Keep that dog away from ours," he said to Bridget over his shoulder. "They'd rip her to shreds."

He found some pizza in the fridge and went to the room without thinking of the dog again.

CHAPTER 19

On Monday morning, Tori's watch phone woke her with a beep. The sound was Dr. B's tone notifying her of a message. She was immediately alert, senses sharp. A glance at the clock told her it was quarter after five.

Please, she thought, *don't let this news be anything horrible.*

The message read: *Does your father have Senator Ethington's personal cell phone number?*

Dr. B had woken her up at five-fifteen to ask that? Did the man have no idea about normal texting protocol?

She wrote, *Probably*. Her father had a lot of senators in his contacts. He liked to talk to people directly instead of going through assistants.

Dr. B texted, *Find it and send it to me as soon as you can.*

You want to talk to the senator? Tori asked.

I want to listen to what he's saying to others.

Oh, Dr. B wanted to bug the phone. She wrote back, *If Senator Ethington is making deals with Overdrake, he wouldn't be foolish enough to use his own phone. He'd use a disposable one.*

True, Dr. B answered. *But most people keep their phones with them all the time. If we have his number we can hack into his phone, use it as an earpiece, and listen in to his other conversations.*

That could be helpful. *I'll get his number,* she wrote. *And if you learn any interesting campaign info, pass that along.*

She was half joking.

Dr. B wrote, *I can't pass along that sort of information. It might make him question whether he's being bugged. It's more important not to tip our hand.*

Tori harrumphed. *You're a Democrat, aren't you?*

Get the number, and I promise to vote for your father.

One voter won over, approximately two hundred million left to go. She closed the message screen on her watch and pulled herself out of bed.

Her father wouldn't give out private numbers, but if she got hold of his phone, she could take the contact information off it. She knew his password; she'd seen him type it in.

He kept his phone on his nightstand, and her parents were light sleepers. Could she sneak into his room and take it without being caught? What would she say if they woke up and saw her making off with her father's cell phone?

Maybe she should ask Dr. B to stop by the neighborhood with a simulator tomorrow morning. If she could fly and see in the dark, it would be a piece of cake to nick her father's phone. But she didn't want to wait until tomorrow. There was an easier way to do this today.

Her father's routine was always the same. His alarm went off at six. He showered, dressed—putting his phone in his suit pocket—ate breakfast, and left for DC. On most days he brought along Aprilynne and dropped her off at the campaign office on his way to the senate building.

Tori went downstairs and made eggs, bacon, and toast for the entire family. Then she walked into Aprilynne's room and flicked on the light. "Hey, I need a favor from you."

Her sister groaned and opened one eye. "What time is it?"

"Almost six. Your alarm is about to go off." Tori sat on her sister's bed with a thud. "So about this favor—it's not hard, and I'll let you have that Ralph Lauren shirt you like so much."

Aprilynne shut her eyes and sighed. "Are you sneaking off somewhere at this hour? There's something wrong with any guy who wants to see you this early."

"I'm not going anywhere," Tori said. "I just made eggs and bacon. I need you to tell Mom and Dad that you made breakfast for them, and they need to come eat it now, before they shower, so it doesn't get cold."

"Why?"

"Because you're a loving daughter. See, it's a win-win situation for you. Plus, you get bacon."

Aprilynne opened her eyes, too curious now to go back to sleep. "I mean why are you doing this?"

"I need a few minutes where I'm guaranteed some private time. I, um, have an important phone call to make, and I want to make sure no one interrupts me."

"An important phone call?" Aprilynne sat up, pushing the covers back. "Let me guess, it involves Jesse?"

"In a roundabout way." Only because Jesse was a Slayer.

"Oh," Aprilynne said, with a measure of understanding in her voice. "Okay, I'll help you out." She stood and ran her hand over her hair, smoothing it down. She'd slept in yoga pants and a sweatshirt, and didn't bother changing before walking to the door. "Breakfast is already done?"

"Yeah." Tori followed Aprilynne out of the room. "And if they ask where I am, stall so they don't try to find me."

"How?" Aprilynne asked.

Tori shrugged. "Ask them how young is too young to get married. That will keep them talking for a while."

"And then they'll look suspiciously at every guy I date."

"But you'll have my Ralph Lauren shirt," Tori said. "And bacon."

Ten minutes later, Tori had the phone number. She sent it to Dr. B, put the shirt on Aprilynne's bed, then went down to the kitchen. Her parents were talking about the dangers of rushing into relationships, and they stayed on that topic for the rest of the morning.

CHAPTER 20

Jesse was getting dressed when his phone beeped with a message from Dr. B.

No school today. I need you for court work. I'm sending someone to your house now to pick you up.

"Court work" meant a mission. Jesse hated these sorts of cryptic texts. The mission could be anything from running a drill to fighting dragons. Whatever it was, he'd better get some breakfast while he could. Flying always made him hungry.

He made his way to the kitchen, winding around stacks of unpacked boxes in the hallway. His family had moved into this house yesterday and everything was still a disorganized mess.

His younger brother, Christian, ate at the table. His prep school uniform already looked rumpled, even though this was the first day he'd ever worn it. He had the same brown hair and eyes as Jesse, but beyond that, their resemblance was minimal, partially because Christian seemed to be stuck in a perpetual slouch.

Jesse searched the clutter on the counter for the toaster, then gave up and poured himself cereal.

His mom paced to a stack of boxes by the oven and dug through the one on top. She wore a black skirt and blazer that made her look more like a business woman than a high school teacher. Her brown hair was still damp from the shower and she hadn't put on makeup yet.

"Have any of you seen my shoes?" She pulled the top box off the stack and opened the second. "I need to make changes to my lesson plan, but I won't have time if I can't find a decent pair of heels."

Jesse's dad came into the kitchen, straightening his tie. He was tall and barrel chested, with graying brown hair that tended to grow too long before he remembered to cut it, and an on-again, off-again beard, depending on whether he felt like shaving. Right now it was thankfully off. "They're in the top box in the hallway. I marked them 'First Day.'"

"Oh," she said, and headed there. "I thought they would be in the box marked shoes."

"Stop worrying," his father called. "You'll do fine today." He took a bowl from a box on the counter—also marked "First Day"—and joined Jesse and Christian at the table. "Kids aren't the only ones to get new-school jitters," he said in a confidential tone. "How are you two doing?"

Christian finished a mouthful of cereal. "I can't believe I have to wear a sucky uniform."

Their father poured some cereal into his bowl. "Uniforms are a good thing. They promote learning."

Their mother breezed back into the kitchen, now wearing black heels. "Conformity doesn't promote learning."

"It does if it keeps girls from wearing distracting clothing. As the father of teenage sons, I would support hazmat suits."

Christian took another spoonful of cereal. "Man, that's one more reason to hate uniforms. The girls won't wear anything distracting."

Jesse didn't comment. His mind was on the mission, wondering how many Slayers would be involved. Would Tori be there? He hoped so.

The phone rang. His mom answered, listened for a moment, then gazed at Jesse. After she hung up, she walked over to the table. "That was Mr. Booker from the FBI. They want you for something this morning."

His father made a low disapproving sound in the back of his throat. "How much testimony does the FBI need? It's his first day at a new school."

"It's okay," Jesse said. "This is more important."

* * *

Fifteen minutes later, Dr. B was briefing Jesse and Kody while he drove them toward Capitol Hill in an inconspicuous-looking beige sedan. Theo sat in the front, typing away on his laptop as if it were a piano and he was playing a concerto—a concerto he hated.

"I want to know what's on Senator Ethington's computer," Dr. B said, slowing the car to merge onto the beltway. "It might lead us to Overdrake or give us forewarning of an attack. Unfortunately, the senator's computer won't be easy to hack."

Jesse didn't bother commenting on that. If it were easy to do, Dr. B wouldn't have called them in.

Theo grumbled in frustration and hit the delete button a bunch of times.

"Senator Ethington has his own server," Dr. B went on, "and it's well protected. We'll need to physically go into his house and install some specialized, undetectable spyware on his computer."

This was worse than Jesse expected. "You want us break into the guy's house? In broad daylight?"

Kody let out a laugh. "At least we're missing school for a good reason."

"Actually," Dr. B said, "Senator Ethington's security

system makes breaking into his house without detection almost impossible. His doors have coded key locks, his windows have alarms, and he has multiple security cameras both inside and outside. It's imperative that Senator Ethington not realize anyone has been in his house, or he'll check his computer."

"So what exactly are we doing?" Jesse asked.

Dr. B reached into his coat pocket and pulled out a small, thin black piece of plastic. It looked like something that had broken off a keyboard. "You're going to plant this disabler chip on Senator Ethington's phone."

"To bug it?"

Dr. B handed the chip to Jesse. "No, we've already hacked into his phone. This is a frequency scanner. Once Senator Ethington carries the chip into his house, it will pick up the alarm system's and the cameras' frequencies and send them to Theo. He's working on a program to disable them so you can break into his home tonight and gain computer access."

Theo pounded something especially hard, and muttered things about wavelength and one hundred and twenty-eight bit encryptions.

Kody scratched the back of his neck doubtfully. "Are you sure Theo can get that working by tonight?"

"Oh yes," Dr. B said, speaking over Theo's angry commentary on frequency-agile computer systems. "Right now, all you need to worry about is a way to get the microchip under the Senator's phone cover."

He gestured to the sack on the car floor between Kody and Jesse. "That has the same model as the senator's phone so you can practice. You'll also find two school uniforms and some glasses. For your cover, you're students from St. Jude, and you want to get a quote from the senator for your school newspaper."

Jesse picked up the bag. "We're going to his office?"

"No." Dr. B slowed the car even further as the beltway traffic became a sluggish crawl. "The senator is in the habit of having breakfast with his aides at different cafés on Capitol Hill— mingling with the common man and all that. Hopefully you'll be able to catch him before he finishes his meal. Booker is already downtown, near the restaurant with the simulator."

Jesse rummaged through the bag until he found the phone, an android with a black cover. He jiggled the case's top. It didn't come off smoothly, but once it was off, he slipped the disabler chip inside easily enough. The hard part would be getting the case open without anyone noticing.

"When you're near Senator Ethington, message me," Dr. B continued. "I'll call him. After he takes out his phone to see who's calling"—Dr. B turned and gave Kody a nod—" you knock it out of his grip."

Kody stretched his hands, warming up his fingers.

"Do it with one of your blasts," Dr. B clarified. "We wouldn't want you to get in trouble for actually bumping into the senator."

"Right," Kody said. "I knew that." He emptied the clothes from the bag onto the seat, then handed Jesse a pair of tan polyester pants, a white button-down shirt, and a blue sweater vest with a coat of arms embroidered on it.

"Wow," Kody said holding up the sweater vest. "Makes you feel sorry for the Saint Jude students."

"My school uniform is just as bad," Jesse said.

Kody pulled off his shirt, picked up the white one, and began undoing the buttons. "These are wimp clothes. If anyone wore this to my school, he'd find himself dangling from a flagpole."

Jesse pulled off his shirt as well. "Rich people don't have to worry about getting harassed at school. They've got lawyers."

Dr. B leaned toward his window then checked the rearview

mirror. "The car behind us is driving erratically. I think they might be following us."

Jesse's eyes went to the rearview mirror, his senses immediately alert. Could Overdrake have found them? "Which car?"

With rush-hour traffic, no one was moving quickly. It was stop and go—mostly stop. Dr. B's car would have a hard enough time changing lanes, let alone going anywhere quickly if they needed to escape.

"The blue one behind us on our right side," Dr. B said. "Two young women. They're behaving strangely."

Before Dr. B finished speaking, Jesse used the camera on his phone to see the car. The women were probably in their early twenties, with long hair and lots of makeup. Not the usual sort of tail. In fact, probably not a tail at all. When he turned to look at them, one woman whistled, and the other blew a kiss and giggled.

Kody peered around Jesse at the car. "Do you know them?"

"No," Jesse said.

Theo looked at the blue car, then glanced back at Jesse and Kody and grunted in annoyance. "Would you two put on your clothes? You're making a spectacle."

Jesse had been so worried about Overdrake that he'd forgotten he was shirtless.

Kody chuckled, lifted his arms in a body builder pose, and flexed his muscles.

Both women in the other car shrieked with laughter. The driver made fanning motions with her hand. The other woman took out a tube of lipstick and began writing her phone number on the window.

Theo lifted his hands in exasperation. "I'm trying to work!"

"The good news," Jesse said, unbuttoning the white shirt

so he could put it on, "is that they're not Overdrake's men. The bad news is we've still got to change our pants."

* * *

Forty minutes later, Jesse and Kody were speed walking toward The Red Kettle Café. The traffic had been bad—it was always some degree of bad in DC, but today's had outdone itself. They might miss Senator Ethington altogether.

Jesse really hoped not. He didn't want to repeat the performance of changing his clothes in the backseat of a car while people in surrounding vehicles watched. And clapped. And threw money.

Because that's what had happened. Traffic had come to a complete standstill, and the women in the blue car made such a big deal of it—rolling down their windows and asking for Jesse and Kody's numbers—that everyone around them noticed what they were doing.

It didn't help that Kody kept striking poses, or that after he took off his jeans, he rolled down his window and twirled them around before putting on his tan pants. Kody had no concept of discretion.

"If any of this morning's ride shows up on YouTube," Jesse said as they walked, "I'll kill you."

"You're too uptight," Kody said. "I thought Greta and Krissy were nice."

"No, they weren't. Nice girls don't try to chuck dollar bills into your car window." Jesse thrust his hands into his pockets. "I still can't believe you added them as contacts on your phone."

"I might want to call them someday."

"I thought Dr. B was going to have a heart attack."

"Yeah," Kody said with a laugh. "It's funny that he trusts us with dragons and armed men but not lonely interns."

Down the street, the café came into view. A green awning stuck out over the door, which somehow didn't match the more pretentious marble that made up the front of the restaurant. Arched windows looked onto the road, giving a glimpse of the people seated inside. They all wore suits or dresses, making the dining room look like a high-powered business meeting.

"We'll need prep school sounding names," Kody said. "Something with a lot of syllables."

"I'll be Sebastian," Jesse said. "You can be Pierpont."

"Pierpont? Is that a real name?"

"Yeah. It was JP Morgan's name. He was one of those robber barons we had to learn about in US history."

"No wonder he went by JP," Kody said.

They'd reached the café door. Kody tugged at the top button of his shirt. He had a neck like a pro-wrestler, and the shirt was too tight. "What school are we from again?"

"St. Jude."

"Wait, isn't he the patron saint of lost causes?"

Jesse raised his eyebrows in surprise that Kody knew that information, then dismissed the omen. "Not today he isn't. Today he's going to be the patron saint of cell phone thieves."

They walked inside and went past the hostess station with a hurried explanation that they were meeting someone. The room was warm, and the scent of bacon and pancakes enveloped everything. Jesse would have felt hungry if he hadn't been so focused on the mission. Despite practicing in the car, slipping the disabler chip into Senator Ethington's phone would be tricky. So many things could go wrong.

Jesse spotted the senator and four other men eating in the middle of the room.

He looked like he did in his campaign spots: stocky, with graying black hair and a contemplative, serious expression. He had a sort of trustworthy air about him that you expected in a politician. Could someone so involved, so high up in the government, be working with Overdrake?

"Let me do the talking," Jesse whispered to Kody. "My mom is a big Ethington supporter, so I know his positions."

They started toward his table, Jesse in front. The clatter of silverware and noise of people talking grew louder, increasing due to Jesse's sharpening senses.

He and Kody were nearly to the table when a man who'd been standing near the wall intercepted them. He was all muscle and height, with a face that seemed permanently fixed in a glower. His shaved head made his earpiece stand out even more. Obviously security detail.

"You're not allowed to come over here," the man said in a deep, severe voice.

Jesse had known Senator Ethington would have a bodyguard or two; Tori complained about them often enough. He just hadn't expected them to be so efficient.

A second bodyguard sat alone at a table behind the senator. His gaze continually swept around the room. He had the build of a bouncer and short, black hair that was gelled into place.

Jesse gestured to the senator's table apologetically. "We want to get a quote from Senator Ethington for our school paper."

"We're from St Jude," Kody put in. He lifted his hand to shake the bodyguard's. "I'm JP. This is Sebastian."

The bodyguard didn't move, didn't take Kody's hand. "You can find plenty of quotes on his website."

No good. "We were hoping for a picture too," Jesse said. He'd brought a cell phone—not his, as he couldn't have anything on him that could be traced.

The bodyguard shook his head. "The senator is meeting with his staffers right now."

So much for Dr. B's assurance that Ethington was eating breakfast out in DC so he could mingle with the common man. Apparently Jesse and Kody were *too* common.

"Can't we please go over and just get his autograph?" Jesse asked. "My mom is a really big fan of his."

The bodyguard looked skeptical about Jesse's explanation, which was ironic, seeing as it was the one thing Jesse was telling the truth about.

"Seriously," Jesse added. "She's a die-hard Democrat. She's even got a donkey tattoo."

The bodyguard's gaze skimmed the room, checking for more interesting dangers than two high school kids. "Some other time. The senator is busy right now."

Plan B was for Kody to walk across the restaurant and knock the senator's phone to the floor from there. The move would be harder to pull off since a hit from that distance would require more force and might seem unnatural. It was one thing to drop your phone; it was another thing to have an invisible force smack your hand so hard your phone flew several feet and slid across the floor.

Jesse didn't want to risk Plan B. "Are you sure I can't get an autograph? It would make me my mother's favorite child for a long time."

The bodyguard remained unmoved. "Sorry."

"Thanks anyway," Kody said, then turned to Jesse. "I'm going to ask that waitress if we can get something to go." He headed toward the back of the restaurant, positioning himself on the other side of the senator's table.

Plan B it was then. Jesse inconspicuously scratched his wrist, pressing his watch button to signal Dr. B to make the call.

The first bodyguard still stood by Jesse, waiting for him to leave or follow Kody. Jesse adjusted his fake glasses. They didn't fit right and had slipped down his nose.

"Haven't you ever done something," he asked, stalling, "and you needed to make up for it by doing something really nice for your mom?"

"No," the bodyguard said, still waiting for him to leave. His lips were pressed into an impatient line.

"Wish I could say the same." Why hadn't Dr. B called yet? Jesse rocked back on his heels, trying to think of something to say to prolong the conversation. "So, if I were to uh, show up at Senator Ethington's house sometime to get his autograph, would you be there keeping the riffraff away?"

The bodyguard's stare quickly became a threatening glare. "I answer his front door."

Senator Ethington reached into his pocket and pulled out his phone.

Finally.

Jesse glanced at Kody. *Not too hard*, he thought. *A gentle shove is all we need.*

A second later, a plate on the senator's table exploded, sending bits of omelet everywhere. Not only did Ethington drop his phone, he let out a startled exclamation too.

Yep, that would be too hard.

The bodyguard who'd been sitting near the senator's table jumped from his seat and pulled out his gun. "Get down!" he yelled. "We've got a shooter!"

People across the restaurant screamed, ducked, and covered their heads while they peered around, looking for a gunman.

The bodyguard near Jesse also whipped out his gun and sprinted toward the table. "Everyone on the ground!"

This just made things worse. Several diners assumed that the rushing bodyguard *was* the gunman, and more screaming ensued, along with people fleeing to the door. Other people huddled under the tables and got out their phones—either recording the event or calling 911.

Jesse crouched as if he were obeying the bodyguards' commands, and made his way as stealthily as he could toward the senator's phone. When Kody blasted the table, the phone had flown from the Ethington's hand, hit a chair and ricocheted back underneath the table. It lay just out of Jesse's reach under a tangle of chair legs.

The continued screaming must have spooked Senator Ethington. He half-stumbled, half-crawled in the direction of the door.

The bodyguard with the gelled hair clearly thought this was the wrong decision. He grabbed the senator by the back of his suitcoat and yanked him to the ground, overpowering any flailing attempts to stand. He then bent over him protectively.

Well, that probably wouldn't make Senator Ethington look particularly presidential when the video of this hit the internet.

Jesse was almost to the phone. As he moved closer to the table, the bald bodyguard pointed a gun in his direction. "You, stop right there! What are you doing?"

So close. "Getting the senator's phone for him." Jesse made a move to pick it up, but one of Ethington's staffers reached down and grabbed it first.

The bald bodyguard glared at Jesse, not buying his story. He grabbed Jesse by the sweater vest, hauled him out from under the table, and pushed him against the wall. Jesse could have fought back—could have thrown the man across the room—but that would have only made things worse. Especially since several diners were recording the event.

He held up his hands as though he was baffled by his treatment. "I didn't do anything."

The guard started patting Jesse down, searching for weapons. "Let's see what you've got on you, punk." He looked over his shoulder at staffers. "Don't let his friend get away." The bodyguard felt Jesse's front pockets, stopping when he felt Jesse's phone. He pulled it out and tossed it to the floor. "Somehow I doubt you're just a couple of school boys."

He was right about that, and Jesse hoped the guard didn't think to call St. Jude. In the distance, sirens wailed a warning; police were on the way. Yeah, this kept getting better. Would the officers do background checks on him and Kody?

The bodyguard proceeded patting down Jesse's legs.

"You won't find anything but my socks," Jesse said. "And I'm pretty sure you're violating my rights. Are you allowed to do this to minors?"

Satisfied Jesse was unarmed, the bodyguard turned to pat down Kody. The gelled-haired bodyguard was still crouching in front of the senator, keeping him on the ground.

Kody stood there, good-naturedly holding his hands up while being frisked. "We came in to get a quote for our school newspaper," he said conversationally, "but this is going to make for a much better story—getting roughed up by Senator Ethington's security." He waved to get the attention of a group of people who were huddled under a booth watching. "Hey, could you send me some pictures of this?"

The bodyguard scowled and stepped away from Kody. "He's clean."

Jesse smirked at the man. "Sorry to disappoint you. Your gunman was probably one of the first people who ran out the door."

The bodyguard let Jesse go and gazed around the restaurant at the remaining customers, who were only now timidly emerging from under tables.

Jesse picked up his phone from the floor and used his extra strength to quietly crush the screen. Then he held the phone up, showing it to the bodyguard. "You broke my phone when you threw it on the floor." He pretended to push a button. "It doesn't work now, and I have to call my mom and ask her to excuse me for being late."

Outside the windows, police cars pulled up, lights swirling.

"Sorry, kid. Use your friend's." The bodyguard still had his gun drawn, but even he realized the danger was over. Senator Ethington had stood up and was wiping off his suit.

Jesse shook his head. "JP's parents took his phone away— a grounding thing. Can I use yours?"

The bodyguard reluctantly reached into his pocket, pulled out a phone, and handed it to Jesse. "Be quick. I've got to talk to the police."

Jesse didn't need to think of a way to create a distraction so the bodyguard wouldn't watch him slip the chip into his phone. The man was busy scanning the restaurant. He was also talking on his mic to the police, updating them on the situation.

After a couple of moments, Jesse handed the bodyguard back his phone. "Thanks. And no hard feelings about my phone. I know you were only doing your job."

Kody strolled over, and Jesse gave him a slight nod, signaling that it was time to go. They walked toward the door, going out with other customers who'd realized that the action was over and it was safe to leave.

They headed down the sidewalk toward their pickup point. Jesse hit the button on his watch to let Dr. B know they were on their way.

Kody checked behind them to make sure no one was paying attention, then muttered, "Okay, I admit it. That boondoggle was completely my fault."

"Yeah. When dishes explode, that's a sign you put too much oomph into the shock."

"All of that fuss and bother, and you didn't even get to touch Ethington's phone."

"Doesn't matter," Jesse said, finally allowing himself to smile over his success. "I put the chip into the bodyguard's phone. He'll go into Ethington's house today—probably do a thorough sweep of the whole place before he lets the senator go inside."

Kody laughed and shook his head. "Well then, looks like that cat got skinned anyway."

"Hey, kid," a man on the sidewalk behind them called, "wait up."

Jesse froze, recognizing the bald bodyguard's voice. Had the man figured out that they weren't who they'd said they were? Or worse, had he found the chip in his phone?

Jesse could grab Kody, fly away, and escape, but that option came with problems of its own. Better to see what the guy wanted before resorting to anything drastic.

He turned, adrenaline making his hands twitch. "Yeah?"

The bodyguard strode down the sidewalk toward them, his expression unreadable beyond its usual sternness.

Kody glanced over, looking for direction. Jesse stayed put, tried to look unconcerned, and waited for the man. "You need something else from us?"

The bodyguard held out a campaign picture of Senator Ethington. "For your mom, kid. When I told the senator why you were in the restaurant, he signed it for you."

Jesse took the picture and let out a relieved breath. They hadn't been found out. "Thanks. Tell Senator Ethington that I appreciate it."

The bodyguard nodded. "Sorry about the pat down. It's just part of the job." He turned and marched back toward the restaurant.

Jesse started toward the pickup point again, feeling the tension drain from him.

After they were out of earshot, Kody said, "There's a name for those times when you think you got caught putting a chip on a guy's phone—a close call."

It was a bad pun, but Jesse laughed anyway.

* * *

Ten minutes later, Dr. B pulled into the parking lot where Jesse and Kody were waiting. The two climbed into the car, and Dr. B headed back into traffic. "How did it go?"

"Great," Jesse said, clicking on his seatbelt. "St. Jude, the patron saint of cell phone thieves, totally came through for us."

Theo didn't speak, didn't spare them a glance. He was typing and deleting with equal vigor. Apparently he still had some bugs to work out of his program.

"Those police sirens I heard earlier," Dr. B said, "those didn't have anything to do with you, did they?"

"They were looking for a gunman," Kody said with a grin. "Fortunately, neither of us was packing heat today."

"Everything went fine." Jesse leaned his head back against the headrest, glad to be done with this part of the mission. "Just don't check YouTube for a while."

Dr. B glanced at them in the rearview mirror. "Why?"

Jesse lifted his head and cleared his throat. "Well, we might have made Senator Ethington look skittish."

"The guy's a wuss," Kody said, and nudged Jesse. "You should call Tori and tell her we ruined her dad's opponent's career. It'll get you major boyfriend points."

"I'm sure we didn't *ruin* his career," Jesse said.

Kody snorted. "Jesse still believes in the senator. Which is nice, because he got the man's autograph. It says, 'To Sebastian's mom, Best wishes.'"

Jesse nodded sadly. "It's almost a really cool present for my mother."

Kody undid the buttons near his collar. "Hey, if you get caught breaking into the guy's house tonight, maybe he can give you one with your real name."

CHAPTER 21

When Tori came home from school on Monday, Brindy still hadn't been found. Tori walked along their property, checking the fence for any sign the dog might have dug under it. She found no holes, no broken places of the fence, nothing that explained Brindy's disappearance.

Overdrake could have easily flown over the fence and stolen her.

Tori dismissed the idea. Overdrake certainly had more important things to do than abduct pets. There had to be another logical explanation. She just hadn't thought of it yet.

She went inside, did homework, ate dinner, helped her mother update the invitation list for an upcoming campaign dinner, then did more homework. It was after eleven o' clock when she finally went upstairs to her room—far too late, considering that she had to get up at six-thirty for school.

Her nerves were on edge, but she chalked it up to Brindy's disappearance getting to her.

It wasn't until Tori flipped her bedroom switch and the light refused to come on that she realized what her subconscious had been trying to tell her: Something was wrong.

She stood in the doorway, hand on the switch, and didn't bother trying to convince herself that her chandelier had blown a fuse. She could feel another presence in the room. Someone was here, waiting for her. Overdrake must have sent someone. Or perhaps he'd come himself.

She didn't scream. Noise would bring her family rushing in, and none of them were armed. Overdrake's quarrel was with her. She would leave her family out of this.

She leaped sideways away from the door and crouched in the darkness.

The other person remained silent. No tell-tale footsteps gave away his location. And yet the tingling at the base of her neck told her the intruder was coming closer.

She opened her eyes wider, straining to see an outline in the shadows. Nothing. All the shapes in the room were dark and shrouded.

Dr. B always told her to rely on her Slayer senses. She pushed away her fear and listened to her instincts.

He was close, but not close enough yet.

Wait.

Wait.

She wasn't sure what she felt exactly—a shift in the air, the body temperature of someone coming nearer, or perhaps a smell too faint to fully register in her brain. Whatever the cause, she knew when the person came within striking distance.

She leapt forward, plowing into him, her anger channeled into action. He didn't fall, only glided backward, wrapping his arms around her. He was airborne and taking her with him.

And then she knew who it was. She recognized the feel of his worn jacket and the scent of his shampoo. *Jesse.* She smacked him in the chest. "What are you doing here? You scared me to death."

"Sorry." He set her carefully back on the floor and let her go. "But I had to make a point." He flipped on a flashlight, illuminating a puddle of light. His brown eyes stared solemnly back at her. "If I can get into your bedroom, so can Overdrake. You aren't safe here." He walked to her desk and turned on the lamp.

She watched him, hands on her hips, still breathing hard. "I can't believe you snuck into my room. I could have killed you."

He smiled at the accusation. "Only if you practiced a lot more." He picked up three light bulbs from her night stand, and his tone turned mildly berating. "You didn't even know someone was hiding in the room until the light didn't work. An intruder could have shot you before that. You've got be more aware of your surroundings." He took the bulbs and flew up to her chandelier. "And how come you're walking around without a single weapon to protect yourself?"

"I came to change into my pajamas. I don't generally carry guns or knives for that." She was glad he'd come when she was fully dressed instead of wearing something embarrassing—her blue fuzzy pajamas came to mind. "Does Dr. B know you're here? Did he authorize this?" She knew the answer even as she asked the question. At camp, Dr. B orchestrated all sorts of surprise attacks on the Slayers. He and the staff had come after them with paintballs so many times, Tori accidentally-on-purpose ripped his paintball gun in half.

"He's down the street with Theo." As Jesse replaced the bulbs, the room grew bright, revealing books spread across her desk and her unmade bed.

Tori sighed and ran a hand through her hair. "Well, you can report that your attack was a success and make me run extra laps next practice—assuming I make it. After last Saturday's jaunt, my parents want to approve all of my activities in advance." She dropped her hand from her hair and pointed a finger at him. "And if you show up at my house again, it had better be to bring me flowers. Because the next person who tries a surprise attack in my bedroom is going to get a lamp lodged in his forehead."

"Next time I'll definitely bring flowers."

She wasn't appeased. She walked closer to the chandelier and looked up at Jesse. "Are you wired? If you are, I have a few things to say to Dr. B."

"Not wired." Jesse landed beside her, close enough to smell his shampoo again. "And good news: Dr. B has a solution to take care of your safety problem." He put a hand on her arm, then let his fingers trail downward. The gesture was half-affection, half-apology. "You're not going to like it, but I think tonight proves it's necessary."

She cocked an eyebrow and waited for the explanation.

"Theo sent a threatening letter to your dad's office, along with some pictures of your family taken through your kitchen windows." Jesse's hand went back up her arm in a soothing motion. "I don't want to say anything bad about Theo—he's the best tech guy there is—but he knows how to conjure a pretty convincing creepy stalker. Anyway, I put a pipe bomb on your back porch. When I return to Dr. B, I'll call you to make sure your family is away from the area, and then Theo will detonate it. Hopefully a minor explosion will convince your parents that you need to move to a safer location until the election is over."

"You're going to blow up my house? *That's* your way of keeping me safe?"

He weaved his fingers into hers and gave her hand a squeeze. "Just a small part of the house—the patio and kitchen door. It might also throw some debris in the pool." He gave her a half-smile. "And by the way, you have an awesome pool. When the fighting is over, you should have the Slayers over for a party."

"It's a date," she said. "And, sadly, this is the only time I'll say those words for the next week."

"You're grounded?"

She nodded.

"Sorry," he said. "I'm a lousy boyfriend. First I get you grounded, and then I use explosives on your house."

"It's okay," she said, resigned. She hated the thought of being forced to move, but at the same time, she understood the necessity. As long as Overdrake knew where her family lived, they were all in danger. "I suppose this might be the best solution."

"We'll all sleep better knowing you're safe." He gave her hand another squeeze. "Especially me, because Dr. B won't feel the need to send me on anymore late night surprise attacks."

"Dr. B never has appreciated the importance of a good night's sleep."

Jesse gazed around her room. She had a canopy bed, but not the frilly sort of princess bed girls had when they were eight. It was a queen size, ornately carved dark cherry wood nineteenth century reproduction. Pretty much everything in their house looked like it had once belonged to Pemberley. Oil paintings hung on the wall. Tori hadn't chosen any of them. Her mother liked buying artwork and needed wall space to hang it all on. The Hafen and Lambourne pieces matched the cranberry and gold in her bedspread.

"Somehow I always expected your room to be pink," Jesse said.

"Eight years ago, you would have been right."

Her anger over the intrusion had faded, and now it just felt odd to have him standing in her bedroom, holding her hand, here among her personal and private things. It felt intimate and dangerous in a different way. The distance between them was so small, and his hand felt warm in hers, comfortable and inviting.

She wasn't sure what to say, and so settled on, "Has Dr. B found jobs for your parents yet?"

Jesse's mom and dad were both teachers and wanted to work at the same high school. Dr. B was having a hard time finding a school with two openings.

"Actually, he did," Jesse said. "They just got jobs at some snooty prep school, and I get free tuition as part of the deal. Starting tomorrow I'll get to mingle with the rich and full of themselves."

"Ah," she said, in a teasing tone. "Maybe some of the rich kids' class and highbrow culture will rub off on you."

"Right. Their Beamers will probably snub my Prius in the school parking lot."

"We might see each other at rival water polo games."

"Sure. I was, of course, the captain of the water polo team at my last school."

She didn't ask which school he was going to or whether he'd be living in Virginia, Maryland, or DC. The Slayers weren't supposed to share personal information. That way, if Overdrake captured any of them, he wouldn't be able to get details from them. For that reason, Dr. B wouldn't send Jesse to her school. Still, she liked the idea of a chance meeting.

A stupid thought, really. Now she would spend the remainder of the school year looking for him at every game.

Jesse was still holding her hand. She wanted to pull him closer, wanted to wrap her arms around him, and tilt her face up to his. She didn't do any of it. That would be crossing the line they'd laid out for themselves. After the last dragon attack, they'd agreed to keep their romantic life separate from their Slayer one. During fights, they had to act as captains, and not be distracted by worrying about each other's safety. The agreement was proof they could do their duties.

She would stay on the safe side of the line. Tori dropped Jesse's hand and looked at her window. It was open a crack, but had been locked earlier. She was sure of it.

She walked over to examine it. The locks were slightly scratched, attesting to having been jimmied open. "How did you disable our alarm?"

He joined her at the window. "Theo is a tech wizard."

"Hmm. He'll have to show me how to do it so I can sneak out."

"Only if you're sneaking out to attend practice." The corners of Jesse's lips lifted. "Or to meet me."

She inclined her head to the side. "Which would you prefer?"

"The latter," he said. "Although since I'm here as a Slayer, that shouldn't be my answer." He shook his head. "But somehow it still is."

It was nice to know she wasn't the only one having trouble sticking to her role as captain.

She gazed down to the yard below. Everything was dark and shadowed; the motion-detector lights hadn't gone off. "Speaking of sneaking out my window, are any of our security cameras going to show you flying around or swooping down and dropping off a bomb?"

"I'm up too high for the cameras, and I lowered the bomb to your porch by wire. The footage won't show who put it there."

"Good."

He glanced at the window. She could tell he was about to say he had to go. After all, Dr. B and Theo were out there waiting.

Jesse didn't speak. He took her hand again, holding it loosely. A goodbye gesture. She tightened her grip. She didn't like goodbyes.

His thumb caressed the back of her hand. They weren't breaking their own rules. Not really. Holding hands could be a sign of friendship, not romance.

Jesse hesitated, then sighed and leaned closer. His eyes went to her lips. He hesitated again, perhaps waiting to see if she would move away. She didn't. She just waited, nerves humming.

He lowered his head and brushed his lips against hers in the lightest of kisses. The touch made her shiver all over. Instead of keeping the kiss short, she slipped her arms around his neck, pulled him closer, and kissed him back. Lines, after all, could bend. That was the whole point of circles, and ovals, and rules about romance.

In the corner of Tori's mind, she knew that if her parents walked into her room right now, things would not go well. She didn't care. Carpe diem. She had no defense against hot guys who flew.

After a few moments, Jesse lifted his head. "This was probably not what Dr. B had in mind when he sent me."

True. She took a step away from him. "Good night."

"Sorry I have to bomb your house."

"I understand." Tori thought of Brindy, and a jab of pain went through her. If they moved, and their dog came back, she wouldn't know where they went.

She wanted to believe that Brindy would come back, that they would find her somehow. An optimistic hope at best.

Jesse gave the window a tug, and it opened, letting in a blast of night air. "I'd stay longer, but I still have to break into Senator Ethington's house tonight."

"You're what?"

"I'm installing spyware on his computer."

"Well, if the whole Slayer gig doesn't pan out, you'll have a great resume as a political saboteur."

He laughed, then dove through the window into the darkness.

She stood there, watching his silhouette soar against the backdrop of the starry sky, then shut the window. She went to check on her family, reminding herself the pending explosion was for the best. Her family needed to disappear where Overdrake couldn't find them.

She found Aprilynne and her mother in their respective bedrooms. Her father was answering email in his den. Standing at the foot of the stairs, she sent Jesse an all-clear message. Seconds later, a sound like cannon fire blasted through the house. The security alarm went off, shrieking in protest. A haze of smoke wafted from the kitchen, setting off the smoke alarms as well.

Her father rushed out of the den, a gun grasped in one hand. Tori had known he kept a gun in his closet safe. She hadn't realized he also had one in his desk. He was more prepared for an attack than she'd given him credit for. As he scanned the landing, he noticed her. She was prepared to explain why she was standing about the house suspiciously: she had been on her way to talk to him. But he didn't ask.

He just pointed to the den. "Go. Lock the door and stay in there until the police arrive. I'll get your mother and sister."

Then he hurried up the stairs. Efficient, calm, and focused. He really would make a good president.

CHAPTER 22

At one in the morning, Jesse was prying open Senator Ethington's second-story window. Or trying to, anyway. It was almost impossible to get any leverage while hovering fifteen feet off the ground.

Jesse had practiced breaking and entering at camp, but he wasn't an expert. The only reason Dr. B had chosen him for this job was his flying ability. It gave him easy access to the den, and he wouldn't wake anyone with the sound of footsteps.

The window was being stubborn, though, and opening it was taking longer than he liked. He had to quell the urge to look over his shoulder to make sure none of the neighbors had come outside and noticed him.

It was one thing to break into a regular person's house. It was another to break into a presidential candidate's home, especially if your parents had contributed to his campaign.

If Jesse got caught, his mother would probably not post bail. He hoped that whatever was on Senator Ethington's computer was worth the risk.

Into his neck mic, he spoke to Theo. "You're sure everything is off?"

"The alarm system and the cameras are dead."

"What about motion sensors?"

"He doesn't have any."

The latch finally gave, and Jesse slid the window open. Silence. No alarm went off, at least not that he could hear. He pushed aside the curtains and glided inside. The room was dark, but Jesse didn't have a problem making out the shapes in front of him. The monitor sat on the desk, the CPU under it.

He floated over, turned on the computer, and inserted Theo's flash drive into the port. Once the computer was booted up, the spyware would download in about ten seconds. When that happened, a light on the flash drive would blink twice, signaling the completed transfer. Booting up would be the longest part of the operation.

Jesse stood completely still, listening for sounds. Half a minute went by. A faint clicking came from down the hallway. Clicking.

And then he realized why Senator Ethington didn't have motion detectors: he had a pet that would set them off.

A dog. Great. They'd checked the outside for animals, but not the inside.

Did Jesse have time to shut the door before the dog came this way? If the dog didn't already know he was here, the noise of shutting the door might alert it.

He glanced at the screen. The computer had to be nearly done booting up.

A large Dalmatian paused in front of the door and sniffed the air. A moment later, it saw Jesse and let out an angry bark.

Jesse waited, watching the flash drive. He needed just a few more seconds.

The dog kept a wary distance, staying in the doorway, but continued barking and baring its teeth. The noise was going to wake the entire house.

Would it be better to grab the flash drive and flee or wait it out? The dog edged closer, growling, until it was only a few feet away.

Jesse was envisioning what his mugshot would look like, and wondered whether it would be splattered across the news, when the flash drive blinked twice. Finally.

He grabbed it and hit the button to shut down the computer. The dog took darting steps toward Jesse. Down the hallway, a door opened.

Done. Jesse dashed to the window, heartbeat racing. He hoped the computer would be dark before anyone entered the room. Once outside the window, he turned to close it. Footsteps were coming down the hallway, too close. He was glad for the curtains; they'd hide him while he tugged the window shut.

The dog's head pushed through the curtain's opening, barking furiously and snapping his teeth. Jesse nearly smacked it with the pane while he shut the window.

"Woodrow!" Senator Ethington snapped. He was inside the den. "Get down from there. What are you doing?"

Going ballistic, that's what the dog was doing. Just as Senator Ethington moved the curtain to check outside, Jesse pressed himself against the outside wall.

The senator stood there peering across his lawn. The seconds ticked by. Jesse didn't breathe.

"Stupid dog," Senator Ethington muttered. "There's nothing out there." The curtain fell closed again.

The sound of the dog barking grew more distant as the senator hauled his pet away.

Jesse peeled himself off the wall, relieved, and flew toward Dr. B's car. He'd visited the two top presidential candidates' houses tonight. He hoped both visits would pay off.

CHAPTER 23

Tori didn't go to school on Tuesday. The family had been up late with the police, and then they had to pack up things and go to one of her parents' friend's houses. The police gave them an escort then left a patrol car to guard the place. The whole experience was surreal.

By the time Tori got up the next morning, her parents had already found a home to rent, a six-bedroom redbrick house behind three security gates. They found the new place so quickly that Tori wondered if they'd had it as a contingency all along.

A group of movers took their belongings from the old house, and by late afternoon, Tori was rearranging things in her bedroom. Pemberley, this time with huge white columns running up the front of the house. Tori's room had its own hand crafted marble fireplace.

Her parents hadn't deemed it necessary to change schools because Veritas Academy, her private school, had strict security measures. On one hand, she was grateful she didn't have to leave her friends. On the other hand, Overdrake knew where she went to school. He might assume she would start someplace new after the move, but it wasn't a sure thing. She wasn't completely out of danger.

When she arrived on Wednesday, she was almost immediately surrounded by people wanting a play-by-play of the explosion. Everybody seemed to know about the attack. Tuesday night, Tori had texted her closest friends to tell them she was moving. Word had spread.

As Tori got her books from her locker, a group of girls gathered around her asking about the pipe bomb.

"Do the police have any clues who did it?"

"No." Tori hoped not, anyway.

"Didn't your surveillance cameras show someone breaking into your yard?"

She shook her head. "Whoever did it was able to avoid the cameras."

The statement brought a lot of disbelief. "All of them?"

"As far as the police have told us," Tori said.

Clint Olson swaggered up to the group. He was the President's son, which made him the celebrity of the school—especially in his own mind. If his father hadn't been so important, he would have been an average, and probably overlooked, type of guy. He didn't play sports or do any extracurricular activities, and only seemed to get good grades because he was forced to. Mostly he liked traveling and name dropping.

"Hey, Tori," he said, making his way toward her. The girls moved for him. People always did. He put one hand on his chest. "I wanted to let you know that I wasn't involved in the bombing of your home."

She got out her notebook for first period journalism. "Well, you *were* on the top of my list of suspects."

Tori's parents could disconnect their professional lives from their personal ones and were as friendly to the President's family as they were to members of their own political party.

She'd never managed to have that kind of generosity toward Clint, though. She remembered all of the President's political insults aimed at her dad. Clint was cut from the same cloth as his father.

"Seriously, though," Clint said. "If your dad is going to play with the big boys, he's got to expect this sort of stuff. It's all part of the game. I can't tell you how many threats my family has gotten. When you've lived with it as long as I have, you learn to brush off danger."

Tori couldn't help herself; she rolled her eyes. She motioned to the hallway, where not one, but two bodyguards surveyed the flow of students coming and going. "I thought you let your security detail take care of it."

"The physical stuff, yeah. But it's the mind games you have to learn to handle. You've got to be cool under pressure." He patted her shoulder in what was probably supposed to be a comforting gesture, but came off patronizing. "Don't worry. All of this will blow over after the election when your dad goes back to being just another senator."

She let out an indignant cough. "Says you and what poll?"

"About half of them," he said.

"Must be the half that are wrong." The warning bell for first period rang, ending the conversation.

"Got to go," Clint said, and sauntered away.

Tori glared at his back and wished she'd said something to wipe the arrogant smugness from his face. The crowd dispersed, leaving only her friend Melinda standing nearby waiting for her. The two had journalism together.

Melinda's dark hair was pulled into a messy bun, held together by a pencil slid through the middle. Tori would have looked slouchy with her hair done that way, but Melinda looked effortlessly pretty and even managed to make the dowdy school uniform seem perky and cute.

"Don't let Clint get to you," she said. "He's just ticked off that everyone is talking about you today instead of the Hollywood fundraiser his father spoke at last weekend. Clint has all sorts of celebrity selfies, but no one cares."

"I'm glad my drama has been useful for something."

They went down the hallway, weaving around students. Melinda shifted her books in her arms. "Oh, with all the bombing drama, you missed meeting Jonathan Richards."

"Who?"

"A hot new senior moved in yesterday. He's in our journalism class."

Hot new senior? Could it be Jesse? Tori quickly quashed the hope. Dr. B wouldn't have sent him here.

"Trust me," Melinda went on, "he's going to make class much more enjoyable."

"Why?"

"Because we can stare at him instead of Dr. Meyerhoff."

Their teacher was overweight, in his sixties, and had long black hair with a bushy beard. Sort of like what Santa would look like if he dyed his hair and tried to be hipster.

"I'm sure staring at the new guy nonstop won't make him feel uncomfortable at all."

Melinda snorted. "He's tall, buff and handsome. Those sorts of guys are used to being noticed."

Tori hoped not. The school already had enough egotistical guys.

She and Melinda ambled into journalism. And there, sitting at a desk near the front of the room, was Jesse. He was talking to the girl in the next desk. Tacy, a cheerleader.

Tori stopped walking, just stood there and gaped loose-jaw at him.

He was here. At her school. Dr. B had sent him here. Why?

Well, who cared why Dr. B had done it? Tori was just glad Jesse was here.

Melinda nudged her. "You might be overdoing the staring part."

Tori moved forward then, still unable to take her eyes off of Jesse. Tacy was smiling at him, flirting as she asked for help with a math assignment. She was a little too enthusiastic about trig in a journalism class.

The bell rang. Tori hadn't reached her desk yet.

"Ms. Hampton," Dr. Meyerhoff called in his usual droll tone of voice. "We're glad you could safely join us today. Please take your seat."

At her name, Jesse straightened and turned in his seat to find her. For a second, his expression held only surprise, then he smiled. One of his genuine smiles full of happiness.

She smiled back and sat down in her desk.

"Mark your calendars," Dr. Meyerhoff said, talking loud enough to be heard over the shuffling of students settling in. "This coming Saturday, you'll need to come to school to work on the newspaper layout. No excuses, folks. This is part of your journalism grade."

He went on about their assignments, but Tori found it hard to concentrate. Jesse was *here*.

Had Dr. B forgotten that she went to school here? Doubtful. Maybe he wanted Jesse at this school because it had so much security. Or perhaps he'd sent Jesse as an extra layer of protection for her.

Whatever the reason, she wasn't going to complain. She used her watch to send Jesse a text.

Why didn't you tell me you were going to my school? Technically the watches were only supposed to be used for Slayer business, but they were both Slayers, and Dr. Meyerhoff wasn't all that interesting.

A few moments later, her watch vibrated on her wrist with a new message.

I didn't know until now. I just started liking this school a lot more.

She wrote back: *Dr. B probably sent you here to keep an eye on me.*

A couple of minutes later, Jesse sent another message. *I just texted him and asked about it. He figures if you have to miss practices, I can pass on important information to you.*

Score. Missing practice had totally paid off. *What about the rule that we're not supposed to know personal details about other Slayers' lives?*

Overdrake knows that rule, Jesse wrote back. *If he ever captured you, he wouldn't expect you to know those kinds of details about me.*

Good point. Tori sat back and tried to listen to Dr. Meyerhoff's lecture. She wasn't very successful. She kept getting distracted by Jesse's broad shoulders and dark hair. It was so odd to see him, a part of her secret world, here at school among the desks and whiteboards.

When class ended, Tori timed her exit so she was walking out with Jesse. They headed down the hallway going the same direction, Melinda and Tacy on either side of them like bookends. They wouldn't be able to talk like they usually did.

Jesse turned to Tori and smiled. To his credit, he looked natural, confident. "Hi. I'm Jonathan."

To avoid breaking his cover, she supposed it would be easier if they pretended they had no past.

"I'm Tori. I hope you like it here."

"I think I will." He smiled again, then added in a confidential tone. "My mom is the new government and world history teacher. In case you have to take one of her classes, I apologize in advance for any of her anti-Republican statements." By way of explanation to those around them, he said, "I heard you're Senator Hampton's daughter."

"I am." Tori decided right then that she didn't ever want to meet Jesse's mother. The woman was bound to dislike her. She would have to see if she could get out of taking any history classes.

Roland, a guy she'd dated a few times Sophomore year, swept over and gave her a hug. "Tori, I left you two messages. Why didn't you call me? I was worried about you."

Tori pulled away as quickly as she could, aware of Jesse watching. "I turned off my phone. I was getting too many messages, and my parents wanted to spend time as a family before my dad goes on the campaign trail again."

Roland reached out and gave her arm a squeeze. "If you need anything, I'm here for you."

She appreciated his concern, and really it wasn't his fault she'd met Jesse and lost all interest in the guys at school, but he didn't seem to be getting the hint. "Thanks. I'm fine, really." Her eyes flicked to Jesse. He was trying to keep any emotion off his face, but a trace of displeasure still made its way through. "Jonathan, this is Roland. He's a . . ."

What to call Roland? *Friend* sounded too intimate— especially the way Roland was standing there with a possessive look on his face. He'd be offended if she said, "platonic acquaintance," but *ex-boyfriend* didn't fit, either. They'd only gone out on a few dates last spring. She settled on, "Roland is a senior like you."

To Roland, she added, "Jonathan moved here from Maryland."

Crap. She'd already made a mistake. Jesse hadn't told her in their hallway conversation where he'd moved from. For all she knew, he had a different backstory. She hoped no one noticed that detail.

"We met yesterday." Roland looked Jesse over the way

guys summed up rivals. "The school hired your parents, didn't they? That's why you moved here?" Roland's words were nice enough, but his tone had an undercurrent: he was pointing out that Jesse's family wouldn't have been able to afford the tuition otherwise.

"Right," Jesse said, also nicely, although Tori doubted he'd missed the real message.

A group of senior guys strutting through the hallway saw Jesse and called out to him. Members of the basketball team, probably trying to recruit him for his height alone.

"Talk to you all later," Jesse said and then headed in the guys' direction.

* * *

The next time Tori saw Jesse was at lunch. He sat at the basketball players' table. She wanted to sit with him, but leaving her friends for a guy she'd just met would look odd. How long would she and Jesse have to pretend they didn't know each other before they could hang out at school without it seeming unusual?

Every few minutes, she glanced at his table. The guys were making a lot of noise, laughing and pounding the table. Jesse smiled and added to the conversation, looking like he fit right in. Once in a while he caught her staring. Every time, he smiled, which sent tingles of happiness through her. And then halfway through lunch, his eyes stopped wandering to her, and his expression had a tightness to it, as though he was ticked off about something.

Maybe he thought she was being too obvious looking at him. But really, that was a normal response. She would have stared at him even if he wasn't her boyfriend.

The rest of the school day dragged. After classes ended, she was supposed to go to the front lobby, where Lars waited for her. Instead, she searched for Jesse in the hallways. She found him at one of the lockers, twirling the combination.

People streamed by, but none paid any attention to the two of them. It was almost like being alone. She strolled up, chemistry book in hand. "So how was your day? Is all our high-brow classiness rubbing off yet?"

"Oh, definitely." Jesse opened his locker. "At lunch, the guys at my table had a contest to see who could drink the most hot sauce. I lost. On purpose."

So that's what the laughing and cheering had been about. "Sounds totally highbrow."

"Then they composed rap lyrics about girls in the lunchroom. I didn't punch Roland when he came up with one about you, but I wanted to."

Tori stiffened. "What did he say?"

Jesse pulled some books from his locker, and repeated the lyrics. "'Tori's story, more sugar than spice. Straight up goddess, not naughty—all nice.'"

"Really?" She hadn't expected Roland to be so good at rap lyrics. "Sounds like he put some thought in to it."

"Yeah. He obviously did." Jesse dropped the books into his backpack, then gave her a penetrating look. "What's the deal between you two anyway? I thought you weren't seeing other guys."

"I'm not. Roland and I dated a few times last year. That's it."

"That's not what he claimed in verse two, which was about the delight of being over at your house until midnight. Last week."

Her head jerked up at the accusation. "He came over for a study group with five other people, and he wasn't there until midnight. He must not have been able to think of anything to rhyme with 'ten thirty.'"

Jesse's dark eyes rested on her." Roland claimed you were alone--ditchin in the kitchen."

"He followed me into the kitchen to help me get drinks. Trust me, nothing song-worthy happened."

Roland had cornered her by the fridge and tried to kiss her, but she wasn't about to mention *that*. Jesse still seemed to sense she was leaving something out though. He let out a huff of exasperation.

"Don't worry. I can handle Roland." She leaned against the next locker. "I've told him I just want to be friends. The problem is, he hasn't seen me date anyone else, so he thinks there's still hope."

Jesse shut his locker and turned to her. "Why didn't you tell people you already had a boyfriend?"

"Because then they'd want to meet you, and when I refused to make that happen, they'd assume I was, for some unknown reason, faking a relationship. Besides, you can't give me a bad time. I bet you never told your friends about me."

"That's because none of them would have believed I was dating Senator Hampton's daughter."

"Now we can both fix our credibility problems." She smiled, feeling an eager giddiness. "How long should we wait until we let people know we're a couple?"

Jesse zipped up his backpack. "I'm thinking somewhere around the next time Roland starts rapping."

Tori turned the problem over in her mind. "We don't want to look like we rushed into anything—especially since your parents teach here. Everything we do will get back to them. For now, we should let people see us talking at school. And I'll send you flirty smiles." She tilted her head seductively and modeled an example.

He leaned toward her, lowering his voice. "You shouldn't do that. It makes me want to kiss you."

She shifted away from him in mock offense. "I'm not the sort of girl who makes out with guys in the school hallway. Please refer to Roland's song, first verse."

"Maybe it's love at first sight this time." Jesse cocked his head, watching her expression. "Or are you embarrassed to admit to your prep school friends you're dating a guy who doesn't drive a Porsche?"

"Of course not." Then, because he still looked skeptical, she added, "I'm fine with your . . ." She didn't remember what type of car he had, which should have proved that she didn't care about those kind of details. "What do you drive, anyway?"

"My parents' eight-year-old Prius, when they let me borrow it. You do realize that most seniors don't have their own cars, don't you?"

"Yes." Actually she'd never given the matter any thought. All of her friends had cars.

He sighed and shut his locker door. Instead of going down the hallway, he leaned against his locker. "Your parents aren't going to like me, are they?"

"Yes, they will. And they'll be happy you drive a Prius. Electric cars hardly ever run out of gas so we'll never be stranded in some deserted, potential make-out spot." She took his hand, then remembered she couldn't do things like that yet and dropped it. "We'll let everyone see us talking together at school, and after a few days of that, we'll tell people we're going out."

"Jonathan?" A woman's voice broke into their conversation.

Tori turned to see a middle-aged teacher walking toward

them. She was tall, and her straight, brown hair was cut below her chin in a no-nonsense bob. The woman had to be Jesse's mother. She had the same dark eyes, and the same way of lifting her eyebrows to indicate disapproval. She was apparently not happy to find a girl at her son's locker.

"There you are," the woman said, closing the distance between them. "Your father is in the office with Christian, making a schedule change. Then we'll be ready to go."

"Okay." Jesse gestured toward Tori. "Mom, this is Tori Hampton. Tori, this is my mom, also known as the new history teacher."

Tori smiled. "Nice to meet you, Doctor . . ." She caught herself, remembering that Jesse went by Richards now, not Harris. "Dr. Richards," she finished. Tori had to be careful not to slip up by using Jesse's real name. She mentally repeated *Richards*, hoping that would help the name stick in her mind.

Jesse's mom smiled back in a forced, uncomfortable sort of way. "Miss."

Tori blinked, not understanding. Why was the woman calling her "miss"? How was Tori supposed to respond? And yet, Jesse's mom was still staring at Tori as though expecting a response. "Excuse me?" Tori ventured.

"It's *Ms*. Richards, not *Dr*. Richards."

Oh. She'd said "Ms.," not "miss."

Tori had used the title doctor without thinking. Except for the PE coach, all of her teachers had doctorates. "Um, sorry," she said, and then worried that she'd sounded sorry about Ms. Richards not having a Ph.D. "I mean, I'm just used to . . . because my other teachers . . ."

This wasn't getting any better. Tori cleared her throat. "I'm sure you're a great teacher." Still not better. The compliment was transparently unfounded. Tori tried to salvage the situation anyway. "You must be a great teacher, because Je— Jonathan is so smart."

"We have journalism together," Jesse said, saving Tori from having to explain how she knew anything about Jesse's intelligence. To Tori, he said, "You were going to put together a study group for our next test, right?"

"Right," she said.

"I'll help you with the drinks," he said.

Tori couldn't help smiling. She'd definitely be holding a study group soon. One that would consist of just the two of them.

Ms. Richards' gaze bounced between Jesse and Tori. She seemed to sense that they weren't thinking about studying. "We should go. Christian and your father are probably done."

"Okay." Jesse slipped his backpack onto one shoulder and gave Tori one last smile. "See you later."

She watched him go with an inward sigh. She was glad he was going to her school, glad she would get to see him every day, but the relationship apparently wouldn't be without complications.

 # CHAPTER 24

After dinner, Dirk's father called him into his office. "I have an assignment for you tonight. You'll be helping out some of my men."

Dirk shoved his hands into his pockets. He didn't like surprise assignments. They were never good news. "Doing what?"

His father walked to the door and motioned for Dirk to come with him. "I've tracked down one of your Slayer friends. I want you to ensure my men are successful drugging him."

Him. That meant Jesse, Kody, or Shang. Dirk felt his stomach tighten, but he followed his father through the house toward the garage. "Who is it?"

His father didn't answer, just went out to the garage. When they were both seated in the Bentley, Dirk asked the question again. "Who?"

"My men will let you know about the target when you get there. Less chance of leaks that way."

What he meant was, Dirk wouldn't have the chance to warn anyone. His father pulled out of the garage and drove down the road that led across their property.

"Why do your men need my help?" Dirk asked. "All of the Slayers would recognize me, and if I'm seen near an attack, the police will suspect me. I should be the last person involved."

Dirk wanted nothing to do with drugging Slayers. Logically, he knew it had to happen, knew it was for the best if the Slayers lost their powers and their memories. But that didn't mean he wanted to be the one to face his old friends and see the anger and hatred for him in their eyes.

His father checked the rearview mirror. "When I sent men after Jesse, he was able to fight them off. I've realized that the best way to catch a Slayer is with a dragon lord."

Then do it yourself, Dirk thought. But he didn't say the words; it wouldn't do any good.

The drive to the airstrip never took long—fifteen minutes when his dad drove the speed limit. Now the trees rushed by. Dirk tapped his armrest in annoyance. "What does it say about your men that they need your son along to do their job?"

His father brushed off the insult. "Slayers sense elevated levels of adrenaline and fear in those around them. My men won't be able to hide those things, but you"—he shot Dirk a look—"you don't fear the Slayers. You should be able to get close to any of them without triggering that type of response."

Dirk huffed out a breath. "You don't think *my* adrenaline will go up while I'm stalking someone who used to be my friend?"

"If you can't find a way to do it," his father said with forced casualness, "then perhaps we should abandon the idea of drugging the Slayers and just kill them instead. I won't always be privy to their locations like I am tonight. We can't waste the opportunity."

Not that—not murder. Dirk felt a sharp jab of dread. "You promised you wouldn't kill them."

"And I need your help in order to keep that promise." He gripped the steering wheel with exasperation. "Can I count on you or not?"

A promise shouldn't be conditional. "If you kill someone, the FBI will get involved. I thought you didn't want that."

"I don't," his father said. "But avoiding an FBI investigation may be the lesser of two evils."

Dirk had no choice really. If he didn't agree to help his father drug one of the Slayers, his men would use guns on the next one they found. "I can do the job," Dirk said. "You don't have to kill anyone."

His father slid him another appraising look. "Good. Then I trust you to take care of it. Don't mess up."

"I won't," Dirk said. He couldn't. Not if he wanted to keep his friends alive.

* * *

As soon as Dirk walked off the plane and onto an airstrip in New York, two Chinese men greeted him. They introduced themselves as Feng and Yen, employees of his father. Which pretty much told Dirk which Slayer was being targeted. "So," he said. "I take it we're going to see Shang."

Feng and Yen didn't comment on that, just sent him stiff smiles, and motioned for him to follow them across the airstrip.

Dirk did, inwardly cursing Shang for bringing this on himself. He knew better than to do anything that would give his location away. Dr. B had told them all repeatedly not to take chances or be careless. So what had Shang done to let Dirk's father find him?

While they walked, Feng handed Dirk a white garment bag. "Your clothes for tonight." No other explanation. Was this a disguise? Where were they going?

They headed down the tarmac toward a parked SUV, where another man waited for them behind the wheel. Also Chinese.

As Dirk made his way to the car, he unzipped the garment bag. It held a gray suit, a pale blue shirt, and a silver tie.

"Shang must be doing something fun tonight," Dirk said. "Am I going to a formal dance?"

The men didn't reply. They just got into the SUV, checking as they did to make sure no one was following them.

Dirk climbed into the backseat. "If it's a dance, I'll need a date. I hope you found someone gorgeous. Right now, I could see myself with a shapely blonde."

Feng and Yen said nothing as they clicked their seatbelts on. They apparently had no sense of humor. They probably didn't have personalities, either.

"Is it a funeral?" Dirk pressed, pulling the shirt from the garment bag. "Or a job interview for someplace with a really lame dress code?"

The driver started the ignition and drove toward the airport exit. Yen cast Dirk a look over his shoulder. "Shang's cousin is getting married today. You'll be attending stag. Sorry for the lack of shapely blondes."

A wedding? "Who gets married on a Wednesday?"

"Today's date is auspicious," Feng said. "Chinese families take such things into consideration."

Yeah, today was going to turn out to be real auspicious. Dirk pulled off his T-shirt, trying not to scowl outright. Shang should know better than to go to a family wedding. He should have realized that his enemies would find out about those kinds of events. But that was Shang's weakness; he was not only loyal to the Slayers, he was unwaveringly loyal to his family.

That loyalty was about to cost him.

* * *

At nine o' clock, Dirk was dressed in the suit and standing

by the large stone fireplace in a hotel lobby. Wooden pillars ran the length of the two-story room, and a deep maroon carpet covered the floor. The whole place looked warm and glowing.

Dirk hadn't gone into the room where the wedding ceremony, tea ceremony, and seven-course banquet had taken place. He'd arrived after all of that. Most of the guests were dancing now, but a few strolled around the building.

Girls in silky dresses and guys speaking Chinese passed Dirk without giving him much notice. He stood by one of the pillars and pretended to text while he waited. Well, it wasn't all pretend. Every ten minutes, Feng texted him, wanting to know his progress on finding Shang.

Patience was never the strong suit of his father's employees. Dirk kept replying with the same reminder: no one was to come into the building until he gave the signal.

Dirk had a tranquilizer gun tucked into the inner pocket of his suitcoat, but he didn't expect Shang to stroll into the lobby and present himself an open target. No doubt he was in some secure corner of the ballroom where he could keep an eye on everything.

Dirk had stationed himself near the fireplace because it was the perfect spot for a photo opp. The huge stone mantel looked like it had been carved in some elegant European village just so people could pose in front of it. Every time someone did, Dirk offered his services.

At nine thirty, two women walked up to the fireplace, cellphones in hand. They were in their early twenties, black hair pulled into sleek buns, and both women wore matching pink bridesmaid dresses. They giggled as they posed for selfies.

Dirk stepped toward them, his flirty smile going full blast. "Need someone to take your picture? I can get a shot so you can see more of those gorgeous dresses."

The taller of the girls gave him an appreciative grin. "Could you? Thanks." She handed him her phone. He took it and then held out his hand to the other girl. "I can take one on your phone too."

She handed it to him, blushing slightly. "Thanks."

Dirk backed up, the phone held in front of him. He'd already closed the camera function and opened the girl's contact list. "Lean closer together," he said, going through the S's. "Your skirt needs to be smoothed down." No sign of Shang's number. He checked Lao, Shang's last name. Not there, either. Sheesh. Didn't anyone have Shang's number?

"You look great now," Dirk told the girls. "Hold it right there." He switched back to the camera function and snapped a couple of pictures. Had it been too much to hope the bridesmaids would know the cousin of the bride?

Dirk switched to the taller girl's phone, holding it up like as if framing a picture, while he went through her contact list. "Are you family of the bride or the groom?"

"Friend of the bride," the shorter girl said. "Min here is Serena's sister."

Finally. And there was Shang's number in her contacts. Dirk memorized it in seconds. "Beauty runs in the bride's family," he said with a wink, "and in her friendships, too."

While the women smiled at the compliment, he took a few more pictures with both cameras, enabling him to find Min's number and forward it to his cell. That way, he had the contact number of at least someone in Shang's family.

Dirk probably wouldn't need it. As soon as Shang felt threatened, he'd either leave the building to draw away the danger, or he'd send his family somewhere safer then stay and fight. Either of those scenarios were workable.

When he was done playing photographer, he deleted his message from Min's phone. He couldn't leave evidence behind.

He smiled and handed the girls their phones back.

"Thanks," Min said and gave him a bashful look. "Are you going to the dance?"

Dirk pulled out his own phone, a disposable one his father had given him for the mission. "In a while," he said, switching his phone to camera mode. "I've got a couple of calls to make first." Without showing any sign he was taking a picture, he snapped one of Min, hoping it hadn't cut off her head. That way his father's men would know her when she left the hotel. In a few minutes, Dirk would text her, pretending to be a friend, and tell her she'd left on a light in her car.

Dirk gave the girls a parting wave and walked across the lobby, already adding Shang and Min's numbers to his contacts. He texted Yen.

Time for you to join the dance. Find Shang, keep him in your sights, and wait for my next instructions.

Yen texted back. *If I go near Shang, he'll sense my adrenaline and know my intentions.*

That's exactly what Dirk was counting on. *I'm in charge of this mission*, Dirk reminded him. *Go in. I'll text you when to attack.*

CHAPTER 25

Shang stood by the drink table with his mother and Puo Puo, his grandmother from Beijing. He was doing his best to ignore their attempts to pick dance partners for him and had altogether tuned out Puo Puo's commentary on the music.

And then something changed in the room. He couldn't tell exactly what, but he involuntarily straightened, his senses growing sharper. His gaze swept the room looking for . . . he wasn't sure who. The Slayers had a subconscious radar for danger, and his had just been tripped.

Someone nearby was overly anxious. Not the normal sort of fear, like a guy worried about being turned down by a girl, or a parent concerned about who was dancing with their daughter. The feeling he sensed was more visceral, more threatening. It was the sweat of someone planning an attack and worried about retaliation.

Shang surveyed the couples dancing and the guests surrounding the dance floor. The room was large enough that he couldn't see everyone, but the people he did see all looked normal. Servers cleared dishes from the tables. No one seemed nervous or suspicious. He couldn't tell who was the culprit.

"Ah," his mom said, "now you're taking our advice and admiring the ladies. Xiaowen is a nice girl. Very smart. Why don't you ask her to dance."

The lights had been dimmed for the dance, making it hard to see facial expressions. The red and gold banners that had looked so bright and festive before looked like swaths of gray. The paper lanterns hanging from the ceiling had turned into dark, vacant orbs. Shang's eye's flicked over the guests closest to him. No one seemed to be paying him any attention. Still, he couldn't ignore what his senses were telling him.

"Something is wrong," he said. He didn't want to scare the women, but he also didn't want them to be caught unaware of the danger either.

"Many things aren't right," Puo Puo said. "The wedding was much too western. Look at all of the people wearing white. It's a funeral color. They'll bring bad luck. So much bad luck."

Shang's gaze still scanned the room. His hands hung by his sides itching to do something. "You should go to someplace safe."

His mother nearly spit out her punch. "I think you're taking Puo Puo's superstitions a bit too seriously."

Shang didn't have time to explain. "Some criminals may be here." Was he the target, or was it someone else? Not knowing was frustrating. He could be sensing hostility completely unrelated to him . . . or Overdrake might have found him. Shang didn't know how to react, who to try and save, he spoke to his mother and Puo Puo. "Go to the lobby. Ask if the hotel has security guards." That errand at least, would keep the two women out of harm's way for a while. And if security guards came and milled around the room, maybe the assailant would think twice before attacking.

Puo Puo made an indignant hurumphing sound. "Security guards? What sort of criminals are you talking about? Why are you trying to ruin Serena's wedding?"

Shang's mother didn't know anything about Slayers or

their abilities, but she did think he was involved as a witness in a drug case. She leaned toward him and lowered her voice. "You worry too much. No one from DC could have followed you here. And no one from New York knows you are here. We didn't tell anyone we were coming."

When Shang's parents had decided to take him to the wedding, he told them it wasn't a good idea. His mother, however, refused to believe that anyone from the criminal case would know enough about his extended family to figure out that his cousin was getting married, let alone think Shang might attend.

He was not so disrespectful as to publicly contradict his mother. He'd only said, "Perhaps we need to worry more, not less."

Now his mother peered around the room. "Do you recognize someone?"

"No," he told her. "But precaution is always a good idea."

She eyed him, clearly debating how much weight to put in his worries. "All right," she finally said. "We'll ask for security guards to look around a bit." She took Puo Puo's arm and led her toward the door, ignoring the older woman's protests.

Shang didn't see his father or sister anywhere. He needed to find them and come up with an excuse to make them leave quickly. Faking illness would probably work.

Shang's phone vibrated, and he pulled it from his pocket. The screen showed a text from a number he didn't recognize, one with a Virginia area code.

You can't stop all kinds of fire.

A chill went down Shang's back, and for a moment he didn't breathe. Overdrake. Somehow he'd gotten Shang's number. Overdrake was the type who liked to play with his victims, to gloat. The message was a reminder that Shang couldn't stop gunfire. He looked around the room again. One of Overdrake's men must be close by and armed.

Shang pressed the side buttons on his watch, sending a message to Dr. B that he was under attack. The distress call wouldn't do much good. The other Slayers were in DC, too far away to help him. Still, they should know.

Was it better to leave the reception and hope Overdrake's man followed, or did he need to stay here to protect his family?

As Shang walked toward the table that held the wedding cake, he called his father and surveyed the crowd to see if anyone was watching him. Several people faced his direction. Any of them could be keeping an eye on him.

The room offered little by way of defense. Bullets would go right through the plastic tables. The chairs were flimsy wooden things.

Shang picked up the knife Serena had used to cut the wedding cake. It was the only weapon available, and a poor one at that. He could throw it to disarm someone, but that action would only work once.

Pieces of cake sat on plastic plates around the table. He picked one up and held the knife below the plate so the blade wasn't noticeable.

Although the phone rang and rang; his father didn't answer. He probably hadn't turned it back on after the ceremony. His father was always saying that technology intruded too much in their lives. Shang hung up. He disconnected the call, deciding to try his sister. Her phone would be on. She embraced technology and all of its intrusions.

Before Shang dialed her number, his phone buzzed with a new text, one from the same unfamiliar number. He searched the room but saw no tell-tale screen lights cutting through the darkness. Whoever was texting him wasn't nearby. That meant there were more than one of Overdrake's men here. One was near enough for Shang to sense his adrenaline, and the other was texting him . . . from where? Shang took his eyes off the crowd to read the new message.

You have such a big family. Have you noticed anyone missing?

Bái mù. Overdrake was targeting his family. Shang's stomach clenched, but he wouldn't let himself feel fear. Fear would only cripple his thinking, and right now he needed a clear mind.

Who was missing?

His phone buzzed with another message. *Turn yourself over, and no one has to die.*

Shang punched his sister's number while making his way toward the ballroom door. He needed to warn his father and sister while finding his mother and Puo Puo. After they were safe, he'd check on the rest of the family, see if anyone was really missing.

Shang glanced behind him to see if anyone had followed.

A man and woman holding hands trailed after him, also moving toward the door. They were suspect. So was the man behind them, heading in the same direction. He looked to be in his twenties, Chinese, in a navy blue suit.

Shang's sister didn't answer her phone. He hung up and called the number again.

This time her voice came over the phone. "I'm in the middle of a dance. Why are you calling?"

"You're in danger. Warn Dad, then stay with a crowd until I come back for you."

"What?" she asked in disbelief.

"The drug dealers," he said. "At least two of them are here. Call Mom and warn her too, and then find dad."

He hung up. He needed to use both hands. Besides, he was

about to leave the ballroom and he didn't want to let his voice give away his location. He stepped into the hallway, slipped his phone in his pocket, and pressed himself against the wall on the far side of the door. He held the cake plate in one hand, the knife in the other, and waited for whoever was following him.

He hoped to see his mother and Puo Puo walking back with security guards. They weren't anywhere around, though.

He forced himself to focus on the door. He hadn't seen his family, but that didn't mean Overdrake had taken them. Shang could only see a slice of the main hallway leading to the lobby. The two women could be anywhere. They were most likely at the front desk right now, trying to explain their worries without giving too much information about Shang's case.

The couple who'd been behind Shang strolled out of the ballroom, laughing loud enough to suggest they'd had too much to drink. They didn't look around or show any signs of nervousness. Shang didn't move, didn't speak, as they walked down the hallway, unaware of him.

Next would be the man. He might be innocent too. Overdrake's man might still be in the room, and Shang would seem insane to anyone who saw him pressing himself to the wall, clutching a knife in one hand and a plate of wedding cake in the other. He could also be wasting his time. He needed to find his family.

Before the man stepped through the doorway, Shang felt him, could almost smell anxiety leaking from him. As soon as the man appeared, Shang flipped the plate across the hallway. The man's gaze followed the movement, and he automatically reached into his jacket pocket.

Shang stepped from his hiding place. Using the knife handle as a club, he hit the man in the back of the head. The man swore and staggered forward, falling. Before he hit the ground, Shang grabbed him by his suitcoat and shoved him against the wall. He placed the knife at the base of the man's throat, holding it tight. "Where are Overdrake's other men? How many of you are there?"

The man didn't say anything, only glared at Shang, breathing hard.

Shang felt along the man's suit and pulled out a large, black gun. He'd seen the type before: a tranquilizer. Three darts in the barrel.

"Thanks for the weapon," Shang said. "I left all mine at home." He tucked the gun into his back pocket, away from the man's grasp. "Are you going to tell me what I want?"

The man still didn't speak. He clutched at Shang's hand, but it was a weak gesture, one without the expected strength. That's when Shang noticed blood on the wall. A stain had formed behind the man's head and was spreading. *Rén zhā.* Shang had hit him too hard.

"Where are the others?" Shang demanded. "Who did they take?"

Still breathing hard, the man sneered in contempt. "Someone you'll miss. If you want to see them again, you'll give me back my gun."

"Who is it?" Shang pressed the man into the wall harder.

"Turn yourself in, and she won't be hurt."

She. His mind flashed to his mother. Had they taken her?

"Who?" Shang repeated.

No answer. Didn't matter. Whoever Overdrake had taken, Shang would get her back. He couldn't waste more time on this interrogation. Any moment now someone would come out of the ballroom, see Shang, and think he was roughing up some helpless guy. They'd call the police. And if anyone saw the gun sticking out of Shang's back pocket, it would make matters even worse.

He pulled the gun from his pocket and pressed the barrel into the man's chest. "Last chance to talk."

The man scowled and remained silent.

Shang wasn't waiting any longer. He pulled the trigger.

The man let out a cough of pain, said every Chinese curse word Shang knew—and a couple he didn't. The tranquilizer wouldn't take long to work, only a minute or two, depending on the drug.

Shang wasn't wearing a jacket, but he could use a place to hide the gun and the knife. Fortunately, Overdrake's henchman didn't need his suitcoat right now.

Spinning the man around, Shang grabbed the top of the coat, and yanked it down. Before the coat was all the way off, the man turned and attempted to swing his fist, which wouldn't have landed even if the guy hadn't been swaying and unsteady. Shang tugged the coat the rest of the way off, sending the man tumbling to the floor.

The man was still swearing. Shang pulled on the suitcoat, regretting again that he'd hit the guy so hard. Blood had oozed onto the collar in places. Hopefully no one would notice. He slipped the knife into the breast pocket, smearing frosting on the lining in the process. Whoever ended up with this coat would get some interesting looks from his dry cleaner.

The man staggered to his feet and took another swing. Shang sidestepped it easily enough. The man lunged forward, trying to grab Shang. He stepped out of the way and let the man fall to the floor.

The gun went into Shang's back pocket again, covered nicely by the suitcoat.

Two women emerged from the ballroom—some of Serena's friends from college—and stopped short when they saw the man on the floor. He rolled over and slurred something unintelligible.

The women peered at him more closely, one putting her hand to her mouth in surprise.

Shang didn't know either of the women personally but spoke to them anyway. "The guy is drunk," he told them. "I was just on my way to tell the hotel staff about him."

"Oh," one of the women said, and both stared at the man, as though unsure what to do. "Is he bleeding?"

Shang gave an exaggerated shrug and strode away before they noticed too many details—like the fact that he'd stolen the guy's suitcoat. As he walked, he went through the coat pockets and found a cell phone. The disposable type. In the recent calls list, he found the number that had texted him earlier. The man and the texter were definitely working together.

He messaged the number: *Where are you?* The owner of the number was most likely with whoever they'd taken hostage. If not, Shang would have to find a way to persuade him to give up that information of her whereabouts.

Shang pulled out his own phone and called his mother. It was a risk; when talking, he'd be less likely to hear an approaching assailant. But he wanted to know whether she was all right.

She didn't answer, and his Puo Puo never used her cell, probably hadn't even taken it with her tonight.

Shang rounded the corner into the main hall and headed to the lobby. If his mother wasn't at the front desk, someone there would know whether she'd come by to talk to request security.

The phone he'd taken from his attacker buzzed, a text answering Shang's earlier question. *We're still on the north side of the building. What's Shang doing?*

He wrote back. *He's looking around for his family and texting.* Which was, after all, the truth.

New plan. Instead of going to the lobby, Shang turned and

strode toward a back door. Once he was outside, he'd go around to the north side of the hotel and catch Overdrake's men unaware.

He took out his own phone. Time to answer Overdrake's messages as himself.

Who do you have?

He pulled the gun from his pocket. Two darts left. Hopefully they would be enough.

A half a minute later a text popped up in reply: *Does it matter? Is there anyone in your family you wouldn't sacrifice yourself for?*

Overdrake clearly didn't know some of Shang's cousins. There were a couple he would only feel slightly guilty about leaving in a dragon lord's clutches.

What exactly do you want? Shang was trying to buy himself some time. He was almost to the back door.

As he reached it, Overdrake replied. *Walk out the front of the hotel and get into the van marked Airport Shuttle. You have five minutes. I would hate to shoot someone.*

Shang would need to be fast. He turned both phones off so they wouldn't ring and give his position away. Gun in hand, he stepped outside.

A single pale lamppost lit a small side parking lot. Empty cars filled most of the spaces. No sight of anyone else. Pine trees and some sort of sculpted hedges lined the property on the north, separating the building from its neighbor. Shang made his way to that corner, keeping in the shadows. In camp, he'd learned how to walk without making a sound, but now the method seemed painfully slow.

He kept his gun at his side and hoped that if any of Overdrake's men saw him they would think he was the man who'd attacked him.

As he came to the corner of the building, he lifted the gun and peered around the side. The trees and shrubs made silhouettes against the night. He saw no people, no hostage. Someone was there though; his senses buzzed with a warning of their own.

That's when he felt a sharp pain in his throat, like an angry wasp's sting. Even before he put his hand to his neck, he knew it was a tranquilizer dart. He only had a few minutes before he lost consciousness—assuming that's all he lost. The drug might do more damage than that.

The two possible results—a drugging that took away his power and memories, or death—shouldn't have been equal in his mind, but the bitterness welling inside him didn't differentiate between them. Either way, his Slayer memories and powers would be gone, and that would be a kind of death. He had let down his friends and his country.

He didn't have time to make it back inside the hotel before passing out. He leaned against the side of the building and searched the grounds, looking for the person who'd shot him. The least Shang could do was return fire.

But no one moved across the grounds. The bushes didn't stir.

The shooter was probably hiding behind the evergreens, and Shang was wasting his last moments of lucidity trying to exact revenge. He retreated around the corner of the building, peeled off the suitcoat, and clumsily used his shirt to wipe his prints from the gun. At least that way, when the authorities found him, they wouldn't know he'd drugged the man inside. As he finished wiping the gun, it fell from his hand. He didn't bother picking it up. Instead, he got out his phone and turned it on. Maybe if he got to the hospital in time, doctor could counteract the drug and prevent it from doing damage.

Wishful thinking, he knew.

He called 911. "I need help," he said, voice already slurring. "I'm at the Ashton Hotel "Outside. North corner." It was hard to speak coherently. He had to concentrate on each word. His head felt heavy and disconnected from the rest of his body. "I was shot. Tranquilizer gun. Send paramedics. Flush out my system."

"You were shot with *what* type of gun?" the operator asked.

He didn't answer. A figure was floating in the air, coming toward him. He blinked to make sure he wasn't hallucinating.

Dirk hovered in front of him, wearing a dark suit, tie, and gloves. He plucked the phone from Shang's hand and ended the call.

"I told you the truth," Dirk said calmly, casually almost. "I didn't want to shoot anyone. Especially not you."

"Traitor," Shang breathed out. He was losing the strength to stand. It was all he could do not to slide to the ground. He looked over to where he'd dropped the gun. It was only a couple feet away, but he couldn't make his legs take him to it.

Dirk didn't acknowledge the insult. "I trained you better than this. You should have expected an ambush. I knew you'd take Yen out and find his phone. I was counting on it. Did you think I would forget how capable you are? I was your captain. I know firsthand."

Shang willed his legs to move; he took a step toward the gun. If he managed to shoot Dirk, the paramedics would find him too. When Dirk woke up he'd be surrounded by doctors and police who would question him, and more importantly, look into his identity.

Dirk went through Shang's phone, deleting their texting exchange. "I'd stay and chat, but I've got evidence to get rid of." He tossed Shang's phone to the ground. "I don't suppose you'll tell me where you left Yen?"

Shang's legs didn't hold his weight. He tumbled forward and would have fallen face first if Dirk hadn't grabbed him.

Dirk slowly lowered him to the ground. "Sorry," he said, and his voice seemed to waver and fade as if he were far away. "Trust me, though, this is better than the alternative."

CHAPTER 26

Jesse was doing homework in his bedroom when he got a warning message from Dr. B saying that Overdrake's men had found Shang in New York. *New York*. Even if Dr. B had thought it prudent to send backup, Shang was too far away for any Slayers to help. None of them could do anything but wait for an update.

Dr. B finished the message with, *I don't believe anyone else's location has been compromised. Nevertheless, be careful.*

For a while, Jesse paced his room telling himself Shang would be okay. Shang was trained and had Slayer senses. Jesse had fought off an attack from Overdrake's men last month; Shang could too. He was as strong and smart. He'd come out on top.

While Jesse paced, he sent Tori a message. *This might be a good time to start carrying weapons around, even if you're just changing into pajamas.*

She wrote back. *I'm armed to the teeth. Okay, not really, but you still don't have to worry about me. I'm safe at home.*

He worried anyway.

An hour later, another message from Dr. B arrived. *Hugh is in the hospital.*

That was Shang's code name because it was close to "huo,"

the Chinese word for fire. *Aside from being drugged, he's fine. I'll keep you apprised as I get more details.*

For a moment, Jesse was too shocked to do anything—even react—but then anger washed over him and settled into sharp fury. Overdrake had put Shang in the hospital. He'd been drugged. He wouldn't be fine. They'd lost a Slayer. And they already had too few.

Jesse's anger had nowhere to go, and nothing he could do with it. This was why people had punching bags. Sometimes you just needed to hit something. He went down to the basement and ran on the treadmill instead. He pushed himself, running and running, until he couldn't go any faster, until he ached with the effort and his lungs burned. The workout wasn't nearly as satisfying as hitting something would have been.

An hour into his run, Dr. B called. Jesse turned off the treadmill and answered, panting. "How is he?"

Dr. B sounded weary. "I'm afraid his memories may be gone. I'd like you to visit him after school tomorrow. He should be home by then."

"Wait, what do you mean, his memories *may* be gone? You're not sure?" Jesse wanted to hold on to hope. Even a thin thread was better than nothing.

"When he awoke," Dr. B explained, "his mother asked what had happened. She was sure a member of the drug cartel tried to kill him. He told her he couldn't remember anything about a cartel, or any case he was supposed to testify in."

Of course Shang couldn't remember. The case didn't exist. If Shang still remembered being a Slayer, he would also have known the drug story was a front.

"I'll arrange for someone to go with you," Dr. B went on. "See if he's retained any memories of being a Slayer."

Part of Jesse wanted to argue that the assignment was

useless. No other drugged Slayers had ever recalled the truth about themselves. Their memories of being a Slayer had transformed into vague recollections of playing camp games. But the other part of Jesse knew he had to talk to Shang, at least to try to reach him.

Still, the visit could be dangerous.

"When Leo and Danielle lost their memories, we talked to them. Dirk knows that," Jesse pointed out. "Overdrake might have people staking out the hospital so he can trail Hugh home. He'll be watching for us."

"Hugh's parents believe he's still in danger. I've already discussed the evasive maneuvers they'll need to take to ensure that he's not tracked from the hospital. It's imperative for you to keep contact with him and convince him to adhere to protocol."

Meaning staying away from alcohol and drugs.

Given enough time—perhaps a year or two—the pathways in his brain that accessed his powers would heal and regrow—but only if no other drugs were in his system during that time. None of the Slayers were allowed to smoke, drink, or ingest anything that changed their brain chemistry. Jesse was so paranoid about the possibility of losing his memories that he even stayed away from Tylenol.

The protocol conversation wasn't one he looked forward to having. How did you bring that sort of thing up without it seeming awkward?

"I'll no longer be able to check on him," Dr. B continued. "He'll think it's odd to hear from his camp director. However, Hugh won't think it's strange for his camp friends to visit."

"I can go as soon as I get home from school," Jesse said.

Dr. B must have heard the discouragement in Jesse's voice. "All is not lost," he said. "Historical records attest that there's a way for Slayers to regain their powers quickly. I just need to find out how."

Dr. B had been searching through medieval records for years, but wasn't any closer to finding the quick cure than he'd been when he first started. Jesse wasn't about to point this out.

"I'll arrange for a drop off," Dr. B said. That meant he'd leave a car on the street for Jesse to drive—less chance of anyone seeing it at Shang's house and tracing it back to Jesse's family. "I'll give you more details as I arrange them." Dr. B then gave Jesse a list of numbers—code for the coordinates for Shang's address. That bit of information—Shang's address, seemed like Dr. B's verdict on Shang's chances of remaining a Slayer. Shang was gone and Dr. B knew it.

* * *

Thursday morning while Jesse got ready for school, Dr. B sent a message. *Edison has a library book to lend you. Pick it up at your convenience.*

Edison was Theo's code name, and "at your convenience" meant outside his house, right now. Jesse had forgotten what "library book" was supposed to mean.

He went out his front door and found Theo sitting in a car parked by his lawn. Sunglasses perched on his nose, and a baseball cap hid most of his curly hair. He rolled down his window as Jesse walked up.

"Hey, Ed," Jesse said.

Theo held out a flash drive that had been put into a Ziploc bag to prevent fingerprints.

"That's the library book?" Jesse asked.

Theo looked at him over the top of his sunglasses. "I don't really go in for all of the codename nonsense."

"Yeah, it gets confusing for all of us." Jesse took the bag and slipped it into his pocket. "Sometimes you have to go along with it to humor Dr. B. What's on the flash drive?"

"Dirt on Senator Whatever-his-code-name-is. Emails about gun deliveries, mostly. There's also an audio file of him talking to an arms smuggler. A shipment is coming through the Newark port tomorrow morning at six."

Theo gestured to the pocket that Jesse had put the flash drive in. "Make sure Tori gets it to her father as soon as possible. If the feds can catch Overdrake's men, maybe one of them will turn on him." Theo started the car's ignition. "At the very least, we've got to keep Overdrake from getting those weapons tomorrow."

Jesse nodded, considering the information. "Shouldn't you turn the recording over to the FBI?"

"That's what I'm doing next," Theo said. "FBI, ATF, and the Coast Guard. I'm one big lending library today."

"Good luck with that."

"I'll need it," Theo said. "The FBI doesn't work very fast or hard on anonymous tips. Let's hope Tori's dad has more pull."

Senator Hampton definitely had pull. Convincing him to use it would be another matter.

CHAPTER 27

On the way to school, Tori sat in the backseat of the BMW, finishing her math. Lars never spoke while driving. He said it disturbed his concentration. Which was fine by Tori. It wasn't like she wanted to talk to him anyway. The man had two facial expressions: scowl and suspicious scowl.

Her phone chimed—a text from Aaron. He was in her contacts as DLJ, short for Dragon Lord Junior.

I still haven't changed my mind.

And she still hadn't come up with a better plan, or one that would dissuade him from contacting his father. Was sending Aaron in as a mole a good idea or a horrible one? Most of the time, it seemed like a horrible one.

Give it more thought, she wrote.

His reply was almost immediate. *Can't. This is the fair's last weekend. Tell Dirk.*

She sighed. Aaron may have been half dragon lord, but he seemed to have inherited the zeal and optimism of a Slayer. She wrote two words: *On Friday*. He had one more day to change his mind. And she had one more day to decide if she could live with Aaron's death on her conscience.

Last night after Dr. B had informed them that Shang's memory was gone, a lot of messages had flown back and forth among the Slayers. Tori spent an hour in tears and another hour wallowing in hot chocolate while wondering how many Slayers would be left when Overdrake attacked the country. Would she be killed off quickly by the dragon, or would she have to watch the few remaining Slayers die first?

Perhaps desperate times called for desperate measures, measures that might risk a twelve-year-old's life. Weren't all the Slayers already risking their lives?

Lars drove to the school's security checkpoint, and the guard waved him through. Technically, Tori was supposed to show her school ID, and Lars was required to show documentation that he was an approved driver, but the school staff knew them both by sight.

A few minutes later, Lars pulled up to the building and waited for her to get out. Even on days when she had a ton of stuff to lug around, he never helped her with it. He said bodyguards had to keep their hands free in case they needed to use them, but Tori was pretty sure he just didn't want to carry her stuff.

She hurried into the school, wishing skirts weren't part of the girls' uniform. Whoever came up with the dress code had obviously never trekked across campus in the cold wearing only tights to keep their legs warm.

Her watch buzzed with a message from Jesse. *Meet me at your locker.*

She'd given him her cell phone number yesterday—a Slayer rule infraction, yes, but it didn't seem so important now that they went to the same school. The fact that he'd used his watch instead of his phone to contact her meant he had Slayer business to discuss. Probably some sort of an assignment.

Meetings at lockers? she wrote. *Are we already at that stage of our relationship?*

Definitely. And besides, I have a library book for you from the doctor.

A library book? Jesse wouldn't be happy she'd forgotten what that was code for. She pushed her way through students milling around the halls and finally answered.

I'd come up with a response that totally made sense if I knew what a library book was. She sent it, realized how the text sounded, then added, *I know what* real *library books are.*

She heard Jesse laughing before she saw him. He'd come down the hallway to intercept her and was shaking his head at her message. She walked over and swatted him. "I read all the time."

He lifted his hands to show that he wasn't arguing the point. "I know. I still remember lugging around all those books you brought to camp."

Back when she'd first enrolled in camp, she imagined she would have time to lounge by the lake and relax with a paperback. It never happened. She'd been too busy training.

She continued toward her locker with Jesse beside her. No one paid any attention to them, but she still kept her voice low. "Any news about Shang?"

Jesse's smile slipped. "No. I'm going to see him after school."

The weight of his words hung between them, heavy and hopeless.

Tori tried for optimism. "Maybe he'll recover before Overdrake attacks."

"Maybe," Jesse said, although he didn't sound like he believed it. He pulled a Ziploc bag from his pocket and handed it to her. A flash drive. "We need an in with someone who's got some authority. Give this to your father as soon as you can. It's evidence of Senator Ethington's involvement in arms smuggling. A shipment is coming through the Newark Port tomorrow at six in the morning."

"A shipment for Overdrake?"

"That's the assumption."

She slipped the drive into her backpack. "I'm surprised Dr. B isn't sending us to intercept the shipment."

She was joking. She didn't really think Dr. B would send them to New Jersey at the crack of dawn to steal assault rifles from under the noses of arms dealers.

But Jesse nodded, as if she'd mentioned a reasonable possibility. "He wants the FBI to track down the smugglers. They won't be able to do that if we steal the evidence."

Really, Jesse was far too willing to go places where people wanted to shoot him.

They reached Tori's locker and walked over to it. "How am I supposed to have gotten the evidence?"

Jesse shrugged. "A mysterious stranger approached you with it?"

"This may surprise you, but I don't meet a lot of mysterious strangers. For that matter, not many boring ones, either. My bodyguard sees to that."

While she twirled her combination, Jesse leaned against the next locker. "Then you'll have to come up with some other credible story. Just make sure you get the flash drive to your dad today before he leaves work. If he has the evidence while he's still on Capitol Hill, maybe he'll show it to other senators and bust Ethington on the spot."

Tori wasn't sure what sort of legal process was needed to remove Ethington from a position of power. Whatever it took, she'd do her part to see that it happened. "Okay. If you need an in, I'm your girl."

Jesse smiled. "Yes, you are."

CHAPTER 28

After school, Jesse picked Lilly up from a bus stop in Vienna, Virginia, and the two of them drove to Shang's home in Fairfax. Lilly brought balloons and a plate of chocolate chip cookies, which made Jesse feel guilty about not bringing anything.

Lilly remained composed on the drive as they hammered out the details of their story, but her red eyes belied her easy tone. Last month, she'd lost Alyssa, her best friend in the Slayers, and now her counterpart was gone too. She looked resolutely out at the road like a martyr determined to endure whatever horrible fate awaited.

After a long pause, Jesse said, "I know how you feel." Specifically, he felt like a part of him had been dragged, roughshod, behind a moving car.

"No, you don't," she muttered.

"He was my friend too." More than a friend. The Slayers were as close as brothers and sisters. Jesse had lost a brother.

"You haven't lost everyone who cares about you." She didn't try to keep the bitterness out of her voice. "I swear, if I have the chance, I'll kill Overdrake myself."

He didn't try to talk her out of her anger. Truth was, one of them really might have to kill Overdrake in a fight. That would be the quickest way to end his bid for a takeover. "You didn't lose everyone who cares about you. All of the Slayers care about you."

She scoffed and went back to staring out the window. "Well, you'll all care when fire is coming your way. I'm the only one who can extinguish it now."

"We care anyway. We always will. We're on the same team."

She made a grumbling sound showing her doubt, but she didn't argue the point. "When we get there, I'll ask Shang the questions."

Jesse nodded in agreement.

"And when we have to lie, let me do it," she said. "You suck at lying."

He glanced over at her then back on the road. "How would you know?"

"Please. I've lived with you every summer since I was twelve."

"Maybe I'm so good at lying that you don't know all of the times I've lied to you."

She rolled her eyes. "You couldn't even sneak off with Tori without everyone knowing. Let me handle any details we have to make up."

They pulled up to a white townhouse and got out. Lilly's balloons jostled against each other, rustling with every step toward the door. She clutched the plate too tightly, holding her chocolate-chip offering as if it could ward off bad news.

Jesse rang the bell. A minute later, a slender Asian woman answered the door and looked them over.

"Hi." Jesse smiled in what he hoped was a casual way. "We're some of Shang's friends. We heard he'd been in the hospital and thought we'd drop by to see him."

Lilly held out the plate of cookies. "I made these for him."

The woman pursed her lips, didn't move to let them in. "How thoughtful. What are your names?"

"I'm Jesse, and this is Lilly," he said. "Shang knows us from camp."

The woman nodded, still not opening the door any wider. "How did you get our address?"

That was trickier to answer—and one of those details Lilly wanted to handle.

She inched forward and lowered her voice to a confidential whisper. "Shang gave it to me." She shrugged sheepishly. "I know he wasn't supposed to tell anyone where he moved, but we've been friends since we were twelve. He knows he can trust me." With Shang's memory loss, he couldn't contradict the story about him giving Lilly his address.

"I see," the woman said, clearly unhappy with the answer. She still eyed them suspiciously. "I'll ask his uncle if Shang is up to a visit." She turned and spoke in Chinese to someone behind the door, then turned back to them. "Just a moment."

Jesse and Lilly awkwardly waited on the doorstep, then heard Shang's voice from inside. "It's okay, Mom. I know them."

The woman—Shang's mother, apparently—opened the door all the way, letting them in.

Shang seemed none the worse for his stint in the hospital. He looked the same—alert, healthy, standing straight, although Jesse wasn't sure Shang knew how to slouch. Jesse looked for a difference in his eyes—some sign that Shang wasn't one of them anymore. He saw nothing. It was stupid to think he would, really. What did he expect? A person couldn't see that sort of thing.

"Sorry you had to wait on the doorstep for so long," Shang

said, gesturing for them to follow him through the room. "My family is being ultra-cautious right now."

The group passed a man sitting on the couch watching TV. He was large, broad shouldered, and wore his dark hair pulled back in a ponytail. If Jesse wasn't mistaken, he had a gun holstered at his waist. He nodded as they walked by.

"That's my uncle Hong," Shang said. "He's staying with us for a while."

He led them upstairs and down a hall to his bedroom. Jesse shouldn't have been surprised that it looked like the inside of an Ikea catalog—the bed was made, desk organized, and no clutter or dirty clothes lay anywhere. Still, Jesse couldn't help but stare in wonder. He hadn't known that real teenagers actually lived this way.

Shang pulled a chair from his desk and offered it to Lilly. "How did you hear about my stint in the hospital?"

"It was one of those weird coincidences," Lilly said, sitting down. "Bess was at the same hospital in New York visiting a relative and she saw them bring you in. The staff wouldn't let her see you, because, you know, she wasn't a relative or anything, but she told us about it. She was really worried about you."

Jesse made his way to a window seat. "If Bess wasn't still in New York, she would have come with us." Despite what Lilly thought of his skills in deception, he managed the lie well enough.

Lilly nonchalantly ran her hands across the arms of the chair. "So how did you wind up in the hospital?"

Even though Jesse knew it wasn't likely, he hoped Shang would say, "I know why you're really asking. Don't worry. I'm still a Slayer."

Instead, Shang sat down on his bed, shaking his head. "I

don't remember most of it, and the police weren't that concerned about making sense of what happened. But my cousin Min and I were both drugged while we were at a family wedding. She doesn't remember much either. She went out to the parking lot to turn off her car's headlights, and the next thing she knew, she was lying on the pavement and people were shaking her awake. I remember less than that. Apparently I told a 911 operator that I'd been shot with a tranquilizer gun, but then they found ketamine in our systems and acted like we were some stupid kids who had OD-ed on a drug trip."

"That's rough," Jesse said. He felt like a piece of his heart had been carved out and left hollow. He'd known beforehand what to expect, but seeing Shang and hearing his explanation made it all worse—all real. He'd lost a brother, and there was nothing he or Lilly could do to reclaim him.

Shang was just . . . gone. The same, yet utterly different.

"I've never used ketamine," Shang emphasized. "I don't use drugs,"

"We know," Lilly said.

"They didn't find any signs of foul play," Shang went on. "Nobody even took my wallet. None of it makes sense."

It actually made perfect sense. Jesse couldn't speak, found it too hard to form words.

Shang hesitated, perhaps deliberating whether to say more on the subject, then asked, "So how did you guys know where I live?" He seemed curious, not suspicious, although it was hard to tell with Shang. He tended to keep his thoughts guarded.

"You told me your address," Lilly said. "Remember? You gave it to me that time we got together at the mall."

Shang cocked his head. "When did we do that?"

She blinked as though surprised he didn't remember. "A week ago. I helped you pick out a jacket, and then we ate at

Panda Express. You went on and on about how it wasn't real Chinese food."

Lilly had told Jesse about the supposed mall trip, but the detail of the jacket was new. And too specific. Either Lilly wasn't as good of a liar as she thought, or it wasn't a lie at all. What had Lilly and Shang been doing together at a mall?

Shang stood, went to his closet, and pulled out a black leather jacket. It looked more like something a biker guy would wear than something Shang would ever pick out.

"This?" he asked.

"Yes," she said brightening. "You remember?"

"No, I just saw it in my closet and wondered where it came from."

Lilly deflated. "You don't remember any of it?"

"Sorry." Shang hung the jacket back up. "I might have gotten a head injury or something when I was drugged. A lot of my memory is gone." He clenched and unclenched his hands, irritated. "The doctors say the memories might come back. It's too early to tell."

Lilly leaned forward, her casual veneer slipping. "What do you remember about camp?"

Shang tilted his head, seemed to think it was an odd question. "Uh, I remember going, and I remember that you guys were there."

"Do you remember which team you were on?" Jesse asked.

"Team?" Shang repeated. "Oh, you mean for the camp games." He shrugged. "It's all kind of foggy. I just remember we went running a lot. I'm glad *that* part of camp is over."

Jesse had anticipated this answer, but it still hurt to hear Shang say it. Each word felt like a stone dropped onto his chest. They'd lost Shang.

Shang, who had always been so thorough and dependable—as logical as Kody was hot-headed. Jesse had always counted on Shang as his next in command in Team Magnus. How would they function without him?

Lilly took in a jagged breath, put her hand to her mouth, and broke into tears.

Jesse had never seen her cry, not in all the years he'd known her. Whenever she was upset, she always got angry, not sad. He would have been less surprised if she'd picked up something and thrown it.

Shang left the bed and went to her, leaning over her chair to put his arm around her. "Lilly, I'm so sorry. What's wrong?"

She didn't answer, just stared at Shang as tears ran down her cheeks.

A look of understanding flashed in his eyes. "Were we . . . dating or something?"

She swallowed, trying to compose herself. "Yeah, something."

They were? When had that happened? Jesse hadn't even suspected, although maybe he should have. At camp they'd gone off together often enough. Still, Lilly had given Jesse and Tori so much grief about breaking Dr. B's no-dating-rule, he hadn't expected her to be guilty of the same offense. He felt a new pang of grief for Lilly. She'd lost more than just her counterpart.

Shang took Lilly's hand, sat on the edge of his desk, and smiled. He didn't seem to mind suddenly finding himself in a relationship with her. "I should have known that a girl had something to do with that jacket. I never would have chosen it myself. The tags are gone, so that means I wore it at least once, didn't I?"

She sniffed and nodded. "All that night. And you looked hot in it too, so don't knock it."

Shang squeezed her hand, and his voice turned soothing.

"Hey, I'm really sorry I don't remember, but I'm sure it's only temporary. I couldn't forget something that big, could I?" He gave her hand another squeeze. "But don't expect me ever to wear the jacket again." He chuckled, trying to joke Lilly into a better mood. "Okay, maybe once more if it makes you happy."

She didn't even crack a smile. "You can't ever drink."

"Was I drunk?" He laughed again and looked over his shoulder at the closet. "Well, that would explain the jacket."

"No," Lilly said. "You weren't drinking. And you can't ever drink or do drugs, or your brain won't heal. You've got to help your memories come back."

"Right," Shang said. "Don't worry. I'll follow the doctor's orders."

Lilly turned his hand so she could see his Slayer watch. "You're still wearing this."

Shang looked at the watch, then noticed she wore an identical one. "Wait, are these some sort of couples' watches? No wonder I didn't feel right taking it off." He ran a finger along the face of Lilly's watch then smiled at her. "Since we're dating, I'm going to have to put my foot down about your fashion choices. From now on, let me pick out my stuff. No more bad-boy jackets or weird watches with a bunch of unexplained buttons."

While Shang was distracted, Jesse quietly slid his own matching watch higher up his arm, out of sight under his coat sleeve. No sense in having to explain why he had one too.

Lilly tapped Shang's watch. "Take it off and look at the back."

"Why?" he asked, even as he took it off. He flipped the watch over, and his eyebrows lowered in confusion. He tilted the watch to better catch the light.

Jesse looked from Shang to Lilly and back again. "What is it?"

"It's inscribed," Shang said, and then asked Lilly, "What does it mean?"

"I don't know," she said. "You engraved it in Chinese. It's a note to yourself."

Shang scrutinized the inscription and grunted. "Yeah, and I should have been more specific, because this doesn't make a lot of sense. 'Go into your room, and pass through has you.'" He looked at them for an explanation. "Why did I write that? What's in my room?"

"It's a clue." Lilly said, her tone growing eager. "After Alyssa lost her memory, you said you weren't going to let that happen to you. So you wrote yourself that message."

Shang lowered his watch. "Alyssa lost her memory too? What happened?" His gaze went back and forth between Jesse and Lilly. "Was it because of the same people who came after me?"

Lilly nodded.

Shang frowned and stood, looking like he wanted to leave the room. "We need to tell the FBI."

"They already know," Jesse said.

Shang's eyes widened with understanding. "Are the two of you involved in the same case I was?"

That was as good an explanation as any. "Yes," Jesse said at the same time Lilly said, "No."

She glared at Jesse. He knew she wanted to tell Shang the truth, tell him everything. But saying things about dragons would only make the two of them lose any credibility they'd gained.

When Alyssa lost her memory, they told her she was a Slayer, and there was a dragon lord named Overdrake who was after them. She thought they were crazy. Better to stick with the truths Shang could actually deal with.

"You can't tell your parents about our involvement with the case," Jesse said. "You can't tell anyone."

Shang took in the information. "I won't."

"Remember Dirk from camp?" Jesse continued. "He's not our friend anymore. You should know that. His father is bad news too."

Lilly stood and spoke to Jesse, her familiar frustration replacing her sadness. "Shang is different from Alyssa. He realizes he's forgotten things." She turned to him. "And you wrote yourself that note, so you know we're not making things up. None of us could have written that in Chinese."

Lilly turned to Shang. "The inscription is telling you to look for something in your room, right? So, where should you look?"

Shang shrugged. "Depends. What am I looking for?"

"Another, longer message from yourself." She glanced at Jesse, then turned away guiltily.

She knew exactly why Shang had written the inscription on his watch. "You mean," Jesse said addressing her, "that Shang hid some sort of account of secret things?" From the time they first became Slayers, Dr. B had forbidden them from recording anything that, if found, could prove they were Slayers. Their parents couldn't be allowed to discover their identities, and neither should anyone else—especially people who might leak information to Overdrake. But now that he knew who each of them were, the rule didn't seem so important. Making a record might even be a good idea, as long as their parents didn't find it.

"If I were to hide something," Shang said, walking to his dresser. "I would put it . . ." He opened a drawer and removed the clothing, stacking it on top of the dresser. "Here." He reached in and pulled out some money from the bottom of the drawer, both Chinese and American, followed by a picture of Lilly.

He turned to her, holding the picture. "Is this what I told myself to remember? You?"

"No," she said, but she smiled at the picture in his hand, pleased that he had it.

Shang replaced the clothing into the drawer then slid out the other drawers, combing through the contents. "A longer message to myself . . ."

Finding nothing out of the ordinary in his dresser, he opened the closet and rummaged through clothes, checking pockets. Lilly went to his bookcase, where she pulled out books and searched for any loose papers among the pages. "The message will probably be written in Chinese," she said.

Jesse joined the search. He checked under the bed, lifted the pictures away from the wall, and riffled through the desk drawers. Jesse even looked behind the dresser, which was hard to do because of the large mirror attached to the top. Twenty minutes later, the three of them had trashed Shang's room, but came up emptyhanded.

Lilly sidled up beside Jesse. "We'll just have to tell him everything."

"He won't believe it if he hears it from us," Jesse said. "Would you?"

Lilly pressed her lips together, apparently unable to bring herself to answer the question.

Shang took his watch off again and flipped it over. "Jing," he read.

"What?" Lilly asked.

"The Chinese symbol for 'jing.' I'm so stupid. The symbols have the same pronunciation, but in this case it doesn't mean 'pass through.' It means 'mirror.' The clue isn't in the room itself. It's inside the room's *mirror*." He walked over to the dresser and examined the edges of the mirror. Then he grinned. "Something's wedged back here. A paper."

He went to his desk, found a letter opener, and worked it into the crack, trying to budge the paper. For several minutes, he maneuvered the letter opener without success. He tried a different angle. "I still can't get it out."

Lilly grumbled something unintelligible, picked up a ceramic pencil holder, and smashed it against the mirror. With an offended-sounding crack, the glass shattered, pieces plunking onto the dresser top.

"In case you don't remember," Lilly told him. "I'm not all that patient. You probably should know that about me while considering my girlfriend status."

"Noted," Shang said calmly, and plucked a long, white envelope from the pile of the mirror's remains. It was addressed to Shang, postmarked with a return address from New York.

Downstairs, Shang's mom called something in Chinese. She must have heard the mirror break.

Jesse hoped she didn't come up to check on them. The mirror chunks might be hard to explain.

"Everything's fine," Shang called back in English. "Just a small accident. I'll clean it up." He opened the envelope, took out a printed sheet of paper and read silently.

"What is it?" Lilly asked.

Shang's forehead wrinkled in confusion. "A rejection letter from a publisher. They wish me all the luck with my manuscript, but feel that contemporary fantasy isn't right for the market at this time."

Lilly edged closer to Shang. "I didn't know you were a writer."

"Obviously I'm not," Shang said. "At least not a good one."

The shards of mirror sat on the dresser like the pieces of a jagged puzzle. Jesse picked up a couple of bigger ones and threw them in the trash can. "You don't remember writing a book?" If Shang didn't remember doing it, then the story most likely involved dragons.

Shang shrugged. "I don't remember writing a novel, sending it anywhere, or getting this letter, but it's addressed to me."

Dragons it was, then. Shang had written about being a Slayer.

Lilly turned to Jesse. "He wouldn't have put secrets into a novel and then sent it off to a stranger to get it published."

Jesse's mom had worked on a book with one of her history teacher friends, so he knew a little about the process. "You don't send publishers your entire book right off. You send editors a letter about the story. If they're interested, they ask for the manuscript."

Shang tossed the letter on his desk. "Why would I tell myself to look for a rejection letter?"

"Because then you'd look for the manuscript," Jesse said. "I think you should find it and read it."

Lilly picked up the letter and scanned it. "*Terror from the Sky*. Sounds like an interesting book."

"It's probably buried in one of your computer folders," Jesse said.

Shang took the letter from Lilly and reread it. "Do you think the story has to do with the drug case?"

"Maybe not the drug case," Jesse said. "But something else."

"We'll come visit again later," Lilly added. "And you can tell us about it." Her voice held more optimism now.

Unjustified optimism. Even if Shang knew the truth about what he used to be, it wouldn't change much. He had still lost his powers and wouldn't get them back for years, if at all. Despite this fact, Jesse didn't feel quite so hopeless anymore either. If Shang knew the truth about himself, the Slayers might not have completely lost him after all.

 # CHAPTER 29

When Tori got home from school, she promptly ditched Lars. This involved telling him that she was doing homework, then climbing out of her second-story bedroom window. Perhaps it wasn't the safest thing she'd ever done, but really, why had her parents ever let her go rappelling if they didn't expect her to use the skill in real life?

She drove to DC to make a surprise visit to her father, speeding when she could. The flash drive lay on the passenger seat like an offering—no, a move in a chess game. It was still in the bag so it wouldn't pick up fingerprints or any traces of fibers from her or her car. She parked farther from the senate building than she needed so she could pretend to have met a mysterious stranger on the walk over. She did, in fact, pass several shadowy people, or perhaps they were just tourists—that was part of the mystery.

Honestly, if Dr. B was going to give her assignments, he ought to come up with credible stories to go along with them.

The senate building was a massive structure of gray granite and arched windows. Columns were suspended in a row halfway up the structure, as though the second floor wanted to belong in Rome, but the ground floor was too practical for such things. The impression Tori always got when she went inside was that everyone imagined themselves to be very important and very busy. Even after you showed your ID to the security guards, they glowered as if you were smuggling explosives in your skirt.

Fortunately, her father's secretary, Mrs. Wright, was friendly. Whenever she saw Tori, she always smiled and asked about school.

Today Tori swept up to Mrs. Wright's desk, blinked back a hint of fake tears, and said, "I really need to see my dad. It's an emergency. I have this problem and I need to talk to him. Can you get me in?"

Mrs. Wright tutted over Tori in concern. "Of course, hon. He's never too busy to be your father." She rescheduled a meeting with a lobbyist, and ten minutes later, Mrs. Wright escorted Tori into her father's office. "You two take all the time you need," she said, then left, shutting the door behind her.

Her father looked up from his desk, far less concerned than Mrs. Wright had been. "Tori. What are you doing here?"

Still trying to come up with a credible story. She sat in one of the chairs and struck what she hoped was a wistful pose. "Um, I needed to get out of the house, so I decided to visit you . . ."

He eyed her, looking nearly as suspicious as the security guards. "Really?"

This was it; she'd just have to go with the mysterious-stranger story. "Yeah. But then on the way, something . . . well, something really weird happened."

"Let me guess," her dad broke in. "Did it involve Lars calling you repeatedly as he tried to track you down?"

"No," she said, taking her phone from her coat pocket to check. "Oh, actually yes, I guess he did." Wow. He'd discovered she was missing a lot sooner than she'd expected.

"Right," her dad said. "Because *that* wouldn't be weird.

That would be Lars doing the job he's paid to do. You, on the other hand, don't seem to have any notion of what a bodyguard is for." Her father pressed the call button to his secretary. "Marylenn, could you call my wife and Lars? Tell them that Tori is here."

Mrs. Wright's voice came back over the speaker. "Already done."

Tori shifted in the chair. "Sorry to worry everyone." The wistful pose had done no good, so she straightened. "But shouldn't I be allowed to visit my father without a tall humorless man tagging along? It's not like the senate building is a dangerous place to go."

Her father tapped his pen against his desk in irritation. "We've talked about this. You didn't tell anyone where you were going, and you didn't answer your phone."

She hadn't taken Lars along because he would have known she'd made up the story about the flash drive.

She gazed at the ceiling, letting out a martyr-like sigh. "I wanted to visit my father—you know, so I could privately talk to you about stuff, like, um, the difficulties of being a teenager. I thought you'd be happy to see me. Now I feel unwanted."

Her father raised an unconvinced eyebrow. "Your desire to spend time with me would be more touching if I didn't know you'd climbed out of your window to get past Lars to do it."

Tori let out an indignant cough. How had Lars known that part? "Was he watching my bedroom door? That's just creepy, Dad."

Her father went back to tapping his pen. "So what was the weird thing that happened on the way here?"

Right. That. Tori's thoughts snapped back to the mission. "While I was walking here, this man came over—he must have recognized me, because he asked me to give you this." She pulled the flash drive from her purse, got up from her chair, and dropped it on his desk. "He said it had incriminating evidence on Senator Ethington. Something about him being involved in an arms smuggling deal that's going to happen tomorrow morning. If the man was right, then you've got to stop Senator Ethington."

With a huff of exasperation, her father picked up the flash drive. "Strange men are approaching you on the street, and you wonder why you have to have a bodyguard."

"The man wasn't strange. He wore a business suit, and he was clean-shaven, and um, really credible looking."

Her father pointed his finger at her. "From now on, you will assume that anywhere you're going, Lars will be with you."

Tori slumped back into her seat. "Dad, I think the thing you should be concentrating on is that Senator Ethington could be involved in criminal activity."

"That's a serious accusation." Her father turned his attention to the flash drive. "If the mystery man had evidence, why didn't he turn it over to the FBI?"

"He said he did, but they're too slow, and this thing is happening tomorrow morning. You can stop it."

Her father put the drive into one of the laptops on his desk, scanned for viruses, and then frowned at whatever had come up on his screen. The frown darkened as he read. Finally, he clicked the audio link. Senator Ethington's voice came over the speakers, muffled but distinct.

I'll make sure the container makes it through customs. Be sure your men are there to pick it up. And don't do something stupid like speeding so the cops have a reason to pull you over.

There was a pause while he listened to the other speaker.

You'll get the money when the inventory is checked. Last time you shorted us thirty AK-103s. We won't pay for guns you don't deliver.

Another pause.

It had better be. Call me when you leave Newark.

The recording ended. Tori's father stared at the computer, his expression still dark.

Tori waited for him to speak. When he didn't, she said, "You're going to make sure the FBI is at the Newark port in the morning, right?"

Before answering, her father scrolled through the documents again. "It sounds like his voice. Might not be, though." He shook his head. "I disagree with Ethington about a lot of things, but I can't believe he'd be involved with smuggling arms." He gestured to the flash drive. "This is probably a joke or a setup to make me look ridiculous."

"It's not," Tori said, perhaps too emphatically. "What if he *is* smuggling in weapons? You can't risk people's safety by ignoring it."

"I'll look into it."

"There's no time for that. The shipment arrives in the morning."

He leaned back in his seat and let his hands fall into his lap. "Tori, I'll take care of it."

"What does that mean?"

"It means I'm not allowed to discuss matters of national security with my teenage daughter. I never should have played that recording in your presence."

"But . . ." The word died on her lips. No matter what she said, he wouldn't tell her anything else. She sighed in resignation. "Okay."

He folded his arms. "Did you actually have something you wanted to talk about, or did you come down here just to pull Lars's chain?"

As if that were an either/or question. She scooted forward in her chair, getting ready to stand. "I guess I should go home and work on my article for journalism."

Her father nodded, his attention back on his computer screen.

"You'll let me know how things at the port turn out?"

"Probably not. Again, it's national security."

She let out another sigh, this one laced with annoyance. "I want to help the country too. I'm capable of a lot more than you realize."

His gaze left the monitor for long enough to give her a tolerant smile. "Of course you are. You're my daughter. But before you delve into politics, espionage, or international affairs, you'd better go finish your homework."

She stood and walked to the door, annoyed. Honestly, her father would never take her seriously. Before leaving, she turned back. "Dad? One more thing. While you're thinking about whether those weapons are a real threat, I want you to imagine one being used against me. Because it could be."

The chance, in fact, was much more likely than he realized.

 CHAPTER 30

A ringing phone woke Overdrake early Friday morning. One look at the screen told him it was Cordero, his man in charge of New Jersey operations. A call at this hour couldn't be good news. Overdrake sat up, still groggy, and answered the phone.

"What's wrong?"

"The Coast Guard was tipped off about our shipment," Cordero said. "They did a surprise check on all cargo heading into Newark."

Overdrake swore and rubbed his eyes. "What's the damage?"

"They confiscated everything, including the ship."

Overdrake swore again, this time so loudly that his wife woke up and gave him a questioning look. He lowered his voice. "Any of our men arrested?"

"Only those on the ship. The port workers are clear. The feds won't find any evidence that leads them to us."

The news could have been worse. This was only one shipment, and his men at the port hadn't been compromised. Still, anger pulsed through Overdrake, first hot and then cold. "If the feds were tipped off, we have a leak. Find it and plug it."

Cordero grunted. "It wasn't anyone in my chain. Capitol Hill got involved and ordered the search."

Capitol Hill? "Who?" Overdrake demanded.

There was a pause as though Cordero had to search somewhere for the name. "Senator Hampton. He pulled strings in the Coast Guard."

Overdrake grit his teeth. If Senator Hampton was involved, then Tori probably was too. Somehow the Slayers had found out about the deal, and Tori had convinced her father to call in the feds.

Now her father would no doubt believe her about other things. Had she already told him about the dragons? Would she admit to being a Slayer? Dr. B had always been adamant that the Slayers not tell their parents about their abilities, but maybe the man was willing to sacrifice having Tori on the team if it meant gaining Senator Hampton's ear.

Overdrake gripped his phone harder. "How many people knew the details of the shipment?"

Cordero's voice slowed. "The seller, the pickup crew, and our inspectors. I reported to Mr. Smith on Wednesday. I used a new cell phone, but he might have been compromised somehow."

Mr. Smith was their name for Senator Ethington.

"I'll talk to him," Overdrake said. "Call if you have more news."

He ended the call and lay back in bed, staring tight-lipped at the ceiling. Cassie put a comforting arm over his chest. "What's wrong?"

He rubbed her arm, his mind still on the phone call. "Nothing you need to worry about." He didn't tell Cassie more than he had to about his doings. That way he never had to worry about whether he could trust her.

He'd learned the hard way that he couldn't automatically trust family.

At least this time, Dirk still had his trust. His son couldn't have had anything to do with the leak. Even if he'd figured out a way to break into Overdrake's files, Dirk wouldn't have discovered anything. Overdrake hadn't written down the plans anywhere. He'd let Cordero handle this operation.

Delegation had a way of leading to problems, but he couldn't do everything by himself. He had to entrust some of the aspects of the revolution to others. Unfortunately, people kept letting him down, kept proving their incompetence.

And now the Slayers had an inside link to his organization. Could they have figured out that Ethington worked for him?

Unlikely, yet the possibility worried him anyway.

Ethington was too confident. The man's ego had grown along with his poll numbers, and now he saw himself as some sort of human version of Manifest Destiny. He'd even hinted that Overdrake needed to listen to *him*, rather than the other way around.

"When I'm in office," Ethington had said just last week, "we won't need a revolution. We'll simply rule the country the way it's supposed to be ruled."

We. Ethington should have understood Overdrake well enough by now to know there would be no *we*. There would also be no bargaining with Congress. No hoping the Supreme Court ruled the way he wanted them to. Overdrake hadn't come all this way to share power.

"When you're in office," Overdrake had retorted, "you will appoint who I want, where I want them, and you will disable the military as I've instructed. When I attack, you will surrender quickly. *That* will be your only important job in office."

This had always been their plan. Overdrake had funded Ethington's political career, made him what he was, and even agreed to let him be the regime's figurehead. But now that

Senator Ethington had the taste of power on his tongue, he was getting harder to control.

Had the senator, in his careless confidence, failed to safeguard the details about the weapons shipment? As a presidential frontrunner, the man had enemies on both sides of the aisle. Maybe Overdrake was jumping to conclusions in assuming Tori was involved.

Then again, he ought to make sure she wouldn't be a problem in the future, just in case.

CHAPTER 31

After Tori ate breakfast, her dad called her into the den and reported that the raid had indeed found weapons. He walked across the room, quizzing her about the informant's appearance, trying to find any identifying features.

"We need to know who that man was. He may have other important information."

Dr. B did have lots of information, but none Tori could share with him. She kept her answers vague. "I don't remember much of what he looked like. I mean, the whole conversation lasted half a minute. Can't you just turn the flash drive over to the FBI and let them deal with Senator Ethington? The weapons are proof he was involved."

Her father shook his head. "I already turned the flash drive over to the FBI. But it's not enough. The file could have been faked, and I'm not sure myself whether the voice actually was Senator Ethington, or just someone trying to implicate him. Some people will do anything to push a candidate off the ticket. Wouldn't be hard to piece together audio of what sounds like a candidate saying whatever you want. We've all got years of recorded speeches to draw on."

"He's guilty," Tori said. "I know he is."

"You may be right," her dad said, pacing in front of the

desk, "but there's not enough evidence to prove it. If I could contact the informant and get more evidence, new leads, things might be different."

Yes, they'd be very different, although not necessarily better. What would her father make of Dr. B's methods, none of which were legal? The authorities needed to gather their own evidence to convict the senator of any wrongdoing.

"The FBI has reason to suspect Ethington now," Tori said. "They'll tap his phone, follow him, do whatever they need to catch him, right?"

Her father sat down in his chair, frustration evident in every movement. "Maybe, maybe not. The FBI is hesitant to spy on presidential candidates. It could be construed as political muckraking."

"Don't they care about national security?"

"Of course they do. But they also have to follow the law in regards to people's rights and civil liberties."

"Red tape." Tori crossed her arms and scowled. "That's what will destroy the country—not bombs or an EMP. It'll be red tape. Don't you ever want to cut through all that and get things done?"

"Every day. But that's not how the system works. Sometimes our hands are tied."

Maybe her father's hands were tied, but hers weren't. Not as long as her parents didn't know she was a Slayer. And right then, she finally stopped wishing she could tell her father the truth.

* * *

Tori's talk with her father put her behind in her morning schedule; she was nearly late to school. Lars had an unhealthy obsession with driving the speed limit, and no amount of assurance on Tori's part that he wouldn't be pulled over for driving five miles over would make him apply more pressure to the gas pedal. In fact, she was pretty sure he slowed down a few times to spite her.

Really, you ditched a guy a couple of times and he got all childish and vindictive.

When Tori finally made it to journalism, she found Jesse in his seat. Tacy sat next to him, leaning over as she talked. She was blonde and beautiful and practically oozing charm all over his desk.

Tori strolled over anyway. She was supposed to act flirty with him so people wouldn't be surprised when they became a couple. Tacy would just have to get used it.

When she reached Jesse, Tori tried to think of something clever to say, even though she wanted to talk about busting the smuggling operation and her irritation over the unlikely odds of the FBI locking up Ethington anytime soon. Of course, she couldn't mention any of that with other people around.

"Hey," she said gesturing to Jesse's polo shirt. "I like your outfit. Where'd you get it?" It was a lame joke, and an old one about their uniforms. Everyone wore red or white polo shirts. Boys wore tan pants, girls red and plaid skirts.

Tacy sent Tori an unimpressed look, a message to back off. Tacy clearly didn't want her time with Jesse interrupted.

He smoothed his shirt. "I bought this at a shop that made me feel like I was enrolling in Hogwarts. You?"

Tori leaned back against the empty desk on Jesse's other side. "I got mine at the same place. Did they give you a wand?"

"I must have missed that aisle."

"That's okay," Tacy broke in. "Not all guys need a wand to cast a spell."

Cheesy line. Granted, a lot of flirting was made up of cheesy lines, but still.

Jesse smiled at Tacy and then glanced at Tori with a questioning look. Was he expecting her to top that?

"She's right," Tori said in an attempt to recapture the flirting high ground. "You have magic potential. Definitely."

Melinda walked up and joined the group. "Who's magical?"

"Jonathan." Tacy turned to him. She had her come-hither smile down. Not too obvious, but still inviting.

Tori tried again. "And if you ever need a magician's assistant . . ." She regretted the sentence immediately. It was borderline pathetic.

Tacy snorted and rolled her eyes. "Do you need someone to cut you in half, Tori? Or do you just want to put on a sparkly costume?"

Melinda laughed uncomfortably, her gaze bouncing between Jesse, Tori, and Tacy.

This was not going how Tori had planned. When had she gotten so bad at flirting?

Jesse smiled, amused, and leaned back in his chair. He was enjoying the fight for his attention a little too much.

"Anything to get out of wearing a plaid skirt," Tori said, in what she hoped was a lighthearted and not skanky manner.

Jesse raised an eyebrow, indicating her answer had come out skanky anyway. "I wouldn't let Roland hear you say that. He might change the lyrics to your song."

Tacy perked up at this bit of news. "Did Roland write Tori a love song? That's so sweet." To Jesse she added, "Roland and Tori are sort of an item."

"So I've heard," Jesse said dryly.

"No, we're not," Tori insisted. "We're just friends."

"Really?" Tacy asked with false innocence. "I thought you were together."

"No, I'm completely free." That also sounded pathetic. "You know . . . I mean . . ." Time to change the subject. "Did you hear about Newark?" She was asking Jesse whether Dr. B had given him the news this morning.

He didn't seem to understand. "No. What happened?"

"Oh, well . . ." She'd have to tell him about it later. "The Coast Guard caught some smugglers."

Everyone stared at her for a moment and then Tacy said, "That's a random piece of news."

Dr. Meyerhoff walked into the room, sipping a cup of coffee as he headed to his desk. "Take your seats, please."

"We'd better sit down," Melinda said, and motioned for Tori to walk with her to their chairs in the back of the room.

Tori started after her, then looked over her shoulder. "Talk to you later, Jesse."

"Jonathan," Melinda corrected.

"Right. I meant Jonathan." Ugh. Tori couldn't believe she'd slipped up. She was no doubt going to hear about *that* later.

After they settled into their desks, Melinda leaned close and lowered her voice. "Okay, as your friend, I think it's time to hold an intervention." She held out her hand to emphasize her point. "I know you think Jonathan is hot, but that was the most dismal attempt of throwing yourself at a guy I've ever seen."

"I wasn't throwing myself at him," Tori whispered back.

Melinda fixed her with an I'm-not-buying-it stare.

"Okay, maybe I was throwing myself at him a little. But *dismal* is a strong word."

"You offered to be his assistant, told him you wanted to get out of your skirt, and then got his name wrong."

Tori slouched down in her seat. "All right, it was kind of dismal."

Dr. Meyerhoff was shuffling through his notes at the front of the room.

Melinda cast a glance at him and then spoke to Tori again. "In the future, if you want to make small talk, remember that throwing out crime facts from other states isn't the best way to do it."

That was unfair. True, maybe, but unfair.

"I have a feeling he likes me anyway," Tori said. "I mean, he smiled at me."

Melinda considered Tori's statement with marked skepticism. "You might be able to salvage your chances if you start acting less needy and strange." She leaned closer, all pep talk now. "Have some pride. Use a little aloofness. Make him work for it. You're Tori Hampton."

Thankfully, Dr. Meyerhoff began his lesson, cutting off any more flirting advice from Melinda. Tori opened her notebook and tried to put thoughts of Jesse out of her mind. She had to force herself to keep her eyes on the teacher so they didn't wander to Jesse's dark hair. Or to his broad shoulders. Or to the way the muscles in his arm moved as he took notes.

She was hopeless, really.

Halfway through class, she heard Overdrake's voice in her mind. He was near a dragon and talking to her.

"Tori, we haven't chatted for a while. Perhaps for too long."

Heat rushed through her, her senses suddenly alert, on fire.

"Dirk might have told you that I've agreed not to hurt you so long as you're not fighting against me. He seems to think there's hope for you as a dragon lord, and he may be right. He knows you better than I do."

Overdrake's voice was light, almost casual, but it had a hard undercurrent to it. "So as a courtesy to both of you, I'm officially warning you to stay out of my business. You can have a long and happy life, Tori. You can have whatever it is Dirk wants to give you. But if you cross me . . . don't think I can't get to you or your family. I can. I can get to your sister, your parents, to anyone and anything you care about, including your dog."

Tori swallowed hard. She'd been right. He'd taken her dog.

"Brindy, isn't it? That's what the tag said."

Tori shut her eyes. She wished she had a way to yell at Overdrake, to tell him he'd better not even think of hurting anyone in her family. Instead she was stuck in class, silently listening, and helpless to do anything.

She gripped her pencil, waiting to see if Overdrake would say more. The teacher's lecture became a meaningless background buzz. Where was Brindy now? Was she still alive?

Students weren't allowed to use phones in class. If she was caught with one out, it would be confiscated. Still, she wanted to message Dirk and ask if he knew that his father had taken her dog.

If Dirk knew that his father had taken Brindy, she wanted to yell at him for letting it happen. If he didn't know, she wanted him to get mad at his father. And she wanted him to find out where Brindy was and take her someplace safe.

She waited until Dr. Meyerhoff was writing on the whiteboard and then rifled through her bag for her phone.

"Do you know how dragons eat?" Overdrake asked. "If they're hungry, and the animal is large—say, human size—they bite their prey in half and eat it in two large gulps. If there's an abundance of prey, however, they just break the animal's back to keep it from escaping. It's a slow, painful death, but one that keeps the meat fresh longer. I'm sure you don't want to see your family end up crippled and waiting for the inevitable. You wouldn't want to make your parents watch your sister be ripped apart, would you?"

Fear and rage twisted inside Tori, making it hard to breathe. Her hands trembled as she searched her bag.

"Imagine your family at my enclosure," he went on. "Because that's what will happen if there are any more unexpected raids on my men."

She heard a whine next to the dragon, the sound of a frightened dog.

"Need more convincing? An object lesson, perhaps?"

A gasp escaped Tori's lips. Was he going to feed Brindy to a dragon?

She'd heard the cries of pigs and the bellows of cattle when being fed to a dragon. Never a dog.

Another yelp came, almost a shriek. It was cut short.

"No!" Tori actually yelled the word. She put a shaking hand to her mouth and listened, hoping to hear Overdrake's assuring that Brindy was okay, that it was all just a threat.

Dr. Meyerhoff stopped writing on the whiteboard in surprise. "You have objections to The Freedom of Information Act, Miss Hampton?"

She stared at him wide-eyed, unable to answer. The whole class had turned to gawk at her, a sea of perplexed gazes.

She heard crunching, the sound of bones breaking.

Tori let out a half-gasp, half-cry. Her stomach turned. She tried to minimize her hearing as much as she could. She didn't want to hear more. Couldn't handle what she'd already heard.

Everyone was peering at her, but she couldn't explain her behavior.

Jesse's gaze went to hers, worried. He, at least, understood that she must have heard something disturbing. He seemed to be waiting to see if she touched her watch to send Dr. B an attack message.

She didn't. Dr. B could do nothing about Brindy. This wasn't a situation that warranted putting the Slayers on alert.

Dr. Meyerhoff looked her over, trying to see the cause of her outburst. "Are you all right?"

"I—I'm sick." She grabbed her bag and stood up. "I have to go." She headed to the door, fighting the tears that pressed against her eyes.

"Check in with the school nurse," Dr. Meyerhoff called.

She was out the door before she could reply.

Overdrake was speaking again. "Leave the Slayers. You aren't really one of them, and they all know that. You're a socialite. Go back to your shopping and your friends. Go back to travel, chocolate, and whatever else you do." His tone grew more clipped. "But stay out of my way, or next time, it won't be a dog you hear."

Tori looked around the hallway, unsure of where to go or what to do. She wanted to leave, wanted to call her family and assure herself that they were all right. She couldn't. Her parents would ask why she was calling in the middle of the day, crying. And if she went to the office and claimed to be ill, the nurse would put her through an array of questions. Tori didn't feel capable of speaking, let alone sitting through the pretense of getting her temperature taken.

She walked numbly toward one of the side doors. She'd go outside and either hide behind a tree on the grounds or disappear into the bleachers until she calmed down.

Be angry, she told herself, *not sad. Let the anger focus you so the sadness can't overwhelm you.* But it was hard to think logically about anything. The memory of Brindy's final cries were looping through her mind.

She turned down a short side hallway that led to one of the emergency exits. They were locked from the outside but had to be kept unlocked from the inside in case of fire. Students weren't supposed to use them except in an emergency.

Through the door's window, she saw trees, fading autumn grass, and the back of the bleachers ringing the athletic field. She reached for the door handle but then hesitated. Had Overdrake figured out she hadn't changed schools when she moved?

What if he'd talked to her just now to flush her out of the building? What if his men were waiting for her out there? They could have breached the school grounds. This could be an ambush.

Tori dropped her hand, from the door undecided. She hated that she'd reached the point where she couldn't even walk out of her own school without worrying about her safety.

Well, forget that. She refused to be a prisoner in her own life. She'd go outside if she wanted to. She needed to be alone.

Tori put her hand back on the handle but didn't push it open. She couldn't afford to be careless. Her life wasn't the only one hanging in the balance. She had to stay safe to protect people against a dragon attack. Her life wasn't her own anymore. Despite what Overdrake said, for her, there was no going back to the way things used to be.

She stepped away from the door, feeling defeated, then leaned back against the wall and slid to the floor. With head in hands, she let the tears come. Everyone in class probably thought she'd had some sort of nervous breakdown, and if she didn't pull herself together before the bell rang, people would see her crying here—and yet she couldn't even go outside for privacy.

This is what being a Slayer had done to her.

A pair of footsteps sounded in the main hallway. She hoped whoever it was would pass by. They didn't. Instead, they came down the side hallway toward her. She didn't want to look up, didn't want to see anyone. But what if it was one of Overdrake's men? Her head snapped up.

Jesse was walking toward her. She slumped in relief.

He sat on the floor beside her and gathered her into a hug, cradling her to him. He was warm and strong, everything she needed. "What happened?" he asked.

She rested her cheek against his chest, took deep breaths, and told him everything.

He let out a sigh, but his muscles didn't tighten in outrage like she'd expected. Instead, they relaxed. Perhaps he'd been expecting worse. "I'm so sorry, Tori."

"He threatened my family," she emphasized.

"We'll warn your bodyguards."

She shook her head. "We get threats all the time. This doesn't change anything, it's just . . . this is so personal." She wiped at her eyes, trying not to smear her mascara into a mess in the process. "You probably think it's silly to get so upset about Brindy, when Overdrake will be attacking cities soon enough."

Jesse kept his hand on her back and rubbed her shoulder, a soft motion a consolation. "I don't think it's silly. Overdrake is striking where he knows he can hurt you. He wants to break you. But you can't let him. "

She shut her eyes. "What if I can't help breaking?"

His hand traveled down her back to her arm and then found her hand. "You're stronger than that. Others paid for our freedom in the past, and now it's our turn."

She didn't answer. He was right. The ghosts of patriots could make a line stretching from one end of the country to the other.

"Dr. B should know what happened," Jesse said. "Do you want me to tell him so you don't have to?"

She nodded. "Thanks." While Jesse pushed the buttons on his watch to call Dr. B, Tori found her phone in her bag and wrote to Dirk, telling him what his father had done.

Did you know about it? she asked at the end.

Overdrake would see the message. She was sure now that he had access to the account. Not long ago, she'd told Dirk she was born for travel, chocolate, and sleeping in. Overdrake had just echoed the same words, telling her to go back to those things. It couldn't be coincidence.

Dirk didn't answer right away. She hadn't expected him to. He was probably in school or busy somewhere plotting with his father's minions. She shoved her phone back into her bag.

When Jesse was done with Dr. B, he put his arm around her again. "Dr. B said to tell you he's sorry about Brindy."

Tori nodded and leaned in to Jesse.

"Someday, all of this will be over," he said. "You won't always have to deal with Overdrake."

That time seemed far away and indistinct, a dream that might blink away. Still, she had to do this—she had to be a Slayer. No matter what Overdrake said, she didn't have a choice. She could feel the eyes of those ghostly patriots all watching her.

"I want to talk about fighting patterns," she said suddenly. "We need to make more changes to them." They'd been altering patterns ever since Dirk betrayed them because he'd known all the old ones.

The topic was an abrupt change, but Tori couldn't bear to sit there like a victim anymore. She had to do something to oppose Overdrake, to defeat him so he couldn't hurt anyone else.

By the time the bell rang for second period, she'd stopped crying, but her eyes were probably puffy and red. She didn't want to face people looking like that, didn't want to answer their inevitable questions. Instead of getting up, she stayed on the floor where she was. Students began walking by, casting glances at her and Jesse.

"Will you be okay?" Jesse asked.

"Yeah. You can go to second period."

Jesse didn't get up or move his arm off her shoulder. "Want to go home?"

"No." She couldn't go to the nurse's office with puffy, red eyes. Anyone would be able to tell that she was upset, not sick, and instead of talking to a nurse, she'd end up in a counselor's office. "What am I going to say when people ask why I randomly yelled, 'No!' during class and then rushed out?"

Jesse thought it over for a moment. "You peeked at your phone and saw a text from your sister saying that your dog had been hit by a car. Everyone will understand."

She nodded. It was a good story and would work as long as none of her friends said anything to her family about Brindy. Tori could probably ensure that never happened. She'd tell her friends that Brindy's death was a touchy subject, and ask them not to bring it up around her family.

"What was your excuse for leaving class?" she asked.

"I didn't give one. I just walked out."

She cocked her head. "Is that allowed in public schools?"

"No. I'm sure I'll hear about it from Dr. Meyerhoff. And my parents."

She sighed. "Sorry to get you in trouble."

His arm dropped from around her shoulders and he gave her hand a squeeze. "They can't get too mad at me for wanting to make sure you're all right."

And she was all right. At least, she would be. She stood, smoothed her hair, and steeled herself to face the world again. "I guess we'd better go to class." She didn't want to be late to second period.

Jesse got to his feet and brushed off his pants. "On the bright side, enough people saw us sitting here that we shouldn't have to do anything else for people to know we're a couple."

She thought of Melinda's words. *You might be able to salvage your chances if you start acting less needy and strange.*

Well, Tori hadn't exactly followed that advice. It was nice to know that Jesse was interested anyway.

CHAPTER 32

Dirk didn't see Tori's message until he came home from school, and then he read it with surprise. That morning at breakfast when his father had told him Brindy actually belonged to Tori and that he planned to use the dog as a warning, Dirk had vetoed the idea. Vehemently.

They were alone during that conversation. Bridget was homeschooled, so she usually slept in. If his sister had been there, their father never would have admitted any of this. Bridget loved the dog and was beginning to consider it her own. Dirk hadn't pointed that out. His father listened to strategy, not emotion.

"I'm trying to convince Tori to join us," Dirk had said. "I can't do that if you're knocking off her pets."

His father had only waved his fork dismissively. "She killed two of mine. I'm just returning the favor."

"No," Dirk said. "You're burning bridges. My bridges. And you'll gain nothing by it."

His father cut through his omelet with more force than needed. "If it means she stays away from future arms deals, that's a gain."

"You don't know Tori like I do. She'll be more determined to fight you if you threaten her."

His father had finally relented, and even promised Dirk he wouldn't use Brindy as dragon food.

Now Dirk reread Tori's message and strode into his father's office, phone in hand, ready to hit something. Maybe his father. The man hadn't kept his word for even an entire day. Didn't a promise mean anything to him? If not, where did that leave Dirk? Could he trust his father about anything?

His father sat in at his desk, reading through reports while Brindy slept at his feet.

Dirk was so surprised he just stood there, gripping the phone.

The dog lifted her head and wagged her tail, whole and well.

"Something wrong?" his father asked.

Dirk lowered the phone. "Why does Tori think you killed her dog?"

His father went back to scanning his reports. "Because it's a good idea to let your enemies know what you're capable of. She'll think twice about crossing me again. She knows I'm capable of taking more than her dog."

"She already knew that. You don't have to torment her pets." Dirk walked over to Brindy and knelt in front of her. He ran his hands over her back, checking for injuries. He didn't find any. His father must have only taken the dog near the dragon enclosure to scare her into yelping.

"You promised me—" Dirk began.

His father cut him off. "I kept my promise. Tori may have heard another dog's demise and assumed it was Brindy's. I never said it was."

Great. His father had still killed a dog. Dirk didn't make an objection. His father already thought Dirk was soft for wanting to spare people. "You say you want my help to lead the country, but you never listen to anything I say. You made things worse with Tori, not better."

His father had made a point today, as he said, but not only to Tori. He'd shown Dirk that no matter what he said, he'd find a way to bend his promises to do whatever he wanted.

Fine. Dirk would make a point of his own. He took hold of Brindy's collar and led her toward the door. "I'm taking the dog back to Tori."

His father looked up from his computer with a smug smile. "Fine. Tell her hi for me. I'm sure she'll be happy to see you."

Dirk shut the door behind him, more bothered by his father's response than he should have been. His father didn't object to the dog's return, which was a good thing. He could have turned it into a power struggle. What bothered Dirk was that he wasn't sure whether his father had said the last sentence sarcastically or not. Was he trying to ensure Dirk and Tori stayed on opposite sides of the fight, or was this whole thing with the dog his father's skewed idea of matchmaking? Did he think Tori would see Dirk as some sort of hero for returning Brindy to her?

If so, his father didn't understand women at all. At least, not Tori.

Dirk led Brindy into the family room, where Bridget had turned the couch and half of the floor into a doll resort. Pink plastic furniture covered everything.

He handed Bridget his phone. "Can you take a picture of me with the dog?"

She slid off the couch and snapped a picture without question. She'd taken so many of Brindy herself, she probably didn't think to wonder why he wanted one. He took the phone and forwarded the picture to Tori.

Bridget pulled a baby bonnet from one of her dolls and

draped it across Brindy's head. "Now can you take a picture of me with her?"

"Just a minute. I'm texting Tori."

Bridget tied the bonnet around Brindy's ears. The dog immediately shook her head, making the bonnet fall off on one side and hang lopsided.

"Is it a love letter?" Bridget asked. She'd met Tori once and thought they were a couple.

"No, I just need to find a way to return the dog to her. She belongs to Tori."

Bridget tried to straighten the bonnet, an impossible task, because Brindy kept licking her hand. "But I want to keep her. Can't Tori share with us? She could come over and visit Peppermint whenever she wants."

"The dog's name is Brindy."

"She can be Peppermint at our house, and Brindy at Tori's."

Dirk sent the message and turned his attention to the dog. "We'll need to get her kennel so she can travel." He would be safer flying the dog to Tori instead of driving. That way, he wouldn't have to worry about being stuck in traffic or followed on the way back. He shouldn't fly to anywhere public, though. Where would a good meeting spot be?

Bridget pouted and held on to Brindy's collar. "Why doesn't Tori come to our house to get her?"

"She doesn't get along with Dad."

"Why?"

Dirk probably shouldn't have even said that much. Bridget knew Slayers existed, but she didn't know he'd been one of them, or that he still had loyalties to the group. She also didn't know that Tori was a Slayer, only that Tori was part dragon lord. By an unspoken pact, Dirk and his father had never told

Bridget the rest, each for his own reasons. Dirk didn't want to let his sister know he'd helped the Slayers kill two dragons, and his father didn't want her to know that he'd set dragons on Dirk and his friends.

"You'll understand when you're older."

Bridget folded her arms and harrumphed. "I will not. I'll forget by then."

"Why don't you get some toys for Brindy to keep her company?" They didn't have dog toys at their house. The guard dogs got bones and leftovers from the dragon. They were happy enough with those.

Brindy, on the other hand, assumed that all Bridget's stuffed animals were, in fact, dog toys, and had turned any she found on the floor into piles of fluff.

Bridget relented a little at this suggestion. She seemed to like the idea of packing up dog accessories. She knelt in front of Brindy and petted her throat. "I'll let you have some teddy bears. Tori will be so surprised."

CHAPTER 33

Tori stared at her cell phone in surprise. She was in her room doing homework and had opened the picture as soon as Dirk sent it. There he was, standing next to a German shepherd. If it wasn't Brindy, it was a dog that looked just like her. What did the picture mean? Did he think Tori needed more proof they'd stolen her dog? Stolen and killed her? The picture of Brindy—her large brown eyes so calm and trusting—made Tori's throat tight. And yet she couldn't believe Dirk would send a picture to be cruel.

Had Overdrake sent it? Was this his way of saying that Dirk had completely turned on her?

Another message popped up on her screen. *Brindy is fine. My dad didn't hurt her. Let's arrange a place to meet, and I'll bring her to you.*

A shiver of hope went through Tori. She did her best to repress it. She wasn't even sure if Dirk was the one sending the message, and now he wanted to meet somewhere? It could be a trap. Probably was a trap. But what if Brindy really was alive?

She wrote back, *Prove that Brindy is really alive. You have twenty seconds to send me a picture of you with her begging in front of you. Say "treat" and she'll do it.*

Tori hit send and waited. If it was Overdrake, he'd need a

lot longer than twenty seconds to photoshop a picture of a German shepherd begging in front of Dirk.

Fifteen seconds later, a picture came back. Brindy stood on her hind legs, paws lifted, looking expectantly at Dirk.

Tori let out a gasp of happiness. Brindy was alive, and Dirk was the one sending the messages. Relief washed over her. Then she took a closer look at the picture and wondered what the white thing tied to the dog's head was. A bandage of some kind? Why did it have frills?

What's on Brindy's head?

Dirk's next message read, *It's a baby bonnet. Sorry about that. Bridget likes playing with her, and you didn't give me enough time to take it off. You also didn't tell me that after you say "treat," your dog barks repeatedly if she doesn't get one. I've sent Bridget to find something, and in the meantime Brindy is checking my pockets for treats. Charming habit.*

Tori laughed and wanted to hug the phone. The weight she'd felt all day was gone, replaced by a grateful giddiness. She wanted to bring Brindy home right now and never let her out of sight again. She wouldn't even point out to Dirk that his father was a jerk for taking her. Not yet, anyway. Not until Brindy was safely home.

She wrote, *Take her to a shelter, and I'll send someone to pick her up.*

No, Dirk answered, *I want to see you. We'll need to pick a place I can fly to while carrying a kennel without being seen.*

Tori's giddiness drained away. Dirk not only wanted to meet her, he wanted to do it in some remote location. Not going to happen. Overdrake probably stole her dog just so Tori would agree to that very thing.

How would I know I'm not walking into a trap?

Same way I'll know I'm not walking into a Slayer trap. We'll trust each other.

Small problem. We don't actually trust each other.

She kept her eyes on the screen, waiting for an answer. Five minutes went by, then ten. Was that the end of their discussion? She'd insulted him, so he was done speaking? What would he do with Brindy?

She couldn't return to her homework, couldn't concentrate on it. After fifteen minutes of waiting, she wrote, *Are you there?*

Still no answer. Another five minutes went by.

She was about to type a plea when his voice filtered into her mind. "Tori, can you hear me?"

He'd gone to the dragons so he could talk to her. That's why he hadn't answered. She wrote, *I hear you.*

"Good. So you can tell by my voice I'm not planning to kidnap you or take away your powers. I just want to return Brindy and talk to you. That's all. I'll come alone. My dad and his men won't know where or when we're meeting, so you don't have to worry about them double crossing me and hurting you."

He sounded sincere, truthful. She also sensed a bit of hesitation, had a feeling he wasn't showing all his cards. But that had always been a part of Dirk. Maybe some hesitancy was part of human nature. People always held something back.

She fiddled with her phone, debating how to answer. Was it safe to meet Dirk? What would he do with Brindy if she refused?

Dirk went on. "I'm the one who has no way to tell if you're lying. I can't see your face or hear your voice, but I'm willing to trust that you'll come without backup, that you won't lay a snare for me." He paused. "Although I'm not so willing that I'm going to tell you the meeting place beforehand. Here's the deal. Tonight, after your family has gone to bed and you can get free, message me. I'll let you know where to go. You can't tell any of the other Slayers you're doing this. They'd insist on coming, and I'm only going to show if you're alone. Yes or no?"

Tori hesitated, then typed, *Yes.*

* * *

Homework was a lost cause. She worked on it half-heartedly, unable to make it through her trig problems. Dirk was right. If she told Dr. B or any of the Slayers about meeting Dirk, they wouldn't let her go alone, and they'd most likely try to capture Dirk. Without him, Overdrake could only control one dragon at a time in an attack.

The Slayers had a chance if they were fighting just one dragon. They'd proven that. Okay—barely proven it. And maybe they wouldn't have been able to kill either dragon without a little luck, but still they'd managed it. But two dragons attacking at once? She didn't like those odds.

Her friends' lives could very well depend on whether or not Dirk was in play during an attack. And here was a chance to capture him.

It wasn't as if Dirk didn't deserve to be tricked. He'd deceived them for years, and tried to lead them into an ambush. But any attempt to capture Dirk could end badly for a lot of reasons. He'd be watching for it. He was smart and trained and probably half expecting her and the Slayers to pull something. He'd arrange their meeting in a way that made it hard—and noticeable—for her to deceive him.

If she betrayed him tonight, he'd never trust her again. Any sort of relationship they'd had would be over; any hope of turning him from the path he was on, gone. And any chance of learning about her dragon lord side would also be lost.

Tori wanted to know how to control dragons, needed that

information desperately. Dirk thought that if she knew more about them, she'd change her mind about being a Slayer. If he trusted her, he might eventually tell her everything she needed to know. This was her opportunity to gain his confidence.

Wasn't that better than coming up with a scheme that would most likely fail? A bird in the hand was worth a dragon in the bush.

She would go tonight, and she wouldn't tell Dr. B or anyone else about it.

She wasn't overly worried about her safety, but she wrote two letters anyway, just to be safe. One was for her parents, telling them about the Slayers and Overdrake. The other letter was for Jesse, explaining her reasons for meeting Dirk. She sealed her parents' letter and put it on her bed. They'd find it if she didn't come back. She put the one to Jesse in the outgoing mail pile downstairs, addressed to the school. When she came back tonight, she'd retrieve it.

That left one more thing to take care of. She'd told Aaron she would tell Dirk about him today. Tonight during their meeting would be the best way. She texted Aaron. *I'm going to talk to Dirk tonight. Do you still want him to know about you?*

He texted back. *Yes.*

Well, she'd expected as much.

She went back to her trig, and waited. After a few hours, her family retired to their rooms and the lights went dark. Once she was certain her parents were asleep, she messaged Dirk. *I'm ready.*

She watched her phone, waiting for his answer. Instead of typing one, he went into the dragon enclosure and answered in her mind.

"Leave your Slayer watch at home. Drive toward Great Falls. Once you're close, I'll tell you where to go next."

Tori didn't like taking off her watch, felt vulnerable without it, but she left it on her dresser and went outside. The house had two garages. One attached to the home, the other separate. She always made sure she parked her car in the detached one so if she had to sneak out, no one would wake at the sound of the garage door opening. She got in and drove through the security gates. They would show she'd typed in the code to open them, but she hoped her parents wouldn't have a reason to check the log.

While she drove, she listened to the sounds of the dragon enclosure. She usually heard a scattering of roars, thumps, and other animal noises, along with the piped-in music Overdrake used to muffle whatever the vets might be saying. Before long, those noises faded, replaced by the rhythmic beat of dragon wings.

Dirk flying toward their meeting spot. Tori received several driving instructions from him. Half an hour later, she was in Potomac, Maryland, sitting in an empty parking lot next to an office building—not the kind of secluded location she'd imagined Dirk would choose. Her powers hadn't turned on, so Dirk was still more than five miles away.

One other vehicle sat in the lot, a covered jeep. Last time Tori saw Dirk, he'd driven a black Porsche. She doubted the jeep was his. Still, she got out of the car and texted, *I'm here.*

"I know you are." Dirk's voice called from behind her. She turned to see him gliding down from the roof of the office building, his blond hair dimmed to brown in the evening light. His blue eyes looked dark too, but she'd looked into them enough times she knew what color they really were—the cheery, open blue of the sky in summer.

He wasn't holding a kennel. Where was Brindy?

Dirk hovered in the air out of Tori's reach, watching her

suspiciously, checking to see if he could sense any deceit or betrayal in her emotions. "Did you tell anyone you were meeting me?"

Only Aaron. How was she going to explain that?

He must have picked up on the spike of guilt. He shook his head in disappointment. "You told someone, didn't you?"

"Not the Slayers," she insisted. "I told a friend I was going to talk to you tonight. It was perfectly harmless. No one followed me. Nobody is lying in wait."

He drifted closer. "Did you bring your Slayer watch?"

"No."

"You don't have anyone tracking your car or phone?"

"I hope not. That would mean my parents are getting way too overprotective. They've already got a bodyguard shadowing me half the time." She was nervous, and it was making her talk too much. She put her hands in her coat pockets to give them something to do besides clenching at her side. "I came alone, just like I said."

Dirk landed on the pavement beside her. She'd forgotten how tall he was, how broad-shouldered. She hadn't forgotten how striking he was. His looks were memorable.

He cocked an eyebrow. "Why did you tell a friend you were talking to me tonight?"

How should she word her answer? She spoke slowly, hiding as much emotion as she could. "I've mentioned you to certain friends. Girls talk about guys. You come up in conversation sometimes. It's a thing."

He'd picked up on her evasiveness, of course, but he seemed to come up with his own reason for it. He bit back a smile. "You talk about me to your friends?"

"Some of them."

"Do you tell them I'm the dangerous bad boy type?"

"Oh, they know."

He was smiling still, that easy, casual expression he wore so well. "But I'm charming, too, so that makes up for my bad side."

"Not always." She folded her arms. "And speaking of your bad side, are you holding to your promise that this meeting isn't a trap?"

If he had changed his mind and meant to overpower her, she couldn't do much to protect herself. Not when he had his powers and she didn't have hers.

"No trap," he said, landing on the ground beside her. "It's all on the up and up."

"So I won't end up drugged like Shang?"

He didn't flinch at the accusation. "I've never wanted you to lose your memories. I can't say the same about Shang. I don't mind that he doesn't remember hating me."

She peered around the parking lot. "So where's Brindy?"

Dirk pointed toward the jeep. "Over there." He glided that direction, and she followed. A kennel sat behind one of the wheels, and Brindy lay inside, sleeping. A fluffy pink blanket covered her, and half a dozen small stuffed animals were wedged around the edges. The dog's muzzle draped over a bright pink flamingo.

"Brindy!" Tori called, stepping closer.

The dog didn't open her eyes. She was breathing, but unconscious. Tori put her hand on the top of the kennel. "What's wrong with her?"

"She's just sedated. I figured she'd freak out less about flying that way."

Tori wished Brindy were awake. She wanted proof that her dog was all right, and she wanted to assure Brindy that she was safe now.

"The stuffed animals are from Bridget," Dirk said. "Oh, and she drew this for you." He pulled a folded piece of paper out of his pocket and handed it to her. It was a crayon rendition of a smiling girl standing by a brown dog. Blue hearts filled the rest of the paper.

"It's Bridget and Brindy," Dirk said. "She wanted you to know how much Brindy will miss her so you'll bring her back to visit."

Tori refolded the picture and put it in her pocket. "Tell her thanks, but I won't be visiting any time soon."

"I'm sorry my dad did this." Dirk shoved his hands in his jacket pockets, looking uncomfortable. "He's so used to getting what he wants by force, I don't think it ever occurs to him there's another way."

"Another way to intimidate me?"

"Another way to keep you out of the fight. When I made him promise not to hurt you, he felt he had to find other methods of persuading you."

Dirk made it sound so civilized, like his father had a polite disagreement with her. "He threatened to feed my family to dragons. Is that sort of thing all right with you?" Really, how could Dirk be this way? How could he hand her cute pictures from his sister and then casually explain his father's motives, as if it were okay to brutally kill innocent people?

"I've told him to leave your family out of it, just like I told him not to kill your dog." Dirk gestured at the kennel to prove that Brindy was safe. "He listened to me about Brindy. He'll leave your family alone too."

Tori folded her arms. "Your father told me that if I didn't stay out of his business, he'd come after my family. You're saying he didn't mean it? How am I supposed to believe that?"

Dirk shrugged. "I never said he wasn't mad at you."

"Mad?" she sputtered. "He told me how dragons killed their prey. You don't do that unless you mean *mad* as in *insanely sociopathic*." She held her hands out, palms up, pleading. "Come back with me. I know a safe place you can go." She meant with his mother. Given half a chance, Bianca would take Dirk.

He reached over and picked up the kennel with one hand as though it weighed nothing. "I'll help you put Brindy in your car." The dog weighed over a hundred pounds without the cage. The ease with which he carried it was a reminder that Dirk had his extra strength now, a reminder that he was dangerous.

He strode to her car, opened the back door, and slid the kennel onto the seat.

"Now let's go somewhere better to talk." He held out his hands and drifted off the ground, a signal that he wanted to carry her.

She shook her head. "I never said I would go anywhere else with you."

Another shrug. "You never said you wouldn't."

She took a step backward. "I don't think our agreement requires me to tell you all of the things I *won't* do."

He grinned, gliding nearer. "I don't know—it seems like a reasonable assumption. I told you I wouldn't lead you into a trap, so I presumed we were listing things we wouldn't do. And while we're on the subject, I won't go salsa dancing, or visit abstract art exhibits, or run away with you to Vegas." He looked upward as if reconsidering. "Okay, maybe you can talk me into Vegas."

"Dirk—" she started.

He didn't let her finish. In one swift motion he flew over, swept her into his arms and took to the sky.

# CHAPTER 34

The cold night air rushed around Tori. She tried to twist out of Dirk's embrace, but her right arm was pinned against him, and he had hold of her left. Kicking was useless against his strength. All she could do was slam her head into his shoulder in protest. He didn't even wince at this action.

Without her Slayer powers, she couldn't hurt him, let alone get away. And even if she could break free from his grasp, they'd already flown too high for her to keep trying. The parking lot was shrinking beneath them, becoming perilously small.

"Put me down!" she yelled. "You said you only wanted to talk!"

She was frustrated with herself as much as she was with him. She'd trusted him and come here without backup.

"And we will talk," Dirk said. "At a different location. Hey, I'm sweeping you off your feet. I thought girls liked that."

He was kidnapping her. Earlier, when he promised he wouldn't, why hadn't she sensed deceit? "How did you do it?" She suddenly wanted to know this information as much as she wanted to be on firm ground again. "How did you lie without me being able to tell?"

"I didn't lie to you," he said. "I'm not kidnapping you. I'm just . . . *borrowing* you for a while."

"That's arguing semantics, and you know it." Was it so easy to fool the counterpart lie detector? Why hadn't she figured that out before?

"I'm doing this for your own good," Dirk went on. Below them, buildings looked like blocks lined up in rows.

She tried to free her arms again. Couldn't. "I left a note for my parents telling them everything. If I don't come back, they'll know who your father is and what he's doing. They'll know your dad has me."

Dirk must have reached the height he wanted. He leveled out, heading toward the Potomac River. "You're so quick to abandon trust. You don't need to be that way." He shifted her in his grip, slipping one arm under her knees and letting her back rest against his other arm. "If we keep going straight, we'll come in range of my dragon, and your powers will turn on. Then you'll have the strength to fight me, although let's be realistic—we both know how *that* match would turn out. I'm bigger and stronger and can call a dragon to help me. So let's agree not to fight, okay?"

"Seriously?" she asked, disbelief giving the word extra bite. "You're taking me somewhere against my will and then asking me not to fight you?"

"I want to show you a dragon without having to haul you there kicking and screaming. That's all I'm planning to do tonight—show you that dragons aren't the monsters you think they are."

Monsters was a pretty accurate term, but she still felt the relief kicking in. He wasn't bringing her to his father. She would have her powers soon. And she might even get Dirk to tell her something about controlling dragons.

They flew over homes, yards, and twisting streets. Darkened, silent places that stared back at them, unaware. "I'm asking you to be open minded for one night. Then you can go back to your car. And if you're not convinced, tomorrow you can go on hating dragons. Just give me your word that you'll come peaceably. Otherwise I'll have to come up with another way to do this, and I'd rather not."

"Meaning what?"

"I haven't let myself plan that far," he said. "If I'd planned a serious kidnapping, you would have detected it." He tilted his face to the side to better see hers. "Of course, that doesn't mean I can't make those plans right now. I could probably find some lonely tower to lock you up in. It worked for Rapunzel." He had the nerve to grin at her. "So what's it going to be? Are you coming willingly, or do I have to invent a nefarious plan B?"

Tori desperately wanted to learn about dragons from him, but she still didn't like this arrangement. She didn't like being tricked and forced into whatever he was planning. He'd proven she couldn't trust him. What else might he do?

"I'll come willingly," she said. "As long as you promise to let me go home afterward." She agreed before she could think of other things she might do instead. Like fight him. Or call Jesse on her cellphone so he could contact the other Slayers. Or kill his stupid dragon. That was the trick. Say it while you meant it.

Dirk smiled. He believed her. "We've got a deal." They'd reached the river and he turned to follow its trailing waters. "I brought Khan tonight. I'll show you how to ride him. You'll love it."

She doubted that, but she'd be as nice about all of this as possible. Dirk could sense her emotions, so if she was genuinely feeling nice, he'd teach her more.

"I'll give dragon riding a try," she said. "But I can't promise to love it."

She forced herself to think of the good times she'd had with Dirk. The letters he'd written to her after camp when she'd been lonely for her Slayer friends. How he'd saved her life more than once. How he helped the Slayers defeat the first dragon—Dirk's own dragon—and warned them about the second attack, giving them time to prepare.

Dirk wasn't a villain at heart. He was a good person who'd been brainwashed by his father.

And he was her counterpart.

She relaxed in his arms and even laid her head against his shoulder, using his warmth to protect herself against the cold rush of wind. He smelled of aftershave and smoke. Dragon smoke, she supposed.

He soared toward a group of wooded islands that spread out in the middle of the river, breaking it into channels. Tori felt a surge of energy—the rush of her Slayer powers turning on. Her vision grew crisp, and she could make out the shapes of the individual trees below. She must be close to the dragon, would reach Khan within a few minutes.

"I can fly by myself now," she told Dirk. "Let go, and I'll follow you."

He didn't loosen his grip on her. "I like holding you."

"Who's not trusting who now?" she asked. "Are you afraid that if you let go of me, I'll be able to outfly both you and your dragon?" She settled back into his arms. "Maybe you have a point. You'd better carry me." She knew Dirk couldn't resist a challenge.

"I've already proved I'm the faster flyer," he said. "I got away from you on Halloween."

"No, I kept up with you until my powers faded."

"I *let* you keep up with me because I wanted to talk to you."

She pulled her right arm away from his chest and wrapped

it around his neck. "Go ahead and tell that to yourself if it helps smooth your ego. I know how important that macho stuff is to guys."

"Fine." He shifted her in his arms, took her hand, then let her loose to fly beside him. She could have broken his grip and darted away, maybe even zoomed away from the river and lost him. She didn't.

Instead, she flew beside him, gliding lower through the night as they headed toward a long island. Hundreds of trees grew on it, all looking like bunchy, jagged silhouettes. From the shore, the trees probably did a fair job of hiding the dragon. But from above picking him out was easy.

Khan was large and black, resting like a cat sunning itself. His wings were folded to his sides, and his tail snaked through several trees. As Dirk and she approached, he lifted his long neck and watched them lazily, unconcerned.

Alarm bells went off in Tori's brain, ringing warnings. Every instinct told her to fight or retreat. The memory of the last two dragon fights flashed through her mind in a panicked blur of images. The fire and screeches, the claws and teeth, all hurtling toward her. The smell returned too, oily and wild—the scent of something before it bursts into flame. She stopped in the air, making Dirk yank backward.

He pulled her forward. "Don't worry. I have control of him."

She reluctantly let herself be towed along. "How do I know that?" She needed to press the point, not because she didn't believe him, but to get Dirk to tell her *how* he controlled a dragon. "That thing could kill me with one bite." She felt like she'd already drawn too close.

"I've been working with dragons since I was a kid," Dirk said. "I know when I have control."

She could make out the diamond-shaped covering on his forehead, a casing dragon lords used so the dragon's signal wouldn't inadvertently create more Slayers while outside.

Khan's large golden eyes followed them as they descended, tracking their movements. Cat eyes, with the same inherent smugness. Even though the dragon showed no signs of aggression, Tori couldn't think of him as anything but fifty tons of different ways to die.

"I went into Kiha's mind once," Tori said. "But I couldn't control her."

"It wasn't that you couldn't control her; it was that my dad wouldn't let you. Big difference." Dirk led Tori toward the ground. They landed in front of the dragon, only a few feet away. Close enough that Khan could have taken them out with one claw. Dirk kept hold of her hand.

Tori completely forgot what point she'd been trying to make. Her whole body went stiff, taut with energy. A voice came to her mind—her own voice this time—shouting at her to rocket away from this place. She took deep breaths to calm herself. Dragons could smell fear in sweat and adrenaline. She wasn't doing herself any favors by acting like a potential dinner.

Khan lowered his head toward Tori. She flinched, straining against Dirk's grip on her hand.

He pulled her closer to him, perhaps to keep her on the ground. "It's okay. Khan is just getting your scent like a dog would. He's curious about you. Think of him as a big poodle."

"Poodles don't want to eat you."

"Well, you never know. They might."

She didn't laugh.

"Watch." He turned to the dragon. "Raise your front leg."

The dragon lifted one of his massive feet from the ground and held it there, claws limp.

"Lower your head."

Khan did, bringing his snout nearly to the ground. He didn't struggle against Dirk's commands, but he also didn't look at him expectantly the way dogs did while performing tricks for their owners.

"Now give us a bit of mood lighting," Dirk said.

The dragon opened his mouth, and a tiny flame twirled around his tongue. The sight would have been funny if Tori hadn't known from experience how dangerous beasts like this actually were. By the light from Khan's flame, his scales looked as black as obsidian and threw glints of reflected light, tiny stars that lay here on earth.

"That's enough," Dirk said. The dragon lowered his foot, shut his mouth, and lifted his head off the ground, bringing it to the level of the trees again.

"I don't have to speak the commands," Dirk said. "I did that for your benefit. Believe me, Khan knows not to hurt you."

Dirk tugged her hand, pulling her over to the dragon until they stood inches from his chest. One lunge, and he could rip her in half, just like Overdrake said. Why had she thought this was a good idea?

Khan peered down at her, his breath spilling around her shoulders. Dirk reached out and ran his free hand along the scales on the dragon's chest. Khan shut his eyes as though he enjoyed the touch or at least was so used to it that it wasn't worth objecting to.

Dirk kept moving his hand along the dragon's chest, petting him. "See? He won't hurt us. Your turn. Touch him."

Tori didn't move. She both dreaded and was fascinated by the idea of running her fingers along the dragon's scales. Mostly dreaded.

"Go ahead," Dirk said softly. "He's perfectly safe."

All that bridled power was sitting in front of her. A living myth. How many people ever got to touch one? She had the chance.

Dirk lifted her hand and placed it onto the dragon's scales. They were smooth and warm, moving slightly with each of Khan's breaths. She meant to drop her hand after a few seconds, but she left it there. She liked the feel of those breaths underneath her fingertips. There was something ancient about them, about the dragon. Touching him reminded her of the times she'd hiked through caves and wondered at the stalactites and stalagmites—beautiful dark things growing hidden away for millennia.

Khan bent his head, lazily sniffed her, then blinked, looking bored, and gazed into the distance. She didn't move her hand, just stared at the dragon, let her eyes drift over his long neck and folded wings, amazed at how docile he was.

"Are dragons always this tame around you?"

"Not hatchlings. Dragons, like horses, have to be broken. Khan is used to me. He doesn't even resist when I take control of his mind."

Tori ran her hand along the scales, fingering the edges where they overlapped. Even though the only light around was the moonlight, the scales still glittered in places. "Did you have control of him while you brought Brindy back to me?"

"Yes."

"How far away can you be before you lose the link?"

"Miles."

A purposely vague answer. He wasn't going to give her any information that could be useful for fighting.

Her hand moved from one scale to its neighbor. "He's different than I imagined."

Dirk glanced at her hand, and smiled in satisfaction. "Admit it, you think he's beautiful."

"Beautiful isn't the word I'd use."

"You're right. He's like living thunder."

And still Tori didn't move her hand away. Some sort of attraction held her there, as though if she touched the dragon long enough, she'd be able to understand his secrets—and control him.

Maybe she could. She could at least try to go into his dragon's mind and experiment. She thought of Bianca's description of the process. *Let the doorway of your connection expand until you can walk through it.*

Tori wasn't sure how to walk through a sound, metaphorically or otherwise. When fighting Kiha, Tori had tried to give the dragon commands, but that hadn't worked, not until she'd shouted one in desperation. And then, suddenly, she'd been there in the dragon's mind. She didn't know how to repeat that feat.

She let the noise in her mind—the part that heard with the dragon's ears—grow louder. It seemed to expand in a circle around her. She didn't have to walk through a doorway. The circle swallowed her and pulled her forward. And suddenly, there she was, inside Khan's mind.

She still stood in front of the dragon with Dirk, yet part of her could also see with Khan's eyes—trees stretching across the island, branches raised to the sky as if in an offering. She smelled decaying leaves at their feet and the river water tumbling over itself not far away. She even smelled the scent of the shampoo she'd used that morning.

When Tori had gone inside Kiha's mind, Overdrake had immediately known. It wouldn't take Dirk long to order her out. Could she find the dragon's control center before then? Where should she look?

Instead of yelling at Tori, Dirk took a step closer so he stood directly behind her. He slid his arms casually around her waist. "See? It's easy for you to step inside. Natural."

Dirk knew and wasn't stopping her? Good. Whatever his reasons, he was giving her time to experiment. Unfortunately, she had no idea how to navigate Khan's mind. She could sense the dragon's thoughts but didn't know how to influence them.

Tori ignored the feel of Dirk's hands on her waist. She was concentrating too hard on the dragon to think about the familiar way he was holding her. She couldn't afford to let her thoughts wander in that direction.

Khan was relaxed, enjoying his rest among the trees. He liked the smells of outdoors and was in no hurry to return to the enclosure.

Where is the enclosure? she asked with her thoughts. *Where do you live?*

A pattern of stars flashed into her mind.

Dirk chuckled into her ear. "Did you catch that? Khan showed you what the stars above his home look like." His hands circled her waist, pulling her closer. "Hope it was useful."

And then without speaking out loud, Dirk's voice echoed in Khan's mind. "Don't show Tori anymore locations." He didn't sound angry, just amused. He seemed willing to let her ask questions as long as they weren't the wrong kind.

What could she ask that would seem harmless but would actually help the Slayers?

Dirk rested his face against her hair. "I've missed you." It was too intimate a gesture, just like wrapping his arms around her waist. Any moment now, he would try to kiss her.

She ought to push him away for Jesse's sake, but she didn't. She needed more time in the dragon's mind. When Overdrake attacked last summer, Dirk had wrested control of the dragon from his father long enough to push it away from Tori. He'd told her that. Which meant there was a way to break a dragon lord's control, at least for a little while.

Knowing how could be the key to defeating Overdrake.

"What have you missed about me?" she asked absently. She'd stumbled into one of Khan's memories, a flight over a sea. Gulls scattered away from him. He dove at one and ate it whole. One bite. The bird was hardly counted as food, but Khan always enjoyed the chase. Now he smelled birds on the island and wanted to startle them from their hiding spots. He couldn't, though. He'd been ordered to lie here.

Dirk brushed his lips across Tori's neck. A small kiss. An invitation to turn around and kiss him back.

She didn't, but didn't pull away from him either. As long as he was busy trying to kiss her, she could stay inside Khan's mind, searching for his control center.

She focused on Khan's thought—that he'd been ordered to stay. She attempted to follow the order like it was a trail that would lead to its origin. She bumped into more bird memories, nothing else. Birds were the only things that were fast enough, nimble enough, to have a chance at escaping a dragon. That made them a challenge. Good sport.

Do you resent being caged up so much? Tori asked Khan.

No answer came, no image flashed in her mind.

Dirk dropped another light kiss on Tori's neck, feather soft and distracting. "You can't ask the question that way. Resentment is a complicated emotion. Dragons don't understand it."

Do you like your home? Tori asked.

Khan misunderstood the question and wondered if it was time to leave.

"What you're really asking," Dirk murmured, "is whether

he's happy, but he's not self-aware enough to know the answer."

Do you want to be free? she asked.

In response she felt the dragon's hopeful anticipation of being allowed to chase birds. Khan knew a flock was near, keeping a wary distance in the trees. Hiding. Huddling. Cowardly little birds.

Dirk chuckled again. "Would your dog understand the concept of freedom? If dragons were smart enough to think like humans, they would have wiped us out long ago. They'd be ruling the world, investing in stocks, and making pharmaceutical companies."

So dragons only had the intelligence of animals. This pronouncement was both a disappointment and a relief. Having a telepathic connection with something that had a high IQ would have been interesting, but at the same time, the smarter the dragons were, the harder they would be to defeat.

"Khan seemed so intelligent when he showed me a star map," Tori said. "I couldn't tell you what the stars look like above my house."

"Dragons are amazing navigators. It's a different type of intelligence."

"How far can he fly in a night?"

"Far enough." Another vague answer. Dirk bent toward her throat again, kissing the spot her jaw met her neck. The touch sent tingles down her back, which she did her best to ignore.

Tori returned to Khan's mind, rummaging through his thoughts. She couldn't think of any useful questions the dragon might actually be able to answer, and she needed to find his control center.

As Dirk's lips left a trail on her neck, it was getting harder to concentrate on that task. Her breathing was going a little jagged. She pushed through different areas of Khan's mind and ran into more memories. Eating. Preening. Eating. Lots of eating. Most of the dragon's memories involved either catching or ripping apart his prey. Catching it was the fun part.

"Wouldn't you rather think about something else?" Dirk asked. "Why do you keep sifting through images of half-eaten animals?"

She was tired of seeing them, but she couldn't admit she was searching for a way to control the dragon. "Khan is so bloodthirsty," she said. "You compared him to a dog. Well, sometimes dogs yank the leashes from their owners' hands. How do you know one day Khan won't break free and kill you?"

"I don't. That's why I'm always careful." Dirk turned Tori around to face him, then bent down to kiss her. This was too close.

She put her hands to his chest, stopping him. "We shouldn't."

He dropped his hands from her waist, and his expression hardened. "Because of Jesse?"

"Because we're fighting for different things."

Dirk's jaw tightened, and he breathed out through his teeth.

And she had ruined her chances of learning anything more about dragons by rebuffing him. He wouldn't tell her anything if he was upset with her. "Because," she added more gently, "how can I fight you later if I kiss you now?"

The words weren't a lie. She still had feelings for Dirk, an empty, aching spot in her heart where he'd once been. She thought of the day last summer when Jesse had broken up with her, remembered the way Dirk had comforted her. She held his gaze, let him see those emotions vibrating through her.

His expression softened. "Then don't fight me." He put his hands on her shoulders, lowered his head, and kissed her. She lifted her hands to his chest again. This time, instead of pushing him away, she wrapped her arms around his neck and kissed him back.

 # CHAPTER 35

Guilt pinged inside Tori. She ignored it. This was for the best, the way her lips were pressed to Dirk's. Only she shouldn't be enjoying it so much. She ignored that thought too. She locked her fingers behind his neck and kissed him, perhaps longer and more thoroughly than was strictly necessary to prove her attraction. But that was because she wanted to be convincing, not because she wanted to keep kissing him.

Behind them, Khan shifted restlessly and grumbled. Tori had somehow drifted out of his mind, but entering it again wasn't hard. She slipped back in and found herself surrounded by Khan's agitation. She couldn't tell the cause of it.

She pulled away from Dirk to ask, "What's wrong with him?"

"I've kept him pinned here too long." Dirk slid his hand into hers, intertwining their fingers. His smile reminded her of the way he'd been at camp—confident, happy, and trusting. He pulled her over to the dragon's side. "Come on. I told you I'd take you for a ride."

The dragon's saddle wasn't like a horse's. Khan was too wide to straddle. A bench was strapped to his back, surrounded by railings. When Overdrake had ridden Kiha, his chair was smaller, swiveled around, and had compartments for ammunition.

This saddle looked like it was designed for sightseeing, not battle. It had no ladders or other way to climb to the bench. Dirk took Tori's hand, and they flew to the seat.

"Here's your first dragon lord lesson," he said. "Always mount from the side. Flying in front of a dragon activates its predatory instincts. You don't want him to snap at you."

Tori sat down and scooted as far forward as possible. "I thought Khan couldn't snap when you have control of him."

Dirk settled onto the bench behind her. "Dragons are like guns. You should be careful even when the safety is on."

"Dragons are like dogs, and now they're like guns. Anything else?"

"Hang on, and you'll see."

She barely had time to take hold of the rails before Khan rose to his feet and leaped into the sky. With wings unfurled, he pushed upward, making the remaining leaves on the trees flutter in distress. He needed no room to take off, no clear path for a running leap. She tucked that bit of information away. She'd fought two dragons, but both were already airborne.

Khan soared upwards with every beat of his long wings. They looked bat-like but worked like birds' wings, sweeping up and down through the air. The ground below them disappeared, and the river became a small, dark thread.

The ride wasn't as smooth as flying under her own power. With each wingbeat, Khan dipped and rose in a comfortable rhythm. It was relaxing to fly without expending her own energy.

"Hold on," Dirk said, then spoke in Khan's mind. *Show her what you can do.*

The dragon dove downward. Tori only had time to gasp before Khan pulled up again, thrusting her back against Dirk's chest. The dragon regained height, spun several times, then plunged downward again. He leaned on his left side and flew that way, then rolled to the right and did a figure eight.

Most people would have screamed at being turned, flipped, and plunged a thousand feet over the ground. Tori laughed and let her head loll back against Dirk's chest. It felt like an amusement park ride.

Dirk's voice came near her ear. "You're never bored when you're with a dragon."

"As though that's a problem for me: I don't have enough excitement in my life."

Khan leveled off and glided away from the river. She sensed the dragon's satisfaction at performing every action Dirk asked of him, perfectly and powerfully. He liked maneuvering in the sky.

A golf course came into view, a sea of grass broken by the occasional clump of trees. Dirk wrapped his hands loosely around Tori's waist. "Isn't this awesome?"

"It's nice." She was purposely understating the event. There was something magical about riding around the night sky on a dragon. No wonder Bianca had fallen for Overdrake. He'd probably made a dragon bow to her, then taken her for a ride in the starlight.

Tori didn't mean to ask Khan about Bianca. Questions just ran through her mind while she was inside his. Had he known Bianca? Had he flown with her?

And then Khan brought a memory forward: A scene of a dark-haired man, not much older than Dirk, helping a young blonde woman onto a seat like this one. She looked breathless and beautiful—eyes shining and cheeks flushed as she smiled at him.

Dirk saw the memory and extinguished it. "Why are you asking about that?"

"I didn't mean to pry. I just wondered if your dad used to do this with girls when he was young. A dragon ride is the ultimate way to impress a date."

"Are you impressed?"

"Very. Are you going to teach me how to make Khan fly like that? It felt like a rollercoaster."

She made the request innocently, but it wasn't innocent. And he knew it.

"I'd be happy to teach you," he said, his voice all purr and possibility. "Right after you promise to leave the Slayers and join me."

"All I have to do is promise?"

"No," he said moving closer. "You have to help me disable the Slayers. That's how I'll know you're really on my side."

She let out a discouraged huff. "You know I can't do that. I can't hurt the others—"

He didn't let her finish. "You won't be hurting them; you'll be keeping them from getting hurt. Fighting dragons *is* how they'll get hurt and killed." He sighed unhappily. "I know what I'm asking is hard, but think about what's best for them."

She was. And stopping Overdrake was best for everyone, including Dirk.

Before she could speak, Dirk did. "The country needs changes. You and I have the opportunity to help solve problems."

"There are nonviolent ways to do that."

"Yeah, and we've seen how well those methods work: we're trillions of dollars in debt, the government is weighed down by bureaucracy, and neither party is capable of solving any real problems—let alone easy ones like fixing crumbling bridges and dams."

Somehow the fact that Dirk knew the state of America's bridges and dams seemed like a bad omen.

"Our enemies keep growing more powerful," he went on, "while we get weaker. You can't deny it; the system is flawed."

"And your father—a rich, violent dictator—would be better how?"

Dirk didn't grow defensive. His voice remained matter of fact. "Democracy has always been a blip in history. Eventually, people get too lazy and hedonistic to rule themselves, and society implodes. It happened in Rome, and it's happening now. The ultimate law in politics is this: If you're weak, someone will conquer you. That's how the world has been for five thousand years, since the first Pharaoh seized control of Egypt and declared himself a living god."

How was Tori supposed to argue with five thousand years of history? She knew far more about past wars than most teenagers, because Dirk liked to tell her stories while he tended the dragons.

She knew all about Hitler's invasions. When Germany rolled across Poland with tanks, Poland sent out the cavalry to fight them. Horses versus tanks. It wasn't much of a battle. The moral of the story: even small forces could run rough shod over Europe if they had superior technology. Ditto for the story of the Mongols sweeping through China because they'd mastered what no one else had—fighting while riding horses.

According to Dirk, fighting from dragons would be revolutionary in the same way.

Khan rose higher into the sky. The city lights below seemed like distant sparkles.

"A representative democracy isn't perfect," Tori said, "but it's the best form of government available."

"Really? Our representative democracy sanctioned slavery, took land from Native Americans, and sent Japanese-American citizens to internment camps. Politicians have always thought of people as expendable tools. Why are you willing to lay down your life to keep those people in power?"

"Because I know my father isn't that way, and I also know that innocent people will die when your father attacks. Why are you willing to lay down your life to *put* him in power?"

Khan's wings struck against the air, beating a rhythm to Dirk's words. "I'm not planning to lay down my life for him; I'm trying to temper him. He listens to me. Remember, I'm the reason the Slayers are still alive, the reason your family is safe. And I'll be the reason that the revolution won't be more brutal than it has to be."

For all of his talk about the faults of democracy, she knew his last statement was the real reason he hadn't left his father. Dirk thought he could rein in the man's darker side. Tori doubted he really could.

"Rulers become dynasties," Dirk continued. "Eventually my father will turn the nation over to me." His posture relaxed, and he leaned in to Tori, resting his chin against her hair. "I want you by my side through all of it. Say you'll help me rule."

Dirk obviously felt certain of victory. Could he be right? Could the country fall so easily? She wanted to believe it couldn't, but all of Dirk's history lessons were beginning to have an effect on her. Nations fell all of the time. Hitler conquered Denmark in a day, Poland in eighteen, and Norway, Belgium, France, and the Netherlands in a few weeks.

"Your proposition is tempting . . ." she said.

Dirk laughed, clearly glad she was considering his offer. "We'll put your dad's talents to good use. He can rule Florida. Maybe we'll throw in Louisiana and Georgia if he agrees to support my father."

She shifted away from Dirk. "You aren't the only one who's been studying history. Dynasties always end up with bad rulers. George the Third went crazy. Cleopatra had her brother and sister killed so she could rule. Richard the Third killed off his nephews for the same reason. You can't skim through a history book without seeing war after war fought to decide who should rule. Democracy is the only way to avoid that fate. We wage our battles at the polls."

"When you studied history, you obviously skipped the Civil War."

It irked her that he was right. The South hadn't accepted Lincoln, so they'd elected their own president and seceded. No blood at the polls, but plenty after.

"Okay, but that only happened once in America."

Dirk laughed again. "If you want, when we're too old to rule, instead of passing on the country to our children, we can reinstate a democracy. The system probably won't last any longer than our dynasty would have, and our kids will be ticked at us, but whatever."

Their kids? He was already planning on having children? She found the assumption simultaneously irritating and sweet. Irritating because the two of them were still enemies and she hadn't agreed to join him, let alone marry him. Plus, she was dating Jesse. Granted, she hadn't acted like Jesse's girlfriend back on the island when she kissed Dirk, but still. A guy shouldn't assume anything until he'd bought a ring and she'd agreed to wear it.

On the other hand, it was sweet that Dirk cared enough about her that he wanted a future with her—that he wanted it enough to offer concessions about how they'd rule together. And he was ready to give her father Florida. As romantic gestures went, that completely beat out flowers.

Dirk leaned against the back rail again. "So what policies do you want to make? The first thing I'm going to do is bring back togas as official business dress. Men shouldn't be expected to wear ties."

He was urging her to join the fantasy, to imagine herself changing things for the better. But thoughts of Bianca returned. She'd probably had similar conversations with Overdrake. Now she was hiding from her ex-husband and she'd lost her oldest son.

"You wouldn't want any of this if your father wasn't making you." Tori turned on the seat so they faced one another. "You can leave him. We can fly Khan somewhere safe."

Dirk shook his head. "What place is safe for a dragon?"

"Are you kidding? People love dragons. The zoos would fight over him."

"A zoo couldn't let him out of his enclosure to fly unless a dragon lord controlled him. I don't want to live my life out in a zoo, do you?"

No. And it seemed cruel to lock dragons up completely when they enjoyed flying so much. Tori was still in Khan's mind, and he was happily scanning the landscape below, enjoying his uncontested rule of sky. No other dragon had confronted him to fight over this territory, so by default, it was all his.

"We could work something out for Khan," Tori said. "The point is, you need to leave your father. If we have you on our side, he won't stand a chance."

Dirk's eyes stayed on hers, asking her to understand. "Even without my help, my father will still take over this country. He has the manpower, the weapons, and the dragons. And he has another son coming. All my defection would do is make him so angry he'd be twice as ruthless. And if I left, I wouldn't have a say in how the government is run."

So that was how it was. Dirk couldn't be convinced.

Tori sagged under the weight of his refusal. "You'll feel horrible when you have to kill people."

"I know," he said. "I suppose soldiers always do."

And there they were, back in the same, circular argument. She would tell him that his war wasn't just one, and then he'd bring up every unjust fight the government had ever forced men to fight in.

How did he make things that should be black and white seem so clouded with shifting gray?

Dirk put his hand on top of hers. "Help me make sure I don't have to kill our friends."

She shook her head. "You know I can't." She pivoted around on the seat, done with the conversation. "You should take me back to my car. It's late."

He didn't turn the dragon.

Was he kidnapping her after all? The fear of that possibility made a deep, instinctual part of Tori splinter. Her attention had already been broken in two—half of her seeing and feeling what happened in her own body, the other half what happened in Khan's. And now the part of her in the dragon's mind broke again, splitting her attention into thirds. She could not only see out of her own eyes and Khan's, but she could also see inside the dragon's brain without being connected to its thoughts. This third part of her seemed like an avatar. She was able to feel around Khan's mind with phantom hands as if wandering around a half-darkened room looking for a light switch.

Everywhere her fingers touched, she found strings of memories. Rows and rows of them dangled in front of her, each one tied to impulses, desires, tangles of sensation She pushed the strings away, and more swung down in front of her. She willed the room to grow lighter and saw that the strings had different colors and tints to them, messy patterns like the underside of a tapestry.

Where is your control center? she asked Khan.

She hadn't expected the dragon to know the answer any more than she knew where things were sorted in her brain. But a section of green and black strings parted, and she felt herself moving through the pathway.

Don't show her anything, Dirk's words sounded in Khan's mind with an echoing quality; she heard them twice.

The instruction was too late. The strings had already parted, revealing an image of Dirk—a perfect replica—standing in the dragon's mind, staring back at her.

He held something in his right hand. Tori couldn't see it clearly, and what she did see made no sense. A hand, maybe, although it wasn't connected to anything.

Now that Tori had seen the place, now that she'd felt it, she'd be able to find it again. She just needed to find the green and black strings and push through them.

In the dragon's control center, Dirk narrowed his eyes. *It doesn't matter,* he said through Khan's mind. *You can't push me out of here.* He held up his free hand. *Go ahead and try.*

Was it that easy? With a running start, she could push him off his spot, make him drop whatever he was holding.

She smiled, hoping she looked confident, and said, *Don't take this personally.*

Then she sprinted toward him. Right before she reached him, she felt herself being picked up. Not the part of her that was in the dragon's mind—her real body.

In that instant, she snapped out of the dragon's mind. She wasn't splintered in three, or two, she was herself again, riding on the dragon's back. And Dirk had picked her up as though she was a rag doll. He held her over the rail and seemed ready to drop her.

She blinked at him, getting her bearings. "Throwing me won't matter. I can fly, you know."

Dirk set her gently back on the bench so that she was facing him. "I wasn't trying to hurt you. I was trying to get your attention." He sat down across from her. "I figured dangling you a thousand feet off the ground would do the trick."

Tori rubbed her temple. She felt like she'd just run a marathon. Her head ached and her senses felt dull now that she no longer shared them with Khan.

"I told you that you wouldn't be able to push me out," Dirk said calmly, then added. "Don't take it personally."

She reached out for Khan's mind again.

"I wouldn't do that," Dirk said. "The point of that demonstration was to show you that if you focus on fighting inside a dragon's mind, you'll leave your body vulnerable. That's dangerous. If you tried hijacking one while my father is barreling down on you with a dragon, he could kill you."

She wiped some stray strands of hair from her face and thought over what Dirk said. "When you pushed your father out of Tamerlane's mind . . . did you leave your body vulnerable . . . to save me?"

He'd been captain of A-team at the time, directing the other Slayers. She didn't remember him even pausing in his duties let alone acting strangely. Of course, she'd been busy fleeing from a dragon at the time, so she might have missed something.

"I've had a lot more practice than you have," he said. "I can split my consciousness into three without losing focus."

Tori wasn't likely to have the chance to practice the split again; still, she was already calculating a new attack defense. If the other Slayers protected her body while she split, she could try to take control of the dragon from Overdrake.

She surveyed the scenery around her. The Potomac River was in sight again, a horizontal line meandering across the landscape. Last she'd checked they'd been flying over a city. "Wait, when did you turn the dragon? Where are we?"

"We're heading back to your car. I told you I wasn't kidnapping you." He gestured to her, emphasizing that she was free. "If you want, you can fly to your car from here. You'll reach it before your powers wear off."

"Well, I could if I knew where it was." She leaned over the railing to get a better look at the scenery. "You know I have no sense of direction." It was true, at least compared to the other Slayers, who all seemed to have built-in compasses, but she also needed a few more minutes to talk with Dirk. She hadn't told him about Aaron yet.

Part of her still didn't want to say anything about him. Aaron's plan to be a mole could go wrong in so many ways.

Khan was passing over the Potomac. They couldn't be far from the parking lot. If she didn't say something now, she'd have to type it in a message, and then Dirk wouldn't be able to use his counterpart sense to gauge that she was telling the truth. He would most likely think it was some sort of trap.

She was supposed to leave Bianca out of the story, but Tori wanted Dirk to know that his mother had loved him, that she'd tried to come back for him, and that when she'd seen his picture she'd cried.

Dirk looked at her questioningly, sensing her inner struggle. Fine. She could use that. "Would you consider switching sides if you had another dragon lord as an ally? You could teach him and me, and then it would be the three of us against your father."

"Tori," Dirk said patiently. "Dragon lords are like Slayers. They have to be exposed to dragon's signal in utero. Your father can't be a dragon lord, even though he comes from the right genetic line."

Tori cocked her head, taken off guard. "Why are you so sure I got my dragon lord genes from my dad?"

"He's running for president. He wants power. Seems like dragon lord genes to me."

"My father's not—well never mind. I wasn't referring to him."

Dirk's gaze shot to hers, finally understanding what she was implying. "Dr. B found someone else?" He sounded hopeful, or at least intrigued.

"In a manner of speaking." Tori spent the next few minutes telling him about Dr. B's tip about the dragon scales and their trip to the Renaissance fair. "We thought we'd find one of your father's men, and we hoped he could lead us to the dragons. Instead we found a twelve-year-old boy named Aaron who looks a lot like you."

"How did he get dragon scales?" Dirk asked, missing the important detail.

"Your mother took them with her when she left your father. Aaron knew they were worth a lot of money, so he's been selling them at fairs."

Dirk didn't miss what Tori was saying that time. Even in the dim light, she could see the effect her words had on him. He looked shocked, then pained. "You're saying I have a half-brother?"

"I'm saying you have a full brother. Aaron told us that Overdrake is his father."

Dirk shook his head. "Not if he's twelve. I would remember having a brother, even if I was only five when he was born."

There was no way to keep Bianca out of this part of the story.

"Your mom left your dad while she was pregnant with him. She didn't want your dad to use Aaron the way he was planning to use you. She came back for a while when you were six and tried to take you with her, but your father wouldn't let her. She had to leave without you."

Dirk silently stared out at the sky, processing the information. "How do you know all of this?"

"Your mom told Aaron about you. She never stopped loving you. You need to know that."

Dirk clenched his jaw, seemed to be chewing on his words. "That's a nice sentiment, but it's not like she would have admitted anything different. The proof is in her actions. She left me behind, and she didn't come back." He made a low rumbling sound in the back of his throat. "How convenient that she got a replacement son out of the bargain."

Tori ached to tell him that no, that wasn't it at all. *I saw your mother. I heard the pain in her voice when she talked about leaving you.* But if Tori admitted to seeing Bianca, Dirk would ask for her address. Tori couldn't give it to him and she couldn't explain why she couldn't. She couldn't endanger Bianca's youngest son that way.

"Whatever you think of your mother, Aaron *is* your brother. Dr. B isn't going to train him, and none of the Slayers trust him because he's a dragon lord. Frankly, they hardly trust me. But if you were to teach Aaron and me how to control dragons—"

"He's twelve," Dirk cut her off. "Do you really want to drag a twelve-year-old into a revolution and put him on the front lines? No." He said it with disapproval that she'd even suggested the idea. Which reminded Tori why she'd cared about Dirk in the first place. He could act cynically calculating about war, but his softer side didn't want a twelve-year-old kid to get hurt.

"Will he still be twelve when your father attacks?" she asked. "I thought the attack was years away."

Dirk didn't answer. His silence wasn't comforting. They neared the parking lot, where her car sat on the pavement, looking like a Hot Wheels toy from this distance.

"I don't know the date of the attack," Dirk said at last. "Whenever it is, Aaron will be too young."

Still not comforting.

Khan flew over the parking lot, making slow circles while Tori and Dirk finished their conversation.

"Think you can find your car now?" Dirk asked.

"Yeah. I guess so." She took hold of the rail, ready to heft herself over it and fly away.

Dirk took hold of her hand to keep her from going. "Next time I invite you to go for a dragon ride, will you believe that I'm not going to kidnap you?"

She let go of the rail and settled back onto the bench. "You want to do this again?" She'd supposed that after she refused to join his side, he wouldn't ask to meet again.

"Next time I'll bring Minerva. You want to see her too, don't you? Maybe she'll have better answers to your questions than Khan did."

"You would let me go into Minerva's mind?"

"Of course." Dirk smiled, purposely tempting her.

He had to know that Tori would try to take control of Minerva, and every time she practiced, she would get better at being able to split her consciousness into three parts. Yet he didn't seem to object.

"Why?" she asked suspiciously. There had to be a trap somewhere she wasn't seeing.

His hands went to her shoulders, and he leaned over and dropped a kiss on her lips. "Because . . ."

He lengthened his explanation with another kiss. And then another. She waited patiently and tried not to kiss him back . . . too much. Then again, she was extracting information from the enemy, so it was okay to encourage him a little.

Finally, he lifted his head. "Because I know that once

you've been inside a dragon's mind, you'll have a harder time killing it." His hands slid off her shoulders. "My father says you had a clear shot at Kiha but didn't take it. Jesse was the one who killed her."

Tori stared back at him, her heart pounding in her chest. He had known about her hesitation with Kiha—and used it against her. He'd let her go into Khan's mind so she'd have a harder time killing him later. This whole evening had been a ploy and she'd walked into it.

She shifted away from Dirk, angry. "In that case, I'd better not meet Minerva."

"Are you sure? You want to practice your dragon lord skills. What other chance will you have?" Dirk smiled at her again. "Maybe I'll even teach you a few things."

He had her, and he knew it. She wanted to keep practicing, but she wasn't going to admit that.

Instead she leaned toward him, slid her arms around his neck, and kissed him as though they really were boyfriend and girlfriend; without reservation.

When she pulled away, he looked at her startled but pleased. "What was that for?"

"I'm hoping it works both ways, and since I kissed you, you'll have a harder time killing me."

He laughed at her reasoning. She didn't stay around to hear his commentary on it. Instead, she flew over the seat rail, down the dragon's side—remembering not to fly in front of him—and glided toward her car.

CHAPTER 36

Tori awoke the next morning to the sound of Brindy barking to be let out of Tori's room. She hadn't set her alarm clock. She'd planned on sleeping in and skipping her journalism meeting this morning.

After all, teachers should know better than to schedule meetings on Saturdays. She needed sleep more than the school newspaper needed her help with the layout. Her decision had nothing to do with the fact she didn't want to face Jesse. Dreaded facing Jesse, actually. She rolled over and shut her eyes. If she avoided him today, she'd have until Monday to figure out what to tell him about Dirk.

Last night when she'd kissed him, it had seemed justified. She'd kissed Dirk so he'd give her access to Khan's mind, so she could figure out how to control him. She'd kissed Dirk in hopes of saving Jesse's life, not to hurt him. She'd done it to protect the country, to prevent death and suffering.

And the time she'd kissed Dirk right before she left, well, she'd done that to make a point. At the moment, her actions hadn't felt all that much out of line considering she'd already kissed him so many times.

As soon as Tori got home, though, the weight of guilt pressed on her. Now it felt like a persistent headache. What had she done? It had been a mistake. All of it.

She'd thought she was buying time inside the dragon's mind with her kisses, but Dirk had wanted her to go into Khan's mind all along. He would have probably let her stay connected to the dragon even if she'd refused his advances.

So she should have refused them. But how could she have known?

Well, maybe she should have realized that going inside Khan's mind would make it harder for her to kill him. She'd already learned that the hard way with Kiha. She'd thought her hesitation was just a personal weakness—a glitch of being too softhearted. Apparently not. It was part of her genetic makeup. Her dragon lord side insisted she protect, not kill, dragons. And that part was activated when she went into a dragon's mind.

Dirk had known what would happen if she went into Khan's mind, and he used that knowledge against her.

Still, one good thing had come from the night. She'd seen the control center of a dragon's mind. She'd experienced how dragon lords split their consciousness three ways—a crucial part of controlling a dragon or pushing another dragon lord out. Dirk had undoubtedly not meant for her to learn that.

Brindy barked again, lifting a paw to scratch at the door. The dog heard people moving around the house and apparently wanted to mingle.

Tori glanced at the clock. It was two minutes after seven. Why was her family up so early on a weekend? She'd only slept half an hour longer than usual.

"Stop it, Brindy," she moaned and turned over.

The dog didn't stop, wouldn't. Tori reluctantly pulled herself out of bed and opened her door. Brindy shot down the hallway, tail wagging, barking wildly.

There was no point going back to sleep now. As soon as her family saw the dog, they would come into Tori's room and ask where Brindy had come from.

Tori followed Brindy down the hallway, yawning. She'd only gotten five hours of sleep. Although that wasn't entirely because of being out dragon riding. After she'd come home, she'd sent Aaron a message saying that Dirk had flat out said Aaron was too young to be involved in the revolution. So she doubted Dirk would tell Overdrake about him.

Tori hadn't expected Aaron to write back until the following day, but he replied almost immediately. *I'll have to find a way to contact Overdrake myself. Suggestions?*

I suggest you listen to Dirk. Stay away from Overdrake for a few years. Wait until you're— She didn't want to say "more mature," that would offend him. *Wait until you're older. He's controlling, and he plays mind games.*

Aaron typed back quickly. *If I wait until after the attacks, it will be too late. Jacob will do something stupid, like go fight the dragons. I'm trying to keep Overdrake from being able to attack. Why aren't you helping me? I thought you wanted to stop him.*

She did want to stop Overdrake. Aaron was right about that.

Aaron sent another message. *I'll list dragon scales for sale online. Someone who works for Overdrake will see the ad eventually and tell him about it. I'll have to go through a lot of buyers, and some of them might be dangerous, especially when I refuse to sell them a scale. But sooner or later, Overdrake, will come for me.*

Really, Aaron was almost as good at manipulation as Dirk. She'd probably regret helping him later, just like she regretted kissing Dirk.

She sighed and tapped out another message. *Fine. I'll write Dirk and say something about you. I'm pretty sure his father is spying on our conversations, so he'll see it. I'll do it on one condition. Before you go to the fair tomorrow, leave your mom a note telling her what you're doing. She has a right to know.*

Done, he wrote back.

Done.

It seemed like such a final word. A dangerous word.

She closed out of Aaron's conversation and brought up her message thread with Dirk. The sound of flapping dragon wings hadn't stopped in her head. Dirk was still out riding.

She wrote to Dirk, *Thanks again for returning Brindy. It means so much to have her back safe. Tell Bridget thanks for the stuffed animals too. Brindy has already chewed off some of their limbs. I guess that's her way of saying she loves them.*

Tori sent the message then sat back, trying to think how to phrase the next few sentences.

Before she could, she heard his voice in her head. "Well, we all have our own ways of showing love, don't we?"

She wrote, *I wanted to talk to you more about your brother. You said Aaron is too young to be involved in the revolution—I agree—but he still needs you in his life. He doesn't have anyone to help him adjust to being a dragon lord like you helped me. He'll be at the North Carolina Renaissance Festival tomorrow. You should go. Start near The Black Unicorn shop. Aaron won't be hard to recognize. He's the twelve-year-old who looks like you.*

Clicking the send link felt eerily like pulling a trigger. She just didn't know who the bullet would strike yet—Overdrake or Aaron.

Dirk didn't say anything at first. She only heard Khan's wingbeats and the air rustling by. Finally, he said. "I can't." Then added, "We'll talk about it next time."

Next time. Meaning when they rode Minerva. He sounded so sure that there would be a next time.

Now as Tori followed her dog down the hallway, she wondered if she should allow a next time. Could she afford to go into Minerva's mind, when she knew that doing so would make it harder for her to kill that dragon?

Brindy bounded down the stairs, all enthusiasm and tail wags, and rushed into the kitchen. Tori's mother let out an astonished cry, "Brindy! How did you get here? Look at you, girl!"

"Brindy is here?" came her father's voice.

Tori trudged down the stairs, went into the kitchen, and recited the story she'd come up with. "One of my friends texted me last night that he'd seen a German shepherd wandering the streets near his house. He knew our dog was missing so he took Brindy inside and texted me a picture. I was too excited to wait until the morning to get her."

"Oh my heavens," her mother said, relieved. She was kneeling in front of the dog and Brindy was doing her best to lick the makeup off her face. "Where was she?"

"Over by Chain Bridge Road." If Tori's parents checked the security footage and noticed how long she was gone last night, she'd tell them she spent a while talking with her friend.

"How did she get all the way over there?" her father asked, petting Brindy and checking her over at the same time.

Aprilynne came into the kitchen to join the welcome-home petting. "I guess this ruins your theory that Brindy was taken by the boogeyman."

"I never said she was taken by the boogeyman." Tori leaned against the counter. "I said she was taken by someone who didn't want her barking while they attacked our house. And if you recall, our house *was* attacked."

"But we're safe now," her mother said with firm insistence, as though the assertion could make it true. "And so is Brindy."

Tori's father straightened. "Speaking of which, you really shouldn't drive off by yourself late at night without letting us know where you're going."

A lecture was coming, maybe more restrictions. Tori edged

toward the kitchen door. "I knew you guys needed your sleep. And speaking of sleep, I'm really tired, so I'm going back to bed."

"You can't," her mother said before Tori finished speaking. "You've got your newspaper layout to do at school this morning, remember?"

"Oh, that." Tori kept going toward the door. "I decided to skip it. The whole class will be there and I already sent in my article. They don't need me."

She should have learned by now that there were some excuses that didn't work on her parents. She could have said she was sick, that the meeting had been cancelled, anything else. Instead of letting her go back to bed, her parents launched into speeches about the importance of fulfilling responsibilities and finishing school assignments.

She barely had time to shower and dress before Lars whisked her off to the school. There would be no delaying her meeting with Jesse. During the ride, she debated what to say and how much to tell him.

On one hand, telling Jesse about kissing Dirk seemed like the honest thing.

On the other hand, what good would telling him do? Telling the truth would only hurt him and make him angry. And since she'd only kissed Dirk as a tactical strategy, why mention it at all and cause Jesse unnecessary pain?

The kisses hadn't meant anything. Not really. She wasn't going to take Dirk up on his offer to rule with him. Or to eventually marry him and have children.

Then again, if she didn't tell Jesse, and he somehow found out about it later, he would know she'd hidden it from him. It would be an admission of guilt. It would be like lying. He'd think she'd cheated on him.

Tori let out a long sigh of resignation. Fine. She'd tell him she'd kissed Dirk.

By the time Lars dropped her off, she'd changed her mind a dozen times. As she walked into the school, she was back to *tell Jesse* . . . until she saw him down the hall halfway to their classroom. He must have heard her footsteps, because he glanced over his shoulder, and when he saw her, he smiled and waited for her to catch up. The smile made remorse thunk around inside of her. He was tall, gorgeous and full of the knight-in-shining-armor, do-the-right-thing Jesse-ness. She wanted to wrap her arms around his chest, sink into him, and forget that last night ever happened.

When she caught up to him, he reached into his backpack and pulled out a stuffed elephant with a pink bow around its neck. "This is for you," he said holding it out. "I was going to go with a teddy bear but when I saw this, I figured an elephant was fitting for a Republican."

She took the toy and ran her hand over its soft, gray material. "Thanks." He was only making this harder. "Did I forget a special occasion? I mean, I didn't bring a donkey for you."

"No occasion. I just wanted to cheer you up. You know, because of yesterday."

"Yesterday?" For a moment she thought he was referring to last night—that he already knew. Why was he looking at her sympathetically and buying her gifts?

"I'm sorry about your dog," Jesse said softly.

Then it made sense. "Oh, Brindy. Right. Great news. She didn't die after all. Dirk brought her back to me."

While she spoke, Melinda came up behind Tori and let out a happy gasp. "Your dog didn't die? I thought she was run over by a car."

Tori cleared her throat uncomfortably. "Um yeah, it turns out she'll be fine. The car was, uh, going slowly, and it was one of those little ones . . . so Brindy was only stunned."

This was the problem with lying. It always came back to bite you. The next time Melinda came over to Tori's house, Brindy would trot over to greet her, and Melinda was bound to mention the dog's miraculous survival to someone in Tori's family.

How would Tori explain that? She couldn't. She'd have to go the rest of her high school years without friends—or anyone who knew the dog story—coming over to her house.

Melinda put a hand to her chest. "I'm so relieved. Did Brindy break any bones?"

"Um, no actually. We got lucky." And to be safe, Tori should also avoid bringing her parents to school functions where her friends might talk to them.

"Amazing," Melinda said.

"Yeah," Tori agreed.

Melinda noticed the elephant in Tori's hand. "What's the stuffed animal for?"

"I gave it to her." Jesse's voice sounded tighter than before. He was most likely thinking about Dirk and wondering how he'd delivered Brindy. "I wanted to cheer her up, you know, back when her dog was dead."

Jesse's eyes narrowed, and Tori could almost see the wheels turning in his mind. Dirk didn't know where Tori lived, so to bring her the dog, they would have had to meet somewhere. A meeting with Dirk could have been a trap—and Tori didn't tell any of the Slayers about it.

She'd been so guilt ridden about kissing Dirk, she'd completely forgotten about the not-telling-the-Slayers-she-was-going-off-to-meet-the-enemy part of last night.

"Ohhh," Melinda cooed over the stuffed animal. "That's so sweet."

"It really was thoughtful," Tori told Jesse. "Thanks again." She set her backpack on the floor and put the elephant inside so she didn't have to look at him anymore. He didn't speak, but she could feel him staring at her, probably going over all the rules she'd broken.

"They say elephants never forget," Melinda said, filling the silence. "The same probably holds true for elephant gifts. Tori will always remember it."

"I don't know," Jesse said. "Tori seems to forget a lot of stuff."

Tori glanced at the classroom door but didn't move toward it. Neither did Jesse.

Melinda's gaze ricochet back and forth between them, noting the tension. "Well," she finally said, "I'm going to journalism now. You guys coming?"

"In a minute," Tori said. "I need to talk to Jesse."

"Jonathan," Jesse said.

"Jonathan," Tori repeated with a wince. How long would it take her to remember he had a different name here? "Sorry. I didn't get much sleep last night."

"Right," Melinda said with a wave." See you guys later." She went inside and shut the door behind her.

Jesse set his backpack on the ground, an indication the conversation wasn't going to be a quick one. "So, what exactly happened with Dirk last night, and why do you look guilty about it?"

This was not going to go well.

Tori fiddled with the strap of her watch. "Dirk made his father promise not to hurt Brindy, so he fed a different dog to the dragon. Which is still horrible. But we've always known he's a horrible person." She was rambling. She stopped fiddling with her watch. "Anyway, when Dirk found out about Brindy, he said he'd return her, but I had to come alone. I knew Dr. B wouldn't let me, so I didn't tell anyone."

Jesse sighed in aggravation and raked a hand through his hair. "Why would you agree to something like that? You know what happened to Shang."

"Dirk promised not to hurt or kidnap me, I could tell he meant it. As you can see, I'm safe, and he didn't kidnap me. Well, mostly."

Jesse raised an eyebrow.

"He sort of flew off with me and brought me to see his dragon. For a while now, he's been saying that if I were around a dragon that wasn't attacking me, I'd love it."

"So did you?" Jesse asked, alarmed.

"Not like I love horses and dogs. But I have to admit that dragons are sort of cool. They're big and powerful and all mythological."

Jesse lowered his voice. "That doesn't make them cool, that makes them dangerous."

"I still don't want to own one, if that's what you're worried about."

"Actually, that's not what I'm worried about."

Tori shifted her stance but didn't say anything else.

"You still look guilty," Jesse said. "What else happened?"

Was she so easy to read? She looked down at her feet. This was going to be even harder than she'd imagined—and she'd known it would be hard.

"I went into Khan's mind. It was easy this time." She glanced back up at Jesse's face. "I was trying to get Dirk to tell me how to control dragons."

Jesse's expression was stern. He was bracing himself. "And?" he asked, as if he knew there was more to the story.

The look pierced her. How could she admit what she'd done? "Dirk kissed me, and I let him because I wanted information."

Jesse stared at her, face going white. "You kissed him?"

"Only so he'd give me information."

Jesse drew in a jagged breath. When he spoke, his words were clipped and hard. "And then Dirk showed you how to control a dragon?" It was clear Jesse didn't believe it.

"Well, not exactly."

"What a surprise." Jesse didn't try to hide the anger in his eyes or the hurt.

Guilt washed through her all over again. "I'm sorry." She took hold of his arm, tentatively reaching for his hand. It was a gesture asking him to understand.

He pulled his arm away from her. "Are you really so naïve about Dirk or are you just making excuses for cheating?"

She might have deserved that, but it still stung. "It wasn't like that. I was able to find Khan's control center."

"You controlled him?"

She wasn't sure if the question was a challenge or whether his Slayer side was kicking in and he really wanted to know. "No, but I got a step closer." She went on, glad for the chance to change the subject. "I learned that to control a dragon, I have to split my consciousness into thirds and send part of myself into the right area of the dragon's mind. The problem is, I can't focus so much on being in the dragon's mind that I don't pay attention to what's happening to my actual body."

"Dirk told you all that? How long were you kissing him?"

"I figured that part out while I was in the dragon's mind."

"Uh huh." A muscle pulsed in Jesse's jaw. "And what exactly was Dirk doing to your body while you weren't paying attention to it?"

Jesse wouldn't be reassured to hear how she'd been so inattentive that Dirk had been able to pick her up and dangle her off the side of a dragon in flight.

"Nothing bad," she said.

Jesse rubbed a hand over his forehead to calm himself. "Okay. Tell me exactly what *did* happen so I don't imagine the worst."

"I kissed him because I thought he would kick me out of the dragon's mind if I didn't. It turned out that Dirk wanted me to go into Khan's mind. He knew I would have a harder time killing a dragon I've connected to. It's a dragon lord thing." Tori held up a hand to stop the protest that was forming on Jesse's lips. "I'm not saying I can't kill him. It will just be harder. The next time we're fighting, I might hesitate again."

Jesse gritted his teeth. "So not only did you make out with Dirk, but your fighting ability has been compromised?"

He made it sound horrible. "Sort of. Although I might be able to break Overdrake's control of a dragon. I'll need someone to protect my body while I figure out how to do it."

"And then you *might* figure it out?" Jesse asked. "Meanwhile we'll have to take another Slayer out of the fight in order to protect you?"

She shrugged. "It doesn't have to be a Slayer. Dr. B or Theo could do it. Or someone who's actually strong enough to carry me out of the path of a dragon."

The plan sounded weak and flawed. She wasn't even sure what would have happened if she had managed to push Dirk out of his position in Khan's mind. She suspected it would have broken his connection with the dragon, but Dirk hadn't given her time to try.

Jesse put a hand to his brow. "So how many times did Dirk kiss you?"

Tori hadn't been expecting the question. She'd been

thinking of ways she could protect her body without taking another Slayer out of the fight. "I don't know."

He dropped his hand, frowning. "He kissed you so many times you lost track?"

She swallowed hard. "You're the one who always says we've got to make sacrifices for the country's sake. That's what I did. That's all it was."

"Right." He leaned toward her, arms crossed. "You weren't thinking of the country when you went off to a secret meeting with the enemy, but when he wanted to make out, you're suddenly a patriot."

"When he kissed me, I was thinking of your safety." And she was, at first. She felt her cheeks growing hot. "Last night I learned a lot of important things."

"Yeah, and I just learned some important things too: Dragon lords can't be trusted." He picked up his backpack then strode down the hall to the classroom.

Dragon lords can't be trusted. He meant her, not Dirk.

Was he breaking up with her?

Did he just need time to cool down?

She held her backpack to her chest, feeling shaky. This had turned out even worse than she'd expected, and she hadn't even told him the part about Aaron. What would Jesse think of her when he found out she was helping Aaron find Overdrake?

Dragon lords can't be trusted.

Jesse hadn't even tried to see her point of view or understand why she'd gone with Dirk. And he acted as if everything she'd learned about controlling dragons didn't matter. It did. It could make a huge difference. If she could figure out how to take control of a dragon away from Overdrake during a battle, she could save the Slayers' lives. And civilians' lives, too.

Wasn't that worth a few kisses?

CHAPTER 37

By nine o'clock Saturday morning, Aaron was showered and dressed. It had taken him longer than usual because most of his stuff had already been packed, waiting for the truck that would come on Monday.

The boxes were one more reminder his life had been dismantled, changed without his permission.

His mom didn't come right out and say that the move was his fault, that he'd screwed up their lives, but the accusation still came across in the brisk way she'd been ordering him around all week. And in the way she'd been throwing his stuff into boxes. She was worried Overdrake might find them as easily as the Slayers had, so now they had to disappear.

She'd even packed up the stuff his stepdad, Wesley, left behind and sent it to him. Just more evidence that he was gone for good. His mom had said that Wesley was only moving out for a trial separation, like the two of them were taking a divorce out for a test drive to see how it fit with their lifestyles.

As far as Aaron was concerned, they were both being selfish.

So his parents argued. So what? Everyone argued sometimes. If you found someone who said they agreed with you about everything, that person was a liar. Liars were the ones you needed to worry about, not the people who admitted they disagreed with you.

Adults were supposed to know how to work things out. They weren't supposed to tear a family apart.

Aaron shoved his Renaissance costume in his backpack: a Robin Hood hat, a cape, and black boots. When he got to the festival, he'd put them on and ask Rudolpho for permission to hang around his shop and pretend to be an employee. Overdrake would expect him to be working somewhere.

Aaron folded the note he'd written to his mother and put it on top of one of the boxes in his room. She'd find it eventually, but not right away. Maybe not even today.

Earlier in the week, he'd told his mother his friend Sergio was having a birthday party today. He'd even created a fake invitation and showed it to her. Sergio lived a few streets over, so last night Aaron had snuck out and hidden his bike in some bushes near Sergio's house. Today after his mom dropped him off at the "party," he'd get his bike from the bushes and ride to the Renaissance Festival. It was only a few miles away, and he knew how to get there. When he'd first decided to sell the scales, he'd scouted out the place to figure out who would be the best buyer.

Now Aaron paused at his bedroom door, trying to memorize how his room looked, or at least, how it had looked before the boxes stood there as a monument to his mistakes.

If he hadn't sold the scales, none of this would have happened.

Aaron had only wanted to make things better for his mom. He'd taken the money Rudolpho gave him, turned it into a cashier's check, and sent it to the mortgage company. His mother's account hadn't been hard to find. The mortgage company kept sending letters about payments being overdue.

The money took care of the back payments, and as an added benefit, his mother believed that Wesley paid it. She'd been so happy.

And now this. They were moving, and his mom was back to thinking Wesley didn't care about them.

Aaron turned from his room and walked down the hall into Jacob's. Like his own room, boxes were stacked everywhere. His brother lay asleep on a mattress on the floor. The headboard and footboard had already been moved downstairs.

Aaron sat down, giving the mattress a jolt.

Jacob opened his eyes, then shut them. "What do you want?"

Too many things to mention. "I'm leaving. I came to say goodbye."

Jacob's eyes opened again. "Where are you going?"

Aaron couldn't tell him the truth. Jacob would tell their mother for sure. "Birthday party. I'll be gone for a while, though."

Jacob looked at him in confusion, probably because Aaron had never woken him up to say goodbye before. "Whose?"

"Sergio's."

Jacob grumbled and turned over. "You're just leaving so you can get out of packing."

"Yep. Plus, I'll get cake."

Jacob picked up a pillow and hit him with it. "Shut up."

Aaron batted the pillow away. "Stay out of trouble while I'm gone." He said the words lightly, but they tore at him. "I know that will be hard for you."

Jacob swung the pillow at him again.

Aaron blocked the hit, then grabbed the pillow from Jacob. "So far, you're not staying out of trouble. You ought to know better than to hit someone stronger than you." Aaron flung the pillow back at his brother to emphasize the point.

The pillow struck Jacob in the chest. With a laugh, he flipped it away and lunged at Aaron, pushing him off the mattress and onto the floor. "You're stronger? Who says?"

Aaron wrapped his arms around his brother, struggling to pin his arms to his sides. "Says every wrestling match we've ever had."

Jacob twisted, resisting the grip. "Not this one." They knocked into a stack of boxes, causing the top ones to crash to the floor.

"Oh, definitely this one." Aaron tightened his hold. He was hugging Jacob goodbye. He was leaving, and his brother didn't know it.

Jacob twisted the other way, broke Aaron's grasp, and got a hand free. Jacob had gotten stronger. When did that happen? Were his Slayer powers developing? He and Jacob slammed into another set of boxes. Those fell over too, only these ones hadn't been taped shut. Things clinked and clattered as they spilled onto the floor.

The bedroom door opened, and their mother marched into the room, surveying the scene. "Stop it! What are you two doing?"

Aaron released Jacob and sat up, breathing hard from the struggle. He plastered a careless grin on his face. "I was just giving Jacob some brotherly advice."

Jacob grabbed the pillow and threw it at Aaron's head. It hit him with a thud.

Their mother gave Jacob a stern look. "I said, stop it."

The box that had spilled contained a dozen of Jacob's pocket knives. A larger collection than Aaron remembered. And it included some hunting knives and daggers. Why had their mother let him have those? Sheesh, he was turning into a little combatant.

She waved a hand at the fallen boxes. "Clean up this mess."

Aaron got to his feet, wiping his hands on his pants. "Can't. I've got a birthday party to go to. Jacob will have to do it."

Their mother turned her stern look on Aaron. "Help your brother first. That's more important."

She meant the words as a reproach, but they didn't feel that way. They felt like permission to leave.

A few minutes later, when he hugged her goodbye, he almost didn't feel bad about going. Almost.

 # CHAPTER 38

Dirk found his father at the breakfast table, sipping coffee and scrolling through the news on his laptop. Cassie and Bridget had just left for the mall. Bridget hadn't wanted to go and had stormed around the house, protesting, "It isn't fair! How come you never make Dirk go shopping?"

Cassie did make Dirk shop occasionally, when she thought his jeans were too worn or his shirts needed updating, but luckily Bridget usually got the brunt of Cassie's fashion shopping impulses.

Dirk poured himself a bowl of cereal. His father had already finished eating, which meant he was probably still at the table because he wanted to talk.

"So," his father said without looking up from his laptop. "How's Tori?"

"Happier now that she has her dog." The thought of kissing Tori made him smile—especially the memory of how she'd kissed him right before she left. "By the way, I told her we'd let her father rule Florida if she joined us."

"And what was her response to that?"

Dirk finished a bite of cereal. "She still has an overly optimistic view of the government, but I'm making progress. Once her father loses the election, she'll see things differently."

"You're making progress?" his father asked. He sounded both amused and cynical. Well, that was fine. His father could be as amused as he wanted to be about Dirk's relationship with Tori, so long as he left her alone.

"Yes, I am," Dirk said.

For a few minutes, he ate in happy silence, but then his father spoke again, "Were you planning to tell me the rest?"

Dirk froze, spoon sagging in his hand. What did his father know? That he'd let Tori inside Khan's mind? About Aaron? No, his father couldn't know about him. Ever since his dad first caught him messaging Tori, Dirk started deleting her messages as soon as he read them.

What was his father referring to? Maybe it was something unimportant, something about school. Whatever it was, Dirk shouldn't act like he was hiding things. He forced himself to continue eating as naturally as he could. "Tell you the rest of what?"

His father turned his laptop around so Dirk could see it. There on the screen were copies of Tori's messages from last night.

Dirk's heart stuttered. His father must have used some sort of spyware. He knew about Aaron.

A surge of anger flared inside Dirk. "You spied on my conversations with Tori? You don't trust me at all—not even enough to respect my most basic privacy."

His father hit the table, making the milk in Dirk's bowl sway back and forth. "If you prove yourself untrustworthy, you don't deserve privacy." He turned the screen back around, making it clatter. "How could you find out about a younger brother—a dragon lord—and not tell me?"

It wouldn't do any good to protest that Aaron was only twelve, or that he had a life of his own—rights even.

"I doubt the kid even exists," Dirk said, keeping his voice even. "I mean, come on—the Slayers claim that I have an unknown brother, and that I can meet him if I go to the fair in North Carolina this weekend. You don't think that sounds like an ambush? Wouldn't you know if you had another son? Wouldn't you have told me?"

His father scanned through the screen again. "I thought you could tell if Tori was lying. Was she lying about the boy?"

"You're saying it could be true?" Dirk knew it was, but needed to pretend he didn't. "You never checked up on my mom after she left? You never saw her long enough to tell if she'd had another kid?"

His father glared at him coldly. "I thought counterparts could detect lies. Was Tori telling the truth or not?"

She was telling the truth, but Dirk just shrugged. "It's not that clear cut. Counterparts sense emotions. I lied to Tori plenty of times without being caught."

"She caught you when it mattered."

His father was referring to last October, when Dirk tried to lead the Slayers into one of his father's buildings. Men had been waiting there to ambush them. Dirk had been so torn up by guilt that Tori knew something was wrong.

"It always mattered," Dirk countered. "I hid who I was from her for months. And if you remember, it was your accent that tipped her off in the end."

His father grunted and returned his attention to the computer screen. "It's possible that the Slayers are laying a snare for us, but it's also possible that I have another son." He let out a muttered oath and snapped his laptop shut. "Before Bianca left, she was acting strangely, and afterwards, she didn't visit you for seven months. I should have known. She would have come back sooner if she wasn't hiding something."

She would have come back sooner. His father's words echoed Tori's, and seemed to be proof that his mother had been at least a little concerned about him. Dirk swallowed, unsure why the words were hard to hear. He'd accepted a long time ago that his mother hadn't cared about him. Shouldn't that be the harder truth to bear? And yet now his father was chipping away at it, and pain twisted through the cracks he was making.

Unbidden, a memory of his mother flashed through his mind. He had been at a friend's house playing and she'd knelt in front of him, crying. "I love you," she said, "and I'll come back for you."

But she hadn't. That was when Dirk had first learned that parents could lie.

His father took out his phone and texted someone. "Keeping a son from me is the sort of spiteful kind of thing she would do, if the boy exists, I'll find him."

Dirk put his spoon on the table. He couldn't pretend he had an appetite any more. "Are you talking lawyers or kidnapping? Because if Aaron goes missing, the police will look for you. That's not what you want."

His father waved away Dirk's words. "Bianca doesn't know where I am or what name I go by now. She won't be able to tell the police anything." He stood up, signaling the discussion was over. "Get dressed. We're going to North Carolina."

* * *

Two hours later, Dirk and his father were strolling across the grounds of the Renaissance festival. The sky was layered with clouds and doing its best to deny the sun's existence. Autumn leaves drifted to the ground like never-ending litter. As good a day as any for a kidnapping.

Dirk's father had sent men to stake out key locations at the fair. Some were dressed as security guards and had bypassed the weapons check at the front gate. If the Slayers attacked, his father's men would easily be able to take hostages to use in negotiations.

Dirk's senses were alert, his powers activated by a simulator in his father's airplane. Slayers weren't the only ones who could use technology to their advantage. He didn't feel anything out of the ordinary—no swirlings of danger to indicate this might be a trap. The only people who were agitated and full of adrenaline were his father's men.

Two dozen of them had fanned out and were searching in a grid pattern for a blond-haired, blue-eyed twelve-year-old boy who looked like Dirk.

The problem was that a lot of boys at the fair fit that description. The men kept snapping pictures and sending them to his father. Every time he opened a new one, he would stare at it as though trying to conjure up a resemblance. He hadn't been satisfied with any of them.

"It would be ironic," Dirk said, "If you got the wrong kid."

The sentence was almost the first thing he'd said to his father since the breakfast table. "Some poor seventh grader is wandering around to get extra credit for his history class, and he's bagged like a safari rhino, dragged into the dragon enclosure, and introduced to Khan. After you revive the kid, you realize it was all a mistake and fly him back to the fair." Dirk shook his head philosophically. "No one will ever believe his story, and he'll go through life with a nervous tick."

"Don't worry. We'll find my son." His father's phone chimed. Another picture had come through. This one showed a kid who was arguably twelve, skinny as a rail, and had hair so pale he didn't seem to have eyebrows.

Dirk shook his head. "Your men think that boy looks like me? Now that's just insulting."

"Idiots. They need to search for someone who looks older than twelve, not younger." His father spoke as he texted new instructions. "My son will be taller, bigger than average."

His men should have known that already. Dirk and his father were both 6' 2" and broad shouldered.

The smell of roasted turkey drifted over from one of the stalls, a reminder that Dirk hadn't had much breakfast.

"I'm getting something to eat," he said and headed that way.

His father wouldn't be happy with him for walking off, but Dirk couldn't bring himself to care much today. Let his father be angry. Dirk didn't want to be here.

He came back a few minutes later with a turkey leg and a soda.

His father let out disapproving grunt. "We're in the middle of a mission. Stop thinking about your stomach."

"We're in the middle of a wild goose chase." Dirk took a bite of turkey. "You don't have another son. It's like you've told me all along. Bianca never came to see me because she didn't care. She wasn't hiding anything. We're wasting our time here."

Dirk knew his father couldn't argue the point; wouldn't change his stance now and say that Bianca had cared about Dirk.

His father ground his teeth together in annoyance. "I'll decide when we're wasting our time." He viewed the crowd, scowling. "I'm going for a better look at a few of the boys. I'll call when I need your help."

His father strode away, disappearing into the crowd.

Good.

With the mood Dirk was in, he was likely to push his father

too far. He still couldn't believe his father had spied on his conversations. Well, Dirk believed it, he just was ticked off about it. He'd have to find a way to detect the spyware and remove it.

Or better yet, he'd leave it on and get a new phone to talk to Tori with. He'd tell her through her dragon hearing that his phone wasn't secure anymore, and then the two of them could write cryptic nonsense on his old phone just to drive his father crazy.

Does the color of the water run clear where you are?

Yes, and do your sheep eat mustard in their pajamas?

Dirk took another bite of turkey and scanned the crowd again. Somewhere out there, he had a younger brother, a brother who didn't know how much danger he was in this very minute.

CHAPTER 39

Aaron sat on a bench by a Ye Olde Chocolate Shoppe, eating a slice of frozen cheesecake. Technically cheesecake wasn't a Renaissance food, but tourists didn't care about authenticity when dessert was involved.

There was only so much to do at a Renaissance fair, and he'd done it all before today, which pretty much left eating as the best thing to do while he waited.

This morning when he'd gone to Rudolpho's store to ask if he could pretend to be an employee, the man's face had gone red and he spat out, "Don't come near my shop again, or I'll tell security I've caught you shoplifting!"

Aaron had blinked at him in disbelief. "You're mad at me? Dude, you're the one who sold me out. You gave my address to a bunch of teenage ninjas who trashed my house. You owe me for that."

"You sold me bad goods!" Rudolpho retorted, shaking his finger. "You knew the scales were dangerous!"

Aaron backed up, hands raised. "Whatever. If anyone comes looking for dragon scales, tell them I'm selling by the Chocolate Shoppe."

Rudolpho kept shaking his finger. "Out!"

Aaron left.

Now he ate slowly, making each bite last. As long as he sat here eating something, people wouldn't wonder why he was alone. He looked like he was just waiting for the rest of his family to join him with their food.

The cheesecake was tasteless on his tongue. An hour ago, his mom texted that he'd been at Sergio's too long, and she was coming to pick him up. He turned his phone off after that.

He didn't want to upset her, but really, he had to do this for Jacob.

Aaron jabbed the cheesecake with his fork. Did his mom suspect where he'd really gone? She'd forbidden him from ever going to another Renaissance festival for the rest of his life. Well, mostly she'd forbidden him from ever having anything to do with dragons, and the festivals had been lumped into the restriction.

At a nearby stage, the audience clapped for a pair of singing nuns. A drummer beat a rhythm for a juggler. Family after family walked by, talking, laughing. Aaron was nearly done with his cheesecake.

Maybe Tori was right, and this was a bad idea. Maybe the only reason he wanted to be a dragon lord was because it sounded important and cool—and completely different from what his life was really like.

Being a dragon lord would mean he was special, needed even.

Aaron took the last bite of his cheesecake. What would be really awesome was if he looked up and saw his dad—his stepdad, Wesley—walking over. Maybe when his mom had realized Aaron was missing, she'd called him. Maybe he would come to the festival to search for him. Wesley would smile when he found Aaron and sit down all concerned, like parents did in the movies.

"I hear you're here looking for your father," he would say. "But you don't have to do that. I'm your father, and I'm coming back. We're going to be a family again."

Aaron looked up. Only the crowd mulled around him.

Another daydream played out in his mind, this one more likely to happen because it involved Overdrake. Aaron had seen pictures of him in his mother's albums. He was tall, with dark hair and the same smile Aaron had inherited—a little crooked on one side. In his daydream, Overdrake came up to him hesitantly, and smiling that crooked smile.

"I'm sorry I haven't been there for you," he'd say. "It wasn't my fault. I just found out about you, and I want to make up for all the years we've missed. Come with me, and you can have anything you want."

That was possible; Overdrake was rich, after all. Aaron's mother had told him that enough times.

He would hold out at first, make Overdrake work to convince him. But he'd finally give in and say he would give living with Overdrake a try.

Aaron looked up. A man was standing about twenty feet away, looking at him. Not Overdrake, just some guy who looked all military-like. Buzzed short hair and beefy arms. He held up a phone in Aaron's direction and took picture.

Weird.

Aaron checked behind him to see if there was something worth taking a picture of back there. The only thing he saw was more people standing around.

He turned to the buzzed-hair guy again, but he'd walked off a little. He shot Aaron a furtive glance as he pushed buttons on his phone.

Was Buzz-guy one of Overdrake's men?

If so, why wasn't he approaching Aaron and pretending to

be a dragon scale customer? That's what someone who worked for Overdrake would do—make sure Aaron was the right kid.

So if he wasn't one of Overdrake's men, who was he? Was Rudolpho pulling something? Maybe his mother had sent some of her friends to search for him.

Whoever it was, Aaron wasn't about to hang around here any longer.

The nice thing about knowing the fairgrounds was that he wouldn't have trouble losing this guy. Aaron got up and strolled down the street. Buzz-guy followed at a slow pace. Aaron took out his phone, turned it on, and walked into the jousting maze. If the man trailed him inside, Aaron would lose him in the maze. He already knew the solution. If Buzz-guy went to wait for him at the exit, Aaron would simply go back out the entrance.

As soon as Aaron turned the maze's first corner, he reversed the direction of the camera on his phone and used it like a mirror to see what the man was doing behind him.

Instead of either following Aaron inside or going to the exit, Buzz-guy stopped at the entrance and talked on his phone, waving his arm at someone. A man in a security uniform jogged over. Buzz-guy pointed to the maze exit and the security guard went in that direction, while Buzz-guy stayed where he was. They were going to watch both exits, catch him whichever way he went.

He bit back a groan. Rudolpho must have made good on his threat to turn Aaron in. Now security was after him. *Crap.* His mom was going to kill him.

Buzz-guy strode toward the maze entrance. Game over, time to run. Aaron darted out of the maze before the man could completely block the entrance and trap him inside. Sprinting down the street, Aaron weaved between and around tourists and trees. The festival grounds were surrounded by a tall, spiked fence to keep nonpaying customers from sneaking in. Unfortunately, the fence didn't offer him a lot of ways out. Buzz-guy was chasing after him. He could hear the man's panting breaths coming closer, catching up. In another few seconds, Aaron would be caught. Would they call the police on him? Could they press charges against him with just Rudolpho's word?

Aaron didn't want to find out, didn't want his mother to have to pick him up at a police station.

A large woman in a billowing dress sauntered the opposite way down the street. A man on stilts marched beside her, juggling bowling pins in large looping arcs. Aaron made a move as though he would go around them to the left, then at the last moment, darted right.

Buzz-guy didn't switch directions as quickly. Aaron heard the woman's angry exclamations and the thunks of bowling pins hitting someone. Hopefully Buzz-guy. Aaron checked over his shoulder. Buzz-guy was on the ground, but another security guard had joined the chase: A dark-haired man with an athlete's build.

Sheesh, how many people were after him? And why were they all in such good shape? Didn't police officers sit around and eat donuts anymore?

Aaron put on a burst of speed. The man had no trouble keeping up. How was Aaron going to lose him? A corner was coming up. Once Aaron went around the building there, he'd have a few seconds until the man caught sight of him again. If he could lose him during those seconds, he'd be able to get away.

Aaron turned the corner and cut through the crowd. The first shop on his right was a fortune teller's shack. He plowed through its doors and then stood inside, panting, as he caught his breath. He'd done it. He'd gotten away.

In front of him, a woman with a turban and way too many bracelets sat at a table with a crystal ball. Another woman, a tourist, sat in a chair across from her. Both stared at him open-mouthed and indignant.

The fortune teller dropped her hands from the crystal ball. "What are you doing in here?"

How could he explain? Aaron shrugged, still panting. "If you could really see the future, wouldn't you know?"

He'd barely finished speaking when the dark-haired security guard burst into the shack. *Ugh.* Aaron hadn't lost him after all. Without a word of explanation, the man lunged at him, arms swinging like a vice. Aaron had no room to maneuver. He leaped onto the table and assessed the situation. Assessing it turned out, was overrated. He needed action. With one swift kick, he sent the crystal ball into the man's chest. The ball hit him with a thud, and he stumbled backward. Six years of soccer practice had just totally paid off.

Both women shrieked in surprise and pushed back from the table. The fortune teller's chair toppled to the ground with a crash of scolding wood.

Aaron jumped off the other side of the table and used it as a barrier between himself and the security guard.

"See what I mean?" Aaron said to the fortune teller. "I bet you didn't see *that* coming at all."

The man wheeled around the table and dove at Aaron. He missed and collided into the back wall, making the whole shack shudder. Aaron dashed passed him, sprinted outside, and ran down the street. He needed a strategy; he needed to be smart about this. He wasn't going to be able to avoid every security guard in the place. At least, not dressed in a cape and hat.

He headed into one of the larger buildings, a sit-down restaurant specializing in serving large chunks of meat. As soon as he was through the door, he slowed his pace and took off the cape and hat. He nodded to the hostess, said, "My parents are already sitting down," and marched past her.

He chucked his hat and cape into a booth he passed, then continued through the dining room. Several people had their jackets draped over the backs of their chairs. He walked toward a guy leaning forward and plucked off his sweatshirt without breaking stride. By the time Aaron had made it back to the front of the restaurant, he wore a maroon hoodie.

He pulled the hood down as far as it would go over his face and made his way toward the front gate. People streamed by him on their way in. A group of fiddlers on the side of the street played so loudly, Aaron couldn't hear footsteps, couldn't tell if anyone was running to catch up with him.

He didn't dare turn around to check; that would give him away.

He forced himself to walk slowly, tried to look natural. He gazed downward as much as possible, hoping less of his face was visible that way. Just a few more minutes until he reached the front gate.

He glanced up and saw a security guard ahead. The man was scanning the crowd, watching everyone going toward the exit. He looked in Aaron's direction.

Aaron didn't want to get any closer. He took a sharp turn and headed into an eating area in between food shops.

Had the man recognized him? Aaron didn't think so, but he wasn't going to have an easy time getting by the guy.

A teenager in a baseball cap sat on a nearby bench, eating a turkey leg. Aaron sank down beside him and hoped the two of them seemed like they were together. He peeked back the way he'd come to see if the security guard was following. No sign of him. Yet.

"If you're smart," the teenager said, "you'll run."

"What?" Aaron turned to get a better look at the guy. He was tall, with football player shoulders, blond hair, and blue eyes. He held a soda and was drinking it casually like he was passing the time of day. Aaron recognized him—or at least thought he did. He couldn't be sure it was really Dirk.

"If you're smart, you'll run," the guy said again. "The front gate is the worst way to go. We're surrounded by two hundred and fifty acres of forest. It would be easier to disappear in there."

The guy knew someone was after Aaron. Did that mean Overdrake's men were the ones chasing him? Why? And where was his father?

"Who are you?" Aaron asked, eyeing him uncertainly.

"I'm your brother. And if you stay here . . ."

Aaron didn't hear the rest of his words. Something sharp penetrated his hood and burrowed into the back of his neck. He let out a cry of surprise and swiped at the thing. A tiny dart fell to the ground.

"What's that?" he asked, outraged. But he already knew. It was some sort of drug, something that would keep him from fighting or calling out for help.

Dirk sighed and put his soda down onto the bench. "That's proof you waited too long to take my advice and run. I'll try not to let this affect my judgment of your intelligence." He gestured to Aaron's feet. "My guess is the boots gave you away. They matched the cape. The hoodie—not so much."

Aaron got to his feet, anger washing over him. He was having serious second thoughts about his plan to go with Overdrake. Tori was right; his father was psychotic. Why else would he have his men do this sort of thing to a son he'd never met—hunt him like some sort of animal? And what sort of person was his brother that he was willingly part of this?

Dirk stood and grabbed hold of Aaron's arm. "It's too late to run now." His voice carried both disappointment and pity.

Aaron tried to jerk his arm away. "Let me go!"

But he couldn't budge his arm from Dirk's grip. He yanked harder, putting all of his strength into it. He didn't manage to so much as pull Dirk a step forward. "Let me go, you freak!" he yelled.

"Do you really think I'm a freak?" Dirk asked with mock offense. "Because if you do, I've got bad news. You're just like me."

"I'm not!" Aaron meant it. He stepped forward and swung at Dirk's throat.

Dirk lifted his free hand, effortlessly intercepting Aaron's strike and stopping it. "I'd let you go," he said, "But in about twenty seconds, you're going to pass out. If you're running, you might give yourself a concussion."

His words were already sounding blurry and far away. Aaron blinked at him. His face was beginning to waver.

Everyone said they looked so much alike. Aaron could see a resemblance, although not as much as other people claimed. Dirk's face had sharper lines, a bigger jaw, and a harder look to his eyes.

They weren't the same at all.

As blackness closed in, Aaron thought of his other brother.

He and Jacob might not look alike, but Aaron was much more like him. Aaron held on to that thought like it would carry him through the darkness.

He was more Slayer than he was dragon lord and always would be.

The end of book three.

Note to the reader: As you can tell, this is not the ending of the story. And yes, I can hear your frustrated scream all the way from my house. When the manuscript reached seven hundred pages and still wasn't finished, I knew I had to break it into two books. Seven-hundred-page paperbacks are only a good thing if you happen to need something hefty to throw at marauders. Otherwise, they tend to fall apart when you read them. I don't want people to pay for a book that doesn't last.

The fourth book, *Slayers: Into the Firestorm*, will be out as soon as I finish it. (I had to take a break and write another book and a novella for series that I'd already committed to). But trust me, no one wants the fourth book out more than I do. Really. True story: My youngest daughter just read this book. I heard her scream twice, then yell, "Mother! Bad author! Bad!" And I knew she'd reached the end. So yeah, she is here in your behalf, making sure the book gets done.

Thanks for your patience.

For any book to succeed, reviews are essential. If you enjoyed this book please leave a review on Amazon. A sentence or two can make all the difference. <u>Please leave a review of Slayers!</u>

ABOUT
THE AUTHOR

CJ Hill is the pen name of author Janette Rallison. She lives in Arizona where she does her best to avoid housework and dragons. She still hasn't decided who Tori should end up with. Fortunately, Tori is only a teenager so she doesn't really have to decide who to spend the rest of her life with. Plus she's a fictional character, so there's that too. CJ is working on Slayers: Into the Firestorm and will decide soon. Probably.

CPSIA information can be obtained
at www.ICGtesting.com
Printed in the USA
LVHW01s0045300917
550248LV00001B/3/P